CARYN ROSE

B-SIDES
AND
BROKEN
HEARTS

till victory
press

B-sides and Broken Hearts

Copyright © 2011 Caryn Rose
Till Victory Press
http://www.bsidesandbrokenhearts.com
http://www.carynlrose.com
editor@tillvictory.com

ISBN: 978-0-9835029-0-6

Cover photograph © Caryn Rose
Cover design © 2011 by Jeroen ten Berge
Author photograph by Debra L
Rothenberg/rothenbergphoto.com

June 2011

ACKNOWLEDGEMENTS

The author wishes to thank: the members of the Seattle Writer's Bloc for invaluable help and encouragement; to Jean, Joel, Mari, Victoria, Heather, Sharon and all my early readers for being the initial fan club; to Uptown Espresso on 4th Avenue and the Harmony Motel for providing refuge; and to every librarian I ever knew for letting me hide in the stacks. Last but not least, to GLR, for unfailing support and unflagging enthusiasm.

This book is dedicated to my mother, who taught me to love books and music with equal fervor

Barbara Janus Rose
1938-2011

JUST LOOK OVER YOUR SHOULDER

TABLE OF CONTENTS

ACKNOWLEDGEMENTS 5

CHAPTER I: 200I 13

CHAPTER 2: 1988 30

CHAPTER 3: 1996 60

CHAPTER 4: I99I 84

CHAPTER 5: I979 99

CHAPTER 6: I99I II3

CHAPTER 7: I993 ....I39

CHAPTER 8: I995 ....I53

CHAPTER 9 : I997 ....I74

CHAPTER I0: 200I I92

CHAPTER II: Los Angeles 2I2

CHAPTER I2: Los Angeles... 233

CHAPTER I3: Los Angeles... 254

CHAPTER I4: Los Angeles... 277

ABOUT THE AUTHOR.. 295

CHAPTER I: 2001

Joey Ramone is dead.

I cannot believe this, so I read the headline again. PUNK ROCK LEGEND JOEY RAMONE DEAD AT 49.

No. This can't be happening. He's a Ramone. Ramones are comic book characters, eternally youthful, and while, sure, the Ramones had gotten older and broken up, they don't die. Not yet. No.

I sit there, alternately staring into space and rereading the news story, as though I'll see something different the next time I look. I am seized by sadness and anger. I can trace my love of the Ramones back to age fifteen. Twenty-two years? It can't really be twenty-two years, can it? I can't have been in Seattle for over ten years now, right?

The Ramones were simple and outrageous, perfect and anarchic. Elegance in blue jeans, black leather and Converse All-Stars. We all wanted to be that cool. Growing up in a New Jersey full of strip malls and spandex, the Ramones were not just a breath of fresh air, they were nothing short of salvation--just to the right of Chrissie Hynde wearing a red leather jacket and lace fingerless gloves on the cover of the first Pretenders album.

A rapid *ding-ding-ding* signaling incoming email pulls me out of my reverie. Just like when Johnny Thunders died, the messages pour in and they all say the same thing: "You were one of the first people I thought of when I heard the news." Why does death dissolve all these barriers when life doesn't? It seems sad and wrong.

The Sunday evening silence bears down on me and I suddenly wonder why I'm not listening to anything. I'm about to head over to the CD rack, but then stop myself; if there was ever an analog band, it's the Ramones. So I walk over to the rows and rows of vinyl, pull out all of my Ramones records, and lay them out flat on the floor in chronological order.

I remember buying the first album at Discount Records out on Route 10 and having the sales clerk laugh at me and tell me I should try listening to some real music, that the Ramones sucked, that they could barely play their instruments. I didn't even try to argue, although it was a matter of honor in those days to defend your music to the death. But how could I argue with someone wearing an Emerson, Lake and Palmer t-shirt? It was one of those old 70's rock shirts, black body with white sleeves and a bad bootleg screen print of the cover of *Brain Salad Surgery*. He had long, stringy hair and John Lennon glasses and I could just tell that he thought he was so cool. Well, he was what passed for cool in the New Jersey suburbs of the late 70's.

Pride of place in my Ramones collection belongs to my autographed *End of the Century* album, signed by Johnny and Joey in thick black magic marker scrawl, carefully shielded in plastic. In the summer of 1980, there was a record signing down in the Village at that cheap record store on the north side of Eighth Street between Fifth and Sixth. I waited in line for hours and when I approached Joey and Johnny at the signing table, couldn't manage to eke out more than "Hi" and "Thank you." At sixteen, they were larger than life to me, and proximity did nothing to alter that perception.

Later that summer I saw them play live for the first time, one August night at the Dr. Pepper Music Festival, held at Wollman Rink in Central Park. The same year had the Pretenders, the Talking Heads, and the Ramones in one week--punk rock heaven for a girl from the suburbs who had no other chance to see these bands. I snuck into the city after school, walked over from Penn Station to the Korvettes at Herald Square and bought tickets. The prices were five dollars for the floor, three dollars for the balcony. It was all general admission, which meant puke brown metal folding chairs that by the end of the season were rusty and dented from thousands of feet jumping up and down on them night after night.

I still have my photos from that show, taken with a Kodak Instamatic from the tenth row. It was the most amazing thing in the world to actually see the Ramones play. Dee Dee counting down every song "1-2-3-4!" Joey standing there, immovable. Johnny's hands a blur of powerchords on his trademark white Mosrite guitar. I was wearing a red miniskirt, black Converse All-Stars and a plain white boy's t-shirt adorned with carefully chosen rock pins, and entirely too much makeup. I jumped up and down on the rusted metal chairs along with everyone else, and sang along and felt happy and free and at home.

In tribute, I put on the first record, the one with the cover that is still so raw and so revolutionary--Roberta Bayley's black and white portrait of the boys in leather jackets t-shirts, ripped jeans and Converse against a brick wall. At the time, that cover was so unlike anything else out there. Nowadays, it's almost a gold standard. Carrying that album around high school didn't earn me any coolness points, since it wasn't *The Wall* or the Grateful Dead. It was Punk Rock. Punk Rock was Bad.

I am now childishly determined to get through every single Ramones album I own tonight, in chronological order. I sit forlornly on the floor, hug my knees to my chest like I did when I was fifteen, and stare, mesmerized, at all the album covers. I turn up the volume some more and sing along really loud, memory after memory I have of the Ramones flashing through my brain. I have to get up every twenty minutes to flip the record, and when I do, I stop at the computer to marvel at who else has crawled out of the woodwork after all these years.

I shake myself out of the reverie of reminiscence and wonder who I should call? I should call Marie, because clearly, my best friend, Ms. Punk Rock 1982 of New Brunswick, hasn't heard yet or she would be burning down the phone lines. And I guess I should probably think about dinner, although I have no appetite. Ian is supposed to come over for dinner. I should call and tell him that I really don't feel like eating. Or maybe, maybe we can go out somewhere and drink beer and talk about the Ramones.

I'm formulating my grand Joey Tribute Plans just as the phone rings. Caller ID advertises that it's Ian.

"Hey, I was just about to call you," I say.

"How are you?" he asks.

"Have you seen the news tonight? Joey Ramone is dead, Ian."

"Uh-huh--I mean, really?" Ian says.

"He was forty-nine. Complications from his cancer."

"Wow. That's a bummer," he says, and then continues: "Hey, I got these tomatoes at the Market this afternoon. These are just the best tomatoes I have ever seen. The guy I bought them from grew them himself. He was so proud of his tomatoes that I just had to buy them. I thought I'd make some bruschetta or something Italian with them. They are just so good. You have got to try them."

I take the receiver away from my ear and hold it in my hand, staring at it as though it's a particularly rotten item I just pulled out of the refrigerator. Ian continues to talk, not realizing I wasn't listening. I think of the line in Elvis Costello's song "No Action," where he talks about holding a girl like he would hold something called Bakelite. I remember when I figured out what Elvis was saying in that line. Bakelite was what they used to make telephones out of. I used to think I was so cool for figuring that out. Of course, no one else I knew cared.

All of a sudden there is silence on the other end of the phone.

"Sorry, I was reading some email--I'm hearing from a lot of people I haven't heard from in ages," I say, by way of apology.

"You weren't even listening!" he says. Ian hates it if you are not one hundred percent focused on him at all times. It's worse if he's cranky about something.

"I think it's kind of fair, considering you aren't listening to me either," I say. I was thinking that, but didn't mean to say it out loud.

"I did listen to you!" he says.

I decide to try another approach, since this one is clearly not going to get me anywhere. He must not understand that I'm honestly upset, that Joey was one of us, that it's not just abstract grief over yet another rock and roll death. Ian would want to console me if he knew how sad I felt right now.

"Ian, I'm really bummed about this. I'm sitting here playing all my Ramones records, in order, and remembering. Remember when it used to be dangerous to like the Ramones?" I say this cheerily, as conversationally as I can manage.

"Lisa, I'm sorry you're upset, but--it's not that big of a deal, right? The Ramones had broken up. They were over long before they had broken up. Let's talk about dinner, and I'll come over and cook," he says. I hear him yawning.

"I thought we could go to Hattie's or the Sunset, I'm sure Max would let us hijack the PA, and we can drink cheap beer and pay tribute to Joey," I say.

"It's a Sunday night!" he says.

"I'm not saying let's get drunk and stay out until 2 a.m."

"I'm really tired," he says. "But it was Sunday, so I was looking forward to seeing you. I went shopping today just for dinner."

"We don't lose a Ramone every day."

"Lisa, I'm sorry, yes, it's sad, but--it's not the greatest loss ever endured by the music world that the author of 'Now I Wanna Sniff Some Glue' is no longer with us." He pronounces the song title in artificial, clipped tones.

"That was Dee Dee," I say, automatically. It was like Tourette's or something. I honestly couldn't stop myself.

"What?" he says.

I pause for just a fraction of a second. "That was Dee Dee. Not Joey."

Ian's intake of breath is loud and ragged. Admittedly, I'm deliberately being a stubborn bitch right now, but I could really fucking care less. He's being--well, I don't know what he's being, but this is my ex-lead guitarist rock-and-roll boyfriend and he wants to talk about tomatoes and doesn't care that Joey Ramone is dead.

"Okay, Lisa, you're upset and you're not being rational and I'm not quite sure why, but it's putting a bummer on my Sunday night and I have a hard week ahead of me. Clearly, I don't feel the same way about the Ramones that you do. I was listening to Rush and KISS and my band never played Ramones songs. I just want to make some dinner, watch some TV, and get ready for work tomorrow."

"Listen, Geddy Lee could die and while it wouldn't affect me personally, I could recognize that it was a loss to the music world and would understand why you were organizing a memorial service at Seattle Center." My anger is starting to escape.

"That's not fair and a cheap shot."

"No, it's not a fucking cheap shot. I'm trying to make a point.

You love Rush, I can't fucking stand them, but if one of them died I would certainly understand why you would be upset about it and I would be sympathetic toward you and I wouldn't cop the attitude of, 'Well, it isn't like Pete Townshend died or something'."

"Rush is the music of my childhood," he says.

"And the Ramones are the music of my childhood!" I say.

"The difference being that Rush are actually musicians," he says, as though he set up this entire exchange just to get that in there.

I can't believe he just said that. He likes the Ramones just like everyone does, right? I mean, not liking the Ramones is like not liking sex. I suddenly realize that I don't actually know how he feels about them. Right now, this whole conversation is echoing back to the stringy-haired record clerk in New Jersey, and it bothers me. What's more, I don't understand it. This is not Ian talking. Not the Ian I know, anyway.

"Wanna talk about cheap shots?" I say, after a minute.

Now there is a big silence on the other end of the phone. This isn't just about the Ramones or Rush, but I'm not quite sure what it is about. Whatever it is, it's making my stomach hurt.

I dive into the silence. "Ian, this isn't about music or talent or validity. This is about you not fucking getting it." I'm angry. I'm angrier than I should be, actually.

"What am I not getting? The historical importance of the Ramones? I'm sorry, please explain it to me." He's almost hissing in response.

Now, I'm really fucking pissed.

"Listen, asshole. This isn't about who's more valid or who's more talented or if I like the Ramones and you don't. You're not having any respect for my feelings right now." I am so upset my hands are shaking and my voice is unsteady. I can't tell if I'm going to burst into tears at any second or start screaming and throwing things. This is not a normal fight.

"It's hard to respect your feelings when they are completely and totally out of proportion," Ian says. "You're out of control right now. I can't talk to you like this. I think you should go take a bath, watch some TV, go to bed early--"

I didn't hang up. Not really. Hanging up involves violence and drama. I just quietly set the receiver down. The phone was on its way back to the cradle by the time he said the words "watch some TV." I mean, God, I love drowning my sorrows in a night of bad TV as much as the next person, but that was all he seemed to do, and seemed to want to do, lately. I went over there a few weeks ago for dinner and found him engrossed in this documentary on nighttime flora and fauna of the Southwestern desert on the Discovery Channel. I'd had a really bad day at work and wanted a hug and a glass of wine. He actually yelled at me to shut up after I tried to talk to him for the third time. Ian didn't even own a television when we were first dating, and had confessed to having a KILL YOUR TELEVISION bumper sticker on his car just a few years earlier.

The phone rings and I see Ian's number on the display. I sigh and pick it up gingerly.

"What happened? Did you hit the wrong button?" I can hear in his voice that he knows perfectly well that I didn't hit the wrong button, but he's not going to accuse me of anything just yet.

"No, I hung up on you." There, I said it.

"See what I mean? You're just overreacting right now. You're way too emotional over this." He sounds almost triumphant.

"So what if I am? Someone important to me just *died*," I say, clearly being too emotional.

There is a pause.

"Do you want me to come over and make you dinner or not?" he asks.

For some reason, I decide to be conciliatory. I am thinking that he is angry about something else and if he'd just come over, he could give me a hug and we'd both apologize, make dinner, snuggle up on the couch and watch a movie.

"Ian, c'mon over. We can make dinner and watch a movie, or I can play Ramones records for you and show you photos and tell you stories. I have lots of great Ramones stories," I say as engagingly as I can. I mean it, though.

"No," he says in that annoying petulant voice of his, which I never respond to and generally ignore. "I'm going to wait until you calm down and get more reasonable about this."

"Then you're going to wait a really fucking long time," I say, and this time I really do hang the phone up. Hard. Like in the movies. It didn't make the same clanging bell sound, though. I think you need one of those old phones to do that. The ones made of Bakelite.

The phone rings again. I ignore it, and walk back over to the turntable and flip over *End of the Century* to side two. "Baby, I Love You" begins to play, in all its glorious Phil Spector over-production. The phone rings and rings, but I put on my headphones, lie down on the floor and close my eyes.

★

What time is it? I must have fallen asleep. I sit up groggily and listen to the wind blowing against the windows. Half-dazed, I look over at the clock; it's almost 11 p.m. I haven't eaten anything, and my head hurts. I struggle to my feet and walk towards the kitchen.

I see that Ian called a few more times after I'd hung up. *I should call him*, I think. And then, "No. I don't want to call him. I don't care if he's angry. I don't want to talk to him anymore." I'm saying all of this aloud for some reason, and that last line catches at my throat. So I say it again, louder.

"I don't want to talk to him anymore."

Well, that's interesting. It's interesting because it's not exasperated or petulant or annoyed or childish or angry, it's just-- flat. It's a statement of fact.

In every relationship I have ever been in, the end never comes in this long drawn out internal debate where I weigh pros and cons and agonize over how I really feel. Or rather, I go through that process but the truth of the matter is, there is a moment, one moment, in which I know it is over. I usually ignore it, deny it, prolong the agony--but that moment is always there.

Maybe it was the night that Ian insisted that we leave the Supersuckers show early for no other reason than he didn't want to be there, despite the fact that I hadn't seen them in eons and Eddie Spaghetti promised to play my favorite song. Maybe it was the night he tried to issue an edict that we weren't going to see Mudhoney because he didn't feel like it, and when I went by myself, he spent the rest of the weekend sulking. (We never missed Mudhoney, ever. We considered Mudhoney a National Treasure that Should Not be Taken For Granted.)

The signs have been there for a while now. I can easily think of other nights, other moments, other conversations where the signal was bad, the connection was broken, and I would look at him like I didn't know who this person was. The moment. You ignore it, because you don't want it to be over.

Right now, I am tired and fed up. I am not filled with love and affection. I don't want to call him and say, this is silly, why are we fighting? I don't care. I feel irritated and resentful and worn out, and I know with perfect certainty that this relationship is over.

I decide to get up and make some soup and read my email. I discover at least a dozen new messages have appeared while I was passed out. I open a can of soup, pour it in a bowl, and stick it in the microwave for three minutes. While it's heating, I scan my inbox. Regina, Jean, Heather--wait, Jake? The microwave beeps that it's finished, and I ignore it.

Jake? I have email from Jake?

Date: Sunday, April 15, 2001
From: jane magazine's #1 bachelor
to: keith richards #1 groupie
subject: gabba gabba hey

hey kid,
Im sure you already heard, tonight we lost joey. we are all bummed out, and you were the first one I thought of. remember when he showed up at our gig at coney island high and we called you screaming and got him to say hi to you on the cell phone? we were all sitting around moping and then christine yelled at us to do something with it. so, mark's writing a song about joey. he went off in a corner and is scribbling frantically. jonathan is ranting that we need to organize a tribute show. scott is just very quiet right now, we're kind of leaving him alone for a bit. me, im just sad.

Its late on Sunday and I dont know if you are still awake but ill be online while we're in here so you can write back too. the fuckers send their love. Christine says, come to la so you can go shopping, and because she misses you. I say come to la so we can get those tattoos we talked about years ago. I found a place on melrose where the clash used to get their tattoos. You know you want to. oh and i miss you too.

  Love ya
  Jake

I read the email once, twice, three times, feeling like that moment in *The Wizard of Oz* when Dorothy's world goes from black and white to Technicolor.

I met Jake and his bandmates my first year in Seattle. I'd just moved from Wallingford to this cheap, rundown house in the Central District, which I shared with the sister of someone I worked with. It wasn't fancy, but my roommate was never there, and it was a house and not a studio apartment above a chilly garage.

Jake, Mark, Scott, and Jonathan lived next door. The first time I saw Jake was when he was mowing the lawn with no shirt on. He was incredibly tall, incredibly thin, incredibly pale, and--at the time--had hair down to the middle of his back, looking for all the world like Ian Astbury and Jim Morrison's illegitimate love child. I thought I had died and gone to heaven. (Of course, later everyone would think he looked like Eddie Vedder, but he looked like Eddie when Ed was still pumping gas in San Diego. Ed just managed to get famous before Jake did. It was a sore point with the rock god.)

The first time I talked to Jake was two months later when the four of them had an impromptu band practice--at 3 a.m. I angrily shoved on a pair of Doc Martens over my bare feet, wrapped a hooded sweatshirt around me and went stomping over there, boots unlaced, in a state of high dudgeon. Not generally a good idea in that neighborhood, but I'd seen these guys and I knew they were students or artists or something, and not selling crack out of their kitchen. I stood on their porch, banging on the door, louder and louder and louder until the music stopped.

Jake was the one who opened the door, and greeted me with this adorable puzzled face, gazing down at me. Even at 3 a.m., he was still pretty gorgeous. But I was tired and had to work the next day. Cuteness had no power over me at that moment.

"Hi. I'm your next-door neighbor. I don't know if you were

aware, but it's three o'clock in the morning. I love loud rock music as much as the next gal, but it's a school night. Could you turn down the volume?" I yawned up in his direction. I suddenly felt very short.

"Wow, I really like your t-shirt!" Jake said, entirely too brightly for three o'clock in the morning.

What was he talking about? I looked down, not having any memory at that moment of what I was wearing. It was my favorite shirt, a picture of Keith Richards standing in front of a sign reading "A Drug Free America Comes First."

"Did you know that picture was taken in Seattle customs?" he said. "Did you--"

"As it so happens, I was already aware of that," I said, cutting off his overly enthusiastic history lesson. "Could you please turn down the volume on your stereo? Just because it goes to eleven doesn't mean that you have to use all of that wattage."

"It's not the stereo, it's us." He smiled really big. Dimples, too, I noticed, even in my sleep-deprived haze.

Bleary-eyed, I inquired: "Us?"

"Our band! We're called Infinite Trainwreck," he said.

Even half asleep, I could recognize a lousy band name.

"Your band name sucks. I don't know if your music does. But right now I need to sleep. Can you please not practice now." It wasn't a request, it was a demand, and so I didn't even wait to hear his response. I stomped over to my house and went back to bed.

The next day I came home from work and there was an exaggeratedly artistic note duct-taped to the front door and a bouquet of supermarket flowers on the doormat. The note was an invitation to come over and hang out and drink wine. And that was how it all started. They were funny and intelligent, and I loved their music. We became fast friends and stayed that way. They would later change their name to Blue Electric, get signed to a major label, and move to L.A.--which is a gross oversimplification of the story.

Although I was in terminal denial about it, Ian hated them. Or more specifically, he hated and resented "Jacob" (he always insisted on calling Jake by his proper name), and the feeling was mutual (although Jake constantly denied that, too). Ian didn't speak to me for two weeks when Jake bought me a Rolling Stones record Ian had talked me out of buying, while Jake refused to return my emails for almost a month after Ian mentioned something about us getting married.

"Lisa, he's a fucking jerk. He's old and sad and bitter that his band didn't hit it big, and he's devoting his entire life to making everyone else miserable for that reason," Jake said over the phone, after I threatened to get on a plane and find him in L.A. if he didn't start talking to me.

"Yes, but I soften him up," I said.

"Yeah, as long as you do what he wants you to, when he wants you to."

"Jake, that is so unfair and not true. I came down to L.A. to the opening show of the last tour, even though Ian couldn't go because of work."

"And he was crabby about it for like six weeks, wasn't he?"

I had no retort to that statement, because Jake was right.

The phone rings again. It's Ian. This time, I pick it up.

"Where have you been? I've been calling all night," he says.

"I fell asleep on the floor with headphones on," I say. I have no energy to be pissed off. But then, it occurs to me that he might actually have been worried. He would go through phases at work when a case in the criminal division would disturb him so much he would check on me constantly, not telling me anything more than there were still fucked up people out there, and reminding me that the police still hadn't caught Mia Zapata's killer.

"I was calling to see if you were ready to apologize," he says.

Well, I guess he wasn't that worried.

Seconds tick by while I hold back my immediate reaction, which is to tell him to go fuck himself and hang up again. More seconds tick by, and yet more seconds. And then I realize that this is pointless, I have nothing to say to him, and he won't hear me anyway.

So I hang the phone up, quietly this time, and unplug it from the wall so I can't hear it ring if he calls back, which I don't think he will. I sit down, open up a new email message, and type:

to: i am a rock god!

from: lisa
subject: joey ramone is dead.

jake. i'm freaked. joey is dead. how did this happen? he's a ramone. ramones don't die.
it's raining (shocker, i know). i have a headache. i just realized that my boyfriend is an asshole and there's no way i can possibly marry this guy. he doesn't care joey is dead.
I would love to come to L.A.. Tell me what your schedule is. and give everyone a hug from me. tell scott that he has to stop buying me sonic youth singles!
xoxo
--l.

I hit send and then start answering the deluge of email prompted by Joey's death. There are so many memories and so many people I miss sitting in my inbox. Leaving New York was such a hard thing, but I had to do it or I would have probably gone mad, killed myself, or both. Too many people I know did burn out, including some of the people whose names are in front of me right now. But these are the ones who made it through to the other side. I watched people I loved crash and burn, burn until there was nothing left. And then I ended up being an innocent bystander at what was probably the worst kind of hit and run destruction of a life, ever. All for the love of rock and roll, like the song says. Stupid kids thinking they will play guitar just like Keith Richards if they mimic everything about him.

It seems so long ago that I woke up in the East Village one morning and decided to move to Seattle. It was the best thing I have ever done.

I am still busily replying to messages when a response from Jake arrives with a loud *DING*.

Date: Sunday, April 15, 2001
From: I wanna be your monkeywrench
to: standing in the shadows
subject: going to california

what are you waiting for? Im not going anywhere. the new house has plenty of room, and girlfriend #87 is no longer on the scene. Do you need a ticket? Call the office tomorrow morning and its yours. But call me and let me have your plane info so I can pick you up myself. Much love

the rock god

p.s. why did you have to go and date a fucking yuppie wannabe loser so you couldn't come and hang out with us any more? good riddance. christine agrees. he didn't even have any money to redeem himself, and he listens to fucking dave matthews. you hate dave matthews.

Jake was right. That should have been the ultimate sign that something was very wrong: Ian had started listening to Dave Matthews.

Dave fucking Matthews was the Antichrist. He was the anti-everything I--we (or so I thought)--cared about in music.

Ian hid the CDs from me and certainly never listened to them when I was around. I only found out about this secret passion (it wasn't even a guilty pleasure, much to my dismay) when I ran into his friend Greg at Larry's Market one night and he asked me if I was coming with them to see DMB at the Gorge.

I looked at him like he was speaking another language.

"Greg. We don't listen to Dave Matthews," I said. "We're the people who drive 300 miles in one night to see Sonic Youth."

"Maybe you don't, Lisa, but Ian bought the tickets and it was his idea."

"No way. This has got to be some kind of perverse practical joke."

"We're even camping overnight at the Gorge!"

"Oh, brother. Well, maybe Ian forgot to tell me," I said, thinking that he had to be doing this as some kind of male bonding thing with his friends. Surely he could not be serious about this.

He was.

"What's wrong with Dave Matthews? I'll have you know, he is an excellent guitar player. Have you ever really listened to any of their records?" Ian said.

I couldn't fault him for being a little bit pissed off, given that I'd spent the day sending him e-cards of Dave Matthews every few hours. That would have been okay, but then I had to ask him if this meant he would wear Dockers and polar fleece out to the Cha-Cha Lounge. He stormed out the door and didn't talk to me for three days.

That's when I knew that this wasn't a guilty pleasure. Oh, well. I just thought it was a minor aberration; you're not always going to have 100% musical compatibility.

(But--*Dave Matthews?*)

That's it, I decide: I am going to L.A.. I've deprived myself of my friends for too long. I'm perusing flight schedules online when it dawns on me: I can wait until tomorrow and get on a plane or I can throw everything in the car and leave <u>now</u>.

I have always wanted to drive to California, but for some reason it just never happened. Roadtripping wasn't that easy in the Northwest; once you hit Portland, the next major city is San Francisco, *twelve hours* later. And, well, life is a little different now.

But like any good Jersey girl, I loved to drive. I loved driving alone, watching the trucks zoom by at night, marker lights blinking like Christmas trees. I loved driving with friends, singing along to bad, tinny Top 40 AM stations, buying tacky souvenirs at truck stops. Driving home from Philadelphia or D.C. and waking up at the same point on the New Jersey Turnpike, where the lights on the refinery turned it into an Emerald City. Staring at the radio relay towers blinking red in the distance and wanting to follow them forever.

I close my eyes and I can see it. I can feel the car moving. I can hear the radio playing and my friends talking, and the yearning for that feeling of freedom hurts somewhere inside the center of my chest.

First things first: I find an old army knapsack in the closet and grab CDs by the handful. Afghan Whigs, always good for bitter tales of lost love. My Springsteen bootlegs, no question. My beloved Rolling Stones, as if I could go anywhere without them. The Who, *Badmotorfinger* by Soundgarden, Motown compilations for that goofy thing you can sing along to by heart in the middle of the night when you're falling asleep despite gallons of fast food coffee. R.E.M. catches my eye; I think of *Reckoning*, and the summer of listening to that album on repeat while a carload of us drove around the East Coast to show after show. The first three Cheap Trick albums and *Live At Budokan*. Elvis Costello. The entire X catalog, mandatory for a trip to Los Angeles. Gram Parsons, Uncle Tupelo, Dylan. The Bowie box set, *London Calling* and *Sandinista*, Lou and the Velvets, Neil Young. I'm not consciously looking for roadtrip music; it's more like inviting friends to keep me company along the way.

And then I pause and carefully, reverentially, pull out the two Ramones CDs I own, *All The Stuff And More*, Volumes I and II. That might not sound like a lot, but being the Ramones, two CDs means I have over sixty songs.

Next, I grab a duffel bag and walk into the bedroom. There's no logic, just happy, free-association packing. This is about favorite clothes, cool clothes, rock chick clothes, all the black clothes that looked so good with my blonde hair but were wasted up here in the land of Birkenstocks and flannel shirts. Finally, I am going to get a chance to wear everything I barely have a reason to. Low-cut jeans, blue and black. Underwear--and I'm gleefully digging the good stuff out of the back of the drawer. I don't think for a minute that anyone but me will ever see it, but that's a good enough reason. Shoes break down into two categories, Converse All-Stars and boots, and I add my sad and lonely pair of high heels for good measure.

I finish getting ready in twenty minutes, exactly. This seems much easier than it should be and I am terrified that I am forgetting something. "Maps are in the car. Phone charger is in the car. Bottle of water is in the car. Sleeping bag is in the trunk..." I recite the list like a mantra to keep me safe, or more likely, make me brave enough to go through with this.

The last thing I need to do is email my manager and claim a family emergency. I deliberately do not change my voicemail, because I don't need Ian calling me at work in the morning and have my message inform him that I am going to be gone for a week or two.

That final business detail complete, I sit back in my desk chair, and take a deep breath. My cheeks are flushed with excitement. I take another deep breath and push my bangs out of my face. There's an air of finality, mixed with a slight tinge of danger, settling about me that I kind of like. Is it finality or resignation? No, it feels more like rebellion. I'm going, dammit. I'm just going.

Balancing bags, I grab the doorknob, take one last deep breath to settle myself, and walk out of the apartment. Outside, it is dark and cool and quiet, that deep, Sunday-night-12:00 a.m. kind of quiet.

Key in the ignition, I start the car, and then slide the faceplate into the stereo, watching the equalizer come to life and illuminate the interior of the car in soft greens and blues. For the life of me, I have no idea what I want to listen to first. I sit, letting the engine run for a while, hands gripping the steering wheel for dear life. It feels like I don't know where I'm going.

And then it hits me--I smile and take the Replacements out of the knapsack, cue the disc up to "Someone Take The Wheel." As I pull onto I-5 in the deep Sunday night blackness, I sing along with pseudo-ebullience; I mean it but I don't quite feel it yet, and I'm hoping that throwing myself into the spirit of the moment will bring me around. I am seized by confusion, I am bursting with excitement, and I am plain old borderline terrified. But I am absolutely bound and fucking determined to face it all head-on for the first time in ages.

Thirty minutes later, I am passing through Tacoma. While I still have this odd raw terror and irrational fear of the unknown churning around my stomach, I feel a lot better, and settle into the rhythm of driving. Fort Lewis. Nisqually Basin. The first sign for the Sleater-Kinney Road exit heralding Olympia. I consider stopping at the next rest stop for coffee, but I'm afraid that if I stop moving I'll be seized by reality, change my mind, turn around, and go back home.

What am I so scared of? I do this all the time--or rather, I used to do this. What is this big gaping hole in my chest? Since when did I get so scared of--well, I don't know what I'm scared of. But I am going to keep driving, and maybe I'll find out.

CHAPTER 2: 1988

It was 8:45 p.m. and I was already late, or at least that's what my answering machine informed me when I arrived home from work. I was late as I was getting changed into the quickest thing I could find (Keith Richards t-shirt and black stovepipe jeans with the zippered ankle vents from Reminiscence snatched up off the floor, spraying perfume over them, oblivious to wrinkles. Red Converse.). I was late while I was throwing a notebook, my cameras, a pile of tapes and a stack of photocopied fanzines into my black Danish schoolbag. I was late as I decided there was nothing I could do with my hair except twist it up into some semblance of neatness and clip it in place with a barrette, almost making me wistful for the short spiky punk hairdo I finally gave up on the year before.

I was still late as I bolted down the three flights of stairs from the two-bedroom railroad apartment that I shared. I was late as I ran up Second Avenue to Washington Street, late as I flew by Pier Platters (where Bill, the owner, helpfully leaned out and yelled, "You're late, they're going on in 15 minutes" as I ran by and waved). I was late jamming seventy-five cents into the turnstiles in the PATH station, frantically hopping down the stairs two at a time and leaping into a waiting train.

I was late getting off the train at Ninth Street, late sprinting up the stairs, late dodging pedestrians down Eighth Street to MacDougal, late cutting diagonally across Washington Square Park where the drug dealers hassled me for fun as I ran by. I was late tearing down West Fourth Street until I finally hit Bowery and those last few blocks south, passing Phebe's and where the Great Gildersleeves used to be and the Amato Opera House, until I finally reached the corner of Bowery where Bleecker dead-ended into it, and yanked open the staple-scarred battered wooden doors to CBGB's.

Panting loudly and dramatically, I frantically fished my ID out of my bag and a fistful of crumpled bills out of my pocket. "You're not late," said the guy at the door, as he cursorily glanced at my driver's license and took my eight dollars. "There are still two more bands before Sonic Youth."

Disgusted, I strode into the club, passing the coat check and the video games, heading for the front of the stage, where I found my friends. There were Patrick and Suzanne and Alison and Alyson (otherwise known as "The Alisons"), sitting on the stage or leaning on the monitors, looking bored to tears. The Alisons were wearing the usual uniform, Staten Island Salvation Army '50s dresses, with fishnets (Alyson's were always red) and black Converse. Suzanne, as always, looked like she should be standing next to the New York Dolls in front of the Gem Spa with her dark curly hair and a mix of thrift store and glam that only she could pull off.

"Don't fucking say it," I said as I approached. "I'm NOT fucking late, and I'm going to fucking kill whoever left a message on my answering machine informing me that there were no opening bands tonight, and Sonic Youth would be onstage by nine." I glared pointedly at Patrick, standing there in his bad haircut from Astor Place, with his post-Ramones ripped jeans and vintage black suit jacket (sleeves rolled up, of course; Sonic Youth buttons strategically placed on the lapel).

"Don't blame me," Patrick said. "I didn't find out until I got here. Something happened to the power down here last night. Some bands from out of town were supposed to play a label showcase, so Sonic Youth said it was okay to add them to the bill tonight. Thurston said it was cool, he likes playing later." He leaned back on the monitor with an air of infuriating superiority. Yes, Patrick was probably the biggest Sonic Youth fan we, or anybody, knew. But right now Mr. *Starpower* fanzine, Mr. I-Know-Everything-About-Sonic-Youth, was pissing me off.

"Whatever. I didn't need to fucking run all the way from fucking Hoboken to the fucking Bowery." I was fuming. I was still fuming when my sore shoulder reminded me that I had a bag full of things that needed to be distributed. I nudged Patrick aside from his place in front of Kim Gordon's microphone, and plopped my bag down in the tiny gap between the edge of the stage and the monitor with a satisfying thud.

Rummaging inside, I pulled out a handful of cassette tapes with handmade inserts. With exaggerated care, I handed out Maxell XL-90s into eagerly waiting hands: "The Replacements at City Gardens. R.E.M. at Maxwell's. Some random dB's show. Hüsker Dü--also Maxwell's." Recordings of live shows, bought, begged or traded.

I was about to hand the last tape to Patrick, except at the last second I remembered the grief he'd put me through earlier that evening, so I pulled it back. He got this panicked look on his face, like he actually thought I wasn't going to give it to him.

"Fucker. Patrick, next time don't make a fucking crisis unless there is one, okay?" I said, handing him the cassette. He looked slightly sheepish, and I almost felt bad for a second.

"Last thing," I said with trepidation, and began handing out copies of my fanzine. Not someone else's 'zine, mine. I finally had the guts and the money and the motivation to do it. Everyone accepted a copy with enthusiasm. Some guy was looking over Alison's shoulder and caught my eye, and raised his eyebrows inquisitively. I handed one over to him, too.

"*notes from the electric blue*," read Suzanne. "Right fucking on, Lisa."

"I was tired of being edited," I said, shaking my head. "The motivation was really not all that noble."

"Bullshit. You published. The motivation doesn't matter, the result matters," she said, reading the last page.

"Is it just poetry?" asked Patrick, flipping through.

"No. Some photos, one short story--but mostly poetry."

I looked around at the crowd, then at the stage. There were roadies or musicians in the opening bands, I could never tell the difference (and sometimes there wasn't one), setting up amps and checking connections and tuning. One band had played, so there were two more bands before SY. I figured I could go get some food, or something, since I didn't get a chance to even think about eating during my interstate marathon earlier in the evening.

I was considering my options when Alison grabbed my hand.

"Hey. I need to talk to you. Can we go outside?" she asked.

"Hell yeah," I said. "I'm starving, and I don't want to stand in here all night waiting for Sonic Youth. There is no air in this place, ever."

"We'll be back," Alison told the others. "Uh, stand big, or something. We want our spots back."

"It's not like anyone will be looking for these spots until five minutes before Sonic Youth hit the stage. Heaven forbid anyone should act like they're actually interested in the band," Patrick said as we walked away.

He was right; our little band of outlaws was an exception. We cared about proximity more than we cared about trying to be cool, so we'd arrive ridiculously early and camp at the front of the stage, or wait in line outside, which was how we all met.

Alison and I walked back outside. There were probably a dozen people hanging around in front of CBGB's, smoking, talking, waiting for friends. I was suddenly overwhelmingly tired and collapsed cross-legged on the sidewalk. To the horror of my friends, this was a preferred position of mine. I maintained that the sidewalk outside CB's was cleaner than any surface inside the club, since at least the sidewalk saw some rain occasionally.

"It's Suzanne," Alison said. "You're not gonna guess who moved into her apartment today."

"What?" I stood back up, temporarily forgetting my fatigue. "Not Kevin. Not that fucking loser junkie asshole. Please tell me I'm wrong." I was so mad I was practically spitting.

"One and the same."

"What is she thinking?"

"She's thinking what everyone thinks. That she can save him," Alyson said.

"He's going to steal everything she cares about. He's going to sell it all. He's going to bring other girls home to fuck in her apartment. How does she think he's going to treat her any differently than the last three women he's been living with?"

"Four," she said. "But remember, they have a 'connection!' He wrote a song about her!"

"And he's told the last four women the exact same lie about the exact same song! Save me from rock and roll musicians, and from women too stupid to see through them," I said, as I shook my head in disgust and sat back down. "Gimme a cigarette." None of us really smoked--it was a tool, a prop, a shield against boredom more than an actual habit.

Alison began to excavate her cavernous bag; it was identical to mine, one of those Danish school bags we all carried. They were made of this canvas that was impossible to destroy, had endless pockets and compartments, and expanded to ridiculous dimensions. You could fit cameras, a limitless supply of tapes and books, clothes, sneakers, duct tape, lunch--you name it. In fact, Alison and I met because one night at Danceteria I put my bag down, turned around for half a second, and turned back again to see a strange woman going through my bag. After I screamed and pounced on her, she explained that she thought it was hers.

While Alison continued to dig, a tall, quiet guy who was leaning up against the wall next to us suddenly bent down, silently offering me a pack of Marlboro Lights. I looked up at him suspiciously, and then over at Alison, who was still fruitlessly furrowing through the bag.

I made the decision to accept the offer--he was cute. I took a cigarette out of the pack, and stood up to get a better look at my benefactor. He pulled out a book of matches and struck one, lighting it for me in the still summer heat.

Alison was still attempting to unearth her cigarettes, oblivious to this recent development.

"Yo! Alison! I'm okay."

She looked up at me and then noticed who I was standing next to. With a barely disguised smirk, she said, "I'm going back inside," and immediately made herself scarce. I didn't even have time to protest.

Bereft of my shield, I had no choice but to face the stranger head on. He was tall and painfully thin, pale skin, dark hair. Uh-oh. This was dead on my type. The face, fucking gorgeous in a quiet understated way. Thin, narrow, cheekbones. Blue eyes. He had been looking off into space, staring uptown, when he seemed to remember I was standing there.

"I'm James," he said, offering his hand. "Sorry to be rude. I haven't been to New York before and this is all kind of overwhelming."

"Lisa. Thanks for the cigarette." I shook the proffered hand.

"I have to warn you, though, you just accepted a gift from a rock and roll musician," he said, deadpan, but with a spark in those eyes.

"Eavesdropping. That's cute," I said, just barely annoyed.

"I'm a songwriter. I have to eavesdrop, that's where I get my best material. I swear, I could not make up the stuff I hear."

My internal light bulb went off. "Songwriter, musician, first time in New York--you must be in one of the bands that got bumped from yesterday?"

"Yeah," he said. "We're here from Seattle. This is our first tour cross-country. Some label guys were supposed to come see us last night--who knows if they'll bother to show up tonight." He shrugged.

"You don't sound all that excited."

"I'm not!" he said. "We're not ready. We don't have enough songs. We haven't played live long enough. If we got signed now, we'd just fall flat on our faces. But our lead singer is convinced that everyone will want to sign a band from Seattle now. Green River and Mudhoney, and the music world will soon be banging down the doors." He rolled his eyes.

I regarded James again. "You have too much common sense to be a rock and roll musician," I told him.

"Thank you. It's a problem. I can't find anyone else who shares my 'common sense,' as you put it. These guys are the closest I could find, but they're still not it. But it's better than sitting home and singing in the shower. At least I'm playing, making music, out touring, seeing other bands, getting more ideas."

"And more material," I couldn't resist.

"Yeah, that too." He smiled, and looked at my shirt. "You know, that picture was taken in Seattle."

It was my favorite shirt ever: Annie Liebovitz's shot of Keith Richards going through customs.

"You're a Stones fan?" I asked, surprised and hopeful.

"Enough to know where that picture was taken."

Now I was impressed, but had zero intention of letting him know. So I settled for a grudging, "You're all right, James from Seattle."

He grinned, flashing these comet blue eyes. Ah, shit. I was done for.

"So how do you like New York?" I asked, ignoring my internal dialogue.

"I think I like it just fine, but I really haven't seen much besides CBGB, the little grocery store across the street--"

"Bodega," I said, automatically.

He looked at me strangely.

"Sorry. It's a bodega, it's a Spanish word that means--well, I don't know what it means, actually, but it's what we call those little stores. Or delis. It's not a grocery store--okay, I'm being stupid. Go on," I said, babbling incoherently.

(*Fuck!* went the internal monologue. *Nice first impression.*)

"Well, I've seen like this one corner, and the--bodega," he continued, carefully. "And then just the drive through the Holland Tunnel to the Travelodge in Jersey City, and then back. The rest of the guys in the band agreed that no one could go wandering off--too afraid someone will get lost, mugged or arrested. Idiots." He shook his head.

Something made me ask, "So how much time do you have before you go on?"

James glanced at his watch. "Half an hour."

I got up off the sidewalk. "Want the dime tour of the East Village?"

He looked at me sideways. I think he thought I was fucking with him or something. After the bodega lecture, I didn't blame him.

"What do you have in mind?"

"It's your first time in New York. You can't just see it standing under the awning at CB's. C'mon!" I started walking north, and then turned to see if he was following. He hesitated slightly and then bounded after me, grinning.

We walked up the Bowery in a strange but companionable silence. James walked with a simple confidence, deliberately observing his surroundings as we walked north.

When we reached the corner of Third Avenue and St. Mark's Place, I began: "Okay, over there--that big white building."

He looked as I pointed east down St. Marks.

I continued: "That's the place that the Velvet Underground played for the first time ever."

"As the Velvet Underground, or were they still the Exploding Plastic Inevitable?" he asked, so quickly that I knew it originated from a knowledge base that was second nature.

"Exploding Plastic Inevitable. Very good." I continued, dumbfounded. "This is St. Mark's Place... kind of the punk rock version of Haight-Ashbury. Manic Panic and Trash and Vaudeville."

"Oh, man...." He gazed longingly down the street.

"No time for shopping, I know. But now you know where it is and you can come here next time you're in New York."

He grinned again. Eyes like blue fire every time he smiled.

"This way," I tilted my head west, and we crossed Third Avenue toward Cooper Union, and then again diagonally to the traffic island. James regarded the sculpture in the center of the island, his arms folded.

"This is the Imagine Cube," I said, doing my best Vanna White. "When John Lennon was shot, someone painted 'IMAGINE' on it in big white letters, and it stayed that way for a long, long time, so we just started calling it the Imagine Cube." I pushed on it, fruitlessly. "It spins... or at least it's supposed to."

"I think you might need two hands... or even four." James moved to the other corner and we both started pushing on it. Still nothing.

"Oh well," I said. "I guess it doesn't turn, but I could have sworn that it did."

We were walking away from the sculpture when a couple, dressed in business attire and carrying briefcases, approached us with concerned looks on their faces.

"Is the cube not turning?" the man asked.

"Doesn't look like it, " I said.

James looked at me, slightly bemused.

"Here, let's all try it," the woman suggested. We each took a corner and started to push. Suddenly--movement! Small shouts of joy as the cube began to turn. All four of us stood back with satisfied looks on our faces, watching it spin.

The couple said goodbye and hurried off. I was about to start talking again, but noticed that James was still standing there, staring at the cube slowly winding down.

"You just had an authentic New York moment," I said after a few minutes.

"Yeah, I guess so!" he said, laughing quietly. "No one at home would talk to total strangers like that, even if you were lying in the street, bleeding. People say that everyone in Seattle is so nice, that we're not like New York, but I maintain that it's a total sham and this incident has now proven me correct."

"Okay, continuing..." I assumed my tour guide mode again.

"Ready."

I faced north and pointed up at the ConEd clock tower in the distance. "Up there is Fourteenth Street, the vicinity of the Palladium and Irving Plaza; a little further west of that tower is Union Square, home of the late Max's Kansas City and Andy Warhol's Factory--at least the most well-known one."

"Where Valerie Solanis shot Andy?"

This guy had to stop impressing me or I was going to propose marriage on the spot.

I recovered and replied, "Correct." I turned left, and pointed. "This is West Eighth Street, which has the best shoe stores in the world; you can find anything you have ever wanted, from Doc Martens to KISS-style '70s platform boots. If you continue down the block, you will pass Electric Lady Studios on your left, not far from the corner of Sixth Avenue." I finished, a little breathlessly. I had never done this for anyone who gave a damn and it was making me inexplicably giddy.

James paused, taking it all in, and then a look of understanding broke over his face, followed by that grin again.

"West Eighth Street and Sixth Avenue?" he said, enunciating deliberately.

"Yeah?" I didn't understand the question at first.

"As in, 'Hey, Keith...'" and all of a sudden, he began a not-bad imitation of an English accent, and I realized with a not-insignificant degree of shock that he was quoting Mick Jagger's opening lines on *Emotional Rescue*, where he asks Keith what he was doing standing on the corner of West Eighth Street and Sixth Avenue. Where had this guy come from?

I wanted to reply in my best Keith Richards but started laughing out loud instead to cover up my nerves.

"Sorry--I'm not laughing at you. I just do a terrible British accent."

"They recorded that at Electric Lady... god! Now I get it! I've looked at maps of New York City and couldn't figure out what was so special about that corner!"

James was crowing in delight. He was so damn happy at that moment. I understood completely, because I remembered exactly how I felt when I walked by Electric Lady one afternoon freshman year and was struck with a similar bolt of realization.

"Jesus. We've walked all of four feet and all this is just--right here," he said.

"Yeah. This city is like that."

He looked at his watch. "I hate to do this, but I gotta get back... I can't leave the guys to set up without me. They get kind of pissed off."

"That's okay, we're pretty much done here... last landmark!" I pointed dramatically across the intersection. "The Riviera: after-show headquarters of the Grand Council."

"The Grand Council?"

"It's what we call it when my friends and I go to the Riviera after concerts and deconstruct the shows until four in the morning...we're kind of pathetic that way," I said. "We keep talking about publishing a fanzine called 'The Grand Council.'"

"Actually, it sounds like a hell of a lot of fun. Seattle closes at, like, two a.m."

We crossed the street and headed back south toward CB's. As we were walking, the realization finally hit that this guy could not be closer to perfect in my world, and suddenly, it was as though I no longer had any idea how to talk to him.

"So where are you guys playing next?" I said. "Are you going to Boston? I love the clubs up there. We saw the Replacements at the Rat a few years ago..." I realized that I was chattering nervously to fill the silence and cover my sudden awkwardness. Before I could make too much of a fool of myself, I stopped and apologized.

"Sorry. I'm babbling. I have a habit of doing that."

"No, no, don't apologize! Jesus!" He shook his head. "I'm just--in shock, still, at all of this. I'm in a band, we're in New York City, we're playing CBGB's, and cute girls are giving me tours of Greenwich Village. Greenwich fucking Village! It's just a little much for me to take in all at once." He paused. "Can I ask a question?"

"Shoot."

"Do you know where the Ramones shot the picture on the cover of their first album? If I came back from New York with just one picture, I would want it to be that."

Oh, god. Be still my heart, was all I could think. But then I recovered and answered him, just as we approached the club again.

"I have good news and bad news," I said. "The good news is that I do know, and they took that picture in the alley right behind CB's."

James looked confused. "So what's the bad news?"

"The bad news is that I wouldn't go back there in the middle of the day with a crowd of fifty people. It's just not safe."

His face fell.

"Think of how many times they stood on the stage you're about to play on," I said. "And there's an equally legendary photo of them in front of that street sign over there, with the club in the background."

The eyes glowed again. He smiled, and I was about to fall fast and hard, when a blonde-haired guy with bad roots leaned out of the door and waved at James, breaking the moment.

"Hey, Jim, we gotta get our shit together."

"Cool, I'll be right there," he said, over his shoulder.

James looked square at me. "We have to load out right after we play, but we're staying to see Sonic Youth. Please come and talk to me after the show, okay? We're parked right over there," he gestured at a beat-up light blue Ford Econoline van with Washington State plates parked just south of CB's. I nodded dumbly and he smiled, flashing those blue eyes again, pulled open the doors and disappeared into the smoky darkness.

I sat down on the sidewalk again and bummed a cigarette off a girl standing outside, hugging the moment to myself for a little while. As I heard the band--James's band--start to play, I got up, opened the doors and headed back inside.

I watched his band (who were called Bone Dry) from the back while I waited at the bar to buy a Coke. I was pleasantly surprised that they didn't suck and that I wouldn't have to lie to him about it after the show. Sonic Youth blew our collective eardrums off, stacks and stacks of handmade guitars lying on the stage, Kim Gordon a fucking rock and roll goddess, Thurston so tall we were always surprised he didn't bang his head on the ceiling.

I took roll after roll of photos. I wasn't really a photographer--I only picked up a camera in the first place so I could take pictures at concerts--but it seemed like we were all trying a million things at once back then. Everyone had a band or a 'zine or took photos or wrote something. It was that time in life when everyone was trying to figure out what they were going to do when they grew up, so they did everything at once and let the dust settle eventually. I tried looking for James before Sonic Youth but it got instantly packed (like it always did) and I didn't want to risk losing my spot, even for those eyes.

After the show, we all piled out of the club into the humid June night, laughing and talking, Patrick scrawling notes from the show into the little notebook he carried everywhere. The light blue van was now half a block north of CB's, and James was leaning up against it. I stood at the curb with the gang, who were trying to figure out where we were going next.

"Uh, could I have a minute?" I said to Alyson.

She glanced over in the direction I was pointing and nodded knowingly. "We'll meet you across the street. I need cigarettes."

I tried to maintain some semblance of being laid back as I walked up to James. He didn't even bother, bounding to attention and smiling big.

"Oh my god! I've never seen anything like that!" he said.

"Don't Sonic Youth play in Seattle a lot?" I asked.

"Yeah, they do, but it's just not the same thing," he said, shaking his head. He paused. "Dare I ask what you thought of us?"

"You guys weren't bad at all."

"That's okay. I'll settle for that," he said, laughing.

"No," I said, "There are some good songs there. You're an excellent guitar player. You have a strong sense of melody."

"Wow," James said. "You listened." His eyes met mine and I wanted nothing more than to look away, make some more small talk, have someone, anyone, interrupt us. But that didn't happen, so I met his gaze and felt my insides twist into knots.

"I think we're going out for coffee and stuff--you guys are all welcome to come with if you want," I finally said, pointing across the street at the gang, who were standing there pretending like they weren't watching me intently.

"Wow, I'd love to, but the van is loaded and we're super-paranoid about leaving it with the gear inside. We thought we'd just drive to Boston."

I sighed inwardly. I really wanted some more time with this guy, although the small voice in my brain kept insisting, *he lives in Seattle.*

"Wait a second." James opened the back door of the van, rummaged inside a medium sized cardboard box, and pulled out a cassette tape.

"Here," he said, giving me the tape. "It's our demo. I know you're not about to join our fan club, but our address is in there..." The sentence kind of trailed off, as though he was suddenly unsure.

"Wait, here..." I rummage inside my bag and pull out my last copy of *notes from the electric blue.* "Something to read on the road. And there's a P.O. box in there; I'd love a postcard from Seattle," I said, amazing myself with my sudden ability to think spontaneously.

He smiled, and started eagerly thumbing through the pages.

"Have a good tour," I said, waving goodbye as I began to cross Bowery in the direction of my friends.

"Lisa?"

I was only a foot or so out into the street, waiting for an opening in the traffic, when I heard my name being called. James came running up and gave me a hug. Just as I was turning away again, he grabbed my hand, pulled me to him, and kissed me on the mouth. It was sweet and serious and childlike in its simplicity, but it made me dizzy.

We stood there looking at each other, James still holding my hand, and then he reluctantly let go, walked back over to the van and waved as he climbed in the back and shut the door.

★

And that was how I met James Rossman. His band went on to Boston, and down to Philly and DC and even as far south as Atlanta, but that was when they imploded and he jumped ship. He grabbed a Greyhound back to New York and took a room at the Y and a job waiting tables at the Riviera, and an ad in the Village Voice looking for bandmates. Of course, I didn't know any of this. I told everyone I didn't care, but the truth was that I was checking my P.O. box every day, just in case.

Three months later, I was sitting on the sidewalk in front of CB's waiting for Alison and Alyson, staring into space and chain smoking in my boredom and exasperation, since this time they were the ones who were late.

"Can I bum a cigarette off you?" asked a voice to my right.

I looked up and it was James. I think I stopped breathing.

"You don't remember me, I'm sure," he said.

I was too happy to see him to play it cool. "You have got to be fucking kidding me, right?"

His face lit up like the Empire State Building in response.

James sat down on the sidewalk next to me and started telling me everything that had happened to him over the last three months. The girls turned up thirty minutes later, walked right by as though they hadn't even noticed, but then turned around and waved excitedly at me once they were out of James's line of sight.

I don't even remember who was playing at CB's that night; we didn't stay. We walked around the Village and went into the Grassroots and sat there drinking beer and playing twenty questions. Not the game Twenty Questions, but the questions you need to ask someone to really to know them. You usually don't do this when you meet someone. You find this stuff out eventually, slowly. Either you see it or someone tells you, but you rarely sit there and ask these things. Who do you love? What makes you happy? What are your politics? Are you a good friend? Do you get along with your parents? What's the first thing that you remember as a child? What is important to you?

And, of course, the vital questions:

"The Replacements?" I asked.

He frowned. He was cute even when he frowned.

"I think Westerberg is a good songwriter. I just have a problem taking them seriously."

"If the songs are good, what's the problem?"

"Ahhhhh, you cannot argue this with someone who is a fan of theirs." He waved his hands in defeat.

"I'm just asking."

"They could be good musicians if they wanted to."

"Then they wouldn't be the Replacements," I said. "Your turn."

James took a sip of beer. "Ladies and gentlemen, the Rolling Stones," he said.

"Is there a question here?"

He looked at me eagerly, drumming his fingers on the table with mock impatience.

"Fine. There is no other band. There is no other album besides *Exile*."

"Taylor or Wood?"

"It's irrelevant." I waved the question away like smoke from my cigarette.

"It's a valid question."

"But it's totally irrelevant. Yes, the albums with Taylor are undeniably better. But he's not in the band anymore, he'll never be again, and besides, Taylor couldn't have played on *Emotional Rescue*."

"Go on." He leaned in closer. I could smell him, a little bit, Ivory soap and a little sweat, cigarette smoke and now cheap beer.

"*Emotional Rescue* gets slagged off as a disco album, but it is the quintessential New York Rolling Stones record. It is New York City in the summer," I said "You know, they filmed the video for "Waiting on a Friend" on St. Marks Place, and then at a bar down the street..."

"You mean right outside? So why are we sitting *here*?" He jumped up excitedly and grabbed my hand. And I never wanted him to let go.

★

We were sitting in the Holiday at 2:30 in the morning. James couldn't sit still all night. I'd mention some place in the Village I liked hanging out at, and he'd insist we go there immediately, which is how we ended up at the Holiday, by virtue of its amazing jukebox.

"What are we doing, James?" I finally asked.

"What do you mean, what are we doing? We're talking."

"We're not just talking," I said, leaning my chin on one hand and looking him right in the eyes. I could see the reflection of the Christmas lights strung along the walls in his pupils.

"We're making up for lost time," he said, meeting my gaze straight on.

It was a little too much for me to take, so I changed the subject. "Who's your favorite songwriter? Who do you want to be?"

"That's easy. Lou Reed. I want to play guitar like Keith Richards and Mick Taylor's bastard son and write lyrics like the reincarnation of Lou Reed," he said, sitting back in his chair with a satisfied look on his face.

"Is this why you didn't go back to Seattle? You wanted to live in New York and be Lou Reed?"

"I didn't go back to Seattle because I wanted to try to find you, and I wanted to be able to walk the same streets as Lou, yeah, sure. It's New York City. It's the center of the universe. I was tired of Seattle...and I hate L.A. I like walking. You can't walk anywhere in L.A."

That comment came out like he just stated his age: "I wanted to try to find you." There was no drama or emphasis or emotion. It was just matter of fact.

"I need another beer," I said, getting up from my chair to try to defuse what I was feeling at that moment. We weren't flirting, there were no coy double entendres and accidental touches or looks. I knew he was coming home with me that night, and that there would be no discussion or games played about it. It was just going to happen. It was as though someone else had decided all of this for us and we were just playing out the scene as directed.

★

Four a.m., closing time. We stayed in the Holiday until they literally threw us out. We could have kept talking until the sun came up.

"Now what?" I asked, my stomach doing flip-flops a mile a minute.

"What would you usually do now?" he asked. He wasn't flirting, he was just--asking.

"Well, the Riviera. Or Kiev. Or Wo Hop. Are you hungry?"

"Not really."

"Okay, then." I held out my hand, and he took it, sliding into mine like connecting puzzle pieces. By this point I had left Hoboken and was living in a tiny studio at the top floor of a brownstone on West Ninth Street between First and A, not far from Tompkins Square Park. We turned left, and started walking to my apartment, up the stoop, through the front door, up the five flights of stairs. I opened the four locks on the dented metal door I'd tried to spray paint red, pushed it open, and stepped inside. James stood out in the hall for a split second, looked at me, and then walked into the apartment.

I closed the door behind him, shut all the locks, put on the two chains, and then turned to watch James doing a slow circuit around the apartment, scrutinizing the photographs and posters and cut-out magazine photos hanging on every spare inch of wall. He was about to make a beeline for the record collection stacked against the far wall when he stopped himself. He held out his hand again, and I stepped forward and grabbed it hard.

We stood there looking at each other for--for I don't know how long. I had stopped wondering or caring about time hours ago. And then he leaned over and kissed me once, gently. Twice, harder. The third time felt like jumping off the roof and we fell into each other's arms for dear life.

I thought I was dreaming. It didn't feel real. It felt too real, too perfect, too good. He smelled good. He tasted good. I loved running my hands through his hair again and again, down his back, I wanted to hold him and kiss every part of him and wrap myself around him. It just worked. We just fit.

When we finally wore ourselves out--James falling back against the pillows gasping, shaking his head and laughing softly, me lying on top of him, my head collapsing into his chest, hair falling across his shoulders--the early morning light was starting to stream in behind the cracks in the curtains. He kissed me on top of my head, wrapped his left hand in the ends of my hair, curled himself around me completely and fell into a deep and total sleep almost immediately. I lay there, watching the light grow and creep into the tiny studio, while tears representing some emotion I'd never encountered before silently streamed out of my eyes, until I finally dropped off myself.

We never talked about how we felt about each other, or if we were going to get into a relationship, it was about the only thing unspoken that night and it was just understood.

Six weeks after that night, James moved out of the Y and into my apartment with his suitcase and his two guitars--a collection that would shortly grow, once his former bandmates shipped his electric guitars to him. He made himself this little space in the corner next to a window, where he'd lean back against the brick wall, and sit and play guitar, and write songs.

James got tired of his job at the Riviera and bought a bike and started working as a messenger, liking the freedom and flexibility it gave him. If he had a song idea, he could finish a delivery and go find a park bench and write it down. I got tired of working as a word processor while trying to figure out what I was going to do with my life, and the owner of the word processing place I worked at offered to teach me about computer programming. I accepted, gratefully; anything was better than typing bad movie scripts by wannabe scriptwriters.

James kept writing songs. Unlike so many musicians who could not wait to make it big, he just kept writing and looking for people to play with and was content with where he was at the moment. It never bothered him when we would walk by Folk City or Kenny's Castaways and would hear people playing who were not half as talented as he was. "It's okay," he always said. "I'm not ready. It's not time. When it's time, it'll happen."

We would go home, and he would fall back into the corner, open a notebook and pick up a guitar. I'd lie on the bed with a book, reading, listening to him play, and thinking that there could not be an existence more perfect than mine.

He made me write, unlike any boy I had ever been with before. He pushed me and prodded me and annoyed the fuck out of me to work on my poetry, on my photography, on anything that was creative. We'd sit there on weekend nights when we were too broke to go out, handing a notebook back and forth, taking turns writing lines. Some of it sucked; some of it was silly; but sometimes, when we weren't thinking too hard and the muse was smiling at us, we'd finish and go back and read what we'd written and it made us hold our breath. Some of them ended up being songs, and James would grab the notebook out of my hand, still reading, and drop back into the corner by the window and play guitar, putting words to music. Some of them ended up being poems, and I'd claim them as mine, kissing him repeatedly as I'd sneak the book out of his hands, and go type them up on the rickety old manual typewriter with the cool typeface I'd bought from a homeless guy in front of Cooper Union.

We went to shows, of course. James was even worse than I was about seeing live music, so nothing changed there. I'd come home from work on Wednesday and he'd be sitting on the floor with the Village Voice open to the club pages, circling shows with a red magic marker, waiting for me to return so we could figure out what we were doing for the next week, what we needed to plan on buying tickets to, what we could afford to see. James even outdid Patrick in his quest to see any band or musician he had ever read about in the smallest review in the most obscure fanzine.

"I haven't been here long enough to be jaded!" he would tease me, when I'd raise my eyebrows at the thought of yet another show at one a.m. on Tuesday night. "I can't be a cynical New Yorker yet--give me a few years."

"No. We already have one cynic in the family."

"Family. I like the sound of that."

I hadn't even realized what I'd said. I would never have said that word if I had been thinking. I swallowed hard and decided not to pursue that line of conversation.

It was the summer of 1989, and the Stones had a new album and a new tour coming. We were plotting and planning with Suzanne, and my old friend Andrea (with whom I'd seen the Stones for the first time in 1981) about what shows we were going to see. We had some semblance of an itinerary from someone who knew someone who had a cousin who had a friend who knew some guy in Brooklyn who had a Stones fanzine. The tour was starting in Philadelphia. There were shows in DC and Boston and a whole string of dates happening at Shea Stadium. We schemed and dreamed and saved money, aiming to see as many shows as we could until we went broke. "I need to see them--we need to see them, Lisa!" James said.

Seeing the Stones with James. Seeing my favorite band in the whole world with the man I loved more than I ever thought it was possible to love, who loved them as much as I did, who understood them as much as I did, who owned three copies of *Exile on Main Street* because he'd worn out two, who picked up every used copy of *Sticky Fingers* he saw because we'd heard a rumor that they were going to discontinue issuing them with the real zipper on the cover, who was as utterly obsessed as I was with every detail about that band.

I would never forget the night I came home and James had made a sixty-minute tape with "Heartbreaker" on one side--just "Heartbreaker"--and "Fingerprint File"--just that song, too--on the other. Thirty minutes of each song.

"I want this for when I'm working, it'll be great for riding the bike uptown!" he said, dancing around the room to the third listen of "Heartbreaker."

"I've heard of mix tapes, sweetheart, but that usually involves *mixes* of different songs," I said, laughing, but understanding completely.

"Nah. I heard this song earlier today on the radio in some deli, waiting for a sandwich, just some crappy AM station, you know? But it was like I'd never heard it before... Here, listen!" James picked up the headphones and plunked them on my head, and turned up the volume, smiling expectantly at me. I didn't know what he was hearing in "Heartbreaker" at that moment that was captivating him so, but I knew what it felt like to hear a song you loved and knew by heart in a totally different way, to feel that flash of lightning hit you again out of nowhere. So I laughed and listened and took the headphones off and danced around the room with him until we fell on the bed, laughing and kissing and suddenly realizing we desperately needed to take each other's clothes off in the worst way possible.

I don't know when the heroin started. I do not know when James decided that he really wanted to see what it was like to be Keith Richards. I can only guess at his motivation, because it was the only one that ever made any sense to me, at all. I had to guess, because I did not know. He didn't tell me that he was even thinking about it, probably because he knew that I would have gone ballistic. But that never stopped him before. We talked about everything. We would talk about other people we lusted after, we would talk about whether or not we should separate and see other people, about whether we should stay together and see other people, about changing jobs and moving, about traveling to Europe and living in Italy for a few months. We talked about money without fighting, ever. We talked about the things that are usually left unspoken.

I wish he had talked to me about it. Although I know now that if he had, I probably would have joined him in that madness because I couldn't have stood to have been left out of something he was experiencing. I wonder, sometimes, if that's why he didn't tell me. I also wonder if my consent would have stopped him, or whether he would have let me come with him. But I don't know why he never talked to me about it. I never would have left him for saying, "I wonder what heroin is really like?" Anyone we knew would have been lying if they said they hadn't wondered. We all saw it up close and personal. We all idolized Johnny Thunders and Keith Richards and knew the words to "Heroin" by heart. People would slip over to that dark side but I was usually not surprised by who chose that path--kids with pasts that I could not imagine (let alone imagine having actually lived), friends with demons and monsters that they had to deal with on a daily basis.

But not James. James would freely admit that his past was not that interesting. He had a nice, normal, suburban childhood. He spoke to his parents regularly, and with great affection. His sister called every other week. My parents adored him, and he wanted to go out to Jersey for Sunday dinner more often than I did--and I liked my parents.

I never saw the track marks, if they were even there. I never saw them because I never would have thought to look for them. He could not have been using that much because he always had money. He worked hard, he always had a straight job. He had money to pay the rent, he never sold his guitars, nothing ever disappeared from the apartment. He was as far from the stereotypical lazy, egotistical, women-using, druggie musician as you could possibly get.

I imagine that he used to wait until I fell asleep every night to go shoot up. I was always gone early in the morning, while his schedule was erratic. Sometimes he worked mornings, sometimes he worked afternoons, sometimes he worked split shifts. There was never any suspicion or jealousy between us so we never watched each other. We never worried if someone was late or not around or didn't call. He worried if I didn't call just because I was a girl and this was New York City, and from a safety standpoint he was probably right. I'd be sitting on the subway with my computer books totally engrossed, a mugger's dream date.

"I'm not worried, look at these books! These are big-ass, heavy books. If anyone tries anything, I'll throw a book at them," I said.

"That's right, the invincible Lisa, queen of New York City. Do me a favor: call anyway, okay?" James said, kissing me on my forehead.

By then I was going to night school up at Hunter, taking some computer classes and getting good at programming languages and other things I never even knew existed.

It always takes me forever to fall asleep, but once I get through the agitation and restlessness I am out. I sleep well and soundly and don't move around at all. So to this day I do not know what woke me up that night. I woke up and James wasn't there. The bed wasn't even warm. It was only a studio so he couldn't be very far away. I thought that maybe he was sitting the dark with headphones on, playing guitar like he sometimes did, when he couldn't sleep or woke up with a dream or idea. But I didn't hear the strings squeaking under his fingers.

And then I sat straight up in bed, alert, I knew something had happened but didn't know what, and without even thinking I rushed into the bathroom and saw James lying on the floor. Cold. A syringe in his right hand. His left arm was still tied off above the elbow with a scrap of white cloth. A blackened spoon on the edge of the sink. I was about to scream and then I realized I had no time for screaming and I ran to the phone and called 9-1-1, and then I started trying to slap James and throw cold water on his face.

And then the ambulance was there and they were shaking their head and telling me, no, I'm sorry, he's dead; he's been dead for hours.

That's when the screaming started.

My neighbors across the hall came over at that point, somehow found my phone book and started calling people. I didn't even see them take the body away. The body. It wasn't the body. It was James.

The next day, and I was reinforced by the Alisons in split shifts, and Raquel and Suzanne. No one would leave me alone for a minute. Not even to run to the bodega for orange juice and cigarettes, the only things I wanted to consume. In the afternoon, I knew I had to let his family know. I was listed as James's emergency contact in what little paperwork he had ever filled out in New York. But I didn't know what to do. No one I knew, I mean really knew, not grandparents or aunts or whatever, had died. What do you do? So I called his sister, and in telling her what happened I had to go through it all over again, and we both screamed and cried together over the phone.

I couldn't go to the funeral; it wasn't a matter of money or logistics, everyone would have loaned me the money if I didn't have it. His parents flew James's body back to Seattle a few days later, and they made it very clear that my presence at the funeral would not be welcomed. This was despite hours on the phone with James's sister going over everything, over and over again, for me as much as for her, trying to find the clue that I missed, the one chance I had to stop him that I must not have seen, it didn't matter. His parents blamed me.

For the next six months, it seemed like all I did in my spare time (and that was any time I wasn't working or studying, both of which I did as much as possible) was try to find someone who knew he was using, find one person that he had talked to about it. I think I went into every bar within a fifty-block radius, Patrick doggedly following me, refusing to let me go alone. I interrogated everyone I knew in the clubs, bouncers, bartenders, soundmen. I made everyone I knew ask anyone they knew who might have used drugs even once if they knew anything, if the dealers recognized him, if any of their user friends knew anything. I never found anyone, anything, anywhere, any clue that would tell me what happened, when he started, why he started, how much he was using, how long he had been using. I would torture myself all night every night, going over everything, going through everything in the apartment, his notebooks and bank statements, his books and photographs and record albums. There was nothing there. Nothing that could tell me the answer to the question I really wanted to know, which was: *why*?

His parents wanted nothing to do with any of his things, for which I was grateful. So I had his records and guitars and his clothes and his songbooks and his socks and his engineer boots that were just a little too big for me. I would sit in the late night darkness in that tiny room that was our whole universe, with one of his denim cowboy shirts wrapped around me and a pair of his socks on my feet, listen to *Exile on Main Street* and hug one of his guitars like it was him. Like it could talk to me, like it could tell me what I had done wrong, where we had gone wrong, how I had missed this one thing, this one big, important thing.

The Stones finally announced their tour, and Suzanne and Andrea bought me tickets, even though it was the last thing in the world I cared about any more. The day before the tour started, Suzanne showed up at the apartment, and went through my drawers and my closet pulling out clothes, while I sat there, on the bed, smoking and staring into space. She was throwing a composition book from my desk into the duffel bag when I finally said something.

"What are you doing?"

"Packing for you," she said, like I was going to argue with her.

I didn't have the strength to argue, to be honest.

"I see that. Why did you throw the notebook in there?"

"You always have a notebook, Lisa."

I shook my head. "Not anymore." It was true. I'd stopped writing. I couldn't touch it, couldn't go near it, and couldn't think about it. The last book I had still had James's writing all over it, in the margins, pages we'd written together, grocery lists, notes he left me if he was going to be home late. Every time I sat down and thought about writing, all I could think about was James, and I had enough trouble dealing with those feelings without deliberately summoning them. So I turned it all off.

The three of us drove down to Philly the next morning, and later that afternoon, I stood there on the field in the September sunshine, not packed down front, but off to the side, still close enough to see every detail. I made the girls go into the crowd--I knew that's where they wanted to be and I didn't want them to hold back because of me. Plus, I wanted to be alone, because I did not know how I would react.

To my surprise, I was fine--I was even having a good time-- until Keith's solo set. When he started "Before They Make Me Run" I was torn between being thrilled to death to see this song played live and ripped apart inside because the impulse to turn to James and say, "Oh my god!" was so physical it was almost violent. There was no James. He wasn't home. I couldn't run and call him. I couldn't go home and jump up and down and explain it to him, knowing he understood. I couldn't write a poem about it for him and hand it to him and watch his face light up as he read it. I stood there, on the field at RFK Stadium in Philadelphia, wearing James's Ray-Ban Aviators to hide the tears streaming down my face as I sang along with Keith, and wondered what I was going to do with all the love in my heart that was still there for someone who wasn't.

James died in July of 1989. It wasn't until March of the next year when I woke up one day after yet another sleepless night, and looked at his guitars and his clothes, his notebook and his pens still there on the windowsill, and I realized that I was never going to get an answer and that it wasn't my fault. That was the day that I went and got boxes from the liquor store on Second Avenue and packed everything up carefully, stacking them in the corner where James used to sit and write and play and look at me and laugh. That Sunday I took the train out to my parents' house in New Jersey and asked them if they'd sell me my old car.

"Lisa, you can have the car if you take over the insurance payments, but you never wanted to deal with parking a car in Manhattan."

"I don't want it for Manhattan. I'm moving."

My parents looked shocked. I'd always believed that New York was the center of the universe and that there was no reason to move anywhere else.

"I'm going to Seattle," I said, not realizing until then that I had a plan. "I've always wanted to drive cross-country. I don't know if I'll stay there, but James said it was beautiful, and that there was lots of music there, and there's some new computer company nearby that I think I can get a job at."

My mother started to cry and reached out to hug me. At that point, she knew the truth.

"Honey. He's not there," she said, stroking my hair like she did when I was a little girl.

"Mom, I know he's not there, but I still feel like he's here. Everywhere I walk in the Village I see him. I might as well see what it's like to not live in New York for a while."

Besides, I thought, his grave is there, and I never got to say goodbye. I may have had some vague unarticulated idea in my head at the time to go to his grave and leave a suicide note and go back to some anonymous hotel room and kill myself... but I knew that was grief and drama whispering in my ear and not how I really felt.

So I packed everything up in the car and convinced one of the Alisons to drive with me, and, in mid-April, we drove through Pennsylvania and Ohio, up past Mount Rushmore, and through Montana. In a week we were in what seemed like another world. There was water and mountains and green everywhere, and, compared to the East Village, it was the Garden of Eden.

My night school professor's recommendation to call a former student got me a job at this new company called Microsoft, and James's best friend from high school, who had visited us once, had a neighbor who was renting out the apartment above her garage. Alyson and I lived in a cheap hotel on Aurora Avenue for a month until all the pieces of my new life came together, and then the day came when I needed to move into my new place, and she needed to go back to New York.

On the drive to the airport, Alyson finally blurted out, "Lisa, you're not going to do something stupid once I'm gone, are you?" I could hear the panic in her voice.

I started crying.

"No. Sometimes I think that I would like to, when it's the middle of the night and I miss him so much and I hate him for leaving without saying goodbye."

Now Alyson was crying.

"I can't believe you're going to stay here and not come back to New York. I am going to miss you. We are all going to miss you."

"I am going to miss you all, too. And I'll miss the Village and sitting on the sidewalk in front of CBs, and pierogies at 2:30 in the morning and sitting at the Rivera until they ask us to leave, and-- well, everything," I said. "But I need to leave until James isn't there anymore. I'm sure I'll just stay here for a year or two, and then I'll be begging you to let me sleep on your futon in the living room until I get my own place."

By this point we were at the airport. We both got out of the car, and I opened the trunk. The two of us stood there looking at each other and then she grabbed me in a fierce hug. Alyson let go, and walked away without saying a word. I was glad she did because I was crying so hard I couldn't have spoken.

I drove back into town and two days later, moved into the apartment above the garage in Wallingford. It was me and four walls, and all the boxes of James's stuff, but they went into a closet. Except for one shirt and his acoustic guitar, which I kept out because I thought I might learn to play it. To me, it was James. I would talk to it, sometimes, when I was tired and lonely and homesick. I started my new job, and loved it. I could work ten, twelve hours a day, which was exhausting but it was what I needed. And there was plenty of music, enough of a scene for me to get involved in again, although at a distance. I tried to find the urge to write or photograph or do something, anything, but it just wasn't there.

Sure, Seattle wasn't New York. But it was my home now, and it wasn't so bad, I had to admit. "I can't sit on the sidewalk in front of the Off Ramp like I could CBGB's, because it's always fucking raining," I explained to Suzanne on the phone. "But it'll do, at least for a while."

That was May of 1990. It was a month later before I finally had the courage to go out to the cemetery where James was buried. I drove out there on an early Sunday morning, after one of those really bad nights where I would sit up and listen to the records we both loved, and wear his shirt and his socks and hug the guitar and try to play it. Around five a.m. I was still tearful and sleepless, but this time, this time I was angry, so I went looking for the address of the cemetery. His sister had given me the grave location right after the funeral. She knew it wasn't my fault.

It was still and quiet and the sun was just peeking over the trees. I walked around for what seemed like forever, trying to figure out where the grave was--the numbers on the piece of paper made no sense to me whatsoever. Just when I was about to give up and go home, I turned around one more time and his gravestone was a few feet away from me. Seeing his name and those dates on that dark grey stone was almost more than I could take.

I collapsed on the wet ground next to the stone and leaned back against it, and then the words just came rushing out: "Fuck you, James. Do you hear me? Fuck you. Fuck you for being stupid, fuck you for not talking to me about it, fuck you for not saying goodbye." I sat there and I cried, I cried until I didn't have any tears left, until I was exhausted.

And then I was done.

As I stood up to leave, I put my hands in my pockets and I felt the guitar pick there. I had gone to visit Jimi Hendrix's grave when I was visiting the tourist sites with Alyson, and it was almost covered in them, left by admiring visitors paying tribute. Smiling a tiny bit, I placed the guitar pick on the bottom edge of the gravestone. I kissed my hand, laid it on top of the stone for a few seconds, and then turned and walked away.

When I was packing to move to Seattle, I had some vague

concept in my mind that I would visit James's grave often. But after that first time, it was like some kind of circle was closed, and I got on with my life. The sleepless nights started to go away. I even started looking for a place to live that was kinder than the cold dingy room above the garage, and ended up with a cozy little house share in the Central District a few weeks later.

What no one knows, not even Jake or Marie, is that I still go. Every year on the day after his birthday. It's like sending him a Christmas card. I stand there in the rain (it is always raining in Seattle in November) and tell him how my year has been, any news I have from New York, and about any musicians who have died that year. I bring flowers and a guitar pick. But once I walk away I don't think about it very much. I don't even talk about it very much anymore. I've never told Ian that James was buried in Seattle, or even that he died. I just refer to him in the past tense as one of my exes.

I still have the acoustic guitar, and that cherry Les Paul he worked double overtime to buy. The acoustic sits out in the music room, my spare bedroom, with the posters and records and memorabilia and artifacts, and I've gone through periods where I've struggled to play it. I will not let Ian touch it. He went to pick it up once and I practically bit his head off. "Geez," he said, "You'd think you were a real musician. Touchy, touchy." And he left it at that. Which was fine with me, because I wasn't going to explain it to him.

And James's Stratocaster, his beloved, beat up, 1975 black Strat that he bought because it was just like Keith's--I gave it to Jake one year. He'd had two guitars stolen out of the van after a show one night. The one guitar he had left was a piece of shit with the pickups held on with duct tape, and he couldn't afford anything new.

On Christmas Eve, I asked him to come over to the house. We walked into my room, and I picked up the guitar where it was lying on the bed, waiting. I handed it to him and he looked at me like I was crazy, and then I told him about James. We had known each other for a year and a half, but it was the first time I had told him the entire story. When I was done talking--and I cannot tell you how long I stood there talking, the words rushing out so fast it felt like they were tripping over each other--Jake sat down on the floor with the guitar in his hands and started crying. That was when I knew I'd done the right thing. Right in giving him the guitar, right in telling him, right in having this person be one of my best friends in the world.

James would have been so upset about Joey dying. He would have gone into the corner and started writing songs about it.

I've been crying silently for a while; my face is wet and hot with tears. Although I'm not that far from Portland now, there's no sign of civilization along the highway and exits are further apart. I think about coffee, I think about stopping and stretching for a while once I cross the border into Oregon. But I decide I'll just keep going until Eugene. There are no ghosts or memories to accidentally run into there. Lord knows there are enough in this car to keep me busy until Los Angeles.

CHAPTER 3: 1996

I met Ian at Rebecca and Tom's Mardi Gras party. Understand, this was not necessarily my idea of a fun Saturday night. Rebecca and I met at the internet startup I went to work for after cashing out of Microsoft. She was an absolute sweetheart, but her friends were all married and a little too cheerleader bouncy for me. But she was my friend, so I went. I even dressed up, digging out this velvet paisley shirt I originally bought to wear to see the Stones in Las Vegas.

As usual, the place was packed. A whole onslaught of people I didn't know and had nothing in common with. I foresaw an entire night of conversations about Swedish finish vs. Pergo. It always made me secretly glad to still be single, even though it made me the recipient of constant, well-meaning pity. I took solace in the company of my geek co-workers, who huddled in the corner to avoid the same conversations I was.

Going to this party was some attempt on my part to try to broaden my social circle. Marie was off on business in Texas for the next six months, the worst possible place for a chick from South Jersey. We talked all the time, but I hated not having my best girlfriend around.

The boys were on the road, in L.A., or somewhere else, almost all the time now. Christine was being a hermit after having been fired--okay, that's not how it was phrased at the time, but that's exactly what did happen--about six months after the band got signed. The label felt they needed a "name" manager to get their affairs together. While she somewhat agreed, she also felt the same way I did, that no one else would care about them as much as she did, and that the guys should have fought harder to keep her. They were just so grateful to finally have a deal that they didn't want to argue with the label and, while she couldn't blame them, it still hurt. So for all intents and purposes, she was incommunicado, and

I let her be.

The music at this party had gone downhill fast. Just when I thought that the worst I was going to have to endure was the ever-bland Wallflowers, our hostess, in an attempt to kindle some party spirit, put on the Macarena, and began to encourage us all to dance. Trying not to visibly cringe, my survival instinct turned me towards the front door. Unfortunately, Rebecca was standing right in front of it. I downed my drink in a quick swallow, held up the empty glass, pointed at the kitchen, and fled for my life.

I was standing in front of the counter trying to decide which of the pitchers of margaritas was non-alcoholic when a voice behind me said, "You couldn't dance the Macarena just to be a good sport?"

I turned around and found myself facing someone I had overheard earlier introduced as a friend of Rebecca's husband. I decided that my wisest course of action would be to pretend I hadn't heard him.

"Do you know which of these is non-alcoholic?" I asked. I had to drive myself home, after all.

"I mean, Rebecca's just trying to be a good hostess," he said.

"You know, I endured listening to 'Ironic' and watching those housewives try to act as though we were listening to Coffin Break or something, and she had to put on that abysmal 'Breakfast At Tiffany's' song twice," I said, feeling a little defensive.

"Whoa! I'm on your side here. Trust me, if 'Who Will Save Your Soul' had come on, I would have been out that door in a flash," he said.

I halted my diatribe, and regarded the stranger critically. No wedding ring, he wasn't sloppy drunk, and appeared to be my age or a little older.

"My name's Ian, by the way," he said, extending his right hand. "I'm sorry, I should have introduced myself earlier."

And he has manners. "Lisa," I said, shaking his hand.

"You know, I had to see that 'Breakfast At Tiffany's' band," he said.

"Why on earth?"

"Because my best friend was dating a girl who loved that song, so he bought her tickets to their concert, and I went along for moral support. Although, to be fair, I can't hate him too much because he's the same guy that forced me to come with him to see this new band called Blue Electric... at the Central!"

I burst out laughing, while he stood there looking at me thoroughly confused, not understanding what he said that was so funny. I stopped my mad cackle and explained: "Blue Electric were my next door neighbors when I first moved to Seattle. They are great, great friends of mine. They will get a kick out of the fact that some guy tried to impress me by saying that he'd seen them back in the day."

(In fact, I would have called Jake on my cell phone at that very moment, but decided to wait. This guy had some potential.)

"You're kidding! They are a great band. I'm not sure they'll be the Seattle version of the Stones, but I like watching them try."

"Jake would love to hear you say that."

"Jake--you talk about him like he's your little brother."

"But he is. I love those boys. I cooked them dinner; I wired them money when their van got broken into on tour... they are my friends and I just love them to death. And it helps that I think their music is amazing," I said earnestly, going into full-scale superfan mode before I caught myself.

At that moment, Rebecca came towards us, headed for the alcohol. She was a little silly drunk, but not too bad. She stopped and looked at the two of us standing there talking. "Oh, you two have met! Good, Tom kept telling me all night that you two had to meet, because you both have that music--*thing*," she said, waving her hands dismissively.

"Have a drink, Rebecca. Have several," I said, steering her towards the drink pitchers. "Just tell me which one is non-alcoholic."

Rebecca poured her drink, gave me a really obvious wink, and went back into the living room.

I sighed and leaned back against the counter. It was 11:30. I figured I could go now without seeming rude. I put my glass in the sink and turned towards the living room.

"Uh, Lisa?" Ian asked. "I don't want to seem like some drunk asshole hitting on you at a party, but--I don't suppose we could go have coffee or see a rock show some time?" He looked almost bashful. It was charming.

I smiled. "I'm on a deadline at work for the next week and a half, but I'm going to see Mike Watt and the Foo Fighters in two weeks," I said, and then waited to see what his response was. This would be the test. "Who?" was not the correct answer.

"Oh, yeah, me too. Have you heard the Foo Fighters' demo? It's amazing, you have to hear this! I have copies everywhere, I will give you the one in my car if you don't already have it, somehow," he said.

"Everyone in Seattle has heard that demo, I think," I said, smiling. "But thank you. Why don't you give me your number and I'll give you a call a few days before the show, and we'll figure out a place to meet beforehand, if you want."

He opened his wallet and handed me a business card. Ian Thomas, attorney-at-law. A downtown address.

"Thanks," I said. "I'll give you a call next week."

"I look forward to it," he said gallantly, with a little bow, even.

I hugged a protesting Rebecca goodbye and quietly slipped out the door as she started organizing Pictionary teams.

★

A month later, I was at Ian's apartment on Capitol Hill. We had plans for dinner at the Broadway Grill. He was running late, so he suggested I swing by and pick him up.

He answered the door in a t-shirt and running shorts. "I just got out of the shower, it'll take me just fifteen minutes to put on some clothes and comb my hair, please make yourself at home," he smiled apologetically, disappearing into the bedroom.

This was our third date. I guessed it was a date, anyway. We went to the Watt/Foo Fighters show, and then we met for dinner the next week because neither of us had had time to meet for dinner before the concert. Tonight the plan was to have dinner and then decide if we were going to the Croc or down to RKCNDY.

I surveyed his apartment with a critical eye. The place was neat but not immaculate, just a few unwashed dishes in the sink. However, it was the entire wall of records (and its matching companion filled with books on the other side of the room) that caught my eye. Obviously, I made a beeline for the record albums. Ray Davies once said that the first thing he did in any new acquaintance's house was check out their record collection, and I was never any different. Lester Bangs also had this thing about checking everyone's copy of *White Light White Heat* to see if it had actually ever been played. I decided that the latter would be a good acid test.

I ran my eye down the rows of albums, looking for the V's. Hmmm. There was something not quite right. The records were alphabetized but there was some odd order, because it restarted at A on a few rows away. Alphabetized, and then in chronological order, I thought. Or was it alphabetized and chronological but with compilations at the end in alphabetical order?

"I have my favorite bands in the order I found out about them, with their albums sorted in the order I discovered them, and then chronological, and then the rest of the collection is strict alphabetical and then chronological." I turned around to see Ian standing there, smiling and looking a little pleased with himself. He had on a white button down shirt, faded jeans, engineer boots, hair still wet, and looked very handsome.

"How did you know what I was looking for?" I asked.

"You were clearly moving towards the end of the alphabet, so I figured you were going to validate your theory about the order against something you knew very well, and in those letters it would have to be the Stones or the Who."

"Damn, that's good."

"Just a lucky guess on my part," he said, shrugging a little shyly.

"Rush before Kiss and the Stones? That makes no sense."

"My next door neighbor was eighteen and a psychotic Rush fan. I was thirteen and had no clue about music."

"So Rush got you into the record store."

"Right. And then I found out about the fun stuff."

"I'm glad you don't categorize Rush as 'the fun stuff.'"

He smiled. "Not a fan. I didn't think you would be."

"Listen, they're totally valid musically. I accept this. But I also think they're pure bombastic overkill, and have no sense of humor whatsoever. I'll never forget reading an article about them in *Creem* in the '80s, where Neil Peart yelled at the journalist for dropping his pen too loudly during soundcheck. It kind of formed my entire impression of Rush."

"I remember that article. And I just thought they were so cool for not taking any shit from a rock journalist. Now I know--they have no sense of humor. But I still love them," he said.

We walked down Broadway to the Grill. They didn't have the best food in the world, but they had good drinks, and the place was always packed and noisy. It was a good choice when you were on a date and weren't quite sure how many awkward silences there would be.

The first night we went out, we were at the show, so that was all we talked about; I didn't learn more than Ian thankfully wasn't one of those annoying people who elbow you all night, yelling, "Isn't this great?!" On our second date, which started at a martini bar, and then moved to Eileen's (one of Kurt Cobain's favorite watering holes) once we both confessed we'd be more comfortable in a dive, we stayed within the safe bounds of the music conversation. Tonight, on date three, I had some vague plans to try to make the conversation a little more personal.

Clearly, so did Ian. Once we'd ordered our first round of drinks, he began asking the classic questions: how long I had been here, how I got here (abridged), how I met Blue Electric (condensed for time). With round two, it was my turn.

"I'm guessing you're a native," I asked.

"Nope," he said. "Chicago. I already know what you're going to say: me, Kim Thayil, and Jonathan Poneman."

"If you tell me that you knew them growing up I will freak."

"No, wrong side of town. Sorry." He grinned. "But *everyone* asks me that question."

"What brought you out here?" I said.

"Well, first I moved to California to go to college, and then law school at UCLA. I wanted to be in L.A. because I had vague ambitions of being a rock star, and my parents agreed to foot the bill for UCLA, not knowing about the rock star part."

"You're a musician!" I said.

"I hid the guitar in my bedroom," Ian said. "Usually, it impresses the chicks, but *you* know Mark Genovese from Blue

Electric," he said. "So I will have to rely on my wit and boyish good looks to win you over," he continued, smiling straight into my eyes.

My stomach did a back flip and confident Lisa found herself staring at her silverware. I would have let the moment hang a little for effect, but now I was dying of curiosity.

"So how did you get from L.A. to Seattle?"

"Well," he said, after hesitating for a minute. "It wasn't working out. I was frustrated. I had some buddies up here who offered me a job--so I moved."

"Define 'working out.'" I said.

"I had graduated from law school, but wasn't working as a lawyer yet. I was in a band with some friends of mine. We had been playing all through college and law school. I only finished law school so my parents would continue to finance my living expenses and keep the band going. And then, one day--literally, one day--it all fell apart. We were on the verge of being signed--I know everyone says that but in our case it was actually true. And then, our lead singer arrived at practice one Tuesday night and told us that he wasn't happy, and that he was leaving the band. He wrote all the lyrics, so we were left with nothing. Hell, even our trailer was his."

Ian was staring out the window into the distance. He didn't look sad; he looked angry, but I didn't feel that I knew him well enough to offer sympathy or solace, nor was I sure that he wanted any part of either.

"Do you still play?" I asked, after a minute or two.

He turned to face me. "Yes! I play with some friends, we actually have a Stones cover band that's mostly a joke, but we do write and play our own material sometimes too," he said.

"Really? A Stones cover band?" Now he'd gotten my attention. "I mean, like the whole deal? Are you Keith or Mick Taylor? How is it I have never heard about a Stones cover band in Seattle?"

"Whoa there. We're not quite In Color. It's more about musicianship and attitude than historical authenticity." With that, I got the first real smile of the evening.

"So where do you play?"

"Some bars in West Seattle, which are the only places that'll really have us. Alki Tavern, the Admiral Benbow. It's fun."

"Will you let me come see you?"

"I'm going to have to practice every night until my fingers bleed if I know you're going to be in the audience, but there is nothing I would enjoy more." Ian smiled again and gently brushed the back of my hand with his index finger. This time, my stomach didn't protest; instead, I got full-on goosebumps.

Despite all the classic signs of heavy flirting, it took me a while before I was positive that we were, indeed, dating. The entire time, I wasn't entirely sure he wasn't just into me as a friend. I had been wrong so many times before, in the exact same situations, that I was going to wait for a very obvious sign.

It was a pattern I couldn't seem to escape: I'd meet a great guy who was really into music. We would hang out and talk shop and trade records and go to shows, but the day always came when they'd call me up and tell me that they'd met this great girl--who owned all of six CDs and hated going to concerts, but for some reason they were convinced that she was *the* woman for them. Some of them even got as far as marrying these women, only to find their record collections relegated to the basement because it didn't fit into the "décor."

So Ian took me by surprise. One Saturday night, we were walking back up Broadway after closing down the Comet Tavern. I had my arm through Ian's for support more than for affection, truthfully. I was very drunk--silly, happy drunk. We'd just seen the legendary L.A. punk band X at Moe's, and John Doe had kissed everyone in the front row (a reference to the opening band, The Best Kissers In The World), which of course included me.

Ian was laughing and making fun of me. "I've never seen anyone actually swoon from a kiss," he teased.

"Dude. You would swoon too if John Doe kissed you. I don't care how straight you are. It's *John Doe*," I said as earnestly as I could, given my condition.

"What about if I kissed you? Would you swoon?"

"You're not John Doe, but we can find out." I thought he was kidding.

He wasn't.

And I did swoon--well, close enough, anyway.

So that was how it started, with a kiss on Broadway in front of the Jack in the Box. We went home and fell into bed, and while it wasn't the height of ecstasy, I'd stopped expecting that years ago. And aside from that, the relationship seemed ideal. We went to rock shows almost every weekend. We went to New Orleans for Jazz Fest, flew to New York for long weekends shopping, visiting my old haunts and old friends. He insisted on going out to dinner with my parents, and he paid the bill. It was nice to be with a guy who was an actual grownup, but still had a place for music in his life.

"He gets it, Marie, he totally gets me," I said to her one night as we sat in Linda's Tavern, catching up, after she got back from whatever godforsaken business trip she'd been sent on. "Monday night I was leaving early so I could go down to Tower on Mercer and buy the new R.E.M. record at midnight--and when he heard what I was doing, he insisted on driving me himself. And--he cooks dinner!"

She nodded halfheartedly. "Mm-hmm."

"You don't sound convinced."

"I dunno, Lisa. He talks a good game but he's almost too nice. Have you seen the dark side? Have you argued yet?"

I shook my head no. "He's super easygoing, Marie. For once, there is no drama."

"See, that's a bad sign. You know it's there, you know it's just stuffed down underneath."

"Maybe he's got his shit together more than we do?"

"How's your sex life?"

I didn't mean to sigh in front of her. "It's just... there. Nothing to complain about, but it's pretty standard, to tell you the truth."

She raised her eyebrows in response.

"Marie, everyone says that sex changes when you get older. It's not bad sex, and it's not no sex, it's just not mind-blowing sex. It's my fault, too. I am way out of practice."

"Are you prepared to give up the possibility of ever having mind-blowing sex again? Are you really ready to settle for this? Lisa. This is not you."

"Marie, you are freaking me out."

"Lisa, he's a nice guy. You like being with him. I'm not saying break up with him. I'm just saying go into this with both eyes open."

"Don't worry, Marie. It'll be fine."

And it was more than fine. I cheerfully sent Ian off with his buddies to see about half a dozen Rush shows in California and the Southwest. I ran down to AAA to get them maps, eagerly helped him buy tickets and pack for the road trip. His friends could not believe that I didn't whine or complain. They were sure there was a catch.

"There is a catch," he said.

"Ah ha! I knew it," they chorused.

"Yeah. She's gonna do the same thing next year when the Stones go on tour, and we're all going to have to help her dial for tickets!" Ian said, with just the tiniest smirk on his face.

All his friends were envious, having had to endure endless pouting and arguments with the women in their lives over this adventure. He was proud and happy; I could hear it both in his voice when he would call to tell me the stories. And it made me happy that he was happy.

I related that story back to Marie as proof positive that this relationship was the real deal.

"And, Marie, remember last week at the Afghan Whigs?"

"Oh, baby, how could I forget?" She sighed deeply into the phone.

"Where was Ian all night? He hung out at the back bar like a good boy, so I could stand up front with you girls and make a total fool of myself."

"Hey, I thought sitting on the edge of the stage and lighting Greg Dulli's cigarettes all night was a classy move on your part."

"Classy, maybe, but pathetic, definitely."

We giggled like schoolgirls and moved on to another subject.

And so, before I knew it, it had been a year. I hadn't intended to make a big deal about the anniversary, but one day I opened the mail to find a Nordstrom gift certificate (in a not-unsubstantial amount) from Ian, with a note reading:

To quote that guy from New Jersey, I'd drive all night to buy you shoes, but it's probably better if I let you go shopping yourself. Buy something pretty, and mark the 16th on your dance card.

He picked me up in his buddy's old Mustang convertible and took us out to dinner at the Cloud Room, a faded vestige of 1940s Seattle. It was one of my favorite places to drink before or after a concert at the Paramount, but it was a little shabby. I knew he would have been happier at the Metropolitan Grill or the Dahlia Lounge. But he knew I would be happier at the Cloud Room.

The truth was, Ian and I were great friends and had a lot of fun. Mark, Jake, and the other guys were on the road so much, Ian definitely helped fill the gap their absence left. I knew I cared for him. I wasn't sure that I loved him, but I also wasn't sure that I didn't. Using my feelings for James as any kind of baseline for a relationship seemed unrealistic and unfair, so I was flying blind.

So after our second anniversary, when Ian started making noises about the future, and even said the word "marriage"--I didn't exactly shut him down. I told Marie, "Well, he hasn't proposed."

"But you have done nothing to deter further discussion of the subject, either," she said.

I sighed and laid back on the couch. "What am I supposed to do? Say, 'Hey, you haven't proposed, and I don't think I want to get married, but I'm not sure' when he hasn't even really asked? Why make it a thing when it's not a thing?"

"And when he does ask, what are you going to say?"

I sighed again.

"Lisa, hon, we're not kids anymore."

"So what are you saying?"

"I'm saying, you can't just let this go on aimlessly forever if you have no intention of marrying the guy, which I don't think you do."

Another sigh. "You're right. But what can I do? It's nice. We have fun. Why end it over something that's not an issue yet?"

"Lisa. It's me, remember? You're not in love with him. I can tell. You need to tell him how you feel, even if you don't know for sure one way or the other."

But I never did. My reasoning was that it wasn't as though he was making any demands on me. We still had separate apartments and led our lives independently. It was comfortable. If he wanted it to be more than it was, well, then I'd make a decision.

A few months after we officially became a relationship, right before Blue Electric came through town, I warned Ian: "We've all known each other for years; we've been on the road; we've been poor together. You're not going to get all the inside jokes immediately." He seemed like he was okay with it, sitting in the corner with a beer, smiling quietly. The boys were still calling me with the usual "You have got to come down here this weekend!" entreaties, and now, sometimes I'd go and sometimes I wouldn't.

Ian appeared mellow about it all, and while he didn't become best buddies with anyone, he didn't seem threatened by the friendship. I tried to not always talk about them or run off every time Mark or Jake would call. I tried to be low-key about it, even though being low-key about anything I care about was almost a physical impossibility. But I wanted Ian to feel comfortable, and I wanted him to feel like he was important to me.

But then things started to change. It was almost imperceptible, nothing I could really articulate until one Sunday morning in the spring of 1998. We had brunch at the 5 Spot at the top of Queen Anne and were walking back to the car when I remembered there was a record fair at Seattle Center.

"So what did you want to do today?" I asked him.

"I don't know," he said. "Any ideas?"

I smiled like the Cheshire Cat. "There's a record fair down at the Center. Let's go for a little while."

"Ah, Lisa, it's already noon, all the good stuff will be gone," he said, but then acquiesced with a nod.

We walked down to the bottom of the hill, paid our two dollars to get into the Snoqualmie Room, and started browsing. Ian was far more systematic than I was at these things, starting at the first table and moving clockwise around the room; I more or less played it by instinct. I liked to walk the room first to get a sense of what was around before diving in.

Which is what I was doing when I saw it.

I saw it clear across the room, hanging on the wall, from a distance of at least thirty yards. I don't know how on earth I saw it, I was so far away that there was no way I could have possibly made it out clearly. I just knew what it was, and started walking as fast as I could. Ian was trying to keep up with me, asking me, "Where are you going? What do you see?" and I couldn't even speak. I was operating on raw instinct.

There it was, the Holy Grail, stuffed inside a plastic sleeve and ignominiously duct-taped to the cinder block wall. The seven inch single for the Rolling Stones' "Have You Seen Your Mother, Baby, Standing In The Shadows." What made this sacred was the picture sleeve, which was a photo of the Stones in full drag. I had wanted to own one of these since I first read about it, since the day I saw one for the very first time, at seventeen, hanging on the wall at Bleecker Bob's on MacDougal Street. Once I had a job and money, I had been looking for a copy of this record for what seemed like forever.

I swallowed hard, pointed at the single, and managed to ask, "Can I see that, please?"

The dealer took it down and handed it to me.

I gingerly held the record, staring in disbelief, not really breathing. Here it was. Bleecker Bob's wouldn't let you touch any of the collectible records until they'd seen your money. Holding it in my hands was so unbelievably different than looking at a photo in a book. I was thirty-four, but the feeling was the same as it was the first time I walked into a record store and found something rare I had been looking for--that feeling of excitement and wonder and elation all whirled together.

I was reaching for my wallet when Ian caught up with me, and I held up the single, beaming.

"Lisa, you're not going to buy that, are you?" he said.

I thought he was teasing me. "Yeah, I think I'll buy this instead," I laughed, gesturing at an autographed Duran Duran album.

"It's seventy-five dollars! I thought you were past the point of spending huge sums on music memorabilia."

"I don't ever remember saying that," I said. That was such a strange statement to make, coming from a man with over 1,200 pieces of vinyl and his own proprietary filing system.

"It's not even in good shape. The corners are dog eared." He pointed to the top left hand corner.

"Ian, how old is this? None of them are going to be perfect. I haven't even seen one of these in person since I was seventeen!" I wasn't sure why I was even debating it with him.

"All the more reason you should wait to find a perfect one. So why not wait?" He was so emphatic that it made me pause.

Slowly, I handed the single back to the dealer. I shivered a tiny bit as I did so and I just shook it off, didn't acknowledge the very physical reaction I was having to this situation.

I didn't mention what happened that day to anyone. Not to Marie, not to Jake, not to any of my Stones friends--if I'd told any of them that I had found the single, they would have been at my house in three minutes flat, clamoring to see it. "Standing In The Shadows" was my alias on the Stones mailing list, for heaven's sake.

So I couldn't rationally explain what happened, or why I didn't buy it after all these years. Ian talking me out of buying a single didn't really seem like a capital offense. I felt silly that the situation bothered me, and also didn't understand why I stopped myself from doing what I wanted to do. It wasn't like me. If anything, it was my fault, not his.

About a month later, I was sitting at work on a Friday afternoon, frantically trying to finish up so I could get home at a reasonable hour, when the phone rang.

"Road trip!" said the voice on the other end.

"Jake!" I grabbed the phone with both hands, delighted. "Where are you?"

"I'm back for a little while. We ran into a creative wall in the studio, so we called a six-week break, and decided to come home for a while. I could sing you a few bars of Thin Lizzy, if you'd like."

"'The Boys Are Back In Town!' You guys should consider covering that," I said.

"Now, that's an idea. We are thinking about doing a secret gig at the Moore while we're here. We'll bill ourselves as Little Boy Blue and the Blue Boys," he said.

"Could you be more obvious?" I said. "Talk about Rolling Stones 101 trivia."

"Lisa, maybe a dozen people will figure that out. You, this girl in Connecticut who runs a fan web site for us, and the five members of the Rolling Stones. Anyway, what are you doing this weekend?"

"No plans, I haven't talked to Ian yet."

"Well, Dead Moon are at the Satyricon tomorrow night, and there's a record fair in Portland this weekend. I say it's time for a road trip!"

"Who's driving?"

"Dude, I am so driving, I am so tired of being driven," he said in an exaggerated L.A. accent. "I want to get into my own car, pump my own gas and pick out my own damn music without a consensus decision."

"You can't pump your own gas in Oregon," I said.

"Right, Oregon and--where else? Oh, that's right. *New Jersey,*" he said, with affectionate emphasis. "So I'll pick you--I mean, you guys--up at eleven o'clock tomorrow morning?"

I hung up, grinning like a fool, and dialed Ian at work.

"Ian Thomas," he said.

"Ian, sweetheart--guess who's in town?"

"Dunno," he said in a half-mumble.

I paused at that reaction. "Are you busy?"

"Kinda. I just want get out of here and I've got a ton of work to do."

"Well, Jake and the boys are in town for a while, and we're going to Portland tomorrow. If you want to come with, cool. If not, cool. But I'm going."

"What's in Portland?"

The words "a record fair" were on the tip of my tongue, but instead I decided to commit a sin of omission. "Oh, Dead Moon is at Satyricon, and Jake wants to spend a few hours at Powell's. He just wants a road trip."

"You'd think he'd want to stay home with the amount of traveling those guys do," he said.

I decided to ignore that. "Are you joining us?"

"I bet anything I'm going have to work tomorrow to get this paperwork done, so--no thanks."

"Dinner tonight?"

"I don't know what time I'm going to get out of here."

"Well, I'll go to the gym and wait for you to finish."

"No, don't bother, it's going to be a while. I'll talk to you next week," he said, and then he hung up.

He hung up. I sat there holding the receiver in my hand and looked at it with a puzzled expression. He had a big case next week and he was just preoccupied, I told myself. But that behavior was almost rude and Ian was nothing if not unfailingly courteous. I shrugged it off and figured I'd catch up with him later in the weekend.

The next day dawned clear and sunny and dry, perfect road trip weather. I was sitting on the front steps of my building, basking in the sun. Jake pulled up in his beloved '68 Mustang, stereo blaring. I bounced down the front walk, opened the door and slid in.

"Hi!" I said, leaning over for a hug.

"Hi backatcha," Jake said, hugging me back. "No Ian?"

"He had to work," I said.

Jake eased the car out into traffic. "That's--too bad," he said.

I decided I'd be grateful that he censored any snarky remarks instead of calling him on it. "Are you really all here? Where are you staying?" I asked.

"The rest of the guys rolled in on the last flight from LAX yesterday. Mark and I are at the house, along with Jonathan. Scott's at his girl's. The prodigal sons have returned home!"

"It's about time."

"Well, don't get too used to it, kid. The move to L.A. is going to happen. From a business perspective, there is no point in being here anymore, and from a personal angle--well, that night at the Croc when I ran into five women I had slept with--"

"Including one that Mark thought _he_ was dating."

"Yeah, it just got a little tricky," he said with a sigh.

"What are we listening to?" I asked, after the sound from the stereo registered in my ears as a Rolling Stones ROIO (recording of illicit origin).

"In the glovebox," he said.

I opened the glove compartment and picked up the jewel case. There wasn't any artwork, just a plain black and white insert with a tracklisting, titled THANK YOU, AHMET ERTEGUN.

"This is--Dallas '78?" I asked.

"Close. Ft. Worth, and yes, '78."

"Any reason for this particular vintage? You generally dislike the '78 shows."

"I dislike them because Mick is generally coked up out of his mind. But I am serious about wanting to do this secret gig, but I want it to be something different," he said, pulling out onto I-5 South.

"Such as?"

"We don't have new material yet, and I don't just want to play the same set as last tour. So I thought we'd do the ultimate Stones cover set--perform a legendary show, in order, down to the stage patter."

"You have always wanted to do this!" I said, excited just thinking about it. "But why not just use *Get Yer Ya-Ya's Out* instead of a bootleg, no matter how well-known you think it is? That way you stand a chance of the audience actually getting the references."

He paused for a second. "I rejected it as too obvious, but you're right, it would make more sense to do that, even though Mark will remind us--repeatedly--that it wasn't recorded at just one show."

"Offer to let him provide a program with annotated references," I said.

"You can do that. I might as well just refer to him as 'my guitarist.'"

"He'd just punch your lights out."

"Exactly."

★

We were walking through the record fair when out of the corner of my eye I saw a familiar image and stopped dead in my tracks, not believing my luck. Jake saw it at the same time and we didn't need to say a word, just exchanged knowing, excited looks as we went scampering down the row to the table. He ran ahead of me for the last ten feet, those ridiculously long legs giving him a decided advantage, and had the dealer taking the record off the wall just as I caught up with him.

"Ah HA!" he said, waving it about. The vendor was alarmed until his wife nudged him and whispered something in his ear, which I assume was Jake's identity. Despite his hair being stuffed into a Mariners hat, Jake's height always gave him away.

"Jake, you fuckhead, I saw it first!" I said.

"Yes, you most certainly did, and I understand that by international treaty, this rightfully belongs to you. However, you are going to let the rock god buy it for you."

I started to protest feebly, but then I remembered what Christine had told me about the band's merchandising grosses from the last tour, and decided it would be okay to let my friend buy me a present. I nodded, and Jake happily pulled out his wallet.

Money changed hands, and Jake handed me the flat brown paper bag. I clasped it to my heart with both hands, smiled, and kissed Jake on the cheek. "Thank you. Just--thank you." I was thrilled to finally have the celebration over this record that it deserved.

The next table was all vinyl, box after box of vinyl LPs in clear plastic sleeves. I started on one end, Jake started on the other. Flip, flip, flip. I just flipped through one by one, while Jake had this weird technique where he pulled the record up an inch mid-flip, never missing a beat.

Flip, flip, flip.

"So what's the plan this year?" I asked Jake.

"Well, like I said, we're off for six weeks. We're not doing anything for the next two weeks... at least not as a band." Jake stopped, and I paused as I watched him pull out the Clash's first album, flip it over, and scan the back cover, checking to see if it was the U.S. or U.K. release. It must have been the U.K. version, because he set it aside for purchase. It seemed like we always knew someone who needed or wanted it.

"I think we'll rent a rehearsal space," he said, "Maybe Soundgarden will let us use their space, since these days, it's probably not getting used for much except watching ball games." He stopped again, pulled up *Blonde on Blonde*, proffered it in my direction. I shook my head no--I think at that point I owned three copies--and he put it back.

Flip, flip, flip.

"Is this creative block as in real creative block, or creative block as in, we cannot stand the sight of each other any further and the last thing we want to do is be stuck in an enclosed space together?" I asked, continuing through my row. W's. Paydirt. I held up a copy of *The Who Sell Out* with the original pop art cover. I owned one but I wasn't sure if Jake did.

"Give that over here," he said, reaching for it. He turned it over, took out the record to inspect it for scratches. It passed muster so he added it to his growing pile of vinyl.

Flip, flip, flip.

"Here, I know you were looking for this," I said, deadpan, and once I had his attention I held up Queensryche's first EP.

Jake rolled his eyes, but conceded the point. "Kid, that thing is actually worth a lot of money," he said.

"Still, gotcha!"

(It was the standing dumb joke. Walk around a record store, pick up the most embarrassing thing you can find, hold it up to your friend and yell really loudly, "Isn't this what you were looking for?" Ian, of course, never got it. He thought it was the most immature thing ever, which it probably was.)

Flip, flip, flip.

Jake continued the conversation: "To answer your question, I think it's a little bit of both. Mark was just burnt out, he was fried. He would just sit and stare at a piece of paper and get freaked out that he couldn't think of anything. I'd suggest he take a break and he'd freak. I'd offer to help write with him and he'd freak. Jonathan would look at him sideways and he'd freak, which, of course, made Scott freak. So Christine, wisely, finally said 'Fuck it,' cancelled the rest of the time we'd booked and sent us packing."

Flip, flip, flip.

I reached the R's and therefore it was time for the mandatory public service announcement: "*Sticky Fingers* with a broken zipper, *Made in the Shade*, *Emotional Rescue* - but no poster. *Some Girls*--" I pulled out the inner sleeve--"it's the reissue cover. Unknown bootleg--" I paused, looking at the plain cover with a black and white photo stuck to it, and turned it over. "Hyde Park. If you don't want it, I'm taking it."

We paid for our purchases, and continued walking through the rest of the room.

"Are people bootlegging you guys yet?" I asked, as we walked by table after table of CD bootleg dealers.

"Jonathan has found a few boots, but only in places like New York and L.A.. Letting people tape since, like, day one has kind of eliminated that market."

"But people will be stupid, and they want CDs now."

He nodded. "I know, but we really could care less. I don't need more money and I know--I mean, I *know*--that anyone buying a live show of ours already has everything we've ever released and then some."

We stood there amidst the cacophony and suddenly reached saturation level at the same moment. There is a moment that everyone goes through at a record show, where you just can't take it another second. That's when you bail, if you're smart. If you stay you will buy things you don't want or already have, or will pay too much, or will buy something you do not want at all, because you are no longer thinking clearly.

We looked at each other, nodded, and headed for the door.

The rest of the afternoon was relaxed and laid back. We walked through the streets of Portland in the sunshine, talking and window-shopping. We made the obligatory pilgrimage to Powell's Books and got lost in the shelves for an hour and a half, and then ended up in Coffee People, going through our purchases and drinking lattes until dinnertime. We grabbed some Thai food and then headed for the club.

Dead Moon, who were a Northwest legend, kicked ass as always. There were only three of them, and Fred and Toody, on guitar and bass, were old enough to be my grandparents. They were the very first band I ever saw live in Seattle, playing their raw, minimalist, scorching, Chuck-Berry-meets-the-MC5 kind of rock and roll. I loved them to death and they never disappointed.

Jake was out in the crowd pogoing around with the punk kids and the bikers and having a blast, while I hugged the far edge of the stage near Toody and alternately watched the band and my friend. No one recognized him, except for a couple of grizzled bikers in colors from Medford, who kept buying him beers and slapping him on the back to his delight and my continual amusement.

We drove back to Seattle in that three a.m. Interstate 5 darkness, stopping in Factoria for gas and at the rest stops for free coffee, having an intense, caffeine-enhanced analysis of a bootleg CD set of *Blood On The Tracks* demos Jake had gotten a hold of. When I got home, I didn't even bother to turn on the lights, kicking my shoes off, climbing into bed in my t-shirt, but carefully propping the new addition to my Rolling Stones collection on the bedside lamp, so it would be the first thing I saw when I woke up the next morning.

★

Ian came to the house for dinner the next weekend, and the first thing he noticed was the single, propped up in the place of honor at the front of my 1960s vintage 45 rpm record rack. I wanted it there so I could see it all the time, because I still couldn't believe that I finally owned one. I never even thought that maybe I should have put it away before Ian arrived.

He didn't say anything, just picked it up and stood there looking at it. For some reason I felt the need to explain, so I matter-of-factly said, "Jake bought it for me--we found it in Portland." If he was so concerned with my finances, well, now he didn't have to be.

Ian put it back with exaggerated care and wordlessly walked over to the table. Uh-oh, I thought. I didn't know what this was, but something told me that it wasn't good.

We served ourselves in silence, and I was about to take my first spoonful of soup, when Ian stopped, hesitated, and finally said: "Why do you insist on letting him buy you presents all the time? How do you think it makes me feel? I can't afford to buy you every Rolling Stones single you want."

This was the problem? I thought. This is about assuaging your masculinity? God, this was stupid. And technically, Ian could afford to buy me whatever he wanted.

But, instead, I put down my spoon and covered his hand with mine. "Ian, I made endless spaghetti dinners to feed those guys, I wired them money at least half a dozen times so they could fix equipment when they were on the road and desperate, I took their first, very bad, promotional photos. Jake could buy me singles for the next ten years and would still owe me money." I smiled gently as I was saying this. It was all so clear to me. It was nothing to get upset over.

"This isn't about paying you back," he said, avoiding my gaze.

"This isn't a romantic gift. It's Jake being Jake."

"To you, records are a romantic gift," Ian said.

"Well, this one isn't. Ian! The Stones are wearing women's clothing on the front of it. This isn't a--Marvin Gaye single or something."

Ian was about to say something, and then he stopped himself. "Okay. If you're sure this is nothing..."

"Ian, I'm very sure. Really. I told you, it's still this exclusive club in the treehouse. Everyone has their thing. Mark sends me first edition books from Paris and London. Scott buys me Sonic Youth singles. Jonathan sends me a postcard every time they're in a new city."

"You've never told me any of this."

I held back from saying that I had, or that I had tried to, but he never seemed interested or like he cared very much before. "Ian, I have known these guys for eight years. I have known you for a little over two. There's a lot of history I have with the boys that will take you years to learn."

He smiled thinly, took a sip of wine, raised his eyebrows and shrugged. "Sure. You're probably right. No big deal. Let's just eat dinner and change the subject."

So I did. But with a sense of vague unease that seemed to be quietly building.

I dialed Marie the second Ian walked out the door.

"Lisa, I can tell you what the problem is," she said.

"Go ahead."

"The real problem, of course, is that Ian refuses to believe that you and Jake never slept together."

"And you know this how?"

"Because it's always about dick size, honey."

I sighed. That was not the answer I wanted to hear.

"And I can hear you rolling your eyes. Don't. There are no vibes between you and Jake. You could not be more platonic, more brother-and-sister. But that makes guys suspicious. They want to know what's wrong with the other guy. Why aren't you together? The usual insecure, proprietary bullshit."

"Well, Ian did ask me about it one night when we were drunk."

"What did he say?"

"We were in the spare bedroom, lying in the beanbag chairs and listening to Charlie Parker. He looked up at that huge subway poster from 'Antique Mirror' that Christine sent me as a joke..."

"The one from the UK? That big-ass huge fucking poster?"

"Yeah, the big blue and green one. I put it up as a joke more than anything else, but I liked it so I just kept it up there--that's the whole point of the music room, it's where fifteen-year-old Lisa still lives."

"So what did he say?" Marie prodded me to get back on topic.

"He stared at the poster for a minute or two, and then looked me right in the eyes and asked, 'Okay, tell me the truth. You and Jacob never ever slept together?'"

"And?"

"And I told him the truth: we didn't."

"That's not the whole truth," Marie said.

"Marie, he asked me if we'd slept together. We didn't. I don't require him to give me an account of every woman he may have fooled around with at a party once."

"But if he had a woman who was his best friend--"

"But he doesn't. Anyway, it's not like we dated; it's not like we had a relationship. Drunken silly groping doesn't count in anyone's book."

There was silence on the other end of the phone.

"Marie, sweetheart, I can hear your eyebrows arching at me."

She sighed. "No, it isn't any of his business. There isn't anything between you guys and you are not required to tell him about everyone you have ever slept with. But it's clearly bugging him."

"And telling him that we almost slept together, but we didn't, is going to make him feel better? If he doesn't believe me that we didn't, how is he going to believe me that not all of our clothes came off? Why do I have to detail to him what happened that night? That's between me and Jake and whomever I choose to share that with. Why the fuck do I have to clinically detail it out just so Ian might feel slightly more secure?"

"It would probably make him feel better if you told him that you guys had done it once and decided it was a mistake," Marie said.

"I resent having to tell him anything, I'm not going to make shit up just to assuage his ego," I said.

There was a pause, and I could hear Marie lighting a cigarette.

"Lisa...do you ever wonder what would have happened if you two had gone through with it?"

Now it was my turn to sigh.

"Never mind, honey. Let me tell you about my latest boy, this will cheer you up," Marie shifted gears. "You will never believe this."

★

Marie was closer to the truth than she knew at that moment. Closer than I was willing to admit to her or myself then, or even now. Yeah. Sometimes I do wonder what would have happened if Jake and I had gone through with it. Maybe it was the wrong time, maybe it wasn't. Someday, when we were old and gray, I figured I'd ask Jake about it, but that was more about not having any regrets than anything else. I never ever thought it was more than that.

But here I am. I left my house in the middle of the night and just started driving. I'm in a car barreling down I-5 in the middle of the night, and my boyfriend has no idea where I am. And while I'm ostensibly heading to L.A. to hang out with my friends, I have to wonder if the real reason I'm going isn't to finally ask Jake that question.

CHAPTER 4: 1991

It was the day after I'd been woken up in the middle of the night by the rock boys next door. It had turned out to be a short workday, nine hours instead of twelve. That felt like a reason to celebrate, so I picked up Thai food on the way home. As I struggled up the front steps, takeout in hand, I almost tripped over something on the top step.

It was a bouquet of tulips, stuck into a salsa jar (with label still intact). I frowned, and bent down to pick up the flowers. That was when I saw the note on the front door. A piece of paper, silver duct tape at top and bottom, with the following carefully inscribed in black magic marker:

Dear Kind Neighbor:

We are very sorry to have disturbed your slumber last night. We appreciate your thoughtfulness in not shooting through our windows like the crackheads across the street did last year. To say thank you, we would like to invite you to have a glass of wine with us this evening around 9 p.m.

With much love,

Jacob Mark Scott Jonathan

InFiNiTe TrAiNwReCk

They'd carefully printed their first names out under their signatures (which was a good thing, since I couldn't have deciphered them otherwise). At first I was slightly annoyed, and then I smiled: It was a nice gesture. More cynically, in New York we would have called it insurance. And hey, that one guy was cute. What would it hurt? I opened the door, put down the food, peeled the note off the door and closed it behind me.

★

Nine o'clock. By now, I'd eaten my takeout in front of the television, and then tried to read a book for a while. I was going to walk over just like I was, and then I decided I could actually make an effort. So I changed into a nice black shirt from Betsey Johnson, long-sleeved and almost slinky, put on the jeans that made my butt look good, and climbed into my red Doc Martens-- purchased because Chris Cornell had sixteen-hole Docs just like them. And just before I walked over there, I grabbed the phone and dialed Marie.

I'd been here about six months, still mostly a loner, when Marie and I met. I had started to recognize her as a familiar face at shows, she was usually there by herself, too, and I guess we were at some kind of level of nodding recognition. She had shoulder length hair dyed blood red, with bold red glasses to match. She was kind of petite but carried a familiar attitude that should have tipped me off she wasn't a local. If this had been New York, we would have started talking to each other as though we were old friends after the second time.

But Seattle was strange that way. Outwardly, everyone seemed really nice and sincere, but underneath it they were anything but, as James had always maintained. It was so odd after New York, everyone there carrying their facade of defiance and defense, but once you got to know them, they were usually the nicest people you'd ever want to know. And part of me was shy. James's death had sent me into this internal world where I spent so much time by myself that it was an effort to talk to people. I'd cry on the phone to Andrea or one of the Alisons every few weeks: "I'd be okay if I just had a best girlfriend..."

"Don't worry, honey. You'll meet someone," they would all say, trying to reassure me.

One random Saturday night at the Off Ramp, I was there on a date with a guy I'd met at a Nirvana show at the OK Hotel a few weeks before. He seemed nice at the time, but had turned out to be a jerk. None of my attempts at conversation worked, everything came back to sex, somehow. I was talking about the Nirvana show, just trying to find some common ground. I mentioned Dave Grohl appreciatively, and suddenly Mr. Jerk turned to me and asked: "So, is he the one you want to kiss?"

I looked at him like he was speaking Japanese. "What?"

"Is he the one you're into?"

"I think he's one of the best drummers I've ever seen," I said.

"So you wanna do Cobain, then? All the girls want to sleep with Cobain, that loser..."

I felt like I had descended into the lower depths of hell, and started scheming how I could escape, and fast. I didn't even care what band was playing that night, I had just picked the Off Ramp as a neutral, public location. That was a New York safety thing that I refused to give up, even if I did live in quiet, safe Washington--home to way too many serial killers for my comfort, I would remind anyone who might suggest that my personal safety measures were excessive.

So I was sitting there at the bar, enduring this painful conversation--which did not improve with the passage of seemingly endless minutes--and working hard to keep his arm from snaking around my shoulders. I glanced across the bar, looking for any distraction, and then I saw her: the woman with the red glasses! She was sitting next to a guy who was loud and clearly drunk. Suddenly, her eyes met mine; she smiled shakily, and then rolled her eyes as she surreptitiously pointed at her date. I smiled in acknowledgement, and nodded my head in the direction of the ladies' room. A look of recognition broke across her face, and I saw her pick up her purse and say something to her companion.

"I'll be right back," I said to the guy I was with. "Little girls' room."

My co-conspirator was inside, leaning against the wall, when I walked in.

"Oh, my god, thank you for doing that," she said with a sigh of relief.

"Don't mention it, I was looking for my own escape."

"What's up with your guy?" she asked, craning through the wall of girls in front of the one mirror that wasn't broken, and brushing her hair.

"He's probably drunker than he looks, keeps trying to put his arm around me, and doesn't believe me when I say I don't want to sleep with any of the members of Nirvana. You?"

"Intravenous drug user, as I learned when he accidentally took off his jacket and forgot he was wearing short sleeves." She stuck out her hand: "Hey, I'm Marie. I see you all the fucking time at shows and I keep meaning to come over and say hi, but people here, they are so damn weird."

"I'm Lisa. Are you not from Seattle?"

"God, no. I'm from New Jersey. I'm an engineer, I got a job with Boeing so I moved out here. I was thoroughly sick of the East Coast, and there was a small matter of a broken engagement. You?"

"Parsippany," I said.

She looked at me dumbfounded, and answered, "New Brunswick."

Both of us grinned from ear to ear.

"What are you doing here?" she asked.

"Microsoft... and, well, let's just say there was a small matter of a relationship that didn't quite end like it was supposed to." I swallowed so the tears didn't sneak up on me.

"Honey, I am so fucking glad to meet you, you do not know. Do you really want to see this band, or can we get the hell out of here? Please tell me you have a car, calling a cab in this town is impossible, and I swear all the taxi drivers are serial killers."

I burst out laughing and she stared at me, puzzled.

"Never mind. I'll explain later. Let's get the hell out of here."

I drove up Route 99 to Beth's Cafe, open 24/7 and home of the twelve-egg omelet; it wasn't quite the Riviera but at least it had some genuine attitude. We sat there in the smoky haze talking until after four in the morning. By that point, we were absolutely convinced that we were long-lost sisters, separated at birth. I'd told her about James, she'd told me about her ex-fiancé Shawn (whom she'd found getting a blow job from her best friend when she'd gone over there to look at her bridesmaid's dress), and spent the rest of the time playing "Were you at this show when..."

"Stones in 1981? MSG? Fuck yeah." I said.

"Springsteen?" she asked.

"How can a South Jersey girl even ask a North Jersey girl that question?" I said.

"Hey, you never know." She paused to take out a cigarette, and offered me one. It was so very, very tempting, but I finally shook my head no.

"What's your poison?" I asked her. "Who's the obsession? I know you have one."

"Elvis Costello."

"Seriously? Wow."

"I think I will scare you if I tell you the lengths I have gone for Elvis."

"I don't think you can scare me, Marie. You're dealing with a professional, here."

"Yeah, but you didn't follow his tour bus through Bridgeport and then run down the sidewalk screaming," she said, shaking her head, but smiling at the memory. "That's a story for another day."

"Um, it is another day," I said, pointing at the clock, which was covered with visible brown nicotine haze.

"Did you see the Clash in Asbury Park in '82?" she asked, drinking her sixth cup of coffee. We were clearly going to be here for a very long time.

"God, yes, all three nights! It was insane. The Shore had never seen anything like that. It was like some kind of inland invasion."

"That was the show that turned me into a punk rocker. I walked into Convention Hall, and just could not believe that there were so many other people just like me... in New Jersey, no less!" She sighed. "Of course, I crashed my mom's car on the way back from the third night, and hadn't mentioned that I was taking it to hang out with a bunch of degenerate punks in Asbury."

By the time we were reeling from caffeine and secondary smoke inhalation and decided to call it a night, if one of us had been a guy, it would have been true love. But we were two straight girls from New Jersey, out in the land of trees and water and bad drivers and equally bad pizza, and it was an instant bonding of kindred souls. We exchanged phone numbers and made plans for the next weekend, and then I drove her back to her apartment on Capitol Hill.

"Where do you live?" Marie asked, as we drove down Broadway.

"Central District."

"You're kidding, right?" she said.

"Hey, I lived in the East Village, remember? This is a cakewalk compared to that. It's cheap, I've got a shared house with a chick that is never there, she's always at her girlfriend's. Maybe someday it'll bother me enough to go find my own place, but I'm already too solitary as it is."

"Well, we're going to change that," she said.

"Yeah," I said, pulling up in front of her building. "I think it's time." I smiled gratefully.

She leaned across the seat and hugged me, and then hopped out and waved madly as she ran to her front door and let herself in--and then ran back and yelled, "See! No one in Seattle does that! They drop me off and drive away!"

Giggling, she ran back to the door, opened it and waved again as it shut behind her.

So I called Marie. "I finally met the guys next door," I said.

"You're kidding! Do tell."

"Their band woke me up last night at three a.m., so I stomped over there and pounded on the door."

"Sometimes I think you forget where you live," she said.

"Marie, I'd seen at least one of them. They mow their lawn. Drug dealers don't bother with yard maintenance."

"Well, go on."

"So I came home today and there was a bouquet of flowers on the front stoop and a note inviting me over to drink wine tonight."

"It's 9:15, what the fuck are you doing on the phone with me? Get over there! Now!" She hung up abruptly, emphasizing the command.

I made one last attempt to do something with my hair and grabbed my keys. I walked across the lawn and was greeted by a note on their front door, instructing me to come around back. In the backyard, I discovered shallow stairs leading to a wooden door illuminated by a single bulb. I approached the door, and after an initial hesitation, knocked.

Almost immediately, someone yanked the door open. It was a

tallish, thin-ish guy with straight jet black hair, pageboy length, dark eyes, darkish skin, definitely Italian, definitely cute. He was dressed simply in faded Levis and a plain white t-shirt, but they hung on his frame with an almost tailored elegance. He held a pair of needle nose pliers in his left hand. All I could think was: *Another one? Oh brother.*

He regarded me with a half-dazed measure of confusion, as though I'd interrupted something, and then a look of recognition broke across his face.

"You must be the girl we woke up last night," he said.

"I must be," I said. "I'm Lisa."

"Well, come on in, Lisa," he said, gesturing me inside. "I'm Mark."

I walked into a big basement room that had been converted into a practice space. Old carpets on the floor, posters on the wall, amps, guitars and speakers--the detritus of musicians.

"Hey, everyone, this is our victim from last night. Meet Lisa," Mark said. "Introductions are in order. Over there on the couch, that's Jake, I think you met him last night. He's our singer."

Jake sprung to his feet almost hitting his head on the low ceiling and ran over. "Jacob McDaniel, at your service," he said, kissing my hand and bowing.

"Are you always such a smart ass?" I said.

He grinned. "I try. I am a lead singer, after all. And in that role, let me continue the introductions, so Mark can go back to being brooding and mysterious in the corner," he said, as Mark walked over to an upside-down amp. He gave Jake the finger in response, and picked up a screwdriver.

Jake continued: "On the couch is our good friend Christine. She used to be the singer in Mark's last band, but has now retired. We are trying to talk her into managing us."

"Kind of hard to manage a band that doesn't play," she said, sweetly. She waved in my direction and smiled. Tall, thin, pale, long black hair, almost Goth but too edgy. "Welcome to the club, we need some more estrogen around here."

"And next to her, that's Scott, he's our bass player."

"Hi, Lisa," he said, as he sat up abruptly from what was clearly a sketch pad and a drawing in progress, and made eye contact, brief and sharp--not unfriendly, but it was a gaze that wasted no time. As soon as our eyes met and he gave me the burst of a smile, Scott resumed his former studied slouch and his artwork. He was wearing tan pants--at first I thought khakis, but realized immediately he wouldn't be caught dead in a pair of Dockers, so they had to be work pants, which were frayed at the hems--a perfectly stretched white t-shirt, and black Chuck Taylors.

"At the stereo over there, taking a ridiculous amount of time to pick out the next record, is Jonathan, our drummer."

Jonathan stood up, pushed his bangs out of his face and glanced over at me. He was average: average height, average shaggy brown hair, average build, wearing an average short-sleeve white button down shirt, untucked, over faded jeans. The highly muscled forearms, however, were dead giveaways that this, indeed, was a drummer, although they seemed in sharp contrast to his All-American Boy demeanor. No guy ever wants to be referred to as "sweet," but Jonathan clearly was.

He looked at me again, more carefully, and this time he did a double take. "It's you!" he said.

Now I did the double take, and realized why he was familiar. "You're at all the Soundgarden shows!" Now I remembered him. Unlike most of the people in an average Seattle concert audience, he was always smiling and obviously enjoying himself.

He came over, wiping his hands on his jeans, smiling. "I could say the same thing about you."

"Guilty as charged." I said, shaking his outstretched hand. "It's nice to finally meet you. I should have known you were a drummer."

"You mean the way I insist on sitting on the stage so I can watch Matt Cameron and don't pay attention to anyone else?" He grinned boyishly.

"Jonathan wants to be Charlie Watts, but he also wants to be Matt Cameron. Which will make for a very interesting illegitimate child once he finally figures out this identity crisis," Jake said. "So Lisa," he continued, "Who else do you like besides the Stones and Soundgarden?"

"Get the woman something to drink and a place to sit before you start the interrogation, dumbfuck," Mark said.

"I don't notice you doing anything about it either, asshole," Jake said, not moving.

Mark abandoned his amplifier repairs and walked over to a small refrigerator. "Lisa, what would you like to drink? We did invite you over for wine, after all."

"If it's all the same to you, I'll take a beer, unless you went out and bought wine especially for me."

"Truthfully, no. Scott works as a waiter at--well, I won't bust him, but he has access to decent wine upon occasion."

"And I know my shit," Scott said, still sketching, not looking up. "These barbarians, Christine excluded, could care less, so let me know if I can ever hook you up."

Mark took a can of Olympia out of the fridge and I nodded. He brought it over to me, and added, "Come over here, grab a pillow, you can sit on the couch, someone will move," he said, glaring at Jake.

This was so cute.

"Process of elimination aside, if he's the singer, you've got to be the guitar player," I said.

Jake started to laugh, as did everyone else. "Is it that obvious?"

"Well, I was about to tell you both to get a room."

"We can talk about that later. Right now we must establish your music credentials, and present ours as well!" Jake sat down on the couch, patted the spot next to him, and looked at me with genuine anticipation. Charming.

I took a deep breath and began. "Okay. Stones. Who. Springsteen. New York punk rock. I grew up in New Jersey, went to school at NYU, hung out at the downtown clubs..."

Scott sat up at the last sentence, and stopped sketching. "Sonic Youth?" It was actually a question.

"Of course. They were the local band."

He fell back against the couch, clasping hands to his heart melodramatically.

"Scott kind of worships Sonic Youth," Jake said. "He and Jonathan are our token Dylan fanatics as well, and Scott is the jazz repertoire representative."

"Yes, wine, Charlie Parker, spare cutlery, and--" he snapped his fingers, "Reefer!" There was a pause. "Not really," he said, sheepishly, as his bandmates cracked up. "It just seemed to go with the jazz trip Jake was laying on me."

"What about West Coast punk?" Christine asked. "The Minutemen?"

"Check."

"X."

"Check."

"Social D?"

"Much respect, as Mike Watt would say."

"Black Flag? Meat Puppets? Anyone else?"

"Not so much. Are you from L.A.?"

"I was born in Orange County. My parents moved us up here when I was seven, and I still hold it against them that they couldn't wait until I was old enough to learn how to surf."

"Let's get back to this Rolling Stones thing," Mark said. "Taylor or Wood?"

"That's not even a question," I said without thinking. And in that moment I flashed back to that moment years ago when James asked me exactly the same thing, and I responded in exactly the same way. I must have gone off for a second or two because when I looked up, Jake was looking at me, concerned. His eyes met mine and softened, and it was like he could read my mind or sense that something was wrong, because he quickly changed the subject.

"Well, I think the time has come to play a little music and show our neighbor what woke her up last night."

Mark looked panicked. "Jake, I'm not sure we're ready to do this."

Everyone in the room let out identical cries of exasperation.

"I think we can deal with an audience of one. Besides, she's passed the audition. She is one of our people!" Jake said.

"What people is that?" I asked.

He turned to me. "If I started talking about busting a button on my trousers, would you think I was coming onto you?"

"Well, you might be, but I would also assume you were quoting *Get Yer Ya-Ya's Out*."

Mark leaned over and high-fived me.

"I even had the off-mic audience comments between songs

memorized by the time I was thirteen," I said. "I wanted to be that girl that kept yelling for 'Paint It Black'."

At that, everyone else grinned stupidly. It was like I said the secret password. Yeah, these were my people.

Jake smiled and met my eyes again. I still found him to be stunningly gorgeous, but now all I was thinking was that I liked this person a lot. It was like that night I bonded with Marie--kindred souls recognizing each other. I immediately felt comfortable with him--I felt comfortable with all of them, but Jake's grey eyes were warm and kind and I could already tell he was a sweetheart.

In order to forestall any further performance discussion, Mark had gone over to fuck around with his guitar, a shiny black Telecaster. He stopped, carefully set the guitar back into its stand, and laid the pick down on top of the amp just to the right of the handle on top. He stepped back, and something in the arrangement must have displeased him, because he inched the guitar stand over a millimeter, and then touched the headstock to make what appeared to be an invisible adjustment to the guitar. Finally satisfied, he came over and plopped himself down next to me.

"Favorite Stones album," he said.

"Well, *Exile* is it for me, you know, there are few albums that are just so totally perfect and complete, but I also really, really love *Emotional Rescue...*"

He half-frowned at me. "Tell me more."

"I know it's not really thought of as their best, or any kind of landmark, and it kind of gets overshadowed by *Some Girls*, but that record was the first one I experienced in real time, if that makes sense... everything else happened before I was old enough to know what was going on. For a girl from New Jersey, that record was New York. I put it on and it's New York in summer, the heat, the smells, I can feel it, I can hear it."

He regarded me again with the half-frown.

"It's a feel thing, it's instinctive... it's not anything that I can really articulate beyond that. I just love that record and I probably play it the most after *Exile*. Now you've probably lost all respect for me..." I felt like I was babbling incoherently.

The frown vanished. "No! Not at all. I was just thinking about what you said, because I barely listen to that album, and I never thought about it that way before. I love how music can give you a sense of time and place, and maybe if I had your context I would feel differently about it."

"You've never been to New York?" I ask.

"No, not yet."

At that moment, Jake walked over and sat down next to us. I got this small sense that it was almost protective in a way, that he didn't want Mark to batter me down too hard.

"But we are going to go there *as soon as possible*," Scott said, almost howling.

"Well, in order to do that, you're going to actually have to leave the basement," Christine said, with exaggerated emphasis in Mark's direction.

"Do you have any Stones bootlegs?" Mark asked, ignoring everyone.

"Of course. *Brussels Affair, Handsome Girls*, a bunch of random ones, mostly '78 and '73. The best ones from that tour are the last shows in Hawaii with Taylor, I think. Hell, I even own a copy of *Cocksucker Blues*."

"*What?* You have got to be fucking kidding me!" Mark said.

"Oh my god," said Jake in astonishment, "We have wanted to see that for years."

"I bought it at some store in the Village years ago."

"What's the quality like?" Mark said.

"I mean, it's a bootleg, but all things considered, it's in really good condition; it's totally watchable."

Jonathan wandered over, and they traded anticipatory glances, and then turned expectantly in my direction. That's when it dawned on me that they really, really wanted me to go home and get it, but were holding themselves back from asking.

"Uh, it's also got some somewhat, erm, risqué footage, and I don't think we know each other well enough yet to sit and watch it..."

That statement was met with blank stares, and I panicked. I desperately did not want to have to remind these boys I just met of certain legendary scenes in that film, involving groupies and an airplane.

I gestured helplessly at Christine, who nodded knowingly and was just about to lean over and whisper something in Mark's ear, when Scott broke the tension by sitting up and proclaiming, deadpan: "Tribal group sex! Shooting up! Naked women! Robert Frank directed the damn thing, for Chrissakes! You are supposed to know this shit, guys, you are bumming me out right now," he said, and then went back to his sketchpad.

Suddenly, Mark became very interested in his guitar setup again, unplugging the power cord and recoiling it with precision. Jonathan excused himself to run upstairs for more beer, and Jake blushed twelve shades of red and stammered apologies.

In an attempt to make him feel better, I changed subjects and asked Jake, "So what do you do when you're not being the lead singer of--what was the name again? Infinite Train Wreck?" I said, with obvious distaste.

He looked at me. "You hate the name."

"I really, really hate the name."

"To answer your question, when I'm not a lead singer, I make pizzas. I deliver pizzas. I wait on tables. I've worked at Muzak. I'm a sometime bartender--basically, I'll do anything that will make money and be mindless enough to not eat up my entire soul. Scott, as you heard, waits tables, Jonathan works at Muzak, and Mark, believe it or not, works as a paralegal. He was supposed to go to law school."

"Who writes the songs?" I asked, even though I was pretty sure I knew the answer already.

"We will share songwriting credits equally when that day comes, but it's essentially me and Mark. We both do words and music, which is a good thing. In my last band, the words were all my responsibility and no one really cared what I sang, which I didn't like very much... but it was a band."

"It beat singing in the shower," I said automatically, as a zing went through my heart. I wondered how long this would this keep happening, when I would finally forget, even a little bit.

Jake glanced at me kindly, and the look in his eyes made me want to talk, so I continued: "That was something an old boyfriend of mine told me about the band he was in at the time...

he was from here, actually."

"Is that how you got out here? Did you move out here to be with him?"

"Yes and no--it's a long story."

Once again, his expression was expectant and inviting and kind, but something in my eyes must have told him that this was dangerous territory for me, because he didn't push it.

Jonathan returned downstairs at that moment, carrying a case of beer. Scott looked up and gestured at him, and Jonathan handed him one. He opened it up, took a swig, and went back to sketching. Not even looking up, he casually asked, "So, Lisa... I don't know what you're doing tomorrow night, but maybe you could look through your video library and bring some cool shit over?"

"You mean, 'Can you please please please bring over *Cocksucker Blues*, we aren't perverts, just psychotic Stones fans who don't know how we're going to sleep tonight, knowing that that video is within one hundred feet of us?'" I said.

He looked up from his sketch pad and winked at me.

Everybody started laughing, including me. I was feeling truly at home in Seattle for the first time.

I see signs heralding Eugene. I figure this might be a good place to stop and get some coffee. I'm far enough away from Seattle that the chance of me panicking and driving back home is slim. There's an AM/PM and a Denny's. I pull into the gas station, and while someone runs out to pump my gas, I go inside for coffee and snacks.

As I'm standing at the register, I look at the rows of cigarette packs behind the counter. As the cashier rings me up, something makes me say, "...And a pack of Marlboro Lights, please." I grab a lighter from the box next to the cash register. I haven't smoked in probably ten years, but for some reason, it seems like a good idea right now.

I stroll away from the gas pumps to a sketchy picnic area along the side. Putting the coffee and bag of snacks down on the ground, I take the cigarettes, pack them down, and peel off the cellophane. Opening the box, I pull one out and light up. I take a drag, and cough hard. A sip of coffee, and then another drag. Whoa. I'm almost getting a high from this, it's been so long.

After a few minutes of standing there and listening to the traffic on the highway, I finish my cigarette, stomp it out, and walk back over to the car. Sorting everything out on the passenger seat, a CD catches my eye: *The Who By Numbers*.

I pull out of the gas station, up the exit ramp, and onto the highway, listening to "Slip Kid." And then as I pick up speed on the highway, I forward through the CD to the song I'm looking for--"How Many Friends." Townshend wrote this in his darkest, bottom-of-the-bottle moments, questioning the sycophants and hangers-on, wondering how many friends he really had. When I used to get into my self-pitying moods, I'd play this one, acting all morose. Which is stupid, because I knew who my friends were. I knew exactly who loved me and I was heading towards them as fast as I could drive.

CHAPTER 5: 1979

I sat on the concrete steps in front of Parsippany Hills High School, chin resting in my hands, waiting in the sunshine of a beautiful blue fall day. It was Monday afternoon and class had just let out. I was waiting for my boyfriend, Eric, to bring his car around from the parking lot. I was anxious and hoped that he wasn't wasting time back there smoking pot or bullshitting with his friends.

At that moment, he pulled up in his sparkly blue 1975 Impala. I used to say it was electric blue, like in the Bowie song, "Sound and Vision." Eric argued that colors could not be electric. I ignored him, and sang the song, to myself at least, every time I saw the car.

I picked up my books and glided over to the car, attempting to look as bored and unhurried as possible. The reason for all the faux coolness was the Who at Madison Square Garden. They were playing five nights, but of course, by the time I heard about it, the shows had completely sold out. So I had been dropping hints to Eric for the past three weeks that I wanted to go. But somehow I knew that if I was too excited, if it seemed like I wanted it too much, he wouldn't want me to have it.

Eric held the wheel, looking straight ahead as I got in. That was odd. He usually at least leaned over and opened the door for me.

"Hey," I said, as cheerily as I could manage to fake. I leaned over to kiss him and he still looked straight ahead.

"Hi," he finally said, as he put the car into first gear and drove out of the parking lot.

"What's up?" I said, trying so hard to contain my enthusiasm that I was gritting my teeth.

"Not much. Bad history test today. Seth got detention." His eyes were on the road and I could not tell how he was feeling.

"Wow, that's bad. What did he do?" I said, feigning concern. I was so not interested in his stoner, loser friends.

"We were in computer class and he wrote a program to print out the lyrics to *Tales From Topographic Oceans*."

I realized that I was supposed to think this was cool, even though I found the band Yes completely bombastic and intolerable. So I kind of smiled and nodded my head, while I thought, *C'mon, Eric, you were supposed to get the Who tickets last night. Did you get them or not? How do you not know that this is the most important thing in the world to me right now?* I convinced Eric to take me to see *The Kids Are Alright* six months earlier, the night the entire world seemed to shudder on its axis for me. The night I discovered what it was like to fall in love with a rock band.

We were almost at my house, and he still hadn't mentioned the tickets. I knew my Mom was home so it wasn't like we would be hanging out. That, and I had a paper to write.

I leaned over, turned on the radio, and tuned it to 95.5, WPLJ. Maybe they would say something about the concert and that would jog Eric's memory. "Behind Blue Eyes" was playing. Immediately, I reached over and turned the volume way up.

Eric leaned over and turned the radio off, sharply.

"Hey, what did you do that for? I love that song!" I said.

"I know you do," he said.

"What's wrong with that?"

"You are way too into that band."

"What?"

"Oh, and I didn't get those tickets. They were fifty dollars each and that was too much money."

My heart dropped into my stomach. Luckily, I had prepared for this eventuality. Time for Plan B.

"Fine. Turn around, I'll just buy them myself. I'll go with Andrea."

"No, you won't," he said.

I was too confused to be angry. "Eric, what is wrong with you? I love this band. I am so excited to see them. This means a lot to me. This is important to me," I said, wondering why I had to say it.

"I told another guy in my homeroom about the tickets and he

went and bought them at lunch." He still didn't take his eyes off the road, but I could see the self-satisfied smirk.

We drove the rest of the way in silence. I didn't know what he expected me to say, if he expected me to just give up that easily? To acquiesce and say, "Oh, you're right, Eric, I really didn't want to go see the Who. We won't go because you don't want to go." I didn't understand what was going on, but I knew I didn't like it.

We pulled into my driveway and I opened the door, got out and didn't say a word. I didn't even look back. At that moment, I was finished with Eric, but I didn't want to break up with him until I put Plan C into action. Just in case he decided to tell my parents what I might be up to.

My mother was at the kitchen table, drinking coffee and reading a magazine. I sat down across from her with a great deal of drama.

"Mom, I just had a fight with Eric. I don't want to talk about it, but I don't want to talk to him if he calls, is that all right?"

"Sure, honey. Are you sure you don't want to talk about it?"

"No, not really. I just think he's being silly. Do you mind if I go call Andrea?"

"Go right ahead, use the phone in my room if you want."

Well, that was easy. It was all I could do to stop myself from running, but I walked quietly into the room, shut the door and dialed Andrea.

"Drea. We are going into New York to see the Who Friday night," I said, in a breathless half-whisper.

"I can't! I can't go... I am so completely grounded. I could not be more grounded," she said.

"What did you do now?" I panicked. There was no Plan D.

"I got a D on my first chemistry homework," she said. "My mother had a cow, she called my father, and he said if it happens again I will be grounded for the rest of the school year. *The rest of the year*," she stressed, anxiously.

"Oh, that's all? Here's the deal: I will come over the rest of this week and help you study for chemistry, if you can drive me to the train station Friday night and cover for me if my mom calls." I said this as though I'd done it a million times. I had watched this kind of thing on TV, though, the ABC *Afterschool Specials* about the bad, fast girls who lied to their parents, cut class, took drugs and got pregnant. I wasn't interested doing any of those things, but I was going to borrow some of their techniques.

"Are you serious?" Andrea said.

"Sure. I like chemistry," I said.

"No! About going into New York all by yourself?"

"Ger, don't freak out on me. I can do this. I know people sell tickets outside; I read about it in *Rolling Stone*. Do we have a deal?" In reality, I had absolutely no idea what I was doing, but she needed to believe that I did or she would freak and tell her mother.

"Can you really help me pass chemistry?" she said. I took that as a yes.

I hung up and walked back into the kitchen, heart pounding.

"Hey, Mom, Andrea is grounded because she got a D in chemistry, and she has a big test next week, so I was wondering if it would be okay if I went over there after dinner this week and helped her study?" I felt like my heart was pounding so loud she could hear it. This was the first big super-conscious lie I had told my parents.

My mother put down the magazine and looked at me. It wasn't a complete lie, though. I did love chemistry and I really could help Andrea. Her problem was that she panicked and blanked out. That's all it was, I'd seen her do this a dozen times already.

"What about your homework?" Mom finally said.

"Well, I have a paper due on *Beowulf* but that won't take long. She really just needs someone she can study with."

"If it's all right with her mother, it's fine with me. I think it's very nice that you want to help Andrea get better grades," she said with an approving smile.

That was so easy it was almost scary, and it made me feel bad about lying to my mother. I briefly considered telling her the truth and just asking her if she would take me into New York Friday night, but if I did that and she said, "No," then I was way out of luck. So I hugged her briefly to cover up my guilt and ran back to the phone.

I went straight to Andrea's house after school all week, and Friday night at around 5:30 we were sitting in her Impala at the train station at Boonton. I was wearing jeans, a white t-shirt, and my prized Red Converse All-Stars, with a denim jacket that once belonged to Eric completing the outfit. I thought I was really cool at that moment. I also knew that I was very scared, but was trying hard not to show it. If Andrea sensed fear, she would freak out, tell her mother, and completely ruin Plan C.

"What train are you coming home on?" asked Andrea, for (literally) the twelfth time.

"I will either be on the 11:30 or 12:30 train. If I'm not on the first one, then I'm on the next one, just come back. This isn't hard, Drea, don't freak out on me. Remember, there will be more chemistry tests!"

I hugged her, picked up my purse--it was a patchwork tote bag with bamboo wooden handles that I had saved up all summer to buy--and got out of the car. I strode into the station and bought a round trip ticket as though I had done this many times before.

The train pulled in, and the conductor stepped off and yelled, "New York Penn Station." I climbed on behind everyone else, found an empty row of seats and sat down near the window, purse held tightly in my lap. I started this trip with fifty dollars, which seemed like an incredible amount of money. We had driven to the bank next to Burger King earlier this week so I could take out money from my passbook savings account. Mom would probably see the withdrawal eventually, but I was just going to say that I had bought some records with the money. That would be bad, but not fatal.

In my head, I ran a quick accounting. I used seven dollars for the train. I had no idea how much a concert ticket was going to cost. The woman at the Ticketron outlet at Discount Records said the tickets cost eight-fifty, eleven dollars, and twelve-fifty. I doubled the price of the most expensive ticket, added some money for the train, and figured I had enough. I hoped I was right.

Leaning my head against the back of the seat, I sat there watching the New Jersey suburbs as they sped by, the train stopping what seemed like every five minutes; the ride seemed longer than I remembered. Finally, as we entered the swamps near Secaucus I could just glimpse the Empire State Building and the

Twin Towers over the hill. We entered a tunnel and a few minutes later, the conductor announced "Penn Station!" over the PA. My heart seemed like it flew up out of my chest and got stuck in my throat. I was there.

Summoning all the nerve I had left, I stepped out onto the platform. There was another train pulling in on the other side, opening up and spilling out what seemed like hundreds of kids dressed just like me, rock t-shirts and jeans and denim jackets and boots and sneakers, everyone chattering excitedly and heading for the stairs. I fell into the crowd, walked up into the concourse, and then followed the masses through the station and up escalators that deposited me outside, facing the big post office.

I took a deep breath. I had gotten myself here; now I had to find a ticket. The box office windows were open, and I decided that would be a good starting point.

"Sorry," said the woman on the other side of the window. "Totally sold out. We had some earlier today."

I stood there on the periphery of the box office and surveyed the action. There were guys walking around quickly and with purpose, almost chanting, "Tickets, tickets, who need a ticket?" I figured that they were probably the ticket scalpers I had read about, but I had no idea how I would go and talk to them. So I leaned against a big round concrete planter and watched for a little while. People would walk up, the scalper took out some tickets, and they either walked away, or they walked with the scalper to the corner and then crossed the street.

Then I noticed some guys dressed like me walking around. They weren't scalpers, I didn't think, but they were talking to every person who walked by them. When they walked by the scalpers they usually laughed and shook their heads "No." "Sorry," I overheard one of them say to a scalper, "Too rich for my blood, brother."

I decided to follow him at a short distance to see what he was doing. As he walked back and forth between the two western entrances to the Garden, he would keep asking everyone, loudly: "Got an extra ticket? I need a ticket. Who has a ticket?"

Wow, I thought. Why didn't I think of that?

Now, of course, the trick would be to actually get up the nerve to do that. So I stood there for a few seconds, gathered some scraps of courage, and started with a group of girls walking by.

"Got an extra ticket?" I said, blurting it out.

"No, sorry!" they said, and smiled at me.

It was easier than I thought it would be, so I tried the next group of people, and then the next random few people walking by. They smiled and shook their heads or said, "No, sorry," and kept walking. After about ten minutes, I decided that it was almost fun.

I was on my third reconnaissance of the area and feeling pretty confident, when I noticed one of those scalper guys was heading towards me.

"Need a ticket, sweetheart?" he asked.

"Maybe," I said, trying to act cool and nonchalant. I was sure he could see right through me.

"I got plenty of tickets, hon."

"Too rich for my blood," I said back to him. (Well, the other guy said that, I was hoping that it would work.)

"Honey, they're only fifty dollars. Good seats, too."

I shook my head and replied, "Sorry, man." Which actually came out sounding cool, even as I thought to myself: *fifty dollars?* Fifty dollars was over ten hours of babysitting. It was my Christmas money from my grandparents, combined.

I walked away and leaned against a planter, feeling kind of dejected. I had been doing so well until Mister Scalper had to tell me how much tickets were going for. After a few minutes of being dejected, I remembered why I was here, and psyched myself up again. I straightened up and started walking toward the next group heading for the Garden.

All of a sudden, a guy came walking directly towards me. He was tall and gangly, with dark shaggy hair and an equally shaggy moustache, wearing jeans, a denim jacket, Frye boots, and a Who t-shirt I was instantly jealous of.

"Hey," the stranger said. "Are you looking for a ticket?"

I turned around and looked to see who was behind me. I realized I was the only one there, so I said, confused, "Who, me?"

"Yes, you. You've been walking around asking people and talking to the scalpers, so I assume you're looking for a ticket for tonight."

I gulped. "Yeah, I am. I just can't afford the scalpers."

"The scalpers are assholes. Never buy from a scalper." He regarded me for a second. "Have you ever seen the Who before?"

"No, never. I'm not old enough," I said.

"Do you mind if I ask how old you are?"

"Fifteen," I said. Something told me it was okay to tell him the truth.

"Where do you live?" he asked.

"Parsippany," I said. "Jersey."

"Flemington," he said, pointing to himself. "I'm Joe, by the way."

"Lisa," I said. I had no idea what was going on. I had an echo in my head about not talking to strangers but this didn't seem to fit the criteria. I didn't think a mugger would introduce himself to me first.

Joe took out his wallet and pulled out what I somehow knew was a ticket for tonight.

"Okay, Lisa from Parsippany, this may be your lucky day. Can you name all four members of the Who?"

I looked at him like he was crazy. "Roger Daltrey, Pete Townshend, John Entwistle, formerly Keith Moon, now Kenney Jones."

"What's your favorite album?"

"*Quadrophenia*."

"Lisa from Parsippany, you have passed the test. Do you have twelve-fifty?"

I stared at him, again not understanding what was happening.

"Lisa. Do you want to see the concert tonight? I would like to sell this ticket to a real Who fan. I believe you are a real Who fan. It cost me twelve dollars and fifty cents. I will sell this to you for twelve-fifty, provided you promise that you never sell a concert ticket to anyone for more than the price that's printed on it. That is scalping. Scalping is not cool."

My hands were shaking as I reached into my purse and carefully pulled out my wallet. I took out ten dollars and three one dollar bills, and gave them to Joe as he handed me the ticket, and then dug two quarters out of his pocket for change.

I held the ticket in both hands, terrified I would drop it, and just stared at it. THE WHO. MADISON SQUARE GARDEN. FRIDAY, SEPTEMBER 14, in computer printing on rainbow-colored cardboard.

Joe looked at me and started to laugh. "Are you waiting for someone or are you going inside now?" he asked.

"Going inside!"

"Let me show you the way, then."

Speechless, still not believing my luck, I followed my benevolent stranger through the turnstiles and began my first solo trip up those escalators. There were hundreds if not thousands of kids doing the same thing. Loud and rowdy, laughing and happy, stoned and drunk, and smoking cigarettes despite the big NO SMOKING signs. It was a little overwhelming.

I didn't realize it at first, but Joe was keeping a careful eye on me. We went up two levels on the escalators and Joe said, "Okay, get off here," and we both stepped off onto the first level concourse. I looked around and checked my ticket, still clasped tightly in my left hand. I was confused and a little overwhelmed. Joe must have known this, because he touched my elbow lightly and said, "Hey, it's this way. Follow me. I know where you're sitting, I sat there last night." We walked through the concourse, me doing my best to keep up with him as I looked in amazement at everything swirling around me.

Joe stopped walking and pointed at an opening in the cream-colored cinderblock wall. "Here we go, this is your section. Walk in and an usher will show you where your seat is. When you get there, turn towards the chairs in front of the stage and wave, that way I'll know you got there okay."

I was about to say "thank you" again, but Joe had disappeared into the crowd.

I walked into the section and gasped as soon as I got through the tunnel. I was right next to the stage! The usher basically ignored me, and I followed the numbers on my ticket to find my row, still in disbelief. Whenever anyone at school talked about going to concerts, they always sat way high up in the upper sections of Madison Square Garden in the blue seats--they called it "the nosebleeds." I sat down, stared at the stage, and thought: *Pete,*

Roger, John, and Kenney are going to be right there. None of this seemed real.

Then I remembered that Joe said to wave when I got to my seat. So I stood up, scanned the crowd, and waved, feeling more than a little self-conscious. Suddenly I heard my name being yelled by a whole bunch of people. First thing I thought was--busted? Is someone from school here? Then I looked down on the floor. I could see Joe standing on a chair and waving back, and a bunch of guys and girls with him also waving and yelling "Lisa!" I smiled and waved back, slightly confused. Who were all those people and how did they know my name?

About fifteen minutes later I was sitting there, still dazed, wondering how I was going to survive waiting until the concert started, when I heard someone saying my name behind me. I whirled around and saw a short, pretty girl with long, dark hair and a big, puffy cap, way older than I was, who pointed at me, said something to the usher, and he let her through.

She walked down to my row, crouched down next to me and quietly said, "Hey, Lisa, I'm Mary. I'm a friend of Joe's. You still have your ticket stub, right?"

I carefully unbuttoned my right jacket pocket, pulled it out and showed it to her.

"Good. I need you to put that away and come with me--trust me on this, okay?"

I nodded yes, and put the ticket back, once again carefully buttoning the pocket shut over it. Once it was safely stored away, I stood up and followed Mary up the stairs. "Thanks for letting me talk to my sister," she said as we walked by the usher. "This is her first concert, I don't want her to sit alone the whole time." The usher smiled indulgently.

Sister? What was going on here?

Once we were out on the concourse, Mary steered me over to a wall. She handed me another ticket stub. "Okay, Lisa, we're going to try some magic here. I want you to follow me and do what I do. Don't say anything, let me do all the talking."

I nodded.

We walked over to another entrance and went inside. I could see that this staircase went all the way to the floor. I followed

Mary down the stairs, down, down, down, until we were stopped by an usher at the bottom. Mary showed him her ticket stub, and then pulled on my arm and I showed him the one Mary gave me, and then we were on the floor.

We walked over to the center section, where the whole showing the ticket stub to the usher routine was repeated. I walked behind Mary as we got closer and closer, until we were so close to the stage that I could see every single detail on it, from guitars to amps, looking just like every picture I had ever seen, and absolutely unreal at the same time.

She was looking at the chalked letters on the concrete floor and stopped at the letter L. I saw Joe and all the people who were waving at me earlier sitting in seats in the middle of the row, and she gestured at me to enter. Coming up behind me, Mary placed her hands on my shoulders and said, "Success!" Everyone in the group kind of smiled and whooped, and patted her and me on the back in what was clearly meant to be congratulations.

I guess I looked confused, because one of Joe's friends commented, "I don't think Lisa understands what just happened, and she kind of needs to understand this in case there's an, um, *situation* later."

Joe patted the seat next to him, and I sat down. Mary sat on the other side. "Okay, so we have seats, but no one actually sits at them at concerts, right? So we figure, what a waste to only have one person standing when we can fit two or maybe even three into that space," Joe said.

My eyes opened wide, and the light bulb went off. "You mean I'm going to watch the concert from here?"

Joe nodded his head yes, and I gasped so hard I almost choked and started coughing. Everyone laughed and pounded me on the back again.

"But why me?" I said.

"We have a rule that we never scalp tickets, but we always have extras. So we like to play a game where we walk around outside to find the biggest fan we can and sell them the ticket. Anyway, Joe came back and told us about you. I told him he shouldn't have left you all alone, and you know the rest," Mary said.

"Now we all need to stand up--otherwise it will be obvious that there are more people here than there are seats," Joe said, looking around nervously.

A minute later, one of Joe's friends pointed at something onstage, and everyone got really excited. Then the lights went down, and what seemed like half of the kids, including Joe, ran down the row towards the aisle and disappeared. There was suddenly a lot of room. And then I looked up at the stage and there was Roger Daltrey right in front of me and Pete walked on with a guitar, hit the opening chords to "I Can't Explain," and I burst into tears. Ohmigod. They were real. This wasn't a movie or a video or a picture in a book or one of the posters on my wall. It was them. They were *right there.* Ohmigod. I was seeing the Who. Ohmigod. The crowd was screaming and cheering and going nuts. I had goosebumps and my stomach was doing flip-flops like I was riding the roller coaster at Great Adventure.

I watched Roger swing the microphone, impossibly high, and catch it every time; there was John on the other side of the stage, standing there, not moving an inch, just like I had read about; Pete was doing windmills and jumping in the air like he did in the movie. I stared at him for a while, forgetting there was anyone else on that stage. He seemed so connected to his guitar, like it was part of him. And Kenney Jones, the new drummer, sitting behind them all. Everything I read talked about how it wasn't the same since Keith died, but I didn't have anything else to compare it to. I couldn't imagine anything more perfect than this anyway. I sang along to every single song. I knew every single word. I was so proud of myself. I was so happy that I was sure I was glowing in the dark.

All of a sudden the lights went down; then they came back up and the stage was empty. The audience started cheering and flicking their lighters, making MSG look like a big rock-and-roll birthday cake. Mary grabbed my hand and yelled, "Come on!" She pulled me out of the row and then down the aisle until we reached a big crowd of people. Suddenly, I saw Joe, and some of the other guys I'd met earlier. Joe grabbed Mary's hand and gently guided her in front of him, and then he tapped the guy next to him on the shoulder and pointed at me. His friend turned around, grabbed my hand, and did the same thing for me.

And then I looked up.

There was nothing in front of me except this big black metal barrier. And then there were a bunch of security guys, and then the stage.

Before I knew it, Pete and Roger and John and Kenney were out there, larger than life and close enough for me to touch, and Pete put on a guitar. They started playing again and we were all singing along. We. I was with people who knew every word. The entire Garden seemed to know every single word. And the guys were screaming: "Pete! Hey PETE! Over here! Pete! 'Naked Eye!' 'Relay!' 'Join Together!'" I got it--they were screaming songs they wanted him to play. They were screaming them because *he could hear them* because *this was the front row*.

I wanted to keep yelling and screaming and crying and singing and just drown, drown in those bright lights, drown in pure electric blue happiness. Colors did have emotions, and feelings, I thought. Eric was wrong. He was so wrong about so much. But he wouldn't have understood tonight anyway.

And then it was over. Pete, Roger, John, and Kenney were all waving at us and hugging each other in the center of the stage, and then the lights came up. It couldn't be over, it felt like it had only been five minutes since the concert started!

"Lisa?" Mary asked. I forgot she was next to me. "How are you doing?"

I smiled really big--and then I flung my arms around her in a hug. I couldn't help myself. I felt like I just wanted to hug everyone. These were my people! They loved the Who. They took care of me.

Now I had to say something.

"Thank you! Thank you all--you were all so nice--thank you!" I said, stuttering a little bit because my heart was still pounding so hard.

Joe looked at his watch and asked, "Hey, Lisa from Parsippany, do you know what time your train is?"

I looked at my watch and started to panic. "I need to run downstairs right now!"

I looked at everyone. I was a dumb fifteen-year-old who could have gotten killed doing this and instead I found these nice people. I hugged Joe and Mary again, and said hurried goodbyes to everyone else as I sprinted for the 12:30 train.

Andrea didn't blow my cover, my mother never found out, and Andrea got a B- on her chemistry test.

And I saw the Who.

As I continue to soar down I-5 through Oregon, I realize that that night was both good and bad. Good in that I did what I wanted to do for the first time in my life, bad in that it showed me the world I really wanted to be a part of. Everything else compared to it seemed dull and boring and pointless. I broke up with Eric the day after the concert. I just wanted to be down in those electric blue and white and green and red spotlights forever, and I knew he would never understand.

It dawns on me that I've never told Ian the Who story, while Jake knows it so well he could recite it by heart. There are so many stories that are part of me, that make me who I am, that I'd never told Ian, but every member of Blue Electric could recite verbatim.

Ribbon of asphalt stretching out endlessly ahead of me, I decide to switch to an AM oldies station and sing along to the likes of Chuck Berry and the Ronettes for a little while. Springsteen has a line in "Something In The Night" about turning the radio up so he didn't have to think. Right now, that sounds like the best idea in the world.

CHAPTER 6: 1991

I had finally been invited--well, more like summoned--to attend an Infinite Trainwreck rehearsal. It had been a few weeks since they woke me up in the middle of the night. I'd been over there almost every other night since that event; just hanging out, listening to records, going to shows, drinking beer. I hadn't turned on the television more than once or twice since then, and it was like having a new lease on life.

But I never got to listen to them play. Mark was terrified of playing live before he thought they were "ready," and he had put the fear of God into Scott and Jonathan as well. Jake, of course, did not agree.

"Jesus, guys, I can hear you play from my house, as already proven," I said.

"We forgot the windows were open," Mark said.

"You're a *band*. You're going to play in public, for people, eventually."

"We're just not ready yet," he said.

I shrugged and dropped the subject. When they were ready to have me hear them play, they'd let me know.

And now here I was, sitting on the floor in front of the couch, and everyone looked nervous as shit. Jonathan kept banging into his drum kit every time he got up to make yet another small adjustment.

Jake finally had enough. "We are starting now. Now. 'Gravel Road.' 1, 2, 3, 4..."

Nothing happened.

He turned around and looked at Mark, then Jonathan, then Scott.

"Did I not just count down?"

They made kind of vague protesting noises.

"One more time. 1, 2, 3, 4..."

This time it worked. They started to play, and Jake began to sing.

Oh. My. Fucking. God.

I was just kind of lounging there, trying not to look at anyone, and honestly, I did not know what to expect. I had been through this so many times with friends who were in bands. Usually, your musician friends are begging you to come watch them play, because they are convinced they are the next Rolling Stones. And usually, they are nowhere near that description.

But Infinite Trainwreck did not seem to have that problem, not at all. I couldn't believe they didn't think they were ready to play live yet! There was cohesion, there was strength, and the first song was just blowing me away. I honestly did not expect this. I thought it would be good. I thought I would like it just fine. I did not expect to be sitting there going, "HOLY SHIT!"

Which is exactly what I tried to say, out loud, when the song was over. But Jake clearly had other ideas. As Mark was still holding the last note of the song, Jake counted down again and they charged into the next one. And then the next one.

The band drove straight through seven songs before Jake finally put up his hand and signaled everyone to stop. By then, how I felt was blindingly obvious, because I was sitting there with my mouth hanging open, shaking my head in utter disbelief. Jonathan even looked up at one point and saw me sitting there smiling, and I could see his whole body relax out of sheer relief.

Everyone looked over at me expectantly.

"Holy shit, guys." I was still amazed.

No response.

"Guys! That was fucking incredible! What are you waiting for! Those were great songs!"

Scott and Jonathan were looking at me like they very much wanted to believe me, but were clearly waiting on Mark to issue the final verdict. Jake wasn't waiting; he just looked excited.

I stood up. "Am I not making myself clear? You don't suck!"

Mark looked at me skeptically.

"Mark. If I really didn't like it, you would know. My body language would give it away. And I would be saying something like, 'Wow, that's a really interesting use of tom toms in that song' because I'd be desperate for something positive to say."

He nodded once.

"Argh! What do I have to do? Jump up and down and say, YOU GUYS WERE GREAT!?"

Jake spoke up. "Well..."

"Yes?"

"I would actually like to see that, so--could you oblige?"

I walked over and pretended to slug him in the arm, and then hugged him as best as I could manage with his guitar still on. Then I walked over to Scott and Jonathan and finally Mark, and did the same thing.

"I have spoken. You do not suck. You are the complete opposite of suck. If you guys don't get your shit together and play in front of people and soon, I will give you so much shit it won't be funny." I deliver this message with special emphasis in Mark's direction.

"Well...maybe," Mark said.

Jonathan threw a drum stick at his head.

Late August. "What are you doing tomorrow?" asked Jake, stuffing his mouth full of spaghetti.

Jake and Mark had turned up a few minutes after my car pulled into the driveway. They were trying to get me to go out with them, and I said I was too tired and needed to make dinner. "You can stay and keep me company if you want," I said, looking in the refrigerator and then the pantry, trying to figure out what I felt like eating. And then I had a thought: "Have you guys eaten yet?"

Their sheepish looks gave them away, so I pulled an extra box of pasta out of the pantry.

So we were eating and talking, and then Jake asked me what I was doing tomorrow.

"I have no plans besides work."

"Can you get out early?"

"Why?"

"Pearl Jam are playing the free concert series at Mural Amphitheater tomorrow, and Mark and I are going."

"Really?" I said, intrigued. Pearl Jam was one of the new bands I hadn't checked out yet.

"Yeah, I think their record comes out on Tuesday," said Mark, trying to sound offhand, as though every band in town got an instant deal with Epic Records.

"How early would we need to get there?" I asked, offering seconds to whoever wanted them.

Jake reached for the bowl. "I have no idea how many people are going to show up. I guess if we got there at five, it wouldn't be too bad."

"Okay, how about I meet you under the Space Needle at five. I can sneak out at four or four-thirty. It's been a long fucking week."

"Lisa, you got home tonight at nine. I think you can leave early," Jake said with his mouth full.

"Hey, this is the deal with my job. Insane hours, but hopefully some day it will be all worth it."

"What would you do if you didn't have to work a day job?" asked Mark.

I was about to reply automatically but then I stopped myself. If I had been in New York, I would have done a million things. Gotten a larger apartment with room for a darkroom, taken a poetry workshop, published a better fanzine.

"I don't know," I finally said.

"You had an answer," said Jake, gently.

"If I was still in New York, I'd have an answer. But I'm in Seattle; my life is a little different now."

"Your life here could be different, too," he said.

I shrugged. "Yeah, but it's not. It is what it is. Anyway, I like what I do, and I'm a long way from any kind of retirement or that kind of money... there's still some pasta left, Mark, do you want it? I don't want to throw this out."

★

Getting out of work early turned out to not be a big deal after all. So I walked out of my office at four, feeling somewhat guilty. I hopped in the car, drove over the bridge in the sunshine, and parked in a lot near Seattle Center a little past 4:30. As I walked up the sidewalk past the tourists coming out of the Space Needle, I saw Jake and Mark reclining on a bench, Ray-Bans on, both displaying rock star attitude so classic it had to be unconscious. It made me smile fondly.

"Hey, you're early!" I said, "What are we doing?"

"We are going over there *now*," said Jake, hopping up, grabbing my arm and pulling me along with great urgency.

"Huh? What's the big deal? How long have you guys been here?"

"We got here around four, we thought we'd go play pinball or something and wait for you, but then we walked by the Amphitheater--" Mark said, rushing ahead of me.

I was panting to keep up with them as we practically sprinted the short distance from the Needle to Mural Amphitheater, which was just behind the kiddy amusement park next to the Space Needle. We came around the corner and the grassy slope that was, basically, the amphitheater came into view. Except there was no grass to be seen, anywhere. The place was completely and totally packed.

We walked around to the back, looking for empty space anywhere, and then Jake stopped. "Come on, follow me," he said, grabbing my hand and pulling me into the crowd. Mark followed, muttering something under his breath. I had no idea what Jake saw, but then again I was half his height. He carefully snaked over blankets and around groups of people, and stopped right next to the soundboard.

"Here, there's a little room," he said, pulling me in front of him, and gesturing for Mark to do likewise. The soundman glanced over at us and looked like he was about to say something, and then did a double take when he saw Mark.

"Mark Genovese?" he asked, walking over.

Mark took off his sunglasses and looked up. "Jimmy?"

"Dude! What the fuck!" The soundman reached over and they shook hands, smiling.

"You're running sound for Pearl Jam?" Mark asked, trying to sound like it wasn't a big deal.

"No, no, for the show--their guy will be back later." He looked around at the crowd, which was still getting larger with every minute. "Why don't you guys stand in front of the board--it'll be easier for you to see," Jimmy said, peering over the front of the board.

"Is there any room?" Mark said.

"Hell, it's my board. I'll make room." He walked over to the soundboard, leaned over, and said something over it. Some people stood up and moved to one side. "Go on over," he gestured, waving at us. We walked around the side and edged our way through the crowd to the front of the soundboard. There were still what seemed like a million people in front of us, but there was no one behind us.

"Good," Jimmy said, once we were settled. "At least I know I don't have assholes standing in front of me who are going to try to rest a beer on the edge of the board, one less thing for me to worry about. Mark, so what are you up to these days? Wild Gift is still officially broken up?"

"Yeah," Mark said, turning around to face him, back to the crowd. "But I've got a new band now--Jake's the singer."

"Wow, really? That's great. Have you played yet? What are you called?"

Mark and Jake exchanged that look again. "No, not yet, we're still getting our songs together. We're Infinite Trainwreck."

"Infinite Trainwreck, huh? Well, dude, I'm working sound at the Central now--when you decide you want to play, give me a call, I will get you a gig."

Mark looked astonished, but tried to cover it up. "That would be cool, dude. Thanks."

"Hey, no problem. I loved your band. You guys should have gone somewhere."

"Yeah, well, our drummer had a little 'problem--'"

"I know. It's too bad about Jason," Jimmy said, commiserating.

"Yeah, well, you can't help someone who doesn't want to be helped, and you know how hard it is to find a drummer in this town."

"I do know that. Do you still talk to any of the other guys?"

"Except Christine, no, not really. Most of them just went back to their day jobs." Mark paused. "What's it like, running sound here?" he asked, probably trying to change the subject, I guessed.

"Biggest problem is that there's this insanely low decibel level we have to stick to because of the sound ordinances. Then it's just defending the board from the drunk and stupid," he said.

"Seriously?" said Mark. "It's an outdoor concert series."

"Yeah, something like seventy-five db, it's ridiculously low. The bands hate it, and I can't believe that the people who live around here can hear the music as much as they say they can, but they gotta keep a good relationship with the city or they will just cancel this thing."

"Maybe someday Seattle will actually think rock music is a good thing," said Mark.

"Yeah, right. Shit, here comes the Pearl Jam sound guy, I gotta get busy. Can you believe this crowd? And it's barely five o'clock! Don't leave without giving me your number--and you can always leave a message for me at the Central." With that, Jimmy turned back to work.

All of a sudden, this ridiculously skinny girl with long blonde hair, wearing jeans and a tank top, pushed through the crowd and stopped right in front of Jake. He looked surprised, and not in a good way.

"Jake, you told me you weren't going to this show!" she said. "And then my girlfriend saw your head sticking up out of the crowd. I told her she had to be wrong, but, here you are!"

"Uh, hi, Joyce. It was kind of a last minute thing," Jake said. "Mark and his girlfriend wanted to go," he said, while the chick glared openly at me. Mark moved closer to me and put his arm around my waist. I was about to smack him one and then the light bulb went off: this must be whomever Jake was dating at the moment. The gesture seemed to placate her, and she sidled up closer to Jake and whispered something in his ear. She couldn't see his face, but we could see him rolling his eyes.

"I think we have practice tonight," he said, taking a step back from her and almost falling into the soundboard.

"Yeah, we have practice tonight," Mark said, trying really hard to suppress a smile.

"You always have practice," she said.

"Well, we are a band," Jake said.

"So when do I get to see you play a show?" she said.

"You'll have to ask Mark," Jake said.

I could feel Mark's forearm tensing up in its place around my waist.

Joyce stood on her tiptoes and kissed Jake entirely too passionately on the lips, and then whispered, "Call me," in what was probably supposed to be a sexy tone of voice. He nodded, and she turned around and headed back into the crowd.

Now I smacked Mark, and then Jake. "Jesus Christ, guys, you think she couldn't tell this was a setup?"

"No," they answered in unison.

"Lisa, she is so incredibly stupid," Mark said.

"Hey!" Jake said. "She's a really nice girl. She volunteers at Children's Hospital on the weekends."

"Between shifts at the Lusty Lady?" Mark said.

"Yes, but what's wrong with that? She's saving up money to go to beauty school," he said.

"You agreed with me that she had no clue this was all faked," Mark said.

"Yes, but I'm the one who's dating her, not you."

"And I'm the one she pretended she was interested in, until you walked by--man, I don't think I've ever seen anyone move that fast," Mark said. "Anyway, I would rather sit in the basement playing guitar than waste my time and money on girls like that."

Jake was about to start protesting again when Pearl Jam came out onstage, and the crowd roared to life.

This was the band of the hour. Mike McCready, the lead guitarist, was wearing a SPIN magazine t-shirt, with a hat that made him look like he was trying to be Stevie Ray Vaughn. Mark had talked a lot about him; lead guitarist envy, clearly. Stone Gossard, the other guitar player, had long hair and Ray-Bans and looked carefully elegant in a t-shirt and tight jeans. So tight, in fact, that Jake looked embarrassed when I pointed it out. Jeff Ament, the bass player, was sporting basketball shorts and some ridiculous floppy hat.

The drummer was all hair and arms flying. "What's the drummer's name," I asked Mark.

"That's actually a new guy--Dave something. He's from

Texas."

"They're already on their second drummer?" I asked, incredulously.

"Third! Like I was saying, drummers are fucking hard to find in this town."

The lead singer, Eddie Vedder, was riveting, even though he looked like he went onstage in whatever clothes he woke up in that morning, and didn't stop to brush his hair either. It was long and wild and he would fling it about, push it back from his face as he sang. He had this huge smile on his face the whole time.

"I don't think I've ever seen anyone so damn happy onstage," I said

"Wait until I get up there!" Jake said.

"No, c'mon. Look at the guy. He's just beaming."

"Do you know his story?" asked Jake.

"No, I don't. Totally clueless."

"He was working in a gas station--really, I swear--in San Diego and a friend of his, who was friends with Stone and Jeff and knew they needed a singer, gave him a tape with rough mixes. He listened to the tape, wrote some lyrics to go with the songs, sent it back up here. They get it, freak out, fly him up here. One week later, he's in the band."

"Wow. That's like rock and roll fantasy stuff right there. No wonder he's so happy."

The song finished, and then Vedder started to sing a lyric about California, and Minnesota--and I had to stifle my startled scream as my nails sunk into Jake's arm. They both looked at me, alarmed, and I was about to explain, "That's a Soundgarden song!" when Vedder announced, "That's a preview of the new Soundgarden album."

"Holy shit!" I said, grinning from ear to ear. Pearl Jam started another song, a little quieter now, and I was still standing there beaming. Yeah, it was silly, but I always thought it was cool when a band mentioned another band that you really dig. And then it dawned on me: "Oh, shit, yeah. They did that Andy Wood tribute record with Soundgarden--and Gossard and Ament were in Mother Love Bone!" I said, to no one in particular.

"Good morning, Lisa," said Jake.

I stuck my tongue out at him.

The next song started, Stone Gossard hitting this great lead, and Mark said, quietly, "Now, I think this song is going to be the hit." Jake frowned and was about to open his mouth, when I said, "Shhh, listening."

They reached the chorus, and the crowd down front was singing along with the band: "I'm still alive." Mark was right, this would be the hit. I liked the other songs just fine but this was a fucking anthem.

They played five more songs, all solid as hell. There was another great power ballad that I thought would be the single--Mark explained, "It's called 'Black,' but Lisa, it's such a fucking weepy tear-jerker love song. They have so many songs that are so much better."

I shook my head, smiling. "Trust me on this one. The girls will love it and the boys will too because it's got a guitar solo."

There was a pretty frantic number toward the end that had Vedder crowdsurfing and then climbing the speaker stacks, grinning and looking out at the crowd. I thought he was going to jump into the audience, but instead he just hopped back down onto the stage and finished the song, not even losing a beat.

"He does that all the time," said Jake.

"Why the sigh?"

"If these guys really become famous, everyone is going to expect this from bands from Seattle."

"Get yourself in shape, boy!" I said, poking his arm.

"I'm too fucking tall to do that. He's short."

"Ooh! Lead singer ego."

"No, seriously, the dude is a midget."

"Shhh," said Mark. "The Jolly Green Giant is a midget compared to you. This song is my favorite."

"What's it called?" I asked.

"'Breath.'"

"Breath" was the last song--no encore, these shows had to finish by a certain time--and we had to wait for the crowd to disperse a little before we could move anywhere.

There was a little bit of tension in air on the ride home, punctuated with dialogue.

Mark: "Jake, we really need to talk."

Jake: "Hey, I'm not the one who doesn't think we're ready to play live yet."

Or:

Mark: "Jake, maybe we could increase our practice schedule?"

Jake: "Hmm, didn't I suggest that last week?"

Jake sat in the passenger seat--okay, more like folded himself like a Swiss Army knife into the passenger seat, all six-foot seven of him (he automatically got to ride shotgun, he never ever had to call it)--staring out the window, lost in thought. Mark was humming "Alive" in the back seat, probably not even realizing that he was doing so.

As we were getting out of the car at home, Mark nonchalantly said to Jake, "Uh, dude? Can we maybe have a band meeting later tonight, after you and Scott get off work? I'd like to call Jimmy next week and see if he can get us on the calendar at the Central soon."

I could see about a million thoughts pass through Jake's face in a split second, but instead of a tirade, he just said: "Sure, Mark. Sounds like a good idea."

After Mark walked away, Jake high-fived me and then gave me a hug. "Call me later if you want some free pizza," he said, running towards his car and off to work.

Everyone has this image of musicians, that in their free time they do nothing more than hang out in dark smoky bars, drinking. In my experience, that picture was always very far from reality. No one in Infinite Trainwreck could afford more than one beer out. So when there wasn't a rock show to go to, they invited their friends over, chipped in for a few cases of cheap beer, and watched videos and movies.

Ever since I'd started hanging out next door, my video library became the Infinite Trainwreck movie rental store. They'd watched everything they owned so many times they were thoroughly sick of them. That was fine with me, it was never fun to watch cool bootleg videos unless you had people to watch them with who also thought they were cool.

Tonight, Jonathan was assigned to select the evening's feature presentation. Jake and Mark and Christine had been taking turns battling the other person for the honors, and tonight, Jonathan claimed dibs on the grounds that he was, after all, the only one who had been to film school, and he wouldn't get sidelined like everyone else did with some other part of my collection.

Yeah, right.

"Jonathan, just pick a fucking video, people are waiting," I said, with some impatience, after half an hour had passed with no visible progress.

"I just cannot get over your library," he said, thumbing through my first edition copy of Patti Smith's *Babel*, purchased on the street in front of Cooper Union for the grand sum of four dollars.

"You can borrow books any time, if you like, let's just pick a movie now please," I said.

He replaced *Babel*, and as he did so, snuck a glance at the top shelf, which was filled with half a dozen three ring notebooks containing plastic pages of slides, and empty black and white photographic paper boxes filled with reject prints. And, alongside them, a bunch of shoeboxes simply marked "J." I could see he was about to ask a question and then thought better of it.

But then he spied my dusty, neglected camera bag, lifted it up and said, "What's this?"

"Oh, it's my camera. I used to take pictures in New York."

"Was there anything you didn't do in New York?" he asked, as he took the bag off the shelf and opened it up.

"Everyone did a million things. We thought we were artists; we were kids."

"You make it sound like it was twenty years ago," Jonathan said.

"It feels like it was light years ago to me."

"Don't you miss it?" He was picking up one of the camera bodies, looking at the lenses and the flash and the autowinder. God, I had almost forgotten I had all that equipment. I hadn't touched a camera since New York.

I shrugged. "Yeah, but I did it for fun, and I knew everyone, here it's such a scene, and everyone knows everyone else--it wouldn't be fun." I didn't want to tell him that the last thing I felt like doing was creating anything.

"What was your usual camera setup?" he inquired.

I took the camera body from him. "Well, this one, the OM1, is manual, so I usually used it for black and white shots when I didn't want to use a flash or for abstract stuff. The OM2 is automatic, I'd have color slide film in here and use the auto-winder on it and probably the flash... depending on who or what I was taking pictures of, and why." I explained all of this with an automatic detachment that was like having an out of body experience, as though the old Lisa was talking. I felt the surge of energy that I remembered every time I picked up a camera and took a photo, or picked up a pen and started writing. I had not felt that in years. I certainly hadn't felt it once since I had moved to Seattle. But that was okay, I kept telling myself, because feeling anything out of the ordinary was always asking for trouble.

Jonathan's face lit up as though he'd had a revelation. "You need to take promo photos for us!"

"You have got to be fucking kidding me. This town is lousy with photographers! Call Charles Peterson or something."

"Can I see some of your photos?" He had spied the empty black and white photo paper boxes I kept my prints in, and unlike most people, knew what they were.

"Jonathan, we need to get back to the house with movies," I said, trying to change the subject.

He threw his hands up in defeat and picked out a handful of Rolling Stones concerts of varying vintage.

Halfway through the second show--a *Steel Wheels* concert in Barcelona or somewhere in Spain, I forget--not amazing, but it was pro-shot--Jonathan announced to the gathering, "Lisa is going to take our promo photos for us."

I whirled around in alarm. "What the fuck? I did not agree to such a thing."

They all ignored me as though I wasn't even in the room.

"Good. I like that idea, have someone you know well take your photos. Keep it in the family," said Christine, approvingly.

"Hello. I have not agreed to anything yet," I said, trying to protest.

"Wow, Lisa, I didn't know you took pictures. Do you have any photographs of Sonic Youth?" asked Scott.

"Who else do you have photos of?" said Mark.

"Yeah, I want to see these!" Jake joined in.

★

So it was two in the morning and all four of them, plus Christine, were jammed into my bedroom, going through the boxes of old black and white photos, holding plastic pages with little pockets containing color slides up to the lamp. I was grateful that my roommate was at her girlfriend's house.

"Lisa, these are all really fucking good," said Mark, going through the fourth box of photos. "Why are you doing not pursuing this, even as a hobby?"

"They're not that good, they're only good to you because of the subject matter. Any band standing in front of CBGB is going to seem amazing to you."

"Hey, don't patronize me. These are good fucking photographs. I know the difference," Mark shot me a look. Jake glared at him and Mark switched boxes with Jonathan, who was sitting on the floor. Scott was enraptured, staring at a photo of Thurston Moore and Kim Gordon onstage at CBGB. No one even bothered to try to move him along.

Christine was sitting in a corner behind the door, holding slides up at the light. She finished going through the book of chromes, and then picked up a box of black and white prints. Suddenly, she stopped, frowned, and held up a photo, looking at me inquisitively.

Oh, god. I thought I had put all of those away.

It was James. Sitting in his space on the floor, exposed brick wall at his back, sunlight coming in through the crooked blinds and streaking across his face and the acoustic guitar in his lap, while he stared down at his hands and a notebook, pen clenched in his teeth. He had no idea I was taking that photo, and that was what I loved about it. James in a creative fugue.

"It's--it's James. My ex-boyfriend. That was our apartment in

New York."

"Oh!" Christine dropped the photo like it was something hot. "I'm sorry!"

"It's okay. I thought those were all somewhere else."

Mark picked it up and regarded it critically. "It's a good photograph."

"Thank you." *Please, please, put it down, Mark*, I pleaded silently. I wasn't ready to explain all of this to them. They knew there was a boy involved in my flight from the East, but they didn't know the details.

Jake held out his hand and Mark reluctantly released the photo. I was steeling myself for additional interrogation but he quietly took the picture, walked back to Christine, and placed it at the bottom of the box. Silently grateful, I breathed a sigh of relief and mouthed "Thank you" at Jake. He shrugged, and went over to Jonathan, who was perusing slides of R.E.M. from some point in the mid-'80s. I could tell Jake sensed something, and it didn't bother me that he did. There was something quietly empathetic about Jake. He acted like the dumb, flighty blonde who didn't take anything seriously, but I already knew that was some kind of defense. Those steel-grey eyes missed nothing.

Jake reached for another box on the top shelf of the bookcase and held it up in my direction. I nodded assent and he opened it up.

"But, wait--there aren't photographs in here. Lisa, what's this?"

"God, I don't even know, I haven't looked in these boxes in so long. Let me see."

I took the box from his hands and realized what it was immediately. "It's the galleys for my fanzine." I had completely forgotten about its existence until that moment.

"Fanzine?" Mark asked.

"Oh, everyone published back then, we all knew someone who worked at a copy center, you could get things run for cheap or free in the overnight shifts. It's really not a big deal," I said.

"Do you have any copies left?" asked Jake.

"I sure hope so--these were the masters I made the copies from." I started digging through the box. "Aha!" There were a few copies of issue one at the bottom, slightly the worse for wear but still intact.

"Can I see?" he asked, eagerly.

"Sure," I said, handing it to him.

"*notes from the electric blue*," he read out loud, and then frowned. "What does that mean?"

"It's kind of hard to explain..." I said. "There's a poem in there--"

"Poem?!" Scott said. "You write poetry, too?"

"Wrote. Past tense."

"Lisa," he said, shaking his head.

"Stop right there. Do you want me to explain or not?"

"I want her to explain, so quiet," said Mark.

"Well," I said, all eyes on me. "It came from the first time I saw the Who, and I ended up in the front row for the encore, and more than anything, I remember the lights, they were white and blue and so bright and overwhelming, I just wanted to drown in them... electric blue is what they felt like. So the whole point of the fanzine was me writing about my love of music, and if my love of music had a color it would be electric blue."

"Like the Bowie song," Mark said.

"Exactly." I said.

"Or you could reverse it," said Jake, almost to himself.

"What?"

"Blue electric," Mark said. He looked at Jake, and then at Jonathan, who started to say something at almost the same moment. Scott got up off the floor and took the fanzine out of Jake's hand.

"What?" I asked again, helplessly.

"Blue Electric," said Mark again. "I like it. A lot. I like the idea behind it. I know what you mean, the first time I saw the Stones..."

"Or the Who at the Kingdome," said Jonathan. "I remember those blue lasers..."

"That feeling, exactly," Scott said. Jake nodded his head in agreement.

"Blue Electric. Infinite Trainwreck is dead. Long live Blue Electric," Mark said.

I stood there, speechless, and overjoyed, and happier than I'd been in longer than I could remember.

★

"Okay, you guys need to turn to your left."

I was standing behind the lens of a camera for the first time in almost three years. Despite my protests and hesitation, it was Sunday afternoon and we were out at Gasworks Park, trying to take the first Blue Electric promotional photographs.

"Could you loosen up, perhaps a bit?" I asked carefully.

Mark scowled at Jake. "Dude, this wasn't my idea." He sat down on the ground with a thud.

"Mark, you are being an asshole," said Jake, sitting down next to him.

"I don't like this. It's so cheesy, it's so artificial," Mark said. "We could be using this time to practice, instead of preening in front of a camera."

At the top of Lake Union, Gasworks was reclaimed industrial land that was converted into a park. The remnants of the old gas plant were still there, so you had a great view of the skyline, the water, and then this old rusty machinery in the background for texture. Later it would become a cliché for every--and I do mean every--Seattle band to get their photographs taken there.

Christine stepped in. "Lisa, why don't you go scout some other locations. We're going to have a little band pep talk," she said, glaring at Mark.

I nodded, picked up my tripod and camera bag, and started walking toward the abandoned gas equipment. A few seconds later, I heard someone running up behind me; it was Jonathan.

"I'm sorry about Mark, Lisa. Don't worry, Christine will get him to cooperate. In the meantime, let me show you something." He walked around the side of one of the tall, rusty, round, metal towers and pointed up. There was graffiti from seemingly a thousand bands all over the place. Then I saw what he was pointing at.

"Wow. Mother Love Bone?"

"Yep, and it's original... up just high enough, and you have to hang off of that little bar to the left in order to reach it... which is probably why it hasn't been covered up."

"That is pretty cool that it's still there. It's like some kind of archaeological artifact, or something."

"Yeah, that's how I feel about it. I thought you'd understand."

I saw Jake's long arms in the distance, waving back and forth like a human semaphore flag. "I think their highnesses are ready now," Jonathan said.

★

I was in the living room of the band house, lying on the couch with a beer, preparing to watch a fashion show. Jake appeared on my doorstep just after dinner, and sheepishly asked me if I'd please come over and help him figure out what to wear for the band's first show. Christine refused to get involved in any more fashion-related discussions, after Jake called her at work for the tenth time.

They'd finally agreed to play in public, and Mark's soundman friend got them on the bill down at the Central in Pioneer Square--the first band on a Wednesday night, but by god, their name was in the ad. They'd been practicing nonstop for weeks now, every single night. I'd been wandering in and out after work and during the weekend, and they sounded good. They were ready. Then again, they'd been ready long before I ever showed up.

So I was lying there, trying to take the situation seriously and not laugh my ass off. Jake would not have come over if he was not in trouble. But it was really difficult to maintain any gravity whatsoever when he walked out wearing black spandex leggings, a pirate-striped t-shirt, the most ridiculous floppy hat I had ever seen, and gold suede boots.

I burst out laughing, lost my balance, and spilled beer all over the couch. I now fully appreciated Christine's predicament.

Jake frowned at me, hurt, and I rushed to assuage his bruised lead-singer ego.

"Why do you have to dress up? Why can't you just wear what you wear all the time? You have a great sense of style. Why are you trying to force it? You guys are not some L.A. glam band. Stop trying so hard."

"We're a rock band, Lisa, I can't just wear jeans and a flannel shirt onstage," he said.

"Half this town considers that a fashion statement."

"That's exactly it--I hate that. Mick Jagger would never dress like that."

"You're not Mick, sweetie."

"Robert Plant wouldn't either."

"It's not 1969."

"Fine, then, what do you think I should wear?" he said, standing there and looking forlorn in that god-awful outfit.

I pried myself off the couch and said, "Let's just go look at your closet. Is your room fit for human consumption?"

"There are clothes everywhere, but, yeah, sure."

I walked down the hall as Jake clumped behind me in those boots. I had to stifle giggles.

He was right, there were clothes everywhere. On the bed, on the floor, on the desk, he must have gone through everything he owned. I began sorting through the morass of clothing, attempting to envision an outfit in my mind. Jake didn't need much to look good. He definitely didn't need spandex.

"Jake--you are thinking Mick, when you should be thinking Keith. Keith 1972," I said.

"What do you mean?"

"Have you ever seen any of those photos from the *Exile* sessions, or from that tour? It was pretty basic. T-shirt, cool belt, boots--" he picked up a foot, and I shook my head--"Suede would be fine, but god, no, not gold."

"I can't afford anything new," he said.

"Band thrift store rule #1: you always spend your money on shoes because it is hard if not impossible to find good shoes in thrift stores. Debbie Harry said that, and I think we agree she would be an expert on this subject."

Jake nodded grudgingly.

"You need cool t-shirts, or even old button-downs, sleeves rolled up--old tuxedo shirts if we can find them. We have to find you a cool belt, but for now this will do," I said, as I fished a weathered brown leather belt with a bronze buckle out of a pile of rejected clothing.

Jake looked at me dubiously. "Are you sure? It's just not very--flash."

"Jake, you guys are not flash. You're not a Bolan or a Daltrey, or even an Iggy. You play guitar most of the time. It's a different dynamic."

"Really? He's not Daltrey? Because I really was hoping for the fringed vest and bare chest," Mark said from the doorway.

"Well, smartass, what are you wearing tomorrow night?" said Jake.

"Whatever I feel like taking out of the closet," he said, calmly.

"Are we talking about clothes for tomorrow?" asked Jonathan, who walked in from down the hall. "Oh, good, Lisa is here, let me show you what I'm going to wear--" he said, as he ran off.

I walked down the hall to the kitchen to get another beer. I was going to need a few more of these if I had become de facto stylist. When I returned, Mark and Jake were arguing, for a change.

"I can't believe you don't care what you're wearing tomorrow night," Jake said. "It's our first show. How can you not care?"

"Because no one is coming to see what we're wearing, they're coming to see what we sound like. Not what we look like," Mark said.

"People come to see what Mick looks like," Jake said.

"We're not the Rolling Stones," said Mark, stating the obvious.

"People come to see what Chris Cornell looks like," Jake said, trying again.

"Yes, but the real audience is people like Scott and Lisa, who come for the music," Mark said. "Those are the people I care about."

At that moment, Jonathan walked in, wearing an outfit consisting of a vintage brown suit jacket, jeans, white button-down shirt, and crowned with a thrift store fedora. We stared at him in abject shock. This was the guy who always wore some kind of white shirt and jeans. Always. The look on our faces must have said it all, because Jonathan sighed, turned around, and walked dejectedly back down the hall toward his room.

Once he was out of earshot, Mark let out a snort of derision.

"Hey, now, that's not fair," I said.

"At least he's making an effort," said Jake.

"I'm making an effort," Mark said. "I'm practicing ten fucking hours a day to get ready for this show. I've been down in the practice room all night while you've been playing supermodel."

"You are hopeless. How is it you do not get this?" Jake said.

I looked at them both. "Cut it out! Just cut it out. Wear what you want. You're not the New York Dolls. Trust me that the Ramones did not have these conversations. Let it the fuck go."

I threw up my hands in defeat and headed home. Some things they were going to have to work out for themselves.

At 6:30 the next night, I rushed down to Pioneer Square, parked underneath the viaduct, and walked around the corner to First Avenue and the Central. Instead of being half an hour late for soundcheck, as I feared, I found Scott, his friend Adam, and Jonathan sitting on the stage, reading the *Rocket*.

"Where are the Glimmer Twins?" I asked.

"I wish I could tell you that they were doing lines in the dressing room," said Scott. "But instead I regret to inform you that the hostilities have recommenced."

"Should I go back there, or am I better off staying very far away?" I asked.

"They're hopeless, Lisa. We tried," said Jonathan. "They're not paying attention to the lowly rhythm section."

I sighed. "Where's Christine? Anyone tried to call her?"

"Christine had to work late; she warned us in advance. We promised it wasn't going to be a big deal," Jonathan said, exasperated.

I sighed again, glanced around for something resembling a backstage entrance, and Scott pointed over his shoulder toward the back.

I walked into a tiny, graffiti-enveloped room right next to the men's bathroom, and found Jake sitting against one wall and Mark against the opposite wall, glaring at each other.

I had clearly entered the room during some kind of standoff. I looked from one guy to the other. No response.

"Uh, hi?" I said.

They glared at me.

"Shouldn't you be soundchecking now?"

"I don't think I can play with someone who doesn't take this seriously," said Jake.

"I take this very fucking seriously, you idiot! I have been practicing for hours after work every night for weeks! How much more seriously should I be taking this?" Mark said.

"You can't even be bothered to change your fucking shirt for this show! People are paying to come see us, can't you make some kind of effort?"

"Once again, I make a major fucking effort in the music. Not how much time I spend modeling my outfits in front of the mirror. If you think I should put more time and effort into that than into practicing, then we need to have a serious fucking talk because I am in the wrong fucking band," he said.

I decided to go out on a limb and risk having said limb sawn off out from under me.

"Jake, it occurs to me that what Mark is wearing is not really the issue here. Would you like to share your feelings with the group?" I lamely tried to interject some humor into things.

"It's just--dammit--if this doesn't work, Mark, you can go play in any band you want to! I'm not that good of a singer. You are that good a guitar player. And you graduated college! You can go and get a real job if this doesn't work. I don't want to be making pizzas for the rest of my life. That's all I know how to do." He sat down dejectedly.

Mark and I exchanged looks of utter disbelief. This man had the voice of the gods, the stage presence to go with it, and wrote lyrics that made you weep. I nodded at Mark and backed out of the room. This was between the two of them now.

I walked out into the bar and a guy in a Jack Daniels t-shirt approached me. "Are you the manager?"

I looked around and realized he was talking to me.

"The manager of what?"

"The manager of the first band--" He looked at his clipboard. "Blue Electric?"

"No," I answered, as I saw Christine through the front windows, running across First Avenue, hair flying. "That would be their manager," I said.

She had barely made it inside when I frantically gestured her over.

"Your band is late for soundcheck and they're not gonna get one if they don't get onstage in the next five minutes," the gentleman in question informed her as she approached.

"Do you know what's going on?" she asked me.

"I'm pretty sure the equipment is set up, but Jake and Mark are having some differences of opinion, for a new and refreshing change," I said.

"Fine. I'll take care of it," she said. "Can you check with the rhythm section for me, while I go diffuse the time bomb?" She strode off with purpose towards the dressing room. I did not envy the two guys about to get Christine on full throttle.

I walked over to my charges. "I've been asked to determine your readiness," I said.

"Wow, not only have we acquired a manager, but she already has got herself a top-notch personal assistant," Scott said. "Yes, Miss Lisa, we are ready. Mark and Jake conveniently started fighting after we set up, and Adam here finished anything those two forgot."

Adam practically stood at attention and beamed. He was one of Scott's boyhood friends, and had been waiting for years for the chance to be a roadie.

There was a commotion behind me, and I turned around to see Jake and Mark, followed by Christine, heading for the stage. I quickly backed away into a neutral location, but all they did was get on stage and start the soundcheck.

Once they were actually playing, Christine came over to me and said, "I'm not quite sure when it was decided I signed up for managing these boys."

"Probably about the same time you decided I was taking their promo photos, and the same time you stayed up all night helping them put together this first setlist, oh, and when you stopped the ad for this gig from going to press calling the band 'The Mark Genovese Experience,'" I said.

"Well, let's see if they keep me. I think I was just a total asshole. They're scared shitless, and they're guys. They're not going to be able to say, 'Hey, Chrissie, lay the fuck off, we're scared.'"

"You got that right. But they definitely needed a swift kick in the ass, and you gave it to them. They didn't need a soft shoulder to cry on at that moment. Remember, they're guys."

She leaned back on the bar stool and listened to the band for a minute, and then continued, "You know, so much went wrong with the band I was in with Mark--I swore I'd never have anything to do with the music business ever again. It made me hate it."

She was quiet again, as the band stopped to run through the bridge of "Bronze Light" a few times.

"But, Lisa, I think I just might like managing this band," she said, smiling.

"I think you already are," I said.

We high-fived each other and turned back to the soundcheck.

The boys weren't going on until 9:30 so we had plenty of time. Jake had one of his coworkers bring down a couple of pizzas for dinner, since it wasn't like they could afford to go out to eat.

And then, before we knew it, the hour of reckoning arrived. There were a few dozen people in the club; not bad for a Wednesday night. Sure, we personally knew more than half of them, but that's what friends are for.

I was chatting with some of Jake's co-workers from Piecora's, when I heard Christine scream, "Hell yeah!" I turned around, and Mark, Jake, Scott and Jonathan were walking onstage, faces in various stages of fear, panic and shock... except for Mark, who just looked--determined. But he was the only one who had actually done this before; Jake's first band had never made it out of his Dad's basement in Lake City.

Jake walked up to the microphone and blurted out: "Happy Wednesday, and thank you for coming... I'm Jake, this is Mark, Scott and Jonathan; we're called Blue Electric. This first song is called 'Down the Road.' 1,2,3--" and the song started, guitars crashing and looks of relief on Mark and Scott's face (Mark because the music was measuring up to his standards, Scott because they were finally on a damn stage), a small smile from Jonathan, having the time of his life, and abject concentration coating Jake's face like latex.

Christine and I moved up through the crowd to be a little closer to the stage, but not so close that the guys would freak out.

After the next song, Scott joked, "Jonathan's good tonight, inne," quoting from the ubiquitous *Get Yer Ya-Ya's Out*, shooting me and Christine a sly smile. Jonathan smirked and did a drum roll. Jake looked blank.

"Christ, Jake has to be a nervous fucking wreck if he isn't catching obvious Stones references," I said to Christine.

At the same moment, looks of revelation broke across our faces and we began yelling: "'Paint It Black'! 'Paint It Black' you devil!"

Mark was standing back at his amp, tuning, shaking his head and rolling his eyes. Jake lost the face of stone and made eye contact with us; we waved and he smiled. Finally, he smiled!

Five more songs, eight songs total, forty-five minutes, and that was it. The first Blue Electric show was behind them, and the boys were packing up equipment and hustling it out to the van. Christine and I stayed at the bar, finishing our beers, staying out of the way until they were done. We had offered to help load out, but were shooed away sternly. "You two did enough already," said Jake.

Mark came strolling up to us. You could see the cockiness in the way he walked, he was on cloud nine and felt great. It was adorable, but I wouldn't shatter his moment by telling him that.

"I would like to congratulate our manager, and inform her and our good friend that the party is moving up to the house. The beer is cheaper and the music is better," he said.

"I guess it's official, then?" she asked, carefully.

His response was to give her a bear hug. Christine's face was a mixture of shock, delight and panic.

"Am I allowed to hug the guitar player?" I asked, hugging him.

"How bad was it," he said, whispering in my ear.

I shook my head and refused to answer. I was not going to humor his fatalism tonight.

He sighed. "Okay, okay. I'm gonna drive up with the guys. See you two in a bit?"

We both nodded, and he nodded back and walked out.

Christine and I went down to the viaduct and got into my car. I turned on the ignition, and the radio came on, heavy metal blaring. As I backed out of the space and headed the car towards home, suddenly these unmistakable drumbeats came thundering out of the speakers and I cranked the radio up until we had distortion. Led Zeppelin! Led Zep was always Christine's favorite band and her first love, despite her shared Stones partisanship with the rest of us.

Headbanging away, hair flying, we screamed the words to each other as we headed towards home. Suddenly, I had a brainwave.

"Hey, feel like a little victory loop down Broadway?"

Christine grinned and rolled her window down in response.

Blasting "Rock and Roll" at the unfortunate inhabitants of Capitol Hill, we took the long way home, Christine glowing, happy and triumphant.

★

Ah ha, finally. So this is Grant's Pass. I've seen the signs heralding its approach for what seems like hours now. Somehow, I managed to not know that there was this freaking treacherous mountain pass that lasts forever in the middle of Oregon. Everyone ominously warns about the Siskyous at the Oregon-California border--if this is bad, and no one ever mentions it, I cannot even imagine what the next pass is like.

I have zero ability to actually select a new CD, since my concentration is steely-eyed, glued to the white line. I would listen to some AM oldies station, but there is no signal up here. So I manage to eject the current disc (*Sandinista*), grab whatever my hand lands on, and wrangle it into the stereo.

As the intro to "Black Dog" comes thundering out of the speakers, I laugh. Cosmic requisition and supply, at your service! That's what Marie always says at weird coincidences like this. I let Led Zeppelin carry me up into the dark black twists of the pass, and can't help but smile.

CHAPTER 7: 1993

It was 8:00 a.m. on a Saturday morning, and the Blue Electric van had been backed down the sidewalk to get it as close to the house as possible. The six of us--the band, Christine and myself--were scurrying around, loading equipment cases and boxes and bags and milk crates full of cables.

Jake was busily loading luggage into the van, when all of a sudden he yelled, "Whose gigantic, heavy duffel bag is this?"

No answer.

"I swear to fucking god I am going to open it up and dump everything in it on the ground so I can figure out who the owner is!"

No answer.

In one swift movement Jake hurled the bag out of the back of the van and plunked it at his feet. I decided it was time to fess up.

"Um... that would be mine," I said.

"What the fuck is in here?! We're going away for THREE WEEKS!" Jake cast his gaze to the heavens and shook his head.

"Mr. fucking drama queen, Jesus!" said Scott in a stage-whisper.

"Books...and boots. That's what makes it so heavy," I said.

"Books?"

"We're going to be driving around the Midwest for three weeks. I will go stir crazy without something to read," I said.

"I know we're going to Kansas, but Christ, they do have bookstores there! You don't have to bring your entire reference library with!" Jake was starting to lose it and we weren't even driving yet.

Behind him, I spied Jonathan and Scott carrying a box I knew contained their personal culture stash (art books, reading material, and Scott's art supplies), and I also knew they had three empty boxes, quietly lying flat under the seats, for their much-anticipated small-town used book store purchases.

At that moment, all I could think was: why on earth did I agree to road manage this tour for them? There must have been some unemployed roadie in Seattle who needed the work, but, no, the band unilaterally decided that they were going to make a statement about the position of women in rock and roll by having their entire crew be female... that, and both myself and Christine got laid off within two weeks of each other, and thus were the only friends in our immediate circle who had the time to drive around America with Blue Electric for three weeks. Christine was officially manager anyway, and had booked the entire tour and could run the soundboard. I could handle lighting and merch and anything else, including, and especially, babysitting the temperamental lead singer.

I decided to end the argument by pulling Jake over to the side and opening up the duffel bag. "See, there's not much in there. It's just a big bag, and it was the most indestructible thing I had. It's my dad's old Army duffel bag, I used to take it to Girl Scout camp."

Jake sighed heavily. That's when I realized it wasn't about the freaking duffel bag. "What is up with you? Why are you so tense?"

His shoulders crumpled in response as though he'd been holding the bag up there the whole time. "I just want this tour to go well. I want the tour to go well so that Mark doesn't quit, so Scott won't go back to his day job, and so Jonathan doesn't go drum for the Screaming Trees."

"Screaming Trees? What happened to Barrett Martin?"

"I don't know that something has happened to him. I just know I saw the Conner brothers talking to Jonathan last month, and I don't want to take any chances. If it's not them, it'll be someone else. Isn't it time for the Fastbacks to get another drummer?" There was a sense of manic desperation to Jake's voice. He crouched down and put his head in his hands. I knelt down next to him and put my arm around his shoulders.

"Let's just get going. You'll feel better once we're on the road and out of the state." I was trying to be sympathetic, but was also conscious of the fact that we were wasting valuable time.

Jake straightened up and shook his hair back. "I'm okay. Let's just get this crap in the van somehow and get the hell out of Dodge."

Christine had been exchanging meaningful glances with me throughout this entire conversation, during which she had she'd finished loading the van--including the offending duffel bag--with the rest of the guys. They were now all leaning up against the vehicle, waiting. When we turned around, everyone sprang back to life.

Mark sauntered over to Jake. "Dude! We are going on tour! Like the Rolling Stones! Like Led Zeppelin! Like the Who! We are a rock band!" His sarcasm had its desired effect, as Jake cracked a smile and started playing along. "Yes! We are--" he stopped, turned, and paused for effect. "We are rock gods!" Jake threw his arms open and imitated Robert Plant on the balcony of the Riot House, that photo he'd had blown up for their rehearsal space years ago. It was on the back wall so he could face it while they rehearsed.

Christine stood there watching this exhibit with her hands on her hips. "Uh, excuse me, Mr. Rock Gods, could we get in the fucking rock god van and get on the fucking road? It's like nine a.m. and I would like to be in Spokane by lunchtime. We do have a gig in Missoula tonight."

We herded them into the van, and rolled out onto I-5 south, heading for I-90 and points east.

Everyone slept until we stopped for pancakes in Spokane, and switched drivers. We held our breath driving through Idaho, Jonathan certain that there would be white supremacists even at the rest stops, although it was beautiful beyond imagining. We drove up, up, and endlessly up through the mountains and down into Missoula, where it was clear and green and beautiful. In what would become a pattern for the tour, we found good coffee and great record stores. The club was tiny but nice and the band played well for the eight people who showed up. Jake informed them that the Police once played for fourteen people in Poughkeepsie, and well, he hoped the audience would remember this day. Mark just rolled his eyes.

We were back on the road the next morning at 8:00 a.m., heading for Minneapolis, a drive that would take two days. After we made it through the interminable mountains that make up most of Montana, North Dakota was flat and the towns were small and there was an inescapable sense of wonder attached to everything we did, no matter how mundane--even walking into a truck stop felt like a brand-new adventure.

Minneapolis was next, the home of almost as much great music as Seattle. We arrived early enough to do some rock and roll sightseeing. I had eagerly planned to try to hunt down the house on the cover of The Replacements' *Let It Be*, while Scott led Jake and Christine on an expedition in search of Prince's Paisley Park studios.

"I hope this is worth it," said Mark, as I followed directions obtained from the club's soundman through leafy Minneapolis streets.

"As long as the house is still there, it's worth it to me," I said.

"I just never got the Replacements. Anyone can get onstage and play a set of twenty-seven unfinished, sloppy, bad covers. We could do it."

"So why don't you?" I asked somewhat heatedly, double-checking the directions. Jonathan leaned over to take the map out of my hands, and gestured left.

"Because we have actual songs to play."

"So did the Replacements. The covers were a reaction to the audience. R.E.M. used to do the same thing for the same reason. It was a lot different being on the road back then, you'd play places that had New Wave night every Tuesday and people wanted to hear the hits;, they had very little patience for anything original."

"You shouldn't care what the audience thinks," Mark said.

"Or you can send them a huge fuck you and play 'Heartbeat, It's a Lovebeat' until they pay attention or leave."

"That's a copout. Just turn up the volume and play louder."

"Have you ever really listened to those songs? Could you write something as immediate and heartfelt as 'Answering Machine?'"

"I like to think that I have," he said.

"Fine, is anyone coming over to the band house and taking pictures of it?"

Mark was just about to explode, when Jonathan leaned over the seat and pointed to our left, silently. There was the house.

"Whoa," I said. I pulled the van over to the side of the road, parked, and then just sat there, as I leaned forward on the steering wheel, and gazed up at the house through the windshield. After a few minutes, I hopped out for a closer look. Jonathan also climbed out, Super-8 camera in hand. He was supposed to be making a film documenting the tour; so far all he'd managed to document was the inside of the van, a bunch of rest stops and gas stations, and a Dairy Queen in Bismarck, North Dakota.

I wish I could have explained to Mark how much the Replacements were our band. They were just a bunch of regular guys who wrote songs about being regular guys. We loved them fiercely, passionately, we followed them all over the Tri-State area when they played, as far south as the 9:30 Club in D.C., as far north as the Rat in Boston. There was no way I could be in Minneapolis for my first and probably only time and not come on this pilgrimage.

I thought back to all my friends, how we all met through the bands of that era, about seeing the Mats at CBGB's one December when they all wore matching striped coveralls, standing on chairs in the back near the soundboard loft. My most vivid memory was during the cover of "Last Train to Clarksville" when this guy in front of us stuck up his middle finger and kept it there through the rest of the show, while we had to hold each other up because we were laughing so hard, having so much fun.

I wondered where everyone was now. Andrea was the only one I still talked to with any kind of regularity. And suddenly, I missed them so much I ached, I missed those nights running around the city like it was our private kingdom, I missed taking over tables at the Riviera or Kiev or the Holiday and having frantic loud conversations because our ears were still ringing from another night at a rock show.

Standing in front of the old Stinson house at 2215 Bryant made me truly homesick for New York for the first time. It was a symbol that represented a time in my life that was full of ridiculously supercharged optimism, when we were all going to be great artists or accomplish big things. The time before James left me, back when everything seemed possible.

I walked back to the van. Jonathan was shooting some footage of the neighborhood, but he put the camera down as I walked up.

Mark was reclined back in the passenger seat, sunglasses on, feet up on the dashboard, looking bored to tears. He sat up as I opened the door. I was about to get in and drive away, when he climbed out of the van.

"Wait."

I regarded him cautiously.

"You can't come all this way and not have your picture taken in front of the house, can you?" He held up my camera, which I had left sitting on the dashboard. We took the obligatory tourist shots, me smiling proudly.

★

The next gig was in Chicago, and somehow, the stars were aligned for Blue Electric that night. There was more than a little apprehension before they walked onstage, since it was the first big city crowd of the tour. But there was no need--the house was half full by the time the band started to play, the audience clearly there to check them out, thanks to some friends of Scott's brother who wrote for the student newspaper at Northwestern. The vibe was great from the first note, and the band responded in kind.

When they came out for the first encore and without a word, started "Around and Around," in honor of Chicago, Chess Studios and the Rolling Stones--inspired by the pilgrimage we'd made earlier in the day to 2120 S. Michigan Avenue (not that there was much to see there)--the place went nuts. With huge smiles of sheer joy and utter relief, the boys played their asses off, laughing the whole time, and walked off stage feeling good, feeling accomplished, for probably the first time since we left Seattle.

"We are much loved in Madison, Wisconsin," Jake said, as we drove out of town the next morning.

"And in Belgium." Mark said.

"Even though we haven't exactly been to Belgium yet..."

"It's just a matter of time."

It was like watching a fucking Marx Brothers routine, Mark and Jake in the front, Mark driving, Jake riding shotgun, or vice versa. The two of them usually competently upheld the tradition of classic singer-guitarist conflict, but ever since Chicago, the forced togetherness of the road seemed to have eliminated the surface tension. Maybe Jake was finally secure enough that Mark (or anyone else) wasn't going to leave the band. Maybe Mark was content because he was playing music every single day and felt like the band was finally going somewhere. Jonathan was content to be traveling, the changing landscape held endless fascination to him. And even Scott was no longer teeth-clenching anxious about the fact that he'd had to quit his job because the restaurant wouldn't give him the time off to do the tour.

I lost the coin toss and had the early morning driving shift from Kansas City to Denver. I was bleary-eyed and completely out of it. I almost considered begging someone to take over for me, but I surveyed the crew and realized that no one else was any better. Plus, fair was fair.

I waited until I was on I-70 heading west before I made any decisions about music. The road was straight and endlessly flat, and everyone else was nodding off or already passed out, sound asleep. Jake was curled up on the floor somewhere, too tall to be even remotely comfortable any other way. Christine had a big floppy hat pulled down over her face. Jonathan's sweatshirt hood was pulled way up over his head so all you could see was his nose. Mark was breathing deeply in the passenger seat, and I couldn't see Scott anywhere, although I could hear his distinctive snores from the back seat.

After a few minutes, I realized that I was going to drive us into a cornfield if I didn't find something to keep me awake. I pulled my bag up onto my lap and shuffled through tape cases until something caught my eye.

The blistering guitar intro to "Search and Destroy" by the Stooges soared out of the speakers and was like the strongest cup of coffee I could possibly imagine. Now, this was morning music! None of that Beatles or Kinks shit that usually ended up being everyone else's a.m. music choice--well, except for Scott who always tried to put on John Coltrane, only to be shouted down, loudly.

"Lisa." It was Mark.

"Yeah?" My eyes were on the road, straight ahead.

"Kid, we're trying to sleep here."

"And I'm trying to drive here."

"There's got to be a compromise."

"I need something to keep me awake. This is working. This is great morning music. Brisk."

"Yeah, like a cold shower," he said.

There were weak murmurs of agreement. See, now I was being evil. I knew this was pissing them off. But I had this slight cranky edge going and I was kind of getting off on it.

"Lisa, please," Mark said.

"Okay, okay. I'll put on something else."

I popped the tape out of the player and tossed it on the console. Picking up the bag, I rummaged carefully, one eye on the road. A small thin smile and another selection was made, and with a click slid into the tape deck.

Bad four-part harmony, trying to imitate a heavy metal band, warbled out of the speakers, and everyone in the van moaned in recognition. It was the Replacements covering "Black Diamond" by KISS, side two of *Let It Be*. Paul's voice was scratchily screaming out from the speakers, and the rest of the band followed manically behind him. I was giggling equally manically to myself. This probably wasn't much better than the Stooges, but fuck them, I got stuck with the early morning run.

Just as I heard Mark sigh, and figured that he was going to begin his campaign again, the song ended, and--I forgot.

I forgot that the next song on this tape was the song that made me fall in love with the Replacements to begin with. One of the most beautiful, haunting, bare and truthful songs ever written began, with that ethereal 12-string guitar intro--"Unsatisfied."

Out of nowhere, stuck in-between a KISS cover and a quasi-instrumental rant against MTV, was the best song that Paul

Westerberg ever wrote. This aching, haunting song about yearning and disappointment, about losing something and resolving--not learning, resolving--to live with it,

"Unsatisfied." I remembered telling James that I wanted to learn to play guitar just so I could play this song. Westerberg sang about seeing your dreams within arms' reach, but then finding out they weren't what they seemed. For a moment, there was no one else in the van with me; I was alone with the song and the grey Kansas morning, wind whistling around the van, the landscape, and my heart--at least for a moment--inescapably bleak.

I'd brought that tape along because I knew we were going to Minneapolis and I knew I would try to find the house. When I threw it in the bag, it struck me that I hadn't listened to it in ages; I just thought I had burned out on it. Now, I remembered why.

I took a long, slow breath. No crying now.

Mark must have seen or suspected something, because I felt him move back from attack position. I turned the volume down slightly and kept heading west, fighting the tears with every breath.

A few minutes later, Mark spoke up, quietly: "Pull off at the next rest stop, please."

I just assumed morning coffee was getting to him, and I couldn't possibly argue with him at that moment, despite van policy being that we only stopped every two hours at the most unless it was a dire emergency.

I pulled off at the rest area and turned off the ignition. No one else stirred, except Mark, who got out of the van, walked across the front, and then knocked on the driver's side window. Not understanding, I rolled it down, with a quizzical expression on my face, almost cranky.

"Let me drive," he said.

My eyes met his in disbelief, and then I realized that, somehow, he knew, or at least understood. Gratefully, I moved into the vacated passenger seat. I wanted to thank him but I was afraid that even one word would cause me to burst into tears, so I simply reached out and touched his arm once he'd settled into the driver's seat.

"Get some sleep, kid, or at least close your eyes for a while," he said, as the van picked up speed on the highway again.

I pulled my dad's old Mets hat out of my bag, covered my face, and wearily let sleep take the place of aching memories.

★

We kept crossing paths with some band from Austin called Snake Oil. Their name was horrible ("Too damn hippie," Jake said), but they were amazingly good--"like Pink Floyd on amphetamines," Scott said. They also had a woman as road manager, the lead singer's ex-girlfriend. She could run sound and lights and sell merch at the same time, and Christine and I were in awe of her. They had an actual guitar tech, too, and the boys salivated at the thought of it. Someone to fix their guitars for them, someone to go out and run around looking for guitar strings.

"You've got to be kidding me," said Sharon, Snake Oil's manager, over an early all-girls dinner in Salt Lake City, the night of our last show with them. "If one of those assholes needs guitar strings, they can go get their own. Keith is not gonna be errand boy. Keith gets the best place to sleep. Keith gets to ride shotgun permanently. They treat the dude with kid gloves."

She turned around as Keith, aforementioned legend, strode into the club, effortlessly balancing four guitar cases. "Hey dude, come over here and meet the wonderful ladies behind Blue Electric," Sharon said.

He seemed just kind of average--average height, average-looking--but then he put down the guitars, turned and walked over and I realized this guy was decidedly not average. He had charisma in buckets. He should be in the band, I thought.

Sharon made the introductions, and when Keith and I shook hands, static electricity caused noticeable sparks to fly. I pulled back involuntarily, while Keith's eyebrows arched in amusement.

"I guess I could make some joke about sparks flying on E Street, but I'm not sure anyone but me will get it," he said.

It was like time screeched to a dead fucking halt. Was the guitar tech for some alternative band from Austin quoting Bruce fucking Springsteen to me? Had some indie band covered "E Street Shuffle" and I didn't know about it?

I decided to make a total fool of myself and cautiously ventured, "If I said, 'Miami' to you, what would be the first thing you thought of?"

"Steve Van Zandt," he said, looking interested.

Oh my fucking god. This was what I thought it was. I realized I was standing there with my mouth hanging open, while he just looked very pleasantly surprised. Who was this guy and where did he come from?

Christine and Sharon clearly had no idea what was going on, so I decided to try to explain. "It would appear that Keith and I are both fans of the work of Mr. Bruce Springsteen."

Neither of us had let go of the other's hand yet.

Christine looked at him, and at me, and at us, and then spun around and walked away, muttering to herself. Sharon looked at the two of us, still holding each other's hand, smiled quietly and followed Christine.

"Well," Keith finally said. "This is quite a surprise." Rich warm brown eyes shot into mine. I felt as though I was suspended in mid-air, but managed to respond: "It's like a password for the underground army, or something."

"You can't be from Seattle," Keith asked.

"Born and bred in the lovely state of New Jersey."

He still hadn't let go of my hand, and I was hanging on for dear life myself.

"South Philly," he answered, pointing at himself. "Best Springsteen audience in the country."

"No shit. That's why we always drove down to the shows at the Spectrum," I said, still stunned.

At this point Keith realized he was still holding onto my hand. He looked down at our hands, looked up at me, squeezed my hand and then gently released it. "So, Lisa from New Jersey, tell me about how you ended up in Seattle and on the road with Blue Electric. And tell me why your band doesn't have a record deal yet..."

We walked towards the dressing rooms and I slid my arm through his, as I started to give him the abridged edition of the Lisa story.

★

Four hours later, we were still talking too much to want to do anything else. It wasn't just Bruce geekery, it was everything. He was learning computers so he could open up a studio in Austin, and wanted to talk programming. He wanted to talk about New York, and Philly, and what we both missed. We talked about our families, and what it was like to transplant yourself so far away from everyone and everything you have ever known.

Of course, when Christine came out to the van around ten o'clock to get guitar strings for Mark and found the two of us making out in the back seat, things got a little complicated. Keith and I went out there, ostensibly, to trade tapes. He didn't have a copy of the Roxy '78 show, and I didn't have the upgrade of the Passaic, NJ show from that same year. So we were going to switch.

We were sitting there, talking intently and listening just as hard, and the next thing I knew, I looked up at him and it was like a moth to the flame, we leaned over and kissed each other, and it was crazy.

Christine opened the door and saw us there, and both of us screamed at the same time. She promptly slammed the door shut, and I extricated myself from Keith and started buttoning my shirt.

Once I was done, I opened the door and hopped out of the van.

"This is good. This is damn funny," Christine said. "Of all the people I expected to find fooling around in the van on this tour, you were not on the list."

"Hey!" I said.

"No, no, I think it's great! Can I open the back door?"

I banged twice on the side of the van and Keith came out, grabbing my ass as he did. Christine shook her head, went around to the back of the van, and busied herself with the flashlight.

Keith leaned me up against the side of the van and kissed me again, hot and dark and full of promise. "Just don't leave without saying goodbye. Promise?"

With that, we walked back into the club and went our separate ways. Christine shot me knowing looks all night, but clearly didn't breathe a word about it to anyone else. We were still giving Jake hell about the two girls we'd discovered in the van with him after the Chicago show.

True to his word, Keith didn't leave without giving me his address and phone number, and insisted on taking mine, writing his details on a piece of paper in a red spiral notebook, tearing out the page and handing it to me. I wrote down mine on another page and handed the book back to him. We stood there looking at each other for a few seconds, not saying anything. Just when I was about to turn away, Keith grabbed my hand and kissed it, before walking over to his van and shutting the door.

I closed my eyes and remembered the last time a boy flew into my life, turned it upside down, and drove away in a van. And then I opened them and tried to push away that memory and replace it with this one, as I walked to our van and climbed in, not looking back.

I'm still fighting my way through Grants Pass. It just goes on forever, it is like nothing I have ever had to drive through before all by myself, even though I had gotten what I had considered true combat driving training on that tour.

It was the only real tour I ever got to go on from beginning to end. I found myself gainfully employed again before long, and the boys started to find people who actually knew what they were doing to go out on the road with them. There were random visits--like the spring I couldn't deal with a Seattle winter that seemingly would not end, and escaped to join them on a tour of the Southwest for a week. And later, of course, once touring was almost luxurious, I could jet off to New York or London or Tokyo for a long weekend.

But of course, since Ian's arrival in my life, running off to random gigs on a whim ended. He never wanted to come with and was always slightly resentful when I would say, "Okay, fine, see ya," and go anyway. So I just stopped going.

Except for the last time they played the United Center in Chicago. They wouldn't take no for an answer, and made all the arrangements before even asking me. I had no idea why until the first encore, when Paul Westerberg (in town to play a show at the Metro) walked out onstage to a standing ovation, and joined the boys in covers of "Black Diamond" (done Mats-style) and "Bastards of Young." I thought I had died and gone to heaven, and the photo of the seven of us taken after the show hangs on the wall in my office.

I move into the right lane, slow down below the speed limit, and turn on the dome light. I need something light, something to keep me awake. I see the blue-tinted cover, a bunch of boys sitting on a rooftop. *Let It Be.*

It's like a long-lost friend is suddenly sitting in the passenger seat. The familiarity of knowing every note and every word of every song is comforting, and I sing along happily. It takes me back to those years in New York, when I felt like nothing was impossible, that we were all invincible, and all we had to do was reach out and pick whatever dream we wanted.

It isn't until after "Black Diamond," ends, volume cranked as loud as I could stand it, that I am caught off-guard with those twelve-string guitar notes. How do I always forget this song is on this record?

I begin to reach down to forward past "Unsatisfied", feeling like it is more than I can take right now, and then stop, swallow hard, and let it play.

When the song finishes, I click back so it starts again, and hit the button so that it would repeat until I stopped it. Feeling like I was now properly girded for the journey ahead, I steeled myself for the next section of ridiculously dark and windy Oregon highway, singing and screaming and letting the tears clean everything out.

CHAPTER 8: 1995

The boys had been on the road for what seemed like forever. They decided that the only way they were going to get any attention was if they went out and made things happen, for as long as it took. Christine was still managing the band, but she couldn't afford to go with, because of course they couldn't afford to pay her. She had a new job she liked and didn't want to fuck it up, and after surviving yet another now-defunct internet startup company, I also had a new gig I was just getting settled into. So they had Adam and one other guy working crew. Adam threw down right before they were about to leave and demanded that he be taken with, that he was committed to the band, threatening to chain himself to the rear axle of the van if they said no.

I was getting phone calls every day, but I was worried about them, worried bad. The phone call I was waiting for was the one where Mark or Jake exploded in my ear that they were coming home because they were finished. The truth was, I wouldn't have blamed them. But it was my job to be the eternal cheerleader. I tried to remain cheery every time someone called with the latest road update.

Then, some promoter who was new in town set up a festival of Seattle bands down at Memorial Stadium at Seattle Center. To try to generate interest, they decided to have a contest where people could vote for their favorite unsigned local bands to play. The winners would get a slot on the bill and free tickets to hand out to their fans.

To everyone's astonishment, Blue Electric won first place by a landslide.

"How did this happen?" Jake asked, long-distance from somewhere in Colorado, with more than a slight touch of wonder in his voice.

"Give the people what they want," I said. "Don't fight it."

"I don't understand how we are on a bill with Soundgarden and and a bunch of other bands who can fill the Moore three nights in a row, when we can barely fill Squid Row," he said.

"That's not true," I said. "Squid Row's been closed for years. And have you ever stopped to consider that maybe the hard work is finally paying off?"

There was silence on the other end of the phone.

"Jake, you should really be more excited about this than you are," I said.

He sighed. "I don't know, Lisa--it's like, how long have we been doing this? It doesn't seem to really be going anywhere."

"Maybe you need to come home and make another record. You have got to be tired of playing the same songs night after night," I said.

"Yeah, and who's gonna release it? More importantly, who's going to pay for it?" I could hear the panic in his voice.

"Jake, you are roadworn and weary and we will talk about this when you are home," I said to him.

★

Christine drove to my house that morning to pick me up. We stopped for coffee at B&O, and then drove down to the Center. The show started at 1 o'clock and Blue Electric were the second band on the bill. As manager, Christine was entitled to a VIP parking pass. That meant that we didn't have to wait in the ridiculously long line of cars waiting to park in the Seattle Center lots, and instead were allowed to park right in front of the stadium.

As we made our way through the Center, I said, "I think this tour has been kind of brutal on the guys."

"Yeah, I know they kind of feel like they are treading water." She yawned again. "This is too damn early."

"Chrissie, I'm worried they're going to pack it in."

That woke her up.

"It would be fucking stupid if they did," she said, as we stopped and listened to Zeke soundchecking inside the stadium. "I swear, they are driving me insane. I know they have worked at this for what seems like a long time, but I swear to god, they cannot see the forest for the trees. They are getting more and more gigs, the gigs they are getting are easier to book, club bookers and promoters know who I am talking about when I call--they are so close. I will personally murder each and every one of them if they try to quit now."

She paused and took a deep breath, and then smiled. "Fuck, it's early, and I'm still cranky. We're supposed to meet Adam near those stupid dolphin sculptures near the fountain, so where is he?"

"They're whales, Chrissie. Whales. The dolphin is not native to the Pacific Northwest."

She glared at me, crankily, as we approached said sculptures. We stood there waiting in silence for a minute or two, and then I heard the distinctive jingle of Adam's keychain approaching.

"Good morning, ladies," he said. He was always so damn cheery in the morning.

We grumbled good mornings.

Opening his ever-present briefcase (in which he usually carried guitar strings, pliers, spare change for pay phones, rubber bands, duct tape, and condoms), he gingerly extracted two laminated passes, hanging on lanyards, and handed one to each of us.

Christine and I high-fived Adam, and each other, and hung the laminates around our necks as casually as possible. It wasn't like we got to wear all-access band passes every day.

The stadium didn't have a lot of backstage facilities, but Mercer Arena and the Opera House were right nearby, so the promoter was using their backstages as well. As we reached the security checkpoint for the Opera House's backstage, once the guards saw laminates, they waved us through. We high-fived each other again.

We followed Adam through a maze of corridors, with music and chatter echoing off the concrete walls. There were roadies scurrying around busily, sleepy musicians beginning to arrive, and the unmistakable hiss of an espresso machine somewhere in the vicinity. At almost the very end of the hallway, we saw a doorway with a sign taped to the door reading BLUE ELECTRIC.

Christine walked up and pounded on the door. "Hey! Are there any rock gods at home?" It swung open and Jonathan stood in the entrance holding a beer.

"Behind every great man, there are even greater women!" He hugged us both.

I collapsed onto a couch with my coffee. "I'm so glad I'm here."

"I'm so fucking nervous, Lisa. Matt Cameron was watching our fucking soundcheck," Jonathan said.

"Right on!" I tried to high five him, but instead, he turned white. "What's wrong?"

"Oh, no. How many times did we all go watch them play together? And now we are playing on the same fucking stage. I think Eddie Vedder is here somewhere."

"Why aren't Pearl Jam playing?" I asked.

Jake ran over, plopped himself down, and smothered me in a hug.

"Too busy fighting Ticketmaster," Scott said. Uncharacteristically, you could always count on him to be a font of useful scene gossip. He claimed it all came from his various restaurant gigs.

"You're on at two?" I asked. It was close to noon now.

"Yeah." Jake swallowed hard.

Despite being on so early in the day, as the band walked onstage at 1:50 p.m., the front of the stage was packed, and there was a decent crowd present in the rest of the stadium. The boys walked out in the sunlight and Jake squinted out over his sunglasses at the crowd.

"Uh, hello. Good morning...good afternoon."

There was a respectable cheer in response.

"We're Blue Electric... um, I assume some of you people down here are the reason we're playing at this show at all...so, uh, thanks." Jake waved at the crowd, and turned and looked at Mark, who was making the "get ON with it" sign with his hands.

"I just wanted to say, we are really fucking thrilled to playing this show with so many great bands, including the mighty Soundgarden..." The crowd cheered loudly, and Jonathan stood up and pointed at his TOTAL FUCKING GODHEAD vintage

Soundgarden t-shirt. "So I'll just shut up now, and..."

With that, Mark struck the first chords to "Antique Mirror" with a look of relief on his face. The band proceeded to play their standard forty minute set straight through, not stopping once, which was exactly the right strategy for a show like this. For all Jake's anguish, this band kicked ass more than ever.

I stood at the side of the stage along with Christine and everyone else. We laughed and danced and yelled insults and sang along, just like we would have at any normal show. I couldn't tell if the guys were having any fun at all. Jake had a look of determination on his face and sang his ass off. Mark just kept plowing into one song after another with a fierce glare, barely looking up at the crowd. Jonathan had his head down and played for all he was worth. (He had told me earlier that he had no intention of looking up during the set: "I already fucked up soundcheck when I looked up and saw Matt Cameron, the last thing I need is to fuck up the set by doing the same thing.") And Scott, as usual, upheld a long tradition of bass players looking bored to tears, while playing so solidly he could have cracked the floorboards while flipping off some frat boys from UW in the front row.

When I realized the band had reached the halfway mark of their set, I decided to take a walk around the stadium and see how bad the sound was. To my amazement, it was fantastic. Whoever was running the soundboard was actually doing their job, even though this band wasn't a headliner. And even better, I discovered that the crowd was genuinely into the show. Even at the concession stands on the sides, people were paying attention.

I made my way back to the side of the stage just as the band finished playing "Blazes." That was usually the second-to-last song in the set, and we were over the thirty minute mark now.

"Okay, this is a song by our favorite band--it should be everybody's favorite band, but..." said Jake.

Some idiot in the crowd yelled something, loudly.

"The Rolling Stones, dumbass, not Stone Temple Pilots," Jake said. "1, 2, 3--"

Jake counted down as Mark strode purposefully to the edge of the stage, looking dangerous, and sliced into the intro of what would turn out to be a searing, raucous version of "Brown Sugar."

They got a full five minutes of applause -- I timed it, staring at my watch and internally urging the audience to continue--but no encore. Not at this show.

"I was shaking so hard that once I got off that stage, there was no way I was going back, even if there was a riot," said Jake, back in the dressing room, drinking from a bottle of champagne.

"Jake! It was great!" I hugged him.

"You're just saying that."

"No, fuckwit, I am not just saying that. You were amazingly good. You even surprised me."

He looked at me, and then looked again. "You're serious."

"I love you guys, I mean, I always have, but--you're on a whole other level now. You really are."

"Yeah, right," said Mark, coming up behind us.

"Okay, fucking cut it out." I said.

"It seems that everyone thinks we are great, except the people who really count. And Lisa, I love you, but your praise cannot change the fact that we have to come back home and deliver pizzas and live on tuna fish again."

"I would change it if I could."

Mark shook his head and walked away, and Jake looked distraught.

"He's getting a little frustrated. I'm worried."

"What? That he's going to quit? Mark wouldn't do it on principle, he'll hang on till the last possible second."

"I'm worried that that last possible second, as you put it, might be rapidly approaching."

"Jake, what the fuck?"

"I don't know how much longer we can keep banging our heads into the wall," Jake began the familiar lament.

"We're not going to have this conversation now," I said. "You just played, if not the best show I have ever seen you play, one of the best. And this one counts. There were an awful lot of people here. You need to be celebrating, not beating yourselves up. So shut up." I hugged him again, kissing him on the cheek.

He beamed, held up the bottle of champagne, and said: "You're right. Let's go have some fun."

A few hours later, after wandering around, getting something to eat, and checking out the other bands, Jake and I were sitting in the V.I.P. area behind the stage, having a beer. All of a sudden, Jonathan came running over.

"Soundgarden are going on in five minutes! Come on!" he said, tugging on my hand. We got up and followed him up onto the side of the stage, past the hangers on congregated at the front, and back behind some equipment cases.

The impossibly tall Jake moved me in front of him, and I crouched down on the stage. Matt Cameron came walking out, and took his place at the drum kit. He saw Jonathan standing there, and smiled and waved. I looked up at Jonathan, who had turned around to see who Matt was waving at. Realizing that we were the only people standing at that particular angle, his face turned white when he realized that Matt was waving at him. He didn't have time to wallow in the freakout, though, once Matt started the bulldozer of a drum into to "Jesus Christ Pose" and all hell broke loose onstage. Jonathan smiled at me--this was our band, dammit--and all anxiety about the future of Blue Electric melted away for at least a little while.

After the show ended, the promoter held a huge party inside the Mercer Arena. It seemed like everyone was there, not just the bands who had played, but seemingly every musician, artist, ball player, quasi-celebrity and related hanger-on in Seattle. It was so funny to watch Mark Lanegan and Eddie Vedder shooting baskets at one end of the arena, Mark so tall and Vedder so damn short. I turned around to see Mark Arm and Steve Turner talking to Mark and Scott, who were completely awestruck that those two guys were paying attention to them. Christine was over with Susan Silver, manager of Alice in Chains and Soundgarden, chatting like they were best friends.

"Okay, Lisa, let's go," said Jonathan conspiratorially, as he grabbed my left arm. Jake took my right arm, and the two of them propelled me through the crowd, clearly with a purpose.

"What the fuck are you doing??" I said in protest.

They grinned evilly, and kept moving. Before I quite knew what was happening, we were standing in front of Chris Cornell, and Jake was turning on the charm: "Hi, Chris, I'm Jake from Blue Electric. Chris, our friend Lisa would love to get her picture taken with you, but she's just too shy--she's been a huge fan for years, do you mind?"

I glared at them both, but then realized that I was stupid for doing so.

He smiled, and said, "Sure."

The earth temporarily stood still while Jonathan got out his Polaroid. Chris put his arm around me and moved his head so it was almost resting on mine. I was finding it very, very difficult to maintain any semblance of cool.

We finished the picture, and I turned to Mr. Cornell and extended my hand. "Thank you."

"You are most welcome," he bowed. *Kill me now*, was all I could think--and then another thought occurred to me.

"Did you get to see the wonderful Blue Electric play this afternoon?" I said, and now it was Jonathan and Jake's turn to glare at me.

"I most certainly did. We've been hearing a lot about them lately. They were quite spectacular," he said.

"See, that's what I told them, but they didn't believe me. I just thought I'd get a second opinion that they'd listen to."

Jonathan was shooting me daggers. I ignored him, and continued. "You know, if you're ever looking for an opening band, I think Blue Electric would be a great match with Soundgarden."

Jake began stepping on my right foot in a feeble attempt to shut me up.

"That's an interesting idea," he said, almost immediately. He turned to Mark and Jake. "So what are you boys up to? Touring, do you have a record out?"

Then the two of them actually had to stop glaring at me, and had to talk to the man, while I stood quietly on the outskirts of the conversation, simultaneously beaming and eavesdropping.

★

It was almost 3:00 a.m., which was unbelievably late for anything in Seattle. Things were starting to wind down. I didn't want to leave, but god, I was really, really tired.

I walked over to Jake and Mark. "Hey, I think I'm out. Should I call a cab or are either of you planning on leaving soon?"

"Mark is rounding up everyone and they're going in the van, but I've got my car," Jake said. "Scott is off doing shots with Matt Lukin and no good can come of that, so clearly it is time to go."

I was sunburnt and tired and happy and just a little drunk. I had a Polaroid of me and Chris Cornell in my pocket. It was so great to see the band doing so well. This day was exactly what they needed. This would help get them through the rest of the tour, the rest of the summer--hell, the rest of the year. At least I hoped it would.

"You're quiet," he said, as we walked through the darkness, the sounds of the party fading behind us.

I smiled, and tucked my hand through his arm. "I'm just-- happy! This is so cool to be a part of!"

"I'm still waiting to wake up and find out that this is all a dream, and that I have to go back to delivering pizzas tomorrow-- which I will after the tour is over. But for tonight, I can pretend that I'm a real musician, a real rock star."

I hugged his arm closer to me. "It will happen, Jake. You have to believe that."

"I'm trying."

We walked up to Jake's car--his precious 1968 blue Mustang, which was nicknamed the Blue Lena, after Keith Richards' car-- and he came around to the passenger door to unlock and open it for me, gallant as ever. I suddenly felt this huge wave of tenderness and affection, and as he moved to let me into the car, I stood on my tiptoes and kissed him in the center of the forehead. I meant it as a thank you, I meant it as the best way I could express what I was feeling at that moment, one physical gesture of affection that was still on the safe side of the "friends" border. But somehow that kiss took on a life of its own and I found myself lingering for more than the few seconds I had planned on it lasting.

When I pulled away, Jake's expression was not what I expected. He looked angry. He stepped back a little and quietly said, "I really wish you hadn't done that..."

I panicked. I really hadn't meant anything--well, not too much, certainly nothing beyond a tiny bit of semi-drunken flirtation--by that gesture. This was not how I wanted to end this day.

"I didn't mean... I mean, it was just..." I said.

"...Because now I'm going to have to do *this*," he said, interrupting me, and before I knew it, somehow I was leaning back against the car and Jake had his arms around me and was kissing me. Once, twice--and then I looked up at him and saw an expression I'd never seen before. It was questioning and desire and surprise, all of which I was feeling myself at that moment.

It was silent and passionate and when we finally broke away from each other, we both stood there, dizzy in disbelief, catching our breath, trying to avoid looking each other in the eye. I knew if I did, I'd be kissing him again, and we were in the middle of a very busy parking lot.

Jake stood by the open door and bowed, gesturing me into the car. I slid in, and out of habit, leaned over to unlock his door. He climbed in, started the car, and we headed towards the Central District in silence.

I didn't know what to say. Small talk was not what was needed at the moment, and it wasn't something we knew how to do, nor was it anything we had ever needed before.

Jake reached for the stereo and turned it on. Led Zeppelin *IV* was in the CD player. He caught my eye and smiled--one of our first arguments was when he played this album twelve times in one day, which happened to be the first day I'd had off in nine, and was home trying to sleep.

So I turned up the volume and we drove back home with Zeppelin on. It was loud enough to fill the void created by the lack of conversation, and had enough comfortable memories attached to it to make the silence less awkward.

He pulled into his driveway and turned off the ignition. The music stopped, and there was that silence again.

"I think we should just go inside and talk about this..." he said.

I breathed a sigh of relief. "Okay. That works."

We headed for my house, which was dark and quiet, unlike the band house, where clearly, the party was going to continue for the rest of the night. I gestured for Jake to follow me to my room. That was nothing unusual; we'd spent plenty of time hanging out in there before.

I opened my door and turned on the light. Simultaneously, I collapsed into a chair, and took off my jacket.

Jake was still standing in the doorway.

"Jake, come in. You can leave the door ajar if you want, or maybe we can get someone to chaperone," I said, teasing him. I sincerely believed that what had happened wasn't anything major. It had just been a moment of stupidity.

Reluctantly, Jake came in the room, shut the door behind him, and leaned up against the door. Just to do something, anything, I started taking off my boots. Uncharacteristically, I'd worn a skirt that day. It was going to be hot, and shorts were anathema to me. I had bought a pair of knee-high black leather boots with a slight heel to wear for the occasion--any excuse to buy a new pair of boots, actually.

"Damn, my feet hurt. I didn't break these in enough first."

There was no sarcastic comment in response to that, and I'd deliberately given him a very wide opening in which he could have made any number of snarky responses. I started to worry that things were going to get weird.

I frowned, and walked over, planning to take his hand and sit him down on the edge of the bed, or in my desk chair, so we could talk about what had happened. "It was too much sun and beer and I was far too silly," I rehearsed mentally. "We can't do this, we're not going to do this, we've been friends too long to change things now."

But when I reached him and grabbed his hand, he enveloped me with one arm, turned the light off with the other, and started kissing me again.

We fell back against the door and this time, there was no hesitation or pretense of hesitation on either side. I kissed him back shyly, but with equal intensity. The kisses were sweet and sharp and filled with the release of years. It was overwhelming. I hadn't really been with anyone since James; I'd had a few relationships lasting maybe six months at the most, but nothing significant or remotely meaningful. Sex was there, and it was nice to have when it was. But most of the time my heart just wasn't in it, and that was what usually made me end things.

But this was different. I was partially in shock, reacting automatically, awakening senses and feelings. I was letting Jake lead. I was trying to stop thinking and just let go. I wanted to let go, give myself over to the moment. But it was hard, like starting an old car on a chilly morning in early winter.

After what seemed like endless minutes of kissing, Jake's mouth moved to my neck. I let out a sharp intake of breath. *We can't do this*, I thought again. *We cannot do this.*

Almost automatically, I started unsnapping his shirt. He was wearing this faded blue denim western shirt, and the snaps came open so easily. He reached down and pulled off my t-shirt in one quick moment, throwing it behind him.

Jake pulled me into his chest for a moment, and we stood there, breathing fast, feeling skin on skin, my head resting on his shoulder. And then he grabbed my hand and pulled me over to the bed, lying down and pulling me on top of him. The kisses started again.

Suddenly, I was thinking: Why on earth hadn't we done this before? Why did it take us so long to get to this? I thought I just had this silly little crush that came and went and only happened when I was sad or lonely. If he had felt this way all along, what were we waiting for?

Then I heard the little voice of conscience or whatever it was that had been keeping a running commentary in my head for the past half hour: *Oh my god. What are you doing? This is your best friend.*

I sat up, twisting myself from away him.

"Lisa, are you okay? What's wrong?"

"Jake. We can't do this," I said. It was like I came back to reality, and the full weight of what almost happened, what had already happened, came crashing down full force.

"I kind of thought we were already doing this," he said, somewhat confused.

"I'm serious." I moved away and slid to the edge of the bed. "Jake, this is going to ruin everything."

"Actually, I thought it was going to make everything pretty fucking great."

I rested my head in my hands. He wasn't getting it.

That gesture assured he did, and he slid around and sat next to me and took my hand.

"We don't have to do this if you don't want to, but I thought it was pretty clear that this was something we'd obviously both been wanting to do or thinking about at least, and I thought things were going pretty well." He tried to sound light, although I could hear he was clearly perplexed, and somewhat upset.

"Trust me, I'm just as confused by this as you are," I said in a very small voice.

"Can you please try to explain to me what's wrong? Do you want to turn the light on? Do you want some clothes?" Now I could hear the alarm and concern in his voice.

"No, no light. Can I have your shirt?" I asked.

He grabbed it up from the other side of the bed and handed it to me. I slid my arms into it and wrapped it around me, hugging myself forlornly.

"Well, if we felt this strongly about each other how did we manage not to see it until now..." My voice trailed off, thinking back to before reality had reared its ugly head.

"Go on."

"Do we really feel this way about each other, or is this just lust? Are you willing to risk our friendship only to find out later that we just lost all sanity for a few moments? I'm not going to have a fling with you, and I don't know if we're both ready for anything more than that. Are we?"

Jake leaned back on his elbows. I could almost see him thinking. Finally, he let out a sigh. I took that as agreement, so I continued.

"I'm not going to gamble our friendship on six weeks of hot sex. I'm not looking for a marriage proposal, but I'm kind of familiar with your dating history and long-term, committed relationships haven't exactly been, how shall I say this, a dominating theme."

He sighed again, and fell back onto the bed, stretching his arms over his head. Jake sat up again, and grabbed my hand. "Well, at least you admit that the sex was hot," he said with that teasing, flirtatious tone of voice I usually heard him using on the continual parade of women. I understood it now because it was working on me. He picked up my hand and kissed the center of my palm. It made me shiver, although I tried to hide it.

I turned around and pulled my legs underneath me, facing him. He grabbed both of my hands and held them together.

"You are strong and wonderful, and I am so happy you are my friend, and I am glad you stopped us before we made a big mistake." He kissed me on top of my head, and then got up and turned around.

"Can I have my shirt back?" he asked.

I peeled his denim shirt off of me, and threw on a t-shirt from the top of the laundry pile.

"You can turn around now."

He turned back to face me, and I tossed him his shirt. "Now get out of here, rock god," I managed to say.

He had his hand on the doorknob and was about to walk out when Jake turned around halfway, not looking at me, and quietly asked: "Are you sure we're doing the right thing?"

"Absolutely," I said. I wasn't sure I believed that, but I knew it was the right thing to say.

Jake glanced back at me, and I smiled as believably as I could. He smiled back. Whether he was faking it too, I couldn't really tell, and didn't want to consider. Blowing me a kiss, Jake walked out of the room and quietly shut the door behind him.

I collapsed backwards on the bed and let out a huge sigh. I had never really thought about what it would be like to be in bed with Jake, and now I sort of knew, and I didn't know how I would ever be able to think about anything else.

The next morning, I was wide awake the minute I opened my eyes, and then remembered what had happened. I looked at the clock, picked up the phone, and dialed Marie.

"Awake and alone?"

She yawned. "Fuck yeah."

"Can you--" Why was I pussyfooting? This was Marie. "I almost slept with Jake."

"I'll be there in twenty--no, fifteen minutes," she said, not even pausing.

Ten minutes later, there was a knock at the front door. Marie was standing there with two double-tall vanilla soy lattes in hand. She walked in, handed me one of the cups, and sat on the couch.

I took a sip, gratefully.

"Okay, what do you mean by 'almost?'"

"Some clothes came off, but not all of them."

"No penetration."

Marie. God love her. "NO," I said.

"But..."

"No, there was no oral action either, get your mind out of the gutter."

"Damn. I really wanted the definitive answer about Jake McDaniel."

"I couldn't go through with it, Marie."

"Why in the ever lovin' earth not?"

I was quiet for a few seconds before saying, "I was scared."

"Of what?"

"Of fucking everything up." I buried my head in my hands.

"Oh, sweetie." She came over and put her arm around my shoulders. "Did you guys talk about it?"

"Enough to make it feel like we had talked about it and enough to make things feel more or less okay, but not quite enough to make me not confused."

We sat there quietly for a while, and then she said, "Lisa, Jake's a great guy. He sleeps with half the city because he is so charming, and because he is looking for the right woman. He is desperately looking for someone he can be with on a long-term basis. If you don't realize that you are that woman--"

"Am I?"

"I think you two need to talk about it. I think your friendship can survive that much."

★

Marie was right, but I couldn't face it. So I kept putting it it off, and before I knew it, the boys were back on the road. I came home to find a cheery goodbye message from all of them, singing "Goodnight, Irene" in bad four part harmony. Jake always called me every couple of days when they were on tour, but they were calls made from rest stop payphones or noisy shouting messages inside loud rock clubs, and not exactly conducive for a serious conversation.

I didn't want to tell Marie that I wimped out, so I kept letting her calls go to the answering machine. She finally cornered me, pulling up in front of the house on Saturday morning after her yoga class.

"I couldn't do it," I said.

She rolled her eyes.

"I'll just wait until they come home," I said.

"If you do not, I will have the conversation with Jake for you," she said.

"No, no, I will. You're right. We need to talk about it so it doesn't get weird later."

Although the truth was that I was less sure, as more and more time went by, that that night wasn't just some weird aberration, some parallel universe we temporarily got sucked into. But, still, it wouldn't hurt to talk about it, clear the air, I thought.

Well, maybe.

★

I came home from work six weeks later, and saw the band van parked out front. I walked into the house and found the answering machine blinking at me.

"We're *home*," said Jake's voice. "And I'm going to sleep for three days. If you haven't seen or heard anyone by Friday, call 9-1-1."

They were home.

I sat next to the phone, staring at it, and trying to understand why my heart was beating faster.

★

I worked fourteen hours on Thursday, so if the guys were awake at any point that day, I missed them completely. On Friday, Scott called me at work and left a message on my voicemail while I was in a meeting: "We're awake now, I think--at least the laundry is clean," the message said. "See you tonight!"

But from the second I walked into the basement that evening, it was clear that it was not going to be the time for any kind of serious, one-on-one conversation with Jake. Instead, it was a night for listening to tapes from the road, looking at photographs that had just been developed, and talking and laughing and pizza and beer--just like old times. There were zero vibes, no odd silences or furtive glances: it was normal as hell. And I realized that I wasn't disappointed; in fact, I was relieved.

Life went on. They were in such a good mood after the festival show. Mark and Jake were working on new songs, practicing every night because they felt like it. So I didn't ask Jake anything. I didn't ask him if we were okay because we *were* okay. And I just figured that at some point it would come up, or it would feel like the right moment to say something. Or it never would, but that would be because it was truly irrelevant.

Three weeks later, I turned onto our block and saw the van backed down the sidewalk, which could only mean one thing: tour. It struck me as odd, because as far as I knew, they had no shows booked--unless something came up at the last minute, like one of their friends cancelled or something. I shrugged to myself, walked in the house and entered a maelstrom of activity.

"Lisa!" Jonathan came running up. "You are never going to believe this..."

The house was a flurry of packing. There were duffel bags and instrument cases everywhere. Adam walked by me, engulfed in equipment cases.

Scott went tearing by, a milk crate filled with equipment cords in his arms. He put it down and gave me a hug. "This is so great!"

I continued to stand there, bemused.

Jake was on the phone in the kitchen, and waved at me, gesturing that he would be finished with the call soon. In the meantime, Mark came up the basement stairs, guitar cases in both hands, and saw me standing there. He put the guitars down quickly and came over. Jake said a hurried goodbye and hung up the phone.

"Sit down," he said.

I walked over to the couch and sat as directed. Jake hung up the phone, and came over. He did not join me; instead, he paced back and forth, and then started: "Last week, I came home from work and there was a message on the machine from a radio station in Austin--apparently, some DJ there saw our show last month, bought the record from us, loved it. He played 'Antique Mirror' on his show late one night--and the phones rang off the hook."

"That's fantastic!" I said.

"Wait, it gets better. People are calling for the song all the time, not just during that DJ's shift. So the station added it to the playlist."

"Holy shit! You're kidding me!"

Mark continued: "So then, DJs in Dallas and Houston are getting calls. So they get the tape from the station in Austin."

Jake paced back over and picked up the narrative: "Long story short, a DJ at freaking KROQ in L.A. gets wind of this, and calls someone up here at a radio station that will go unnamed, but they did do us the courtesy of saying that we played at the festival and did well and that Chris Cornell thought we rocked. So the guy in L.A. plays the song. Phones ring off the hook."

"Will someone get to the point of this story before I kill you all, right here and now??" I said.

"We are going on the Aerosmith tour!" said Jonathan, who was coming up the basement stairs, carrying the bass drum.

"What?!" I was sure I did not hear him correctly.

"Aerosmith's manager somehow got a hold of our phone number," Mark said.

Jake's turn: "He heard the song. Some promoter he knows saw us in Denver, and told him we were great. He called last night and Mark talked to him for a while, but I honestly thought it was bullshit. But then this morning, their booking agent calls and invites us out on tour with them."

"Aerosmith is asking an unsigned band to come on the tour?" I was still in disbelief.

"Well," Mark said.

"Holy mother of god, if someone doesn't tell me what the fuck is going on," I said.

"There have been a few messages from A&R people. At first it was just the local weasels and I ignored the messages, we've been through this before. But this morning there were two calls from L.A.. A&M and Geffen," Mark said, now practically shouting with glee.

Oh, my god. It was happening. It was finally happening.

I looked at them all, standing there, so excited that they were flushed. My pulse had shot up through the roof in the last five minutes myself, so I understood.

"So what is happening now?" I asked, calming down a little.

"We have to pack, we have to drive to L.A. tomorrow night, we need to be there by Monday morning to meet with the booking agent. From there we are going to somehow get our own booking agent, and a bigger van," Jake said.

"Honestly, Lisa, I think we'll get to L.A. and they'll tell us it's all bullshit. But I'm willing to gamble on the chance that it's not. Worst case scenario, we guilt them into getting us some shows in California and we come home," said Mark, while Jake glared at him.

At that moment, Christine burst into the house, hair flying.

"Lisa!" she said, excitedly. We hugged fiercely.

"I don't know what I'm going to do, this is insane. I may have to get a cell phone, a beeper, or both," she said, flustered.

"Well, you know, I'm not exactly going anywhere," I said.

Jake looked at me wistfully. "I figured you would be packing already if you could come with. Are you sure you can't get some time off work?"

"Jake, I get two weeks a year, and I like this job."

He looked dejected. "Fuck."

"And I can probably help you a lot more from here. I can handle press, for one thing," I said.

"You're absolutely right," said Christine. "That will be great."

"And my dad is fronting the money to press up some more copies of the last record, so we will need some help getting that done, too," Jake said.

The rest of the night and the next day was a blur of packing and errands and getting Christine a cell phone, last minute emergency guitar repairs, visits to family and girlfriends. The band house was lit up with a continual stream of well-wishers. The CDs weren't finished, they would have to be shipped. The promo photos and bio were duplicated and sitting in my house, half of them packed in the van to take down to California.

But then, before we knew it, it was time to go. I was standing outside the house in as the sun began to set over the Olympics, while the six of them--Adam turned up in the morning, having quit his job at the last minute--raced around, making last minute adjustments to the impossibly full van, someone running into the house every five minutes because of yet something else forgotten.

"Guys, I guarantee you that wherever you are going, they will have stores there," I said.

And then, everything was done. There was nothing left to do except say goodbye to me, a line of silent hugs, no one saying much. Then one by one, everyone climbed into the van. Slowly, carefully, Jake behind the wheel, the van drove down the street and headed for I-5 south and adventures unknown.

I stood there watching until I couldn't see them anymore. And then the quiet was overwhelming. The house looked about as forlorn as I felt. I was so unbelievably happy for them. But I was also sad in a way, because it was all going to change now, and I wouldn't even be there to see it happen.

Christine was right--it was like having two jobs. Nine-to-five at my real job at the internet start-up du jour, and then answering press, taking messages, and shipping CDs and press material all over the country: Topeka. Nashville. Charlotte. Cleveland. Minneapolis. Des Moines. Oklahoma City. What began as a three-month tour turned into a year and a half on the road. And in that year and a half, they got signed, took six weeks off in New York to make the second album, and then flew off to Europe to play festivals the next summer. I didn't see them again until I came over to England in August to see them play at the Reading Festival, on extended vacation time courtesy of yet another failed start-up.

There were short bursts of visits home, mostly to see family and get more clothes. I was worried that I would hear from them less and less, now that there was a record company and a real road crew. But instead of frantic calls asking for another 1,000 photos to be duplicated and shipped to points unknown, now I was treated to the phone calls I'd been waiting for, the hysterical laughing calls about meeting Bob Dylan or Tom Petty asking them to come out on tour next year, being backstage at Madison Square Garden, playing the Orpheum in Boston, the Fox Theater in Atlanta, the Auditorium Theater in Chicago, being able to go see them do some of these things, the things we'd always dreamed of. I was thrilled.

But I never did get to ask Jake if we were okay. And after a while, it seemed to no longer matter.

Except now. Now, when I am on the road in the middle of the night, rolling through sheer blackness, with only little silver saucers full of music to keep me company. Ian is history, and for the life of me I have no idea what my future is.

CHAPTER 9 : 1997

Ian was dragging his feet, acting like a three year old who didn't want to go school. He kept walking in and out of his bedroom with different shirts on, going into the bathroom to look in the mirror, and then walking back into the bedroom and changing again. Then it was his shoes. Chuck Taylors, no. Workboots, no. Doc Martens, no.

I finally grabbed a pair of One Stars and thrust them at him. "Wear these and let's go <u>now</u>," I said, losing all pretense of patience.

"I don't know what you're all freaked out about," he said in response. "It's not like you have to fight the crowd to be down front or something."

"My best friends are headlining Key Arena and I would like to enjoy every possible second. It's six-fifteen, I told Jake we'd be there in time for soundcheck, which has now long passed!"

At that moment my cell phone rang.

"Hello?" I said, not relishing explaining to any member of Blue Electric why I was not at Key Arena yet.

"Lisa!! Where the hell are you guys?" It was Jake.

"Hi Jake, we're just ready now." I looked at Ian and made it clear that this was not a question, but rather a statement. "We'll be there in like fifteen minutes, I promise." Thank god we had VIP parking or we wouldn't be.

"How about I just send a car up? Would that be better?"

"Jake, I love you."

"He's already on the way, actually. I had a feeling you guys would be running a little late. The driver will call your cell when he's downstairs."

At that moment, call waiting beeped. I clicked over to the other line.

"Yes, hello, we'll be right down." I grabbed my jacket and

looked at Ian. "Are you coming or not?"

He glared at me and picked up his denim jacket in what seemed like slow motion.

We walked downstairs in silence and got into the town car. I sat back in the cool dark interior and smiled. "Now, this is the life."

Ian sat there in a glum, obvious silence. *How fucking oppressive*, I thought. I sighed inwardly, and then decided to be the good girlfriend.

"Ian, what's wrong, sweetheart? Do you really not want to come? Is the boys' club getting to you? I know that it can be really irritating if you don't get all the inside jokes."

He looked at me silently, displaying no emotion.

"I can't guess what is bothering you." I leaned my head against the seat back and closed my eyes. I resented him for taking me away from the guys, I was angry that he was putting a downer on one of the best nights of my life. If he didn't want to go he just should have said so and I could have gone alone.

"It's just weird," he said after a few minutes. "They're your friends, sure. And when they were just another band, it didn't seem like a big deal or anything. But for the last six months, they've been on MTV, they're in *Rolling Stone*, Tower Records has a freaking display with their records in it..."

"It's just an end cap," I said, not able to stop myself from correcting him, and then realized that wasn't going to help. Changing tactics, I continued, "Local heroes make good. They do that for everyone."

"Lisa, they're your friends, but they're not my friends. They'll never be my friends. I'll never be calling Jake McDaniel on a Thursday night and inviting him to go shoot pool at Temple Billiards. It's bad enough when we're all hanging out on some random weekend. But they're headlining a tour, they are hardcore rock stars now. I'm an outsider; I accept this. But now I'm *really* going to be an outsider..."

The car pulled into the back gate of Key Arena, down the ramp, and into the loading area inside the arena. We got out and I handed Ian his laminated pass. He carelessly shoved it into his pocket, and a security guard pointed us towards a corridor.

We reached a dressing room door with a sign reading BLUE ELECTRIC--BAND ONLY. I showed the security guard my laminate, and he knocked and the door swung open.

The dressing room was packed with loud, happy people. It was absolutely vibrating with excitement. Ian saw a table with refreshments and silently headed that way. I was about to follow him, when Mark saw me from across the room and headed in my direction.

He greeted me with a quick, tight hug.

"How are you feeling?" I asked.

"How do I always feel before a show?" he said.

"You're just not human, Mark Genovese." Before the tour started, the record company had somehow arranged for them to use Neil Young's house on Kauai for a month. Jake learned to surf, Scott started oil painting, Jonathan took scuba diving lessons, and Mark holed up practicing six hours a day. Then he'd let himself go windsurfing, for exactly two hours, before picking up the guitar again for an hour or two with the rest of the guys after dinner.

"This is what I do. It's what I've always done. It's what I always wanted to do. This is my universe and I am the king. There's nothing to be nervous about."

"You're so lying."

"The day you tell me Keith Richards is in the audience watching, then I'll be nervous. Until then, I'm fine." He smiled and walked away.

Realizing that Ian was nowhere in my line of sight, I whirled around in a panic. Then I spotted him, standing in a corner talking to Adam. Well, at least he was making an effort to fend for himself. Maybe I wouldn't have to worry. Maybe he would have fun tonight, calm down about the boys, and we would all live happily ever after.

And maybe Keith Richards is in the audience, Lisa, said the voice in my head.

I managed to get hugs from Jonathan and Scott, both of whom were overwhelmed by their families, who had finally come to terms with the fact that their boys might just be doing okay with that crazy rock and roll. Scott had a look of "Oh, god, please save me" agony on his face as his mother tried to get yet another second cousin on the guest list; I think I might have heard him whimper a little as I walked away. Jonathan, with his usual good nature, was enduring an aunt loudly regale anyone within earshot with yet another embarrassing story of something cute he did in the third grade. "I go onstage in less than an hour," he whispered in my ear, as I offered condolences mid-hug, "Then I'm free of all of these people for the next year and a half!"

I headed over to talk to Suzie, the band's first hardcore fan, the sweetest person I had ever met. She grew up in a tiny town in Eastern Washington and happened to be in Seattle one weekend with her parents, looking at the University of Washington, back when the guys were still playing clubs. They were playing an all-ages show at the First Avenue Theater, she talked her parents into going with her, and the rest was history.

She was sitting in a chair with a tiara on her head, with a grin that could only be described as "shit-eating" on her face. Suzie was just the most dedicated, die-hard fan you could imagine. She was the first one to buy tickets when there were no more than two dozen people coming to the shows. She would turn up in the most unexpected places, like Tucson, Arizona on a Monday night. Some nights she was the only person in the audience. She kept track of the date and location of every show, and hounded the band to save their setlists so she could keep a listing of every song they played. "Someday this will be a big deal," she always said.

At first we were all a little freaked out by this red-haired girl showing up everywhere and watching the shows with a single-minded, devoted concentration. But after a while, we realized that she was exactly like us, doing what we had done with other bands. She could be trusted to do just about anything, from running the merch table to putting her in a taxi uptown, rushing Mark's black Les Paul to Manny's Music when he desperately needed a vintage pickup replaced, four hours before a show at the Felt Forum.

And now she was getting her just rewards. Good for her. I always liked Suzie. She reminded me of, well, me, at that age.

"Well, Suzie, you look like you're having a good time," I said.

She sprung up off the chair and grabbed me in a bear hug. "Lisa! I can't believe it. Jake called me himself to invite me to the show--they sent a car to come get me! He even called me before the tickets went on sale so I didn't have to camp out at the box office!"

"And that laminate is good for the whole tour."

She beamed at me. "Yes, Christine told me: this is my laminate and I will have two tickets under my name at the box office for every show. And I have her cell phone number in case there is a problem."

She sat back and sighed. She looked almost dejected.

"Suzie, what's wrong?

"Well, it's so easy! It doesn't seem fair."

I didn't mean to, but I laughed out loud. I put my hand on her shoulder, and said, "You can go camp out in the rain if you want to, sweetheart, no one will stop you. But it's a long tour, and the distances between shows are a lot further. They want you to be safe."

"I know, I know, but it almost doesn't seem the same if I don't have to work for it," she said.

"But you did work for it, Suzie, you did work for it." I gave her a hug, and was going to check on Ian, when I saw Christine walk into the room and lean exhaustedly against a wall. She'd been running in and out of the room since I got there.

After a disastrous interlude with a "professional manager" who had been recommended by the record company, but who managed a dozen other bands and could never remember anyone's name except Jake's, Christine was managing Blue Electric again. There were flowers, there were apologies, Jonathan made a experimental film in which they all begged her to come back. None of it worked until Mark and Jake wrote a song and they all stood in her front yard, playing a short acoustic set. She figured they had suitably humiliated themselves enough at that point, so she quit her job at the ad agency and was thrust into a major tour (already planned, the band timed the firing of the former manager deliberately). Despite the fatigue, I could tell she was walking on air. This is what she was born to do.

As I approached, she was standing with Mark and his mother and I could see the bags under her eyes. Already, and the tour had barely started.

She gave me a huge hug. "Can I admit that I'm more than a little scared?"

I hugged her tight. "We will drink and celebrate later, I promise."

At that moment her walkie-talkie began to squawk. She hugged me one more time and strode purposefully out the door.

I was leaning against the wall, looking for Ian again, when someone hissed into my ear: "Hey baby, come here often?"

I smiled, as Jake put his arm around me and kissed me on the cheek. "Can I tell you that I am *really fucking nervous*," he said in a stage whisper.

"At least you're not having an argument with Mark because you don't like what he's wearing."

"Oh, I already did that. Fat lot of good it does me. He looks like he's going out to fix his car."

"I think he looks just fine."

Jake shrugged, and looked at his boots.

"You're really nervous, aren't you?" I asked.

"Oh, no, I'm not nervous, I'm just playing in front of every single person I have ever known, gone to school with, made pizza for, every woman I have ever slept with, my grade school teachers, my parents' friends... shall I go on?"

"I don't think every woman you have ever slept with is here. The capacity is not big enough."

That worked. He cracked a smile.

"Excuse me, please," Christine was taking command now. "Thirty minutes to show time. Could everyone please clear the room except for band members. Thank you very much."

I turned to find Ian so we could leave, when Jake grabbed my arm: "That doesn't mean you!"

"Yes, it does."

I studied his face, and he was clearly beyond nervous. But then I looked at Ian, waiting impatiently, and back at Jake. Jake had at least six other people who could take care of him. As I inwardly shook with frustration, I hugged him tight, and assured him: "You'll be fine. I'll see you out there." He looked at me kind of helplessly as I walked out of the room. I didn't want to leave, but I knew that I didn't want to deal with Ian later if I stayed.

I walked into the packed hospitality room. Every Seattle musician, big or small, must have been on the guest list, and they were all present and accounted for.

"Wow, everyone's here, huh," I said, as I almost stumbled into a group of people consisting of Krist Novoselic, half of Alice in Chains, and Ben Shepherd to boot, and made my way across the room to Ian. He was standing uncomfortably in a corner. I slid my hand into his.

"Having fun?" I asked, and then immediately regretted it.

The initial glance was sharp, but then immediately softened. He looked fine. Not angry, not upset, just normal, calm.

"I'm fine."

I was about to press the subject when the new tour manager came up to escort us to the stage. When we got there, I was positive the stage was going to break in the middle from the weight of the hangers-on on either side. We were positioned just behind the monitor board, with several rows of people, none of whom I knew, standing in front of us.

We had just settled in when Adam pushed his way through the crowd and grabbed my hand.

"Come with me, now!" he said.

I looked at him, puzzled.

"Now!" he said.

I glanced briefly at Ian, who replied with an annoyed shrug. At that moment I abandoned any pretense of trying to be the patient, understanding girlfriend, and let Adam pull me through the crowd. Fuck Ian. Why the hell couldn't he let me have a good time tonight?

"You are not watching the show from there," Adam said, as he escorted me through the throng, "And I'm not sure who sorted out the sidestage seating arrangements, but I don't much like them." He led me onto the stage, behind Mark's amps. I looked at him like he was crazy. "I'm supposed to stand here?"

"Mark insisted," he said, as he wheeled a small stool out from behind an equipment case and carefully dusted it off. "Now I need to hop to it." He hugged me quickly and scurried off into the darkness.

The house lights went down, the crowd burst into applause,

and I could see a flashlight coming up the steps and knew the guys were right behind it. Despite myself, I burst into tears. I was glad that no one, especially Ian, was anywhere near me.

Mark was at his amps, looking backward, adjusting something. As soon as he saw me there, his lips curved up in a small, sly smile, obviously pleased that his orders were carried out. And then he saw that I was crying and I could see that there were tears in his eyes, too. Taken aback at this display of emotion on his part, I replied with the Keith Richards Rasta salute--fists to heart, head, sky--and he blew me a kiss in response.

He turned around just as Jake stepped up to the microphone and said, "Hello, Seattle..."

The crowd applauded wildly.

"God, I have always wanted to say that..."

Ten thousand people laughed.

"Doesn't it sound stupid?"

More applause.

"But I feel like we do know each and every one of you personally--and we're glad we're here, friends and neighbors alike, and we could not have started this tour anywhere else. This song is for you, I wrote it one night sitting in the OK Hotel..." Some people started to cheer already, knowing what it was. "It's called 'Antique Mirror,' and no matter what anyone says, this song is for you, Seattle."

Mark windmilled into the opening chords and the entire arena went apeshit. I could see kids in the last rows of the upper section in the back jumping up and down, people were flashing lighters, the fans in the fan club seats were pogoing and singing and waving signs. Everyone was on their feet, and I was fucking crying again. I turned sideways to look at Jonathan and he had his head down, grinning like a maniac and hitting the drums for all he was worth. Suzie, over on the other side of the stage, was jumping up and down, red hair flying, just like she was in the front row again. Jake arched his head back and started to sing, and it was, instantly, complete and total pandemonium.

★

Three hours and a curfew violation later--Jake was even lecturing the security guards to let people dance in the aisles: "Ya know, that's what Eddie Vedder would do..."(only to find out later that Eddie Vedder was in the audience--Jake was mortified)--the show was over and we were all at the after-show party at the Wild Ginger.

"We could never afford to eat here," said Mark, "So we figured we'd make the record company pay for all of our friends to eat here."

"That's what they're there for," Jake said, a little drunkenly.

Several hours later, we were all very drunk, very loud, and deliriously happy.

"We're going to the house to watch the sunrise," Jake said.

About twenty people piled out of the Wild Ginger and into a line of waiting cars and vans. Ian looked at me wearily. "You don't have to come with, hon," I said, for probably the fiftieth time that night. "You can just go home."

"No, I'm going," he said. I shrugged and got into a limo with Mark and Christine. Ian climbed in besides me and stared out the window in silence. *Why doesn't he just go home?* I thought. Why was he here? All night he'd been like this but refused to leave.

The latest version of El Casa de Blue Electric was almost too nice to be a band house. On the eastern ridge in West Seattle, it had a panoramic view of the Cascades and downtown. The lights sparkling across the water made the house seem like a palace, and made the city seem beautiful and magical. It was dark and quiet and still, except for the horde of crazy drunk rock people that were stumbling up the steps and into the house. It was built in the '50s or '60s and clearly nothing had been done to modernize it, which was why Mark got it for such a low price.

But it was big and slightly isolated and had enough room for everyone, even though only Mark and Jake were living there at the moment. Jonathan had already moved to L.A., since he was getting involved in outside film projects, and Scott was living with his girlfriend, Leslie, a photojournalist he met when *Interview* magazine decided to do a story on the band.

There was space for a music room downstairs, another room in the basement they talked about making into a studio, and about five bedrooms upstairs. It looked like they had just moved in, even though they'd had this house for a while now. Mark bought it right after they got signed, thinking it was a good investment.

I was lying on the carpet downstairs in the den, next to Christine and Marie, watching a Rolling Stones bootleg video from the 1973 tour on the big screen TV. We were drinking tequila straight out of the bottle, smoking cigarettes and giggling like a bunch of giddy schoolgirls. This was what I should have been doing all night, I thought, not babysitting my sullen boyfriend. He'd gone off with the boys to check out the rehearsal space, and I was grateful for the break.

The video cut out in the middle of a crazy version of "Midnight Rambler," and there was sudden silence. Before one of us could reach over and grab the remote or find another video, the lull was suddenly punctuated with loud voices yelling in the music room. I recognized one of the voices as Ian's and went running as fast as I could, given my present condition, although I was sobering up rapidly.

As I entered the room, I ran into Jonathan leaving with a look of disgust on his face, but he stopped and turned around once he saw me. Ian and Jake were standing there with guitars, glaring at each other, body postures defensive. Mark was sitting behind the drums, looking pissed off. I was surprised to see him there--I was probably a better drummer than Mark Genovese--and then it hit me: Mark was drumming because there were three guitar players in the room and there was no way Jake or Ian would have conceded the guitar role to the other.

I could read Jake's body language and realized he was beyond furious. He was gripping the neck of his guitar so tightly that his knuckles were white. If that guitar hadn't meant so much to Jake, he probably would have hit Ian with it already. I hoped to fucking hell that Jake didn't mention to Ian that I was the one who gave him the guitar, and that it belonged to my dead ex-boyfriend, but right now they were clearly being so stupid that it wouldn't have surprised me if he had.

I stepped into the middle of the room and said, "Does someone want to tell me what's going on here?"

Silence. I glanced at Jake and he looked away. I peered over at

Ian and he wouldn't even meet my gaze.

"I'm waiting."

More silence.

"What the hell is happening here?" I said. I was so not liking this, and I didn't even know for sure what it was about. But I had a sinking feeling in the pit of my stomach.

Mark raised his hand and stood up. "They were fighting about you," he said. "Ian told Jake to stay away from you, and Jake told him he was a yuppie loser asshole that didn't deserve to be with you. It started with Jake telling Ian he was a poseur guitar player and he never would have made it, and went downhill from there. There was more, some aspersions as to the respective masculinity of each of the parties, if you get my drift, but that was the discussion in a nutshell." He nodded at me and sat back down.

Jake glowered at him. "Whose side are you on?" he said.

"Hers," Mark said.

Now I needed to deal with Ian. "What the fuck did you think you were doing? Who the fuck do you think you are?" I said.

"I'm your boyfriend," he said.

"Right. My boyfriend, not my fucking owner."

"I can't deal with him calling you all the time, and sending you presents, and 'oh please get on a plane and come see us in Tokyo.'"

"Wait, I send her presents too, dickhead," Jonathan said, but shut up after Mark gave him the look of death. I was thankful for the intervention because I had enough on my hands already.

"I'm her friend, asshole, I've known her longer than you have," Jake said, oh so helpfully.

"Jake, shut up. I'll get to you in a minute," I said.

"I cannot deal with the specter of your rock star ex-boyfriend constantly in our life. You have their photos everywhere, you play their music all the time, you are always talking about them," Ian said.

"Ian, Jake is not an ex-boyfriend," I said.

"Oh, yeah, sure, like I believe that."

We all started protesting at once. Like I told Marie a million times, it didn't make any difference what I said or didn't say, he would never believe me. I was astounded that this clearly was what had been bothering him all night--wait, all night? It had probably always been bothering him.

"Ian, Lisa and I never dated, we were never an item. Trust me on this one. She is one of my oldest and dearest friends, but she was never my girlfriend. Anyone can confirm that." Jake was trying to be cool and level with Ian. I appreciated that.

"Nothing ever happened? Ever?"

Jake and I traded furtive glances and we both looked at the floor, as Mark and Jonathan echoed what Jake just said.

Yeah. That one night after the festival show, where some of our clothes came off until I got some sense into me. I didn't have to tell Ian about that. It was none of his business, it was before his time.

I decided to change tactics.

"Jake, what the hell is your problem?"

"He's a jerk. He won't let you come see us. You aren't coming to Portland, you won't go to Vancouver, you didn't come to soundcheck today, you barely made it to the show tonight! He's jealous. It's bullshit. You belonged here with us."

"She belongs with me, jackass," Ian said. "You don't really want her, you just want to go back to Southern California and date some other twenty-one year old model. Lisa, he's just using you. You're his consolation prize when there's nothing else around. I can't believe you don't see that."

I burst into tears and stormed out of the room. I flew through the den, ignoring the distressed looks of the girls as I scooped up my purse, the bottle of tequila and someone's American Spirit lights lying on a table, slammed through the door and down the stairs. Halfway down I realized I didn't have a car, and that I was in no shape to drive if I did. I sunk down onto the steps, hugged my knees to my chest, and rested my head on my legs, shaking miserably.

This was supposed to be my big fun night. They always said, "When we make it, we will make it together." They swore up and down that they were taking their friends with them when they became famous. Now we were finally here, and instead of having the time of my life, I was trapped in some adolescent playground fight over nothing. I loved Jake to death but that was over between us--not even over, it never even was. I thought Ian and I had a grown-up relationship. Instead this was all one big nightmare.

I put my head in my hands and started crying again, and then I heard someone coming down the stairs behind me. I straightened up and patted my eyes dry and tried to look as normal as I could.

Mark sat down next to me. "Excuse me, is this step taken?"

"Funny."

He put his arm around me. "Men are assholes, aren't they? Are you okay?"

"No," I said, snuffling.

"Do you want one of the girls instead?"

I snuffled again, and shrugged. "I want to run away. I want to go to the beach."

Mark dangled a set of keys in front of me. "C'mon. Let's go."

I looked at him, and then back at the house.

"Kid, they're both still fighting about who was going to go after you. That's when I walked out. Let them beat the shit out of each other and then they'll feel better. Christine and Marie came in to referee, it'll be fine. In the meantime, let's go listen to the waves."

I grabbed his hand and we got up and walked down the stairs.

"Where's your car? What are you even driving now?"

He pointed down the street. I didn't even know what to look for. We started walking and then I saw it. A big red Ford Fairlane convertible, top down, gleaming in the streetlights.

"Oh, Mark!" I sighed in admiration.

He grinned proudly. "I just bought it last month. Finally, I have a cool car of my very own. I know, it is just so cliché, but fuck it. Let Scott and Jonathan drive brand-new Volvos like every other Seattle musician."

"Mark, it's awesome." I ran my hand down the hood. It was truly beautiful.

He put the top up, opened the door for me, and then slid into the driver's seat. "Let's do the loop, down to Alki and around?"

"Sounds good to me." I leaned my head back, closed my eyes halfway, and curled my feet up underneath me. Mark hit the stereo and *Sticky Fingers* blasted into life, first song, side one, as though on cue.

We drove past the lights on Alki silently, down Beach Drive, all the way along the waterfront until we hit the dead end at the bottom of Lincoln Park. Mark turned the car around, and parked it on the side of the street.

"Feel better?" he asked, gently patting the back of my head.

"A little," I said. "Can we get out and walk a little? There's a bench out near the water I like to sit at."

We walked across the grass, over to the shoreline, and sat down on the bench. I looked out at the black water and the waves gently rolling in. I thought about the situation awaiting me back at Jake's house, and sighed. A tear rolled out of my eye and down my cheek before I could stop it.

"No, you can't do that." Mark put his arm around me. "The whole point of this was to get you to stop crying."

"Mark, it's so stupid. Jake and I are not like that, we don't have those feelings about each other. So why does he care? And Ian, I don't get Ian, I don't know what he wants all of a sudden... I've never seen this side of him before, I don't like it."

"Jake just misses having you around. He misses being able to call you at 2:00 a.m. with girl problems; we miss being able to send you a ticket to New York to come see us on the spur of the moment. I miss being able to call you and play you song ideas. Jonathan misses being able to call you from a store and get your advice on what color shoes to buy. And who else would go to poetry readings with Scott?"

"But you guys can always call, I always want to talk to you!" I said.

"Yeah, you do, but we don't want to intrude. And now that you have Ian, you can't just make a decision Thursday night to hop on a plane Friday morning to go to New York."

I sat there, silently. He was right; the first few times I just said no because I genuinely wanted to be with Ian, and figured there would be other chances. I did all that and Ian still ended up being jealous.

Something started to ring and I looked at Mark. "Cell phone-- sorry about that. I forgot I even had it." He took it out of his back pocket and answered: "Hello? Yeah, I've got her. She's not rushing back. Put him in a car and send him home, I'm really done with his bullshit for tonight."

He shut the phone and leaned back against the bench, looking angry and pleased with himself at the same time. "In case you were wondering, that was Christine, who, thank god, took charge of the situation when the two boys decided to resort to blows in the backyard. She said she briefly considered letting them kill each other just for the entertainment value, but couldn't find the video camera." He paused. "I don't mean to rush you, but are you ready to go back?"

I nodded yes, and we walked back across the grass to the car.

When we got back to the convertible, I turned around, wanting to give Mark the biggest hug ever for taking care of me. He was still standing on the sidewalk, looking out at the water with an odd look on his face. I tugged on his shirtsleeve to get his attention. He smiled, and I flung my arms around his neck and hugged him tight.

"Thank you for taking care of me," I said. I started to pull away and he wasn't letting go. I looked up and his black eyes were sparkling again and he leaned down and kissed me, hard and for real. It was as deep and dark and endless as those eyes.

He stopped, and I was breathing hard. "I think we should get back," I said, overwhelmed with unexpected emotion. Mark gently let go, and just as gently took a few steps back.

I opened the door and got in the car, and Mark walked around and got in the driver's side. He put the key in the ignition and then looked over at me. "I'm sorry," he said, "That wasn't fair what I just did."

"What?"

"Kissing you just to see what it would be like."

"What wasn't fair about it?"

"You're upset, you're vulnerable, I bring you down here to comfort you and then take advantage of it." He banged his fist on the steering wheel, angry at himself.

He was about to start into another tirade, and that was when I leaned over and kissed him, which managed to shut him up nicely.

After a few minutes, we realized the steering wheel was getting in the way, so he slid over to my side of the car and we were still kissing.

"Mark, this is trouble."

"I know."

"I don't care."

"Neither do I."

So the kissing continued, getting even hotter. I wasn't thinking that I shouldn't be doing this because I had a boyfriend. I was thinking, *Why isn't kissing Ian like this*?

Suddenly, Mark pulled away and moved back to his side of the car, breathing hard. "This is so not a good idea."

I looked at him, at that hair, those warm hands, his long legs in those tight faded jeans... and sighed hard. But I knew that he was right.

I leaned over, kissed Mark on the forehead, and then started fixing my hair in the side mirror. I didn't want to have to look him in the eye. "Thanks for the introduction of reality," I said, as Mark started the car and pulled out onto the road, en route to Jake's house.

A pause, and then Mark ran his hand back through his hair. "What was this? It doesn't have to be anything, or it could be something. I don't know."

I sighed. "I think it was about a moment..."

"And maybe some other things that I don't think we really need to talk about."

"Do I hear regrets?" I asked.

"No. I'd do it again right now," he said.

I swallowed hard. "Mark, I love you, you are my friend and my brother, but I don't think this is meant to be a love for the ages."

"Unlike you and Jake."

"Don't say that."

"I'm just calling it like I see it. He's an idiot if he doesn't see it. You're an idiot if you keep going out with that yuppie asshole. I got to have a crazy, hot moment on one of the greatest nights of my life with a woman who I love and adore and am really glad to know. That's more than a lot of people get to say in their whole lives."

We drove back to the house in silence. I got out of the car, and walked up the stairs in my bare feet. When I reached the top, there was Jake, sitting on the front step. Mark regarded me, and then Jake, and then silently walked inside, closing the door behind him. I watched him walk away with more than a touch of regret.

Jake gazed up at me, looking for all the world like a three year old boy at that moment.

"I'm sorry," he said.

"Oh, Jake," I sat down and put my arm around his shoulder. "It's okay. I didn't know that this was bothering him so fucking much."

"What are you going to do about it?"

"I don't know."

"I don't think you should be with him. Because I don't think he really loves you."

I sat there quietly. There might have been some truth to that, but I almost resented Jake saying it. He was not one to talk, since he claimed he found true love on almost a monthly basis.

"Jake, I have a lot of time invested in this relationship. He really is very sweet," I said, amazed at my ability to fabricate.

He shrugged. "Kid, it's up to you. As long as he's not hurting you, we will accept anyone you want to have in your life. I just think you could do a lot better."

"Yeah, well, thanks."

We sat there in companionable silence, watching the early morning light break over the Cascades.

Mark and I never talked about that night ever again. He never mentioned it to anyone, either--there's no way anyone in our little family could have resisted making a joke about that situation.

After that surreal night in West Seattle, Ian and I somehow made it through that week and that month and that year and seemed to be back on the right track. That was about the time that he started talking about us getting married. No one asked and no one answered, it just was said and then became assumed. I wasn't sure how I felt about this but he wasn't pushing me to set a date or move in with him. If that was what he needed to feel secure, then my guilt was going to let him have it.

The boys were off on tour for the next year anyway, which helped. Everyone took turns emailing me reports from the road. Verona, Lisbon, Boston, Detroit, Toronto. There was a standing plane ticket ready to bring me anywhere in the world. This was what the boys had dreamed about, this was the place that we had all worked and prayed and hoped and helped them get to--and I hated missing it. But I immersed myself in my work and pretended that it didn't matter.

But it mattered a lot then, and it never stopped being important to me. The thing that I gave it all up for didn't matter at all now. At least I am finally getting my priorities in order. Every minute, I move closer to the people who count.

I'm still fighting my way through this endless mountain pass, but it's time to change the CD. I stick my hand in the knapsack and pull jewel cases out, tossing them on the floor of the passenger side as I reject them. And then I find something I wasn't sure I brought, but is exactly what I'm looking for. I slip the disc in, and then forward through it until I reach the song I need. "Country Feedback," probably the best thing R.E.M. has ever done, with its biting, aching lyrics about regret and loss, lost opportunities, and despair. Instead of making me feel worse, somehow, this song always made me feel better, made me feel less alone, knowing I wasn't the only one in the world who thought and felt this way.

The soaring steel guitar carries me further into the Oregon mountain blackness.

CHAPTER 10: 2001

Something is ringing, shrill as hell, loud enough to raise me from what felt like the sleep of the dead. I try to turn over, to get away from the noise, but then I hit my head on something hard and plastic. Blinking my eyes open, it slowly dawns on me that I am in my car. For the flash of a second, I cannot remember why, and am not entirely sure I'm not in the middle of a nightmare. I open and close my eyes several times in rapid succession, just to be sure, and then the ringing thing starts again. That's when I realize it's my cell phone.

"Hello," I say.

"Helloooooooooo! " It's Jake. OH! It's *Jake*. Now I remember what happened, and why I am sleeping in my car in a Motel 6 parking lot.

"Hang on," I say. I put the phone down so I can move the seat back upright and pick it up again. "That's better... hi."

"What is up? It's 11:30, I just called the office to find out what flight they'd booked you on, only to have Virginia inform me you had not called yet! What's the deal?"

"Um, I'm in Oregon."

"What?"

"Um, I was pissed off last night and I didn't want to stay there and wait until morning, so I just packed up the car and started driving." It sounds kind of ridiculous now, even to me.

"What time did you start driving?" he asks.

"Midnight?" It's a question. I'm not really sure.

"Lisa, have you been driving all night? Where are you, exactly?"

"Just over Grants Pass. How did I not know that I-5 goes through a horrific dark narrow twisting mountain pass right in the middle of fucking Oregon? No one ever talks about Grants Pass. It's always the Siskiyous!"

"You decided to drive to California. Lisa. You're the same

woman who hated driving the three and a half hours from Seattle to Portland!"

"Jake, don't yell at me. I'm not turning around now. I can do this. I want to do this."

"You realize it's like ten more hours."

"I did six, seven last night, that's New York to Cleveland on a good day. After that, ten will seem like a breeze in the daylight," I say, trying to convince myself.

"Are you sure?"

"Well, it's too late to turn around now. I don't want to drive eight hours just to get back to Seattle, you know?" I pause, finally awake enough to feel the emotional hangover from last night's events.

Jake must sense this, because he backs down. "You keep your phone on, all right?"

"I'm not the one who turns it off all the fucking time," I say.

"Call every few hours, okay? If you get voicemail, leave a message."

"I'll be fine, Jake, I'm a big girl."

"You're driving. Lisa, what happened with Ian?"

"Nothing, really. That's the thing. We just had a fight. I told him Joey Ramone was dead, and he told me that it was no great loss to the music community that the author of 'Now I Wanna Sniff Some Glue' was no longer with us."

"But that was Dee Dee!" Jake says, in what I know was an automatic response.

"I don't want to talk about it anymore or I'll start thinking about it again, and I've spent the whole night trying to not think about it."

"If I don't hear from you by Sacto, I will call the state troopers, and some of them are big Blue Electric fans. So don't fuck around with me."

I hang up before we can go another round on the subject. I guess it might seem a little flighty, a little impetuous, a little not-Lisa to just pick up and leave the house. But this used to be me. Hey, the Replacements are playing in Boston, let's go. Wow, that Dream Syndicate show was so great, I'd love to see it again--how about DC this weekend? It is me, after all. Maybe that's why I did it. About fucking time.

I begin driving up the pass through the Siskiyous into California, bracing myself for the worst. But after last night, it seems laughably easy. There is more traffic on the road, to be sure, but it's nowhere near as bad as those mountains in that darkness in the middle of the night.

Coming down the other side, there's no more green. It's dry and brown and starting to be desert, and I can see a big snow-capped mountain peeking through the cliffs on my right. Mt. Shasta, I guess, not really knowing for sure, wishing for a map. I drive down, down, down, and there's a sign welcoming me to California.

In the distance, smack in the middle of nowhere, a little tollbooth-like station seems to materialize out of the blue. The juxtaposition of the tiny building against the huge mountains and large open space around it makes it appear incongruous and unreal. The image that flashes into my head is from some old school Bruce Springsteen story, about a cherry-red flying saucer with Cadillac fins and 'Little Melvin and the Invaders' painted on the side pulling up and asking Bruce and Clarence for directions in exchange for three wishes.

I pull up to the booth and to my eternal disappointment, inside is some kind of California State inspector woman.

"Do you have any fruit or plants?" she asks.

"No, ma'am." I have to stop myself from giggling.

"Would you like a map?"

"Can you tell me how to get to the New Jersey Turnpike?" I cannot help asking, trying to keep a straight face.

Confused, she hands me a map of California, and I drive off, the laughter finally bursting out of me. I'm feeling a sense of wonder that is making me giggle out loud. I throw on some Chuck Berry, wish I had a convertible, and lose myself in the road.

★

I'm driving through small towns with names like Weed and Cottonwood. There's more winding through mountains, but again, nothing nearly as bad as Oregon. The first exit I see in California is exit 893, which is kind of frightening, and San Francisco shows as 383 miles, which seems impossibly far away. Oh, god. What am I doing?

The cell phone rings again just as I'm pondering this thought. I'm driving too fast to look at the display, so I just answer, praying it's not Ian.

"Hello?" I brace myself for the worst.

"Okay, what is up, lady?" says a female voice.

"Oh, Marie! Hi!" I am so glad to hear from her right now.

"I've been calling all morning, I knew you'd be bummed about Joey. Then, I sent you email, and I get an out of office message saying you are out for two weeks?!"

"Uh... I'm in California." Here we go again.

"*What*?" Ouch. That almost hurt.

"I'm in Northern California, somewhere."

"WHAT?"

"You're sounding like a broken record, as my mother would say."

"Where are you, exactly?" she asks.

"Exit 3,478, or something similarly ridiculous."

"Where are you going? What are you doing? What happened?" Then her tone changes. "It's Ian, isn't it, you had a fight."

"I'm going to L.A.. Yes, we had a fight. No, I don't want to go into it right now," I say, as I hear her start to line up her questions in a row. "Jake emailed me in the middle of it--or rather at the end of it--and said, come to L.A.. He told me to fly today, I didn't want to wait, I didn't want to give myself a chance to change my mind, so I got in the car and started driving."

There was a pause, and then: "So, you're going to see Jake?"

Boy, did she change gears fast.

"I'm going to see the boys, and Christine, too. They're in the studio, working on the next record."

"But you're going to see Jake," she says, again.

"Marie, I know what you're getting at, and--okay. Yeah. Maybe. Maybe I'm going to try to figure some things out."

"Ooh, I knew this would happen someday!" She's practically squealing and I badly want to hit her.

"Let's not start planning my bridal shower, toots. All I know is that Jake for once doesn't have a girlfriend right now. I'm staying there because he's the one I talked to--it could have been any one of them--I'm just going."

"But you are going to have a conversation about--IT."

"What the fuck is up with you?"

"Lisa! This is a milestone! You have left the old boyfriend after five years! You are going to see the only other man in your life who is even a remote possibility. There are tons of unanswered questions there. Be real. This is me you're talking to."

"Can we not make it into more than it is?" I don't mean to snap.

"So when will you get there?" Good, she's not going to push me. I can't even think about this yet. This was not the reason I got in the car and started driving last night. I just wanted to go.

"Tonight, late, probably around 10."

"Are you checking in with someone?"

"Jesus H. Christ, I am thirty-seven years old," I say.

"And there are serial killers at highway rest stops," Marie says. "I watch *Dateline*."

"Thanks for that image. Now I will not stop to pee until Los Angeles." I pause as I remember something. "I need you to call Ian and cover for me."

"Talking points?" She sounds almost delighted.

"Just tell him that I have gone out of town for a few days, make him think Joey's death has triggered a spontaneous trip back to New York. I want to buy some time before I have to deal with this." The very thought made a wave of tiredness wash over me.

"Can I do anything else for you?"

"Yeah. Can you go down to CB's tonight and have a beer for me? For Joey?"

"Oh, Lisa, now I'm going to cry. Consider it done. Drive carefully, hon."

I'm reasonably sure that Marie never did like Ian. She never said anything, but it wasn't like the three of us went out a lot together, if you know what I mean. I think he was happy that her job sent her around the country on multi-month postings. I don't know anything anymore. All I do know is now I'm seeing all these things about my boyfriend and my relationship that I should have seen years ago. Was I really going to marry this guy?

Of course I wasn't. But I stayed in the relationship anyway because there never seemed any good reason to end it, the same way I stayed in jobs I hated until I was presented with an obvious end. Ian and I never fought; we rarely even argued. He wasn't a blatant asshole. He was handsome. He was smart. He had a good job and a decent sense of fashion. This relationship just wasn't It. And I can't believe he didn't see it as much as I did right now. I can't believe I didn't try to change it, and just sat there and let my life happen to me, instead of being an active participant. This trip wasn't me? No, my life wasn't me.

Taking Mr. Springsteen's advice yet again, I roll down my windows, turn Chuck Berry back up as loud as I can, and pick up speed.

The sun set hours ago and I am now driving along the long flat straight road in darkness. No streetlights, nothing except a sky full of stars, a few other cars and the endless supply of trucks that have been escorting me the whole way down. I am flying at this point. The posted speed limit is 70 and I have been going my careful, only-nine-miles-over-the-speed-limit-so-maybe-the-cop-won't-think-I'm-worth-it, seventy-nine. But then other cars passed me like I am standing still. So I push it to eighty-five, and then ninety, and even in good moments ninety-five. When am I ever going to have a chance to go ninety-five on the highway again?

There is a moment just outside of Sacramento when the furthest point on the I-5 signs said LOS ANGELES for the first time and I erupt in this ecstatic, involuntary whoop of triumph. Fuck yeah! Los Angeles! Then, every passing mileage sign: 398... 287... 245... 183 is the most recent one, and at my current rate of travel, I will be there in a little over two hours.

I stop for dinner around seven, and call Jake. He picks up on the first or second ring.

"Where are you? I've been waiting for you to call."

"The middle of nowhere."

"No, seriously, where are you?"

"I'm telling you, I saw a sign back there that said Middle Of Nowhere."

"Smartass. How many miles on the last sign?"

"183."

He whistles. "Jesus, woman, are you driving or flying low?"

"I will remind you that I am from the great state of New Jersey."

"Fair enough," he says. "Listen, we're supposed to go out to dinner with some record company weasels tonight, but if I'm running late someone will be at the house by ten o'clock to let you in. Is that okay? I don't know that I can get out of this," he says, sounding equally worried and apologetic.

"Jake, I don't care. When I get there I am going to walk in your front door and collapse where I stand, so it doesn't matter if you're there. I will not be coherent or good company."

"When are you ever good company? Did I miss this?"

"Fuck you."

"I love you too, kid."

I hang up, pocket the phone, and stretch backwards, twisting back and forth in the slight dry wind that was blowing, squinting up at the dark night sky, full of stars, so far away from anything resembling a city. I feel a million miles away from anywhere right now, restless, rootless. And I don't know what's waiting for me when I arrive.

Two hours later and I am wondering where L.A. is. Does it just somehow emerge out of this flat desert wasteland like an oasis in the dunes? I didn't exactly stop to look at topography maps before I got in the car. I-5, straight shot to L.A.. What's so complicated?

Then there's a turnoff where trucks are sent to the right and cars to the left, and it feels like we're going into a landing pattern. I veer to the right, and then I see a sign reading: Grapevine.

Holy shit! This is the infamous Grapevine I have heard so much about. Now I understand, it's a mountain pass, I can see a long line of headlights coming down diagonally. This must be the gateway to L.A..

There is only one thing I want to hear as I enter the City of Angels, one person I want with me on the home stretch. I slide a disc into the stereo and begin the climb up the Grapevine. "All right, Los Angeles: Bruce Springsteen and the E Street Band!" says the radio announcer. It's the legendary 1978 Roxy show. It begins with Bruce talking over an excitedly whooping audience, apologizing for everyone not being able to get in. He asks for reverb on the microphone and then it's "Peggy Sue," the way only the E Street Band could play it. I smile so big, smile with such a sense of relief and comfort.

I listen to the opening chords of the next song and sing along almost absent-mindedly, when I suddenly feel like I've been electrocuted, this jolt of sheer stark recognition. It's "Badlands," a song from *Darkness On The Edge of Town*, which means it's a song I've heard at least hundreds, if not thousands of times in my life, on record and live, in person and on bootleg. But now I've got context. I've spent the last twenty hours driving through darkness and daylight, mountains and desert, through tears and elation, and now I am listening to Bruce sing this on an L.A. stage twenty-two years ago, in the city I am just about to enter, and it is now completely, totally and utterly different. I sing along so loud I have to turn up the volume and even then it's almost not enough, shouting the words to "Badlands" as hard as I can.

The tears are running out of my eyes nonstop, it is relief and release and triumph and exhaustion and nostalgia and longing and fear and excitement all together and all at once, crystallized and given voice and feeling and shape and substance by the music. I'm here. I drove from Seattle to Los Angeles. I did it. I let out another big whoop at the top of my lungs.

I keep singing, I am hitting the steering wheel with the clap-clap-clap-clap-clap-clap-clapclapclap drumbeat that Max plays on the verses. How can this happen? How can a song that meant so much to me when I first heard it at fourteen, a song about dreams and hope, suddenly mean just as much right now, suddenly the words apply exactly to my life twenty-two years later? And how can it affect me in the same way, how can it lift me up, transport me, elevate me, inspire me, give me meaning and, well, hope?

So there is this sense of amazement and thanksgiving

enveloping everything else that I am feeling. Just when I think I am numb to it all, when I think I can't stop dwelling on how incredibly much my life sucks at this moment, how crazy and stupid and nonsensical I am being, running away from home at thirty-seven... here's Bruce. In his innocence and enthusiasm and excitement, he sweeps out of nowhere and gives me something to hang onto when there isn't much left on my side of the fence.

Landfall! I reach the bottom of the grade and I've truly arrived, I am in the Valley. I roll down the window and let the warm night wind blow into the car, and I reach into my bag and pull out those forbidden cigarettes. I light one up, realizing this is probably the only place in Los Angeles where I can legally smoke inside. I feel just like that kid who's hiding in order to smoke the cigarette she stole out of her mom's purse.

I keep going down I-5, carefully glancing at the directions to Jake's house, watching for the exit. I have no clue where I am or where I'm going, or how it fits into the rest of the city. I am so geographically challenged when it comes to L.A. that it's not funny. A city you cannot walk never made any sense to me.

Somehow Jake bought a house before anyone else did. His dad came down to go house hunting with him, and despite his strict instructions that he be shown houses that were small and unpretentious, he ended up with an almost-mansion. The house had just gone on the market the day before, the seller was desperate, and Jake had the cash to put down. He got some incredible deal on more house than he ever planned on buying, for less than he planned on spending (as his dad pointed out), so he bought it. I'd never seen this place; the few times I'd been down before Jake had had some woman living with him, and the negotiations were too complicated. So I usually stayed with Christine in her condo in West Hollywood.

Finally, the exit! I drive up a wide boulevard, and then take a left. I'm watching for landmarks, Jake told me to watch for trees, and then a wall on my right and an open gate...and I have arrived. What looks like Mark's red Ford Fairlane is sitting in the driveway. I park and gratefully shut off the engine.

I sit there in the silence for a second or two, breathing an enormous sigh of relief. Oh my fucking god, I am finally here.

I'm gathering up all my crap--CDs, books, papers, everything that was in my purse or backpack and is now all over the passenger seat and the floor in front of it--when someone whips around the side of the car and tries to open the door. It's Mark, jumping up and down excitedly. Mark Genovese, jumping up and down.

"Open the motherfucking door, kid!"

I give up on trying to sort the mess out and unlock the door. He flings it open, grabs my arm and practically yanks me out of the car.

"Kid!" he says, flinging his arms around me in the biggest hug ever, which I return with every ounce of strength I can muster. I close my eyes and rest my head on his shoulder, squeezing him gently around the shoulders. I'm home, is all I can think. I'm home. My eyes well up with tears and I can't stop it.

"Hey, hey...!" Mark pulls away gently, alarmed. "Oh, god, Lisa, what is wrong? Are you okay? That wasn't the greeting I thought I was going to get..."

I wipe the tears from my eyes with the back of my hand and look at him. "No, no, it's okay. I'm just so tired, and it was such a long fucking drive, and it took fucking forever, and--" I stop. "You know, David Bowie never had a bad guitar player, ever."

Mark frowns, but then rolls with it: "I know. He always would bring these fucking dynamite guys out with him--Ronson, Earl Slick, Stevie Ray...hell, even Reeves Gabrels was no slouch. What made you arrive at this sudden revelation?"

"It was a long drive, sweetheart, it was a long drive."

"Did you just throw the box set in the car or what?"

"That, and the rest of the catalog that I actually own on CD. I discovered that, somehow, I do not own *Alladin Sane* on CD? I almost stopped somewhere and bought it."

I suddenly need to yawn and stretch at that moment badly, and I do so, like a cat. It's then that I realize how utterly exhausted I truly am. My first, second, third, fourth and fifth winds are fading fast. I grab some things out of the car and walk with Mark over to the house.

As we reach the front door, I say, "You know, when Jake said, 'I'll make sure someone is here waiting for you,' I was expecting a housekeeper or something."

"Yeah, well, we had that weasel dinner tonight--record company people from, like, the Netherlands, and Belgium. Jake could not get out of it, but of course, I'm only the guitar player, so no one noticed I left early. All they wanted was the singer."

"Doesn't everyone?" I say. He rolls his eyes in response.

Mark opens the door and ushers me in. I look around and give a low whistle. The house isn't huge or ostentatious, but it is sure as hell impressive. It was too dark to see what it looked like outside, but inside is California mission style Spanish architecture, this round tiled entrance hallway with a circular staircase going to the second floor. There is a huge wrought iron chandelier hanging over it all, and doors or dark hallways leading off into distant rooms going around like spokes on a wheel.

"I forgot, you haven't been here since he bought this place," Mark says, putting my duffel bag down on the floor.

I am turning circles in awe. "No, the last time I was here, it was the rented bungalow in Topanga Canyon."

"That was his Joni Mitchell period."

"I would laugh, except that *was* his Joni Mitchell period."

"Do you want the tour or do you want to see your room?" Mark asks.

"I would love the tour but I don't know that I'm going to make it much longer," I say.

"Okay, follow me," Mark picks my bag up again and begins walking up the stairs. I follow behind him silently. It is quiet and cool and white and feels like a refuge. I'm beginning to understand why Jake bought this house.

We walk down the hallway past several doors and then Mark stops at a door on the left-hand side. He opens it up and says with an exaggerated bow, "The guest room, milady."

I walk in. The carpet is beige and so thick I practically sink up to my ankles. There are French doors with gauzy curtains, looking like they open out onto a balcony of some sort. There's a huge cozy green velvet armchair in the corner and a bunch of matching floor-size velvet pillows in the other corner. And in the middle of the room, an enormous cast-iron bed.

"Nice." I say, surveying the room hungrily. It's more than nice.

It's wonderful. I look at the framed poster hanging above the bed and laugh. It's from the 1997 Stones shows in Oakland when Pearl Jam opened. We all went to those shows together.

"There comes a point where you just run out of room," Mark says.

"Ah, I thought that was in my honor."

"Lisa, there are Rolling Stones posters in every room in this house, including the bathrooms. Like I said, after a while, you run out of room."

I sit down on the bed gratefully and fall backward.

"Okay. I'm saying goodnight. I know we could sit and talk until dawn, and I would love nothing more, but you need to sleep. It'll take you a while to wind down, and even then your body will still feel like it's moving for a few hours. I know this from the road."

I hop up with energy I didn't know I had and fling my arms around him, hugging him gratefully.

"I'm so glad you were here, Mark. I don't know if I could have dealt with an anonymous housekeeper type person."

"Sandy's really okay, you'll like him--but there was no way I was going to let you pull up to an empty house."

I sigh, remembering.

"Joey Ramone is dead, Mark."

"I know, kid. I know."

He walks out of the room and closes the door quietly. I fall back on the bed and curl up with my head on the pillow. I'm almost asleep when I realize I really don't want to sleep in these sweaty clothes. I get up, take off my Chuck Taylors and socks, and pad over to the bathroom. I peel off my clothes, drop them to the floor, and turn on the shower. I step in and stand there with my eyes closed under the hot water.

It's then I start crying for real. The enormity of everything, Ian, Joey dying, feeling old, missing my friends, the mess my life seems to be hit me like an anvil. I lean against the wall, rest my head against the cool tile, and just let myself sob, big heaving silent sobs, the hot tears mixing with the water spraying on my head and down my body.

Finishing the shower, I dry off and climb into pajamas--or

rather, the old faded black Soundgarden t-shirt and gym shorts that are my version of pajamas. Although Mark was right--my body still feels like it is in the car, moving forward--within seconds I fall thankfully into a deep, dreamless sleep.

★

When I finally struggle into consciousness the next morning, the room is pitch black. I have no idea what time it is, and I'll have to get out of bed to check my cell phone. So I decide to just get up, pull on a t-shirt and jeans, and pad barefoot down the stairs. I'm wandering down a hallway, looking for someone, when a Latino gentleman with long hair and wearing a Grateful Dead shirt sticks his head out of a door and surprises the hell out of me.

"Hi! You must be Lisa. I'm Sandy, I work for Jake."

"Oh, yeah. Hi. Mark told me about you."

"I'm glad he did, you would have freaked otherwise."

"Maybe just a little," I say.

"Jake had to do more record company stuff this afternoon--he left about half an hour ago. He said take it easy, hang out, they'll all come up later this afternoon and you're having a barbeque. Can I get you anything? Breakfast? Coffee?"

"Coffee would be great... but..." I decide to just say it. "Los Angeles is not exactly known as the land of decent coffee."

"Remember who I work for?"

"You have a point there. Sure. Coffee. Maybe some fruit?" I ask somewhat tentatively. I follow Sandy into the kitchen. Oh god. I now want to live here because of the kitchen, and I don't even cook. It's airy and white, with terracotta tile on the floor, big shiny steel appliances--and an old round wooden table in the corner near the windows. Jake had one like it in his house when he was growing up and it reminded him of his mom. He always said he'd get one when he could afford to have a big enough house with a big enough kitchen to fit a big round table in.

So I begin the morning on the deck, sipping coffee and eating papaya and mango, listening to a live Elvis Costello radio broadcast from 1981 I found in the CD collection. Jake always had this secret obsession with Elvis Costello, it was like he was afraid to admit it or something. Marie, of course, spent six months trying to hook up with him once she learned this secret, which was amusing to watch even if nothing ever materialized from it.

★

Later that afternoon, I'm standing in the French doors that open onto the deck, just kind of lazily surveying the sunset over the horizon, and then I remember.

Ian.

Oh, shit. I've been here all fucking day and I didn't think about him once. But it's unfair to keep him waiting; at some point, he will honestly worry. So I head up to my room, shut the door, and dial Seattle.

"Where are you?" he asks.

"Ian, I'm fine. I'm just not in Seattle. It doesn't matter where I am. I just needed to get away."

"You could have told me! I was worried."

Were you really? I think.

"It was late, and it was spontaneous," I say.

The silence is suddenly very large.

"Ian, I think..." I'm about to launch into a whole speech but then realize I am suddenly very tired again. "Ian. It's over. We're done."

"What?" Well, that surprises me. He's actually taken aback.

"Ian, c'mon, you haven't been happy for months, I haven't been happy, that has to mean something."

"Well, we just haven't been trying hard enough."

"What's that supposed to mean? It sounds like it came out of a magazine, things you're supposed to say when you break up."

"That's not fair."

"Then tell me exactly what you mean by that. What should we be doing differently?"

"You're being totally irrational right now. I can't have this discussion with you on the phone. You need to come back to Seattle so we can work on saving this relationship." Again, it sounds like he is reading lines written for him.

"What does that mean, Ian? What do I have to do to save it?"

"We both need to get some perspective and realize what's important."

"So what would be first on the list?" I ask, with genuine interest.

Ian has no response. I didn't think that he would.

"Ian, it's over. That's all. You know this as well as I do. I am breaking up with you. We are not engaged, we are not dating, we are not in a relationship."

"You're going to give up this easily? Over a rock star dying?"

"Ian, that's not what it's about."

He starts to say something and then stops. So I continue: "Ian, do you love me?"

"What kind of question is that?"

"I think it's a really valid question given that we're supposed to be engaged and stuff and that we're fighting now about whether to end a relationship. Do you love me?"

"I'm not a very expressive person."

"That's not what I'm asking. I'm asking you if you love me. Do you want to grow old with me? Do you want to be with me for the rest of your life? Can you see that far? Do you kiss me out of desire or consolation?" I secretly relish working that Jeff Buckley quote into the conversation, because I know he will not get it. But I always quietly thought of Ian every time I heard that song. It was more truth than I ever wanted to face, until now.

Silence. A very heavy silence.

"Will you still love me when I'm sixty-four?"

His response is an exasperated sigh at the end of the phone, which I expected. That song always makes me laugh. Talk about cheesy. But having that melody in my head is exactly what I need right now because it's impossible for me to be maudlin, hearing the *boomp-boomp* of the tuba in my brain.

I continue: "Because I can't say that about you, truthfully, and I don't know that I ever could."

Silence again, and a sigh. "When are you coming back to Seattle?" he asks.

"I don't know. I have plenty of vacation time. I'm going to play it by ear."

"Will you call me when you're back?"

"I'll call you, sure, and if you need to talk more or get closure or I don't know what, yeah, sure. But don't think that I'm going to come back and change my mind about everything I've just said. It's not all going to stop being true because I'm back."

"Take care of yourself, Lisa," he said, suddenly quiet. No more bluster.

I swallow hard and choke back the tears. "You too, Ian."

I lay back on the bed and stare blankly at the ceiling, feeling empty and alone and lost, like I had let go of the last tether I had holding me down on the planet. I want a cigarette, a beer, a bar with a good jukebox or a band playing loud music in a dark smoky club somewhere. I want to connect with energy and life and remind myself I am alive.

And I am in L.A., with my friends, and can have exactly what I want, right now.

A hour or so later, I'm back in the library, trying to force myself to concentrate on a book, when I hear commotion in the entrance hall. I put the book down and run around the corner, and to my delight, find all of Blue Electric standing there.

I tacklehug as much of them as I can manage at once.

"Look at you all," I say. "Where's Christine?"

"She had to phone Australia, so she said she'd be late," Jake says.

"Damn her," I say. I want everyone here, now.

"What are we doing? Why are we standing here? Let's go outside, put on some tunes, get some beers," says Jonathan.

"You go out, I'll go talk to Sandy. Be there in a second." Jake disappears in the direction of the kitchen.

Scott grabs my hand and the four of us walk out onto the deck. I collapse gratefully into a lawn chair, and he and Jonathan sit down across from me. Mark leans against the railing, looking out into the fading sunset. Jake comes up the stairs a few seconds later and asks, "Any music requests?"

"If this particular group of individuals has to reach a consensus, we'll be sitting in here in silence forever. Just put something on," Mark says. "Anything at all will do."

Jake nods in assent, and clatters back out. Mark drops into a chair next to me. Bob Dylan starts to play softly from the hidden outdoor speakers.

"So," he says, smiling gently at me.

I glance across at Jonathan and Scott and they are looking at me inquisitively. I realize I'm going to have to get this out of the way, so I don't have to relay the story four different times.

"Guys. I'm fine. It's okay. You all hated Ian."

They all protest, and I interrupt: "Stop, already. I know it. You had good reason to. He was always an asshole around you. He never even made a fucking effort. And he was jealous and resented you, so it was mutual. But it's over. There was a phone conversation, it sucked, but I'm done."

"Wow," says Jake.

I nod.

"When are you going home? Do you know?" Scott asks.

"I don't know. I just want to hang out here for a while and not think about anything, not be in Seattle, not have to work or think about Ian, not have to see anything or anyone I don't want to."

"Well, since that sounds like Jake's daily existence, you should be just fine," says Mark.

"Hey, asshole, I'm the one who makes all the record company meetings," he says.

"And they only want to see you anyway, so what's the point in me going?" Mark say.

"Boys, we're not doing this. She just got here. Save it." Jonathan says.

"What are we eating, Jake?" Scott asks, trying to change the subject.

"Sandy is going to grill some stuff for fajitas--does that work?" Jake inquires of no one in particular.

Everyone murmurs yes.

"Fine, then we're just waiting for Chrissie. If she's not here in fifteen, I'll go call." Jake looks around. "Lisa, not that I want to abandon you or anything, but I have some demos I need to play for Mark."

"Go, go." I wave at them. They regard me apprehensively.

"Seriously, go. I'm fine. I'm here for a while. You're working on a record. Go."

"If you're sure--" Jake says, tentatively.

"Oh, Jesus Christ, please go. Now. I'm not an invalid. I'm not having a nervous breakdown."

The two of them get up and walk towards the screen door. Jake stops, turns and says, "Scott, you might want to hear this one too, it's the song I seem to be having difficulty, erm, explaining how it sounds."

"That's putting it mildly," Mark says under his breath. Jake shoots him a glare.

"Oh. That one." Scott gets up too.

"I'll stay and keep Lisa company. I have no issues with the song. I understand exactly what you're saying, Jake," Jonathan says, moving to the chair next to mine.

The guitar player, singer and bass player disappear out of sight, and after a moment, Jonathan reaches over and puts his hand on mine. "Are you sure you're all right? I mean, this is us, Lisa."

"Ah, I'm fine. I mean, it's not a small thing, ending a relationship of almost five years, but it was time." I lean my head back against the seat and close my eyes briefly. "It still doesn't feel real, none of this feels real."

"Why the hell did you drive?" he asks, after a few minutes. "You could have been on a plane this morning and here in two hours."

Everyone keeps asking me this, and I keep avoiding it. "Because I was afraid that if I went to sleep, the next morning it would all be back to normal, I wouldn't remember how angry or upset I was, and I'd just pick up where I left off. I've felt like this about Ian for a long, long time, I've realized in the past forty-eight hours, and..." I am suddenly very tired again.

"And it was time to go," Jonathan finishes the sentence for me. That was it, wasn't it? I nod.

"Exactly. There was no point in prolonging the agony, or trying again, or talking it all through--he didn't get it. I'm not sure he ever did. I knew it was over, so I left." Big sigh. "That and I kept thinking about 'Prove It All Night.'"

"Why?"

"Well, the title at first, it was kind of the theme song I had in my head--" I pause, and think about how to explain it to him.

Suddenly, I have an idea. I hop up, and beckon to Jonathan to follow me. We go into the library, and then I realize what I need is in the car. "Wait here," I tell him.

I run up to the guest room to get my car keys, and then outside to my car to rummage through the knapsack full of CDs. I come back into the library, grinning, and turn off the CD changer.

"What is this?" Jonathan asks.

"My favorite Bruce bootleg."

He rolls his eyes. He isn't much of a fan.

"No, no, just one song, I promise. It will explain everything."

I'm forwarding through the disc, obsessively remembering the setlist from this show, in order. "Here we go. 'Prove It,' as we Bruce geeks like to call it. This version is the ultimate one, as far as I'm concerned, it's sharp, it's focused, he delivers the lyrics with precision, the band is just on." I hit play, and the song begins.

I'm sitting on the floor beaming up at Jonathan, who is enjoying it more than he's willing to let on, I suspect. Then the second verse starts and out of nowhere, and it's like the lyrics reach out and wrap themselves around my heart in a stranglehold. Bruce singing about desire, dreams, and the price you pay, about wanting and yearning and facing it all head on. In other words, everything I had done, and more importantly, everything I hadn't had the courage to do.

Before I know it, I start crying. I am crying hard, and uncontrollably, and Jonathan rushes out of the room, while I hug my knees to my chest and rest my head on my thighs, crying and crying, tears just flooding out of my eyes. The words just touched too close to home, were too true, too real.

Suddenly, someone is kneeling next to me. Without looking up, I know it's Jake.

"Lisa?"

I snuffle in response.

He wraps his arms around me, hugging me tight. "It's okay. It is."

"Jake, I spent five years with him. Five years! It was nothing, it was a waste, I wasted all that time...!"

"Shhhh."

"How could I do that? How could I be so stupid? Why didn't I listen to anyone?"

"Why are you beating yourself up now?"

"Because--" And I realize I can't say it, can't say that I wanted what I had with James so badly, that I just hoped and prayed that I would come close some day, that it made me so incredibly angry that I lost so much, so long ago.

I'm still sitting there crying when Jake stands up. "Okay, that's it. You're going to bed. I'm giving you a Valium, and you're going to sleep."

"No Valium."

"A shot of Jack, then."

"No."

"Dammit, Lisa, stop being so fucking stubborn."

I realize that I am overwhelmed, and exhausted, and that this is probably not all that healthy. I also realize that there will be plenty of time to process this later. I nod yes wearily, and follow Jake upstairs to the guest room. He goes out of the room and comes back with a pill and a glass of water, which I swallow.

"Please go to sleep, Lisa."

I nod again, helplessly.

He kisses me on the top of my head, and is about to leave the room when he turns and says, "But if you can't sleep, don't lie here in agony, please come wake me up, I don't care what time it is."

I nod, and he walks out of the room and closes the door.

I slide out of my jeans and undo my bra under my clothes, too overcome to try to change or brush my teeth or wash my face. I climb under the covers and pull them tight around me. Although sleep is the last thing I expect or think I want, as soon as I relax enough to let my eyes close, I feel myself drifting off. Choosing not to fight it, I slip into welcome oblivion.

CHAPTER II: Los Angeles

When I open my eyes the next morning, I'm disoriented and groggy. For a second I can't remember why, and then I recall with dismay the details of the previous evening.

I collapse back onto the pillow and close my eyes, trying to console myself that it all had to come out sooner or later, and I preferred sooner rather than later.

I struggle out of bed, shower and change. T-shirt and jeans-clad, I wander downstairs, heading for the kitchen, desperately needing coffee to clear the cobwebs.

Jake is sitting at the kitchen table, reading a book. I'm surprised to see him, and he's equally surprised to see me.

"How are you doing?" he asks, gently.

"I'm still tired, a little out of it, but I don't feel overwhelmed."

"So what are you up to today?" he asks, pouring coffee into an enormous mug and handing it to me.

"I think I just want to spend a day or two doing nothing, Jake... just sleep and read and sleep some more. I think I need it." I take a grateful sip of caffeine.

"Well, your wish is my command," he says. "We're in the studio--I should actually leave in a few minutes--but if you need anything, just call."

So that's what I did. Nothing. A huge part of me just didn't want to talk. I turned off my cell phone as soon as I was done talking to Ian and didn't want to turn it back on just yet. I emailed Marie and told her I was alive, but needing space. For the next two days, all I did was sleep, eat, and wander around Jake's enormous, wonderful house. I sat on the deck and stared at the skyline for hours, I started reading my way through the library, and I made a huge mess of the CD collection, pulling out disc after disc I needed to hear.

When Jake came home Thursday night, he found me lying on the couch with three books stacked up next to me and Jeff Buckley playing on the stereo, entirely too loud, the carpet strewn with rejected jewel boxes.

"Life! Finally, this house has some life," he says.

"Jake, it's not like you've been in this house alone the entire time," I say, puzzled, looking up from my book.

"If I had come home and found any of the women I have ever dated listening to a Jeff Buckley bootleg and reading Richard Meltzer... well, let's just say I wouldn't be single now."

Of course, that is exactly what I am doing. And I remember Marie's prediction, and slowly take a deep breath. I try to surreptitiously look up at Jake, who clearly also realizes the implications of what he's just said, and is trying to gauge my reaction while pretending to be busy adjusting the equalizer.

After I don't react, he changes the subject: "How about you come down to the studio tomorrow night?"

"Really?" I hop up from the couch, excited.

"You have been welcome all this week, we just thought you needed a break... but yeah. I think it's time. We want you to hear what we're working on."

"Oh, god. I can't wait!"

"Hungry?" he asks. "I have to be back at the studio by seven. I was going to have Sand get some Thai food--sound good?"

I nod yes.

"Okay, back in a few," and Jake strides out of the library, whistling.

I fall back on the couch and take the visible, deep breath I've been wanting to for the last five minutes of the conversation. Clearly, I'm not going to be able to avoid the subject. I resolve to call Marie after he's left for the studio.

★

"Okay, this is your phone call," I say long-distance to New York City, the second I see the Mustang disappear down the driveway.

"So, what's up? How's the house? How are the boys? Have you talked to Ian?"

I decide to answer the questions backward. "Yes, I talked to Ian, we have officially Broken Up. The boys are wonderful. The house is amazing. What's up? Marie, you're right, either I'm going to bring up the subject of me and Jake, or he's going to bring it up, but it almost came up tonight."

"Yesss!" I imagine her doing victory laps around her couch.

"You know, it's not like I'm sending out wedding invitations, Marie."

"Lisa, I only want to finally see you happy."

"But I'm not sure any more, Marie. I'm not feeling anything towards him. There are no vibes. I've been here three days now and it's been completely and totally normal and comfortable."

"What's wrong with that?"

"What I had with Ian was completely and totally normal and comfortable. If Jake is truly the love of my life, there should be-- *something*."

"Fireworks?"

"I don't know, I should have that pit in my stomach, my heart should go flip-flop, I should be thinking about him all the time."

"And you're not." I hear her lighting up a cigarette.

"No. Not even a little. I could not possibly be thinking about him less."

"Well, you guys have been friends for so long, you don't just shift gears overnight."

I fall back into the couch with a sigh.

"Goddamit, Lisa, you need to Have The Conversation once and for all, and put an end to it either way."

I'm about to sigh again, and it feels wrong and pathetic.

"You're right."

"What?"

"I said, you're right. Don't make me repeat that."

★

I must have fallen asleep as soon as I hung up the phone,

because I woke up the next morning with a pillow under my head and a comforter placed over me, with a note taped to the television:

Came home and found you passed out. I'll pick you up at 4:30, call the cell if you need anything.

A big JAKE is scrawled at the bottom, taking up half of the page.

He rolls in at 4:30 sharp and honks the horn, and I go running out to the Blue Lena and hop in. Radiohead blasting out of the stereo--"Mark got some demos from their guitar player," Jake says, by way of explanation--we head off down the winding roads to the surface streets and drive into Hollywood.

Jake parks the car on the street and says, "Okay, we're here." Just off Sunset. The building we're parked next to could not look less like a recording studio, more like an abandoned club or restaurant. He hits the intercom and announces, "It's Jake--" The door buzzes and he pushes it open.

We walk in and I am stunned. I feel like I am in the fucking Hotel California or something, but in the best way possible. Crazy '70s-style wood fixtures, mirrors and gold records. The guy at the desk greets us offhandedly: "Hey, Jake..."

Waving back in acknowledgement, Jake pushes open a door next to the front desk and I hear muffled guitars playing. We walk down a narrow carpeted hallway, and turn into what looks like the deck of a pirate ship. "Here's the control room," he says, ushering me in. It's fucking wild, like being in some weird sci-fi spaceship, only everything is wood and carpeting--with the huge control board in the middle of it, amps and machines and effects and things I do not understand stacked in every available space.

Christine and a guy I am introduced to as "Nick the engineer" are back behind an enormous control board. Through the window into the studio, I can see Scott, Jonathan and Mark, with Adam playing tambourine, joyously playing away.

Christine waves and hits a button, and suddenly the control room is filled with the sounds of three-quarters of Blue Electric playing "Sheena Is A Punk Rocker," with Scott on lead vocals.

"Hey!" says Jake, striking a mock-dramatic pose. "He's stealing my gig!"

Jake runs out of the control room and into the studio, picks up a bass, unplugs Scott, and plugs himself in instead. Striking a Dee Dee Ramone pose, Jake begins to try to play bass, which causes the song to fall apart (it was almost over, anyway) because they are all laughing too hard to play.

There is some clearly amused discussion, and then Jake steps up to the mike and starts to sing "Blitzkrieg Bop." They work their way through that, followed by sloppy but affectionate versions of "Pinhead" and "Teenage Lobotomy," having the time of their lives.

When the medley has finished, the guys put down their instruments and come into the studio, still laughing.

"Man, that was great," Mark says. "That felt good."

"I know. It's hard to remember that Joey is fucking **gone**," Scott says.

"Is there any kind of a tribute show planned? Do you know, Lisa?" Jonathan asks.

I shake my head. "Not a word, but they have been doing these shows for Joey's birthday, even before--" I stop, a little choked up.

"I'll make some calls," Christine says. "In the meantime, gentlemen, shall we?"

"I can't wait for you to hear this record, Lisa," Mark says, as they walk back into the studio. "I am so proud of this. It is going to be the hardest record we have ever made, but my god I think it is going to be the best."

Nick points out a spot towards the front of the control room where I can sit and be out of the way, Christine settles into her spot in the back behind the board, and so tonight's session begins.

Lights are low, candles are lit; as always, the guys spend a lot of time turning the studio into a version of every rehearsal space they ever had, Scott and Jake taking the lead on this particular project, with help from Adam. He arranged for Stargazer lilies in vases all around the studio, and the scent mixed with the candles and the heat is almost dizzying. There's this weird blue-red light overhead in the studio that's dimmed down about as far as it can be, it's reminding me of the sky before a huge summer thunderstorm.

They begin recording, overdubbing on a song or two, double-tracking vocals, adding new layers of instrumentation, taking breaks to assemble back in the control room and listen to their work. It's fascinating to watch them work like this.

★

It's 9:00 p.m., and Mark has been trying to get a solo just right for the last three hours. In hushed tones, Jake tells me that this song will likely end up being the focal piece of the album, which explains why Mark is wearing himself out. He's in the studio tearing out solo after solo, and then comes into the control room, listens to the playback, shakes his head, and goes back and plays it again.

Every solo sounds better than the last one, and every time we think he possibly can't blow our minds any further, he does. Mark must know this, which is why he keeps pushing himself. His shirt is drenched with sweat and he refuses to change. He doesn't want to lower the lights, take a break, have a drink. Another take, another trip in to listen to the playback. He puts on headphones while the rest of us listen through the studio monitors. His eyes are closed, his head is down, and his face is pale from the effort he is exuding. One last screaming note dies out, and we sit there in silence and wait for Mark's verdict.

Jake looks at him expectantly. Mark meets his gaze, they lock eyes for a few seconds, and then he shakes his head no. "Not yet," he finally says. "It's not how I hear it in my head."

"You're going to drive yourself crazy."

"It'd be a fine way to go," Mark says.

"Take a break?" Christine asks, quietly.

Mark shakes his head no. "One more time," he says.

"Maybe turn the lights out? Should we leave?" asks Jonathan.

Mark stops, and thinks. "No. I want an audience. I feel like I am not connecting."

"Connecting with what?" asks Jake.

"If I knew, I wouldn't have been playing for the last three hours and nine minutes."

"Want to try another room, Mark?" Scott asks. "Could be the

acoustics, could be the vibe, hell, could be the temperature."

"I wish it was that simple, dude, but I don't think so." He stops, regards me sitting there quietly, and asks, "Lisa?"

I look at him in surprise. What on earth can I possibly tell him?

"I'm the wrong person to be asking, I know nothing about this stuff."

"Bullshit, don't give me that. What do you feel? What's your gut?"

I think for a second, and then answer: "If you say you need connection and audience... well, this is kind of silly, but when you said that, the first image that flashed into my mind was Jimmy Page onstage at Madison Square Garden, spotlight on him, the rest of the venue all dark... very classic, very true, but also something very lost."

He stops and stares at me, dead on. Then he smiles, just a little, and turns to look at Christine.

In a split second, she smiles big with understanding. "That can mean only one thing," she says. "The Fabulous Forum. Sure, it can be done. I'll have to make a couple of phone calls. You guys wait here."

★

Three hours later, we are all standing on the floor at the former Great Western Forum in Inglewood, about fifteen minutes away from the studio. Christine made some calls and, while she won't let on exactly what strings were pulled, we were granted entry to the darkened venue around midnight, walking through the deserted backstage tunnels.

"I don't even want to know how she did this," Jake says, whispering.

"Why are you whispering? There is no one here except us," Scott says.

"There are ghosts here, for sure... come on, this was Zeppelin's favorite venue in the States. They played here, I don't know how many times," Jake says.

"Sixteen," Christine finishes the sentence, meeting us as we emerge through the tunnel onto the floor of the arena.

"Including..."

She snaps her fingers and the sound system, left over from a Christian rock festival that was being held at the venue, bursts into life with what was unmistakably live Zep. Nick waves at us from behind the soundboard.

"5/31/73. It was all I had in the car," she says.

"John Bonham's twenty-fifth birthday," says Jonathan. "Not too shabby."

At that moment, Mark walks out through the tunnel. He insisted on driving himself. Whether he planned it or not, he definitely made an entrance. His face lights up when he hears what is being played.

"Way to go, Chrissie, now I have *that* to live up to."

"You hate Zeppelin," she says.

"No, I hate what they became. But this is what, early '70s? They were the masters of their domain back then." He looks around. "So what are we waiting for?"

"Adam and Nick are getting set up... and we're waiting for a few other people." She glances at her watch, and checks a text message on her phone.

"People?" Jake asks.

"Well, if this solo is going to be the ultimate classic rock screaming solo, Nick and I decided that it would be good if we had some live recordings of it, too."

"And how, exactly, do you propose to do that?"

At that moment, Christine's cell phone rings. "Yes, this is Christine. Who do you have out there? Jared, Bruce and JB? That's who we're waiting for, please walk them in."

Everyone stares at her, clueless, except Jonathan, who asks, "Christine, are these guys who I think they are?"

"Oh, that's right, you worked with them on the last Christmas album. Yes. The best tapers you guys have."

"How on earth did you find them?" Jake asks.

"Well, as we were just discussing, I found them when we were putting together that live compilation you sent out last Christmas, when the record company temporarily lost our board tapes, and we had to find something fast. Suzie suggested we talk to the tapers, recommended a few names. I swear, they were more professional than most people I work with at the record company."

A security guard comes through the tunnel in the back of the arena, with three guys wearing baseball caps trailing behind him, all carrying backpacks or little bags and folded-up stands under their arms. Christine walks over to them, shakes hands all around, and gestures in the direction of the band. All three shake their heads "No," vigorously. One guy reaches into his bag and hands Christine a small mountain of CDs.

She walks away, the tapers confer briefly, and then split up. One guy heads right in front of the soundboard, another one walks up the empty house until he was about one-quarter of the way back from the stage, and the third climbs up on the soundboard and begins conferring with Nick, who takes out a handful of cords and begins hooking them up to the board.

"What on earth are they *doing*?" Jake asks.

Jonathan comes to attention. "These are local guys, right? So they have been taping here for years and know exactly where to stand in order to get the best sound." He shakes his head. "Impressive."

"Exactly," Christine says, as she rejoins us.

"What did you say to them?" Scott asks.

"I asked if they wanted to meet you guys, and they all, very politely, declined, but they did want you to have these," and with that she hands out about half a dozen CD-R's, some in jewel cases with beautiful artwork, others in plain white sleeves. "They felt these were the best shows from the last tour, in case we were thinking about releasing live discs while you guys are on hiatus."

"Were we thinking about that?" Scott asks.

"No, but I am now," Christine says, examining the artwork closely.

I walk over to Mark, who has wandered away from the group, and is standing in front of the stage while Adam sets up his amps. He meets my eyes with a gaze of dark vehemence out of nowhere. I touch his face with the back of my hand and he grabs onto it, hard, as though it is the only thing tethering him to the planet. We stare at each other for a few more seconds and then I walk away, taking a seat about fifteen rows back. I sit dead center, while

Adam, Mark and Nick finish their preparations, soundchecking, adjusting microphones, talking to the tapers, checking levels. The rest of the guys take seats scattered through the front section.

There is a lull in the previous flurry of activity, and all of a sudden the house lights go out, and the stage lights go up in classic rock show white and blue.

"Mark, I'm sorry, I couldn't get you a follow spot, it's a union thing, apparently, or so they insist," Christine says over the PA.

"No, that's quite alright. This will do just fine," he says, standing in the center of the stage, looking up at the darkened venue, and taking a few deep breaths.

I sit there by myself in the fifteenth row watching him, anticipation so thick I could swim in it, absolutely sure that this is going to be like witnessing a test blast in the Nevada desert.

The playback of the song starts, and I am holding my breath, counting the beats, I've heard this so many times tonight I already know where the solo is supposed to start.

And now here it is. From the very first note I get goosebumps, the hair on my arms stands on end. It's the same solo he has been playing all night, but with a deeper color, a different quality of emotion, a far greater depth. There may not be anyone in this arena, but Mark is playing like every one of the 17,000 seats is filled.

I close my eyes and let myself drift into the music, listening to those notes soar and echo around the arena.

The solo ends, the playback dies down, and I realize I am dizzy. I am dizzy because I have been holding my breath. It is quiet; no one is saying anything. The house lights are still down.

Mark shades his eyes, and looks back at the board. He doesn't say anything.

"That was fabulous for me, but how was it for you, brother?" Nick asks over the PA.

Mark's response is to nod his head once, and to take his guitar off and hand it to Adam.

"I'm just going to listen to everything, Mark, to make sure we're good on all the tapes," Nick says.

Mark nods again, walks to the front of the stage and jumps off onto the floor.

It sounds like everyone else is back at the soundboard, listening, but all I want to do is to stay right where I am as long as possible, eyes closed, because I still want to be in that place I was while Mark was playing.

After a few more minutes, the magic has faded away, at least a little, so I open my eyes and find Mark is sitting next to me. I turn to meet his gaze, my eyes still wet. We don't say anything out loud but it feels like we are saying everything, just looking at each other.

He reaches down and grabs my hand. I can feel something in him let go, let out everything that he had been holding inside for the last few hours. I start to cry again, just a little bit, because I cannot believe that he is letting his guard down that much in front of anybody. Jake is the emotional one of the pair. This is not something Mark would ever do, or had ever done, and all I can do is hold his hand as tightly as I can.

After a few minutes, he picks up my hand, kisses it, and lets it go, relaxing back into the chair. "That was pretty cool," he says. "I just pretended I was some combination of Keith, Townshend, Jimmy Page, and--you'll love this--Eddie Van Halen. Suddenly it all worked perfectly."

Nick's voice comes over the PA again, and the house lights begin to flicker on. "We're good, Mark, unless you want to hear playback."

Mark stands up and turns around, walking towards the board. "Call me crazy, but I know I got it." He passes one of the tapers, busy dismantling equipment, and stops. "Thanks for helping us out. Can I ask what you thought?"

"I would have paid double full ticket price just to see that," the taper says, as he folded up his mic stand.

"That's good enough for me." Mark reaches out and they shake hands.

At this point, I am walking back to where everyone has congregated by the soundboard.

"I'm going home," Mark says, "And I'll see you all back at the studio tomorrow night." Quietly, with his usual grace and dignity, he heads for the backstage tunnel and disappears into the darkness.

"Fucker, he just wanted to make a dramatic exit," Jake says.

"Fucker is entitled to do whatever the fuck he wants after that mind-fucking-blowing solo," Scott says.

"Nick, let's call it a night," Christine says, standing up.

"You can say that again," he says.

★

Christine has called a twenty-four hour moratorium on work, and we are all headed out for a night on the town. I finally get to dig out the rock and roll wardrobe, put on makeup, really do something with my hair, and go Out. Jake and I arrive at this ridiculously chic Japanese restaurant, where the six of us sit around the table and eat until we are stuffed and laugh and laugh and laugh. Even Mark. He strolled into the restaurant looking rested and happy, and jumped right into the conversation like nothing happened last night.

"Christine, it's just not human." I say.

"Maybe it's not Mark. Maybe it's an alien," she says.

"What are you two whispering about?" asks Jake.

"You, of course--it's all about you, sweetheart," I say.

He pokes me in the arm with his chopstick in retort.

After the sushi, we pile into the cars after much debate about what bar we are going to, and end up--okay, I still have no idea, but it looked impressive. Christine and the boys are standing outside waiting for us, but as soon as the bouncer sees Jake, everything changes.

"Goddammit, everyone wants the fucking lead singer," Mark says under his breath, only half kidding, as we are now ushered in with some degree of fanfare and shown to a prime corner booth. The bar is dark and wooden and split level and does not look like some place these guys would hang out in, as it is far too elegant.

"You're right--I mean, who cares about the guitar player, anyway?" I say to Mark.

"Hey, what are you doing tomorrow," he asks, as we all settle in and order drinks.

"I have no plans, remember? I'm a free spirit."

"Want to come down to Venice for the day?"

"Wow, yeah. That would be great."

"I'll come up and get you around lunchtime."

"Cool." I smile. This will be fun. I can't wait to see what his place looks like. Jonathan told me that Mark had put so much work into it that he might as well buy it, but he just kept refusing to for some reason.

"So I had an idea today," Christine says, when the second round of drinks has arrived.

"Ooh! An idea!" Jake says, sitting up at attention.

"Oh, shut the fuck up. This is why you pay me the big bucks."

"We pay you? And all this time I thought it was out of the goodness of your heart." Scott says.

She ignores them. "How would you guys like to play a show next week?"

Everyone's faces light up. It's like she hit some kind of ON switch.

"I'll take that as a yes."

"Where?" Jake asks.

"I thought the Roxy, maybe the Palladium--wouldn't you like to play the new stuff in front of someone? Get some kind of reaction?"

"Connect," says Mark, quietly, leaning back with his arm resting across the back of the booth.

"Exactly," Christine says.

"How are we doing to do this?" Jake asks.

"I figure all we need to do is email the fan club. I can get us a venue in a day or two."

"I like this idea," says Jake. "It will be so good to get up in front of people."

Mark, Scott and Jonathan all turn and glare at him, almost in unison.

"What? I was just saying. I know we agreed, no tour. But maybe it wouldn't kill us to do a dozen fan club shows or something? Small venues? Two, three weeks on the road max?" He's trying to be engaging with that puppy dog look of his. I know it works on the girls, but I can't imagine it's going to work on his bandmates.

There's silence, while everyone mulls this over.

Mark speaks first: "You're right. It wouldn't kill us. But I am absolutely not doing arenas and I am absolutely not doing anything but the fan club shows, and they have to be fan club shows. Period."

"That's a yes?" Jake asks, hopeful.

"It is. If Christine thinks we can do it."

"We can do it," she says, "The record company won't be thrilled, but--I think it's a really good idea, and it's a nice thing to do for the fans."

"Jonathan? Scott? Any objections?" Mark asks.

"No more than two or three weeks," says Jonathan.

"As long as it's small theaters or clubs, fine with me," says Scott.

"Consider it done," says Christine.

"Now, no more business," Scott says. "Dammit."

"Let's do something really outrageous," Jake says.

"Maybe I should wear lots of eyeliner and black leather," Mark says.

"That would be my idea of fun," I say.

He throws back his head and starts to laugh. "Okay, only if you teach me that punk rock trick about lighting the eye pencil on fire..."

"Deal!"

"Lighting the pencil on *fire*?" Jonathan asks. "And then you put it near your *eye*?"

It's 2:00 a.m., and Jake and I walk out of the bar with everyone else trailing behind us. I am giggling madly and feeling no pain. Add to that a serious dose of euphoria--I am happy and I am relaxed.

"People should go home, and sleep," Christine says. "If you guys stay up all night it will defeat the purpose of the break."

There are some murmurs of protest that change quickly to agreement. Hugs, handshakes, and everyone heads for their cars.

"All right then. Let's hit it," Jake says in my direction, turning towards the direction of the Mustang. We get into the car, and head towards the freeway. I'm leaning back against the seat, propping my head up on my hand against the door. It's a feeling of comfort and contentment and utter peace, despite my alcoholic elation. Me and Jake, together again, riding in a car somewhere.

He hits the freeway and turns on the stereo. This car always had a state of the art stereo, but now that Jake has money, it's insane. "I spend so much time on the road here... I swear I get my best listening done in the car," he'd said after he told me how much the whole thing cost on the way to the restaurant, cranking one of the bootlegs from the 1972 Hawaii shows, Mick Taylor's last shows.

"Any requests?"

I shake my head. "Up to you."

His hand moves to the CD changer and hits button six, which can mean only one thing: *Exile On Main Street*. He's had *Exile* in his car on a permanent basis since the day he bought it. It never gets old and it fit every mood you could ever have.

Shooting effortlessly through the neon darkness, Jake driving with casual precision, the music so loud and so clear, and all I can think at this moment was how much I love this person. And with almost blinding clarity I realize: it's not love like I want to take all his clothes off, it's love as a friend, as my friend, as someone I utterly cared for and trusted and feel safe with.

Everything is perfect, and nothing should be any different. Jake and I are not meant to be more than we are. I don't want anything more than what we have right now, what we have always had.

I feel a lightness, a sense of relief.

We pull off the highway, and follow the winding streets up to the house, still not talking, still listening. As we get out of the car, Jake hesitates, and then says, "Let's go downstairs, I have something I want to play for you."

He opens the basement door and beckons me to follow.

At the bottom of the stairs is the studio. It is a medium-sized, dark, low room, carpeted in shades of brown, with a big couch and two easy chairs, along one wall, and filled with half a dozen guitars, and hordes of amps, tape machines, and other mechanical looking boxes.

"This is the mad inventor's studio. I think I spend more time here than anywhere." He smiles, and points at the couch. I walk over and collapse into it. It is big and deep and soft, made of this luscious dark brown velvety material.

"Nice couch."

"I've fallen asleep in it more times than I care to admit," he says, plunking himself down on the other end. He looks like he is about to say something, and then stops himself. Instead, he gets up, walks over to a reel-to-reel machine, turns on some other buttons and switches, and the tape starts to play.

"Hi there, we're Blue Electric, and we suck," Jake's voice drawls out of the speakers. "But somehow we got invited to play tonight, so we hope you don't suffer too badly."

I sit up and stare at him in disbelief. "The KNDD Christmas show!"

"Memory like an elephant," he says, smiling.

"Where did you get this! I thought they didn't tape it!"

"They didn't. This local guy who taped every Christmas show got it. One of our fans found it and sent it to us, and we converted it so we can send it out to the fan club for Christmas--on vinyl."

"Oh my god!" The tape is still playing, the first song of the set, one they never recorded and doesn't exist anymore: "Circles In Motion!" I exclaim in wonderment.

Jake winces. "Yep."

"It really wasn't that bad," I say.

"Oh, but it wasn't that good either. And Mercer Arena just made us sound like mud."

"Mark broke three guitar strings in the next song."

"Right, and we didn't have spares for some reason."

"And the only person who was willing to loan you an instrument was the dude from Presidents of the USA..."

"Who played with *two* strings. Right. Kim Thayil was hanging out backstage, and he pulled rank and made someone give us a fucking guitar."

"And then you went into the Stones medley."

We're still listening--there's a lot of commotion, and crowd noise, and then you hear Mark play the intro to "Rusty Cage" and screech "THANK YOU, KIM!" Then he hit the opening chords to "Satisfaction".

"Oh, god. I had almost forgotten about this!"

"So had we. It arrived at the office one day, and luckily we have Suzie opening the fan mail. She recognized the date immediately, ran around screaming for five minutes, and then called me."

They're on "Let's Spend The Night Together" now. They did five Stones songs in a row, one after the other, and then were told to get the hell off the stage. Christine and I stood down front and to the side, dancing our asses off and laughing hysterically. The band were unceremoniously booted out of the backstage as soon as their set was over, and were told they'd never play that show again. Sure, until they had the #10 album in the country, and suddenly all was forgotten. Nothing made them happier than the day they stood around Christine's desk while she informed the program director, on speakerphone, that Blue Electric was not going to play their show, and then reminded him exactly why.

Jake sits down in one of the easy chairs and looks over at me. I'm still engrossed, memories from that night flashing before my eyes. I can't believe they found this tape after all those years.

I finally look at him, and realize he hasn't taken his eyes off me the entire time. "What?" I smile.

"That was a long time ago," he says.

"Not that long ago," I say with great fondness.

"Lisa..." he looks down at his sneakers. "Do you remember that night after we played that big festival..."

Oh, my god, we're going to talk about this. I don't know how he knew, how he read my mind, but I shouldn't be surprised. It's Jake. He has what I used to call "super-Lisa-radar."

"That was the night I met Chris Cornell," I say, brightly. "Kind of hard to forget THAT..."

"Are we not going to talk about this?" he asks, looking helpless.

I pull my legs under me and pat the couch, beckoning him over. Jake comes over and sits down tentatively.

(The tape is still playing. "Paint It Black" is on, Jake hamming it up for all that it's worth.)

"Listen, sweetheart, yes, I remember. Of course I remember. But this isn't what this is about. Or maybe I thought it might be, but I don't think it is. Do you?"

"I don't know. We never got a chance to find out. Things got a little out of control, we never did talk about it, you had Ian, I had-- a few relationships."

("Brown Sugar," song number four. It is so incongruous to have this kind of heavy discussion with this absolutely comical show playing in the background. But it's a good thing; it will keep this conversation from turning morose, or too fucking serious.)

I take his hand and hold it for a few seconds, thinking about what I am going to say. And then I say: "Jake--yeah. It was kind of an unfinished movie. I didn't think about it for a really long time, and then when I was driving down here, I did think about it. For a few hours I did think I was going to come down here and ask you if you wanted to try to have a relationship. But ever since I got here, I haven't been so sure any more."

(Song five, and the last one: "Stray Cat Blues." "This is for Chris Cornell and everyone in Soundgarden," Jake dedicates the song. Soundgarden covered it first, but I don't think anything tops Blue Electric's frantic, almost punk rock version.)

I continue: "I realize that I do love you, but it's not that kind of love, I'm pretty sure."

(The sound just abruptly cut out. The irate soundman literally pulled the plug on them three quarters of the way through the song, so Jake couldn't even say goodbye.)

Now we're sitting in silence again.

"Jonathan said that we were just both too scared of finding out the truth." He blurts this out, still not opening his eyes.

"Arghhhh... I don't know. Do you feel that way towards me?"

Now he lifts his head and looks up. "Lisa, I love you, you are one of my best friends in the whole world. I can tell you things I'd never tell anyone else, we are so alike, we think and feel the same way about so much... sometimes I think, God, why do I even bother with anyone else--there's Lisa--okay, I don't know how to keep talking about this without insulting you."

"What? You're not attracted to me? That's not an insult. It's a feeling, it's there or it's not. It's that simple."

"It's not that I'm not attracted to you, it's just that I'm not in love with you. Obviously I was attracted to you or we wouldn't have ended up in bed in the first place."

I push my hair back from my face. Why is this conversation harder than breaking up with Ian was?

"Jake, I think we are soul mates. I think we will be friends forever. But I don't think we're destined to be together..." I say, looking at him carefully. Taking a deep breath, I continue: "If you think that maybe we're just clouding the issue because we're afraid of fucking up the friendship, or just afraid of facing something that could be IT, then, well, it's not exactly going to be painful to give it a try." I smile, and exhale. That took a lot to get out.

"See, I just don't know," he says, sounding despondent. "My track record with relationships is so incredibly bad..."

"Okay. Let's try this." Throwing caution to the wind, I lean over and kiss him on the mouth: once, twice, and then Jake gets over his shock and starts kissing me back. After about a minute or two, I pull away gently. It was nice, to be sure, and there was some kind of automatic reaction in my body, but it didn't feel like being struck by lightning.

All these years of wondering aimlessly about this, and what I finally discover is that I really don't want to sleep with him.

"Jake, I don't think this is us. If this was a love for the ages, we'd still be at it and our clothes would already be starting to come off."

He starts laughing. He's laughing, and then grabs me in a bear hug. He is laughing so hard I can feel his body shake.

"God, I love how you can just say exactly what you think. I really wish I did want to take your clothes off, because we would have one hell of a relationship. Whew."

"Sigh of relief? That's not doing much for my self-esteem, buster." I punch him in the arm, playfully.

"You don't understand--everyone was in on it, Christine taking me to lunch and telling me that this was my last chance, Jonathan was relentless, even Scott--as we were leaving the restaurant tonight, he leaned over and said in my ear, 'If you break her heart, I will break your legs.'"

"What time is it?" I ask.

"It's almost four."

"Jesus, Jake, I have got to sleep. This is not a good schedule for me to be on..."

"Lisa," Jake says, and then stops.

"Yeah?"

"Why are you going back to Seattle, anyway? Do you like your job that much? You're always complaining that the apartment is too small and you hate it, the weather drives you insane, Marie is always somewhere else, you can't buy cool shoes in Seattle..."

I look at him. "What am I supposed to do? Move down here?"

"Why not?"

The expression on my face must have said, "What the fuck are you talking about?" because he continues: "We can hire you at least temporarily," he says, shutting down my protests. "Christ, you're like the only one of our friends who we haven't given a job to. But if you want to keep working with computers, there are companies down here. Can't you afford to not work for a while?"

"Probably two years, but not forever."

"It would be really nice to have you down here," Jake says, turning on the charm and beginning the offensive.

"Until you go on the road and leave me for a year," I say.

"Well, as our feature discussion this evening highlighted, we're not going on the road for a year, but even if we did, I'm telling you, there are jobs for you to do," he says.

"If I worked for you guys, I would probably hate you all, and hate the music, and I never wanted that." I look at the clock above the console. "Jake! I am not making life-changing decisions at 4:30 in the morning...or at least not more than one. I have got to get some sleep."

I get to the top of the stairs and head straight for the staircase up to the bedrooms, waving behind me as I walk up the stairs. I am halfway up when I hear Jake:

"Lisa?"

I stop, and turn around. The look on his face is filled with confusion and uncertainty.

"Are we doing the right thing?"

"Jake. Go to sleep. You're tired. I'm tired. Yes. We are doing the right thing." I blow him a kiss, and keep walking up the stairs.

I get into the room, close the door, and fall on the bed without turning on the light. Curling up on top of the covers, I hug the pillow and think, as the tears rise in my eyes again: If I don't love

Jake, and don't want to be with him, why am I crying? Why do I feel more than a little sad and lost right now?

CHAPTER 12: Los Angeles

I'm in the front seat of Mark's cherry red Ford Fairlane, top down, driving down the Santa Monica freeway towards the ocean. It's early Sunday afternoon, and the weather is straight out of a Beach Boys song.

"I can't believe you still have this car," I yell over the wind.

"I love this car. It is my dream car. Why would I give it up for anything?"

"Now you sound like Jake."

"Hey, I haven't put three times the money the car cost me into this thing."

"It's more like five times, and you bought this car fully restored." I'm teasing him, but I know he's going to take it seriously.

"Listen, my parents bought me a brand new Honda Civic when I turned sixteen. Jake's dad bought him the Blue Lena and said, 'You figure out how to fix it.'"

We're off the highway now and driving down a commercial boulevard filled with traffic. I'm craning my neck, trying to see the ocean as we drive, and then Mark turns into a small side street and I can see the water at the end of it. The houses are all different shapes and sizes, modern ones, old rundown clapboard houses, a mix of architecture and styles. He pulls up in front of a short, three story blue quasi-Victorian building and parks in front of the garage.

"This is it."

Nonplussed, I stare at the house. I was sure he'd be turning into one of the modern concrete buildings. Mark doesn't seem to notice.

"Let's go for a walk--I can show you the house later. The sun may not be out all day," he says.

We stroll down the street towards the water. The wind is

blowing and I can smell the ocean. He's no more three or four blocks away. We reach the end of the street and it dead-ends into a wide plaza.

I look around me. There are rollerbladers and bicyclists, food stands and souvenir stores, all of it so incredibly tacky, overpriced and majorly commercial. Typical for a seashore town, but not typical of Mark Genovese.

"Welcome to the Coney Island of the West, Venice Beach," he says, with a sweep of his hand.

"*What?*" I am horrified.

Mark realizes his blasphemy and tries to backpedal. "Well, that is what they used to call it. No, it's not Asbury Park, but in California, this is a beach town, so just get over it right now."

"Like you would know about the Jersey Shore." I remain indignant.

"We played the Stone Pony in Asbury Park."

"Yes, I remember. You kept calling me and trying to convince me that Springsteen was there, and sent me a Polaroid of the men's room door, with a note saying, 'Brucie definitely touched this once!'" Hell, they'd sent me a Polaroid of the urinals, too, with a similar dedication.

He throws his hands up in the air in the universal symbol of surrender. "Do you want the grand tour or not?"

I nod, and he turns me to face the ocean.

"Okay, this is Venice, obviously. North of here is Santa Monica. South of here is Manhattan Beach, then Redondo Beach, then Long Beach, and way way way south is San Diego."

I hear the sounds of skateboard wheels behind us and move out of the way. A pack of four teenagers swoop by us, bad mall punk clothing and equally bad haircuts. One of them glances sideways, and then swerves to a stop. His friends realize he isn't with them anymore and they stop, look back at us, and then pick up their skateboards and walk in our direction. I'm thinking--what, skate punks gonna hassle the rock star or something? But the first kid walks over to Mark and they shake hands, gravely.

"We found a bass player," the kid tells Mark. He couldn't have been more than thirteen or fourteen.

"Really? Congratulations." Mark says.

"This is Joey," the kid says, indicating a Hispanic kid with a crooked mohawk. Mark and Joey shake hands.

"So do we still have a deal?" asks the first kid.

"Dominic, I told you. You have to do your own work first. Practice, get your shit together, get some gigs, play for people. When you've done that, let me know and I'll come see you. If I think you're taking this seriously, I will let you have twenty minutes on my stage the next time we play in L.A.. But I'm not doing that if I think you're fucking around."

Dominic nods.

"If I let you on my stage and you suck, it'll hurt you more than not playing the gig."

He nods again.

"Do you guys have a practice space?"

"Yeah. My dad is letting us use his garage down in OC."

"Are you practicing?"

"Every Sunday."

"How long?"

"Three, four hours."

"Do you all practice on your own besides that?"

Dominic nods vigorously, but the other kids kind of stare off into space, at their shoes, off at the ocean.

"Dudes, you have got to play on your own. It doesn't happen when you sleep."

"Do you still practice?" This was one of the other kids now.

"Every fucking day," says Mark.

"You're shitting me," the kid answers.

"Like I said: it doesn't happen by me putting the guitar under my pillow. I'm not gonna get better if I don't practice. I worked hard my whole life so all I would have to do all day is play the guitar."

"Man, I wouldn't play the guitar, I'd be getting high, fucking chicks," says Joey, kind of checking me out. Whoa, I'm being scoped by a sixteen year old.

Mark shoots him a sharp glance, and the kid backs off. "First of all, this is my friend Lisa, not a 'chick.' Show some respect. Second of all, if you're getting high all the time, you're gonna suck. Third of all, if that's the only reason you want to be in a band, then forget it." He starts to walk away from them, beckoning me to follow.

"No! No, Mark, wait!" It's Dominic again. Mark stops.

"Dominic, do not waste my fucking time. I told you that the first time you asked me to give you guitar lessons. You may have your shit together, but I'm not sure your friends do."

Dominic looks like he is about to cry. It's kind of touching, actually.

"Mark, I'll show you. Give us a few weeks, maybe come down to practice or we can come play in your studio?"

Mark pauses. "Maybe. Drop me a note when you think you're ready, we'll talk about it. Cool?"

They shake hands again, and then Dominic and his friends skate off, heading north.

I look at Mark. "What was that all about?"

"They're skate punks, they hang out on the beach..."

"Mall punks is more like it," I say. "They wouldn't know the Circle Jerks if Keith Morris himself bit them on the ass. Those were skate punks!"

"Lisa! What year is it? Punk is dead, long live punk. They think they are outlaws, I prefer to indulge them in that fantasy, instead of lecturing them about the good old days."

I am pouting.

Mark sighs, exasperated. "Do you want to hear the story or not?"

"Go on."

"They saw me eating lunch down here one day, and then the next day Dominic came over and asked me if I was the dude in Blue Electric, and I said yes. He just kind of nodded and skated away. A few days later, I saw him again, and he had this really bad Kmart electric guitar strapped to his back. He asked me if I gave guitar lessons. I was going to tell him to get lost, thinking he was fucking with me, but then he explained that he really wanted to learn how to play and had some books at home and he couldn't follow them. Oh, and that everyone else he knew either sucked, or played like Dave Matthews, and that wasn't what he wanted."

"Wow. Smart kid. Go on."

Mark points at a hot dog stand, advertising "Real New York

Hot Dogs!" and I shake my head no. If this is considered the Coney Island of the West, I shudder to think what they consider a 'real' hot dog.

"So it turns out that he's left-handed, and was trying to play right handed, and he could barely fucking read, I'm surprised he figured out anything--I mean, his hands were cut and scabbed over because he was just playing wrong, strings were too tight, the guitar wasn't even in tune..."

We're passing a street musician, who's playing a reggaefied version of "Sympathy for the Devil." I wince, but Mark grins and we stop and listen for a while. He takes a ten dollar bill out of his pocket and throws it in the guitar case after the third verse. "Keep it up, Dave," he says to the guitarist, who nods and says, "Thanks, Mark," and we continue walking.

"So I bought some strings for him, restrung the guitar left-handed, wrote out some charts for him, taught him how to tune the thing--the kid has almost perfect pitch, it's uncanny. He'd written songs already, using his own kind of notation system that only he understands... anyway, I gave him a few lessons and he really didn't need more than that. Once he had an instrument that was in tune and had the basics down, he was off and running."

Mark stops, and points out at the sand. I nod yes. I take off my shoes and we walk towards the water. A few feet from the waves, I stop and plop down on the sand. He looks down, and then sits next to me.

"Finish the story," I say.

"Okay, so he's playing, he has this piece of crap amp that he got with the guitar, but it's something. But his stepfather was giving him trouble about playing the guitar, yelling at him, shit like that. All I can think is, at least this kid isn't doing drugs, at least he's got something he cares about. So I drove out to his house one weekend."

"You're kidding me."

"With my entire discography in the back seat."

"Again, you're kidding me."

"Well, I wanted the guy to take me seriously. Turns out I didn't even need to do it, the whole reason Dominic knew who I was in the first place was because his stepdad is a fan! Has all the records, has the first single on the original label... the whole nine yards. I walk up to the front door and knock on it and the dude almost lost it. He thought his wife entered him in some radio station contest and he was the winner."

"You were the prize of a radio station contest?"

"Oh, shut up. So I go in and explain to this guy that I've been giving Dominic guitar lessons and that his stepson is really talented and needs support, and the guy starts to freak out. 'Dominic! This is the old guy in Venice who's been giving you guitar lessons?!'"

"'Old guy,' that's good."

"Yeah, I kind of liked it myself. His stepfather thought it was one of the street musicians or something, had no fucking idea. Dominic said he didn't tell him because he didn't think he'd believe him. Dude said he was right, he wouldn't have believed him. So they make me stay for dinner, and by the end of it he's promising to buy Dominic a better amp and an actual tuner, and to clean out the garage so he has a place to practice."

I'm stunned by this whole story. I mean, Jake's the one who would offer to drive fans back to Marysville after shows, while Mark would be sleeping in the back seat of the van, pissed off as hell. Not that Mark's an asshole, he just doesn't have the same natural generosity of spirit that Jake was brought up with. It isn't the kind of thing that would have been exactly encouraged by his father.

"Is that it?"

"No, of course there's more. I'm about to leave, when Dominic's mother gets involved in the discussion. She very shyly tells me that Dominic's grades are not all that hot, and maybe there was something I could do to encourage him to do better at school. So I tell Dominic that if he passes all his classes, I will let his band open for us the next time we play in L.A.."

"Whoa."

"What the hell, I can give some kids twenty minutes on the fucking stage, it's not a big deal, no one will see them anyway, everyone's looking at the ticket and saying 'Three bands, I can show up at nine.'"

"Did it work?"

"Did it work? The kid is getting As and Bs. He just doesn't want his friends to know, it wouldn't be cool for some reason."

"Does anyone else know about this?"

"No, but now I'm going to have to fucking tell the guys, since it looks like I'll have to come through on my promise. And we have almost no shows this year, as you heard last night. No one will mind, really. I didn't want it to be a big deal. I just thought I'd help some kid learn how to play guitar, get him off the street."

The wind has picked up and I shiver a little. Mark gets up, brushes the sand off his jeans. "Come on, let's keep walking. We'll find some food, get coffee, something." I reluctantly get up and leave the waves behind, and head back towards the walkway with Mark, still kind of awed at the whole saga.

We approach a restaurant with a whole line of outdoor tables. I am of course ready to sit outside, but Mark is shaking his head.

"Mark, it's just not cold! Come on! You're from Seattle!"

We walk in the restaurant and the hostess, an older woman with graying hair, greets him enthusiastically. "Mark! How are you! Who is this lovely lady with you."

"Carol, this is an old friend of mine from Seattle, Lisa. Lisa, this is Carol."

"Where do you want to sit, you two?"

"Lisa wants to sit outside."

Carol smiles, and walks us outside to a table. The sun is shining and it's more than warm enough. We sit down, Carol leaves us with a menu, and walks away.

"One menu?" I ask, quizzically.

"She knows what I'm having."

"Mark, does everyone on this beach know you?"

"Well, it's my neighborhood."

"You didn't know anyone in our neighborhood except me."

"Everyone else in our neighborhood was a crack dealer, or thought we were crack dealers."

"Almost true, but--"

"It's an outdoor neighborhood, during the winter there aren't that many people here except on weekends," he shrugs. "I told you, I like it here. It's got that veneer of California fake, except it's like a--New Jersey version of California," he says, grimacing.

"Like you know so much about New Jersey," I say, my East Coast pride rising one more time.

"Let's not start that again." He pauses. "It's just--real. It's more real than Seattle was."

"The Central District was pretty fucking real, Mark," I say.

"Lisa, I spent, what, three years in the CD? The rest of the time I lived in Magnolia with my family, I was totally sheltered, I went to good schools, I lived at home when I went to college. It wasn't until I started playing guitar that I moved out, and even then it was to an apartment on Queen Anne, nice and civilized. What musician lives on Queen Anne?" he shakes his head.

Carol comes back, I order a chicken sandwich and lemonade, and she just smiles at Mark and hurries off.

"This isn't real, but it's more real than the rest of L.A.," he finally says. "And it's not trendy, like where Scott lives--they think they're the fucking East Village down there, and they're not. I can't explain it any better than that."

I put my hand on his arm. "No, you explained it pretty well. I get it." Well, I sort of get it. Or maybe it's that I never thought about Mark like this before. Never put all the pieces of the puzzle together.

We eat our lunch while people watching and trying to outdo the other with sarcastic comments. Carol returns after we've finished, while we're sitting in the sun, and asks, "Coffee?"

"Ah, no thanks, Carol," Mark answers, before I can make eye contact with him to find out if I want to order coffee here.

"Okay then, I'll just put this on your tab?"

"Yes, thanks."

"This is not a place you want to be having coffee," he whispers across the table.

"Is there anywhere in L.A. besides Jake's house that I do want to have coffee?"

"Actually, yeah. C'mon."

We leave the restaurant and walk for a few blocks. Mark turns left, away from the beach, and stops in front of a store with an old wooden screen door.

"Now, *this* is where you want to get coffee," he says, opening the door and ushering me in. It's tiny, but could be any espresso joint back home. "Breathe," he say.

I take a deep breath and I smell it. Coffee roasting. Good coffee.

"Wow," I say in admiration.

"Yeah. They do okay... if I can get someone out of the back. Hello?" he says, loudly.

A few seconds later a guy emerges. "Mark! How ya doin'," he asks jovially.

"Pretty good, Pete. You?"

"Can't complain. How's the record going?"

"It's going," Mark says.

"Got it. You don't want to talk about it. Trust me, brother, I get it. Who's the pretty lady with you?"

"This is my friend Lisa from back home... so let's give her a double tall skinny latte, no foam, and please prove to her that she can get decent coffee somewhere in the state of California."

"Your usual?"

"Yes, please."

Pete turns and busies himself grinding coffee and pulling shots. I am amazed that Mark still remembers what I drink. Jake never had to be told when he made coffee runs, I never thought to consider that Mark might also remember.

I look at Mark again. I try to look at him as though I haven't known him for a good portion of my adult life. I try to forget everything I assume about the person I currently know as Mark, and I'm surprised by what I do see. He's always been a good-looking guy, but age has turned him into strikingly handsome. He still favored the simple wardrobe he always did, jeans and t-shirts. A button-down shirt was dressing up big time as far as he was concerned. He's chatting with Pete and doesn't sense my intent gaze, and I'm thankful for that.

You think you know a person and you go through life with those comfortable assumptions, and almost never change or adjust them. People freak out when people they know change; it's probably not the changes that alarm them, it's the fact that they have to adjust their way of thinking about the person. It's not even fair for me to be laughing at Mark or teasing him for what I've seen today. Sure, I don't think Mark knew my old roommate's name, and now he seems to know the entire fucking neighborhood. I accept that maybe I don't know Mark as well as I think I do. I think about how much my friends have changed from all the years on the road, all the years living outside of Seattle. And I'm suddenly overwhelmingly sad. All this lost time, all these lost opportunities.

"Here we go. Skinny latte, no foam, and one triple Americano." Pete presents us with our drinks, interrupting my interlude of self-flagellation. They both look at me apprehensively and I realize that I am expected to sample my drink and pass judgment. I prepare myself for the worst, and take a sip.

"Wow!" I take another sip. "That is fucking good coffee, pardon my French," I say, astonished.

Pete takes a little bow. "Thank you, ma'am. That's high praise, coming from a friend of Mark's from the home country."

"You're from Seattle?"

"Born and raised in Ballard."

"How did you end up here?"

"I used to be in a heavy metal band, long before your time. We came down here in the early '80s, trying to make it big--long story short, I was smart enough to save my advance from the record company and use it to buy this place after the band fell apart." He smiles at Mark.

"Well, thank you, Pete. I am delighted to make this latte's acquaintance."

Mark snorts, and then laughs out loud. "We'll see you later, Pete." Screen door banging behind us, we walk out.

We continue walking away from the beach, sipping our coffee, and return to Mark's house. Coming in through the garage, Mark punches buttons on his security system, and pushes the door open.

"Follow me," he says, bowing. "This is my studio. Not quite as cozy as Jake's, but it works for me."

Guitars. Amps. Guitars again. Guitar cases, flight cases, microphones, tape decks, mixing consoles. I walk around the room, inspecting carefully, and then I look up, and cannot believe what I see hanging on the walls.

Carefully displayed, in simple frames, is every single poster that the band ever had on the walls of their early practice spaces. Bowie from *Ziggy Stardust*. Robert Plant on the balcony of the Hyatt House. Mick Jagger in *Performance*. Keith from the 72 tour. Led Zeppelin on stage. A big Soundgarden poster from *Louder than Live* and the Who circa 1979, both of which were donations from me.

"I can't believe you have all the posters! I never stopped to think about what happened to these," I say.

"Well, no one did, really. When we gave up the last practice space in Seattle, they got packed up and somehow I ended up taking them. Then I basically forgot about their existence, and one poster tube looks pretty much like another. When I moved in here, I opened up a box and there they were, so I had them framed, since they are somewhat historical now," he says.

"It's amazing how many memories there are just in looking at all these posters together again."

"That's kind of how I feel about it." He grins.

Mark Genovese sentimental about possessions that weren't guitars or amps or effects pedals? This had to be a first.

"Okay, let's go upstairs, you get the grand tour!" We walk out and the door clicks shut behind us. "The first floor used to belong to a surfboard company. About two months after I moved in upstairs, they were moving out, so I just asked the landlord how much he'd charge me for the whole building. Plus, that way--no neighbors. I just built another room inside of what was already there to soundproof it."

"Now I understand why Scott says he doesn't understand why you don't just buy this place."

He shakes his head no. I decide to not pursue it.

We get to the top of the stairs and the door swings open on a big, sunny living room. Persian carpets and a big L-shaped sofa, bookshelves and paintings interspersed with framed posters, guitars on the walls. I turn around and around and around, taking it all in. Yeah, this is Mark.

"Through there is the kitchen. Originally there was a separate dining room, I just knocked the wall down to make this room bigger."

There's another staircase in the corner, and Mark heads over to it. I follow behind. There are photographs in the stairwell, early photos of the band, later photos, live photos, promo photos, groupings of photos that Mark or someone took of the guys hanging out, groups of friends, playing baseball, standing in front of the Kingdome. It's the entire history of Blue Electric.

"Your photo is up here, in case you were wondering," he mentions as he climbs. That promo photo I took at Gasworks, all those years ago. It's nicely framed and everything. I beam up at him.

"C'mon up here. It's my favorite part of the house, aside from the studio."

We reach a landing, and then another flight of stairs. Mark gestures down the hallway. "The bedrooms are on this floor, I've got two and a half. The half is junk storage since I don't know what to do with it yet."

We climb up the last flight of stairs. This time there's no keypad, but instead several huge locks bolt across the doorway.

"New York style," I observe.

"Sorry for the overkill on the security system, but it is Venice, and as you noticed, everyone knows I'm in the vicinity, and thanks to the internet, everyone knows exactly which house is mine."

Mark throws the door open. We're on the roof, and there's a nice little deck with lawnchairs and an umbrella. I collapse into one of the chairs, put my feet up, and smile at Mark.

"We forgot the beer."

He shakes his head, and heads back down the stairs.

It's sundown now, and we're still here. My shoes are off, my hair is down. The light is fading slowly over the ocean. There are about a dozen empty beer bottles surrounding us. Why does beer always taste better out in the sun and wind?

"Sunset over the Pacific. Damn," I share my thought with Mark as though it is a great revelation.

He lowers his sunglasses--still those damn Ray-Bans--down his nose, and turns his head slowly to look at me.

"Profound as usual, Lisa. Thank you for not disappointing

me."

"Oh, fuck you, Genovese."

"Back atcha, but I was actually being somewhat sincere."

Now it's my turn to lower my sunglasses and peer inquisitively over them in his direction.

"You really said it all. You're right. Sunset over the Pacific. How did I get here?"

"You worked your ass off, that's how you got here," I say, putting down my empty Corona bottle. It falls over. "Oops."

"Never mind, we'll get it later--here," he gestures, reaching into the metal tub that was full to the brim with ice and bottles when he hauled it up here several hours earlier. He hands me another bottle.

"So you're really not going to tour when this record's done?" I ask, leaning back in the chair again.

"Nope."

"Why? You love touring."

"Wrong. I love playing live, onstage, in front of an audience. I hate the endless travel, I hate the large venues, I hate dealing with record company and radio station idiots after every show. Especially radio station idiots."

"So close your backstage."

"There are still people we have to meet... but, yes, that is a solution."

"Play small venues."

"Then people get shut out, and that's not fair. Not to mention how much we hate scalpers."

"Play two weeks at one venue. Let Mohammed come to the mountain. That's what Joe Strummer said when the Clash didn't want to tour for *Sandinista* and just were going to play those two weeks at Bond's Casino."

"And since I know that you were there, what happened when they did that?"

I pause, remembering running around Times Square, being chased by NYPD on horseback, as they broke up one of several riots that week due to those shows. I sigh, and fall back against the chair again.

"No, no, these are all good ideas. We've thought of them all, we've been around this a million times already, it seems. There's just no good solution."

The light is starting to completely dissolve from the sky right about now. I love this time of day. The magic hour. Nothing seems real, everything has this lovely haze around it.

"Mark, why is this record so important?" I ask, after a few minutes of silence.

He sighs. "Because I think it might be the last one."

Talk about a cure for drunkenness. "What?" I say, sitting up as straight as I can manage, given the circumstances.

"Lisa, we did it all, we did everything we wanted to do and all the things we never thought we would do."

"But--"

"I just think it might have run its course. I don't know. I haven't talked about this with anyone else, actually," he says. "I don't know that I want to talk about it that much. I don't know what's going to happen. Maybe after a year off I'll want to come back and I won't feel like we're just marching along without stopping to ask ourselves, do we want to keep doing this?"

"What are you going to do on your year off?" I ask.

"New York City," he says with a grin.

"What?" I lose my balance and almost fall out of the chair. "New York?"

"Well, it's not like I haven't heard you talk about it as the center of the universe for the past ten years."

"You hate New York!" I say.

"No. I hated a particular moment in New York when someone stole the first Les Paul I managed to scrape up money to buy. I hated another moment in New York when CBGB's flooded and we couldn't play after driving two days straight to get there. And, okay, I really wasn't fond of that moment when someone slashed all our tires and we missed our show in Boston. Otherwise, I like New York just fine."

"You're serious."

"So I'm going to go to New York, and rent an apartment in the East Village, which will make Scott jealous as fuck, and I'm thinking about a solo album."

Now I have to say something. "Mark, I do not feel like I know you anymore. Nothing you have done or said today--"

"Seems like something I'd do," he finishes the sentence for me. "I know. I'm not sure I know who I am anymore, either. Or--" He stops, takes a drink, stares at the ocean. I wait.

"I think for so many years, I had to act a certain way because my father expected me to be that way. When I went out on my own, I had no idea how to do anything differently. It's honestly taken me all this fucking time to stop and think about everything I do, everything I think, everything I believe." He takes a drink of beer. "It's like every action I take, I look at it and say, 'Is this what I really want to do, or is this just automatic?'"

"That's very Zen, Mark.'

"Funny you should mention that. I've been reading about Buddhism... really fascinating shit. Living in the moment. Be here now. I mean... it's not like I haven't had fun and I'm not proud and my life isn't great, it's just that I'm not sure I was totally here every second of it. Whereas Jake just kind of wallows in every moment of the day."

"Well, that's Jake, it's not you."

"I know, but I think he might be on to something. Don't tell him I said that."

At that, I burst out into a cackle. Ah, thank god, nothing has really changed all that much.

"What do you want to do for dinner?" Mark asks.

"We're eating? I thought this was dinner."

"We should eat something... we could call out for pizza."

My expression must register the appropriate degree of horror, because he replies, "Oh, Jesus fucking Christ. Fucking New Yorker. You haven't lived there for over ten years and you're still a pizza fascist. I cannot believe you."

"Pizza, coffee, we all have our dogmas."

"Fuck you."

"Back atcha."

"Let's go downstairs and look at delivery menus. This is L.A., we can literally have anything from any restaurant in the city delivered here... and I am the big rock star, after all. I can afford it."

"That's too bad, Mark, because I was buying tonight."

"Rich software chick versus big rock superstar? I think I win."

★

In the end, we can't decide. So we order Chinese from one place and sushi from another. It ends up being entirely too much food for five people, let alone two, but it is delicious and slightly decadent, and we don't have to leave the house.

"Movie?" Mark asks, eating a bite of tuna roll.

"What did you have in mind?" I ask, lost in a carton of Moo Goo Gai Pan.

"*Rock and Roll Circus*?"

"Got anything I haven't seen sixteen million times?"

"That's right, I got my copy from you originally. You'll have to get up and look," he says, gesturing with his chopsticks in the direction of a bookcase.

Somehow I struggle to my feet and in a food induced semi-coma woozily make my way across the room.

"Oh, shit," I say. It's an entire bookcase full of DVDs, every rock movie ever, and probably a hundred concert bootlegs.

"It slides," he says from his corner on the floor.

I cautiously push the bookcase to one side, and it slides quietly, revealing an identical unit, exactly as full as the first one, but with hand-labeled VHS tapes, again, rock films and shows. I look at him and shake my head in awe.

"Hey, I offered to make a decision for you," he says. "I think you'll like DVD number thirty-seven."

★

What did we watch? God, what didn't we watch: The Who. Led Zeppelin. The Clash. Lou Reed. Stones bootleg after Stones bootleg. Around 3:00 or 4:00 a.m., the Stones concert we are watching dies out suddenly in the middle of a bad, coked-out 1978 performance of "Angie."

"Oh, lord, Mark," I say, wanting nothing more than to stretch out right where I am and fall asleep. "We are, officially, drunk."

"Clearly, I'm not driving you home tonight," he says.

"No shit." I drop my head back against the couch.

We're sitting on the floor at this point, coffee table with the dinner remnants pushed back against the other side of the room. Mark is lying on the floor in front of me, head on a pillow resting almost on my legs. He stretches out and his arms graze my thighs. I kind of look up at the brief touch but don't think anything of it.

"Is there anything left to watch?" I ask.

"Hey, kid, we've barely scratched the surface." He turns over so he's lying on his stomach, looking up at me. I can see him out of the corner of my eye, and something makes me pick my head up.

Those eyes. They are glinting like there's a light shining off them somewhere. I chalk it up to track lighting and me being very drunk. But then I look again, and something makes my stomach turn over. Mark is just looking at me, evenly, but something, something makes me lean over and kiss him on the forehead.

He smiles affectionately, and then stops. There must have been something in my face, because he gets up, sits on the couch, and pats the cushion. Holding out his hand for support, somehow I pry myself up off of the floor and sit down next to him. He puts his arm around me and I rest my head on his shoulder.

"Okay, what are we going to watch next?" I ask, with my eyes closed. I can feel him leaning his head against mine.

"Is that what you really want to do now?" he asks, quietly.

No, it isn't.

I pick my head up and look at him as levelly as I possibly can. And I realize I'm not really that drunk, and that what I am feeling is something completely different, surprising--hell, shocking. I realize that I have brand new feelings about the person sitting next to me right now.

All these thoughts are racing through my head when Mark leans over and kisses me quietly on the mouth. He pulls back a little bit, like he's gauging my reaction, and that's when my internal dialogue said "Shut up and kiss the boy already." I rest my hand against his face and lean in to kiss him.

Everything is suddenly quiet and still. Then Mark pulls away, breathing hard. He stands up, and looks down at me with some gravity.

"What are we doing?" he finally asks.

"I think you know exactly what we're doing," I say.

"Lisa, I was just being mischievous, which was wrong and unfair, but--"

"You don't get to use that excuse this time, Mark Genovese," I say. Now it's my turn to stand up. I face him, and put my arms around his waist, looking right into his eyes.

"This is not a small thing we're about to do," he finally says.

"It better not be." I do not know where I am finding this newfound carelessness, but it is very much there.

"Lisa," he says, and then stops.

"Are we going to stand here all night and talk, or are we going somewhere?" I ask, sliding up against him as close as possible and resting my head on his shoulder. I want this.

He doesn't say anything, so I ask again. "What do you want, Mark?" I can still feel the hesitation in his body.

Minutes pass, and then Mark answers me:

"Everything. I want--everything."

He turns away, grabs my hand, and pulls me in the direction of the stairs.

We walk into his bedroom and he shuts the door. He takes a visibly deep breath and walks towards me. I put my arms around him again and kiss him as hard as I can. There are another few moments of hesitancy and then he is walking me backwards, and we fall onto the bed, kissing and kissing and kissing and kissing.

Hours, seconds, minutes, days, lifetimes later... I don't know how long we have been here. I know that the lights are out except for a small reading lamp over his desk. I know I have felt and kissed and touched every inch of his body. I am hardly shy in bed, but this is different somehow. This is different and enormous. My life is changing at this moment.

It is battle. It is mutual conquest. It is triumph. It is sliding the last bolt into place. It is silence and surrender, it is letting go, opening up, letting every layer drop away, all pretense, shyness, hesitation. Walls, barriers, chains, bounds, letting go, letting go. It is possessing and being possessed. There is anger and rage and passion and heat and sadness and joy and pure naked lust. There are no boundaries, rules, taboos. Everything, Mark said. I want everything. And it was everything, it is everything and then the sharp bright flash and I drop into a moment of nothingness.

Gradually, my breathing returns to normal, although Mark's chest, his arms still crushing me against him, rises and falls at an accelerated rate. Words would be useless now. As the world around us comes back into focus, so does the feeling of cold air and a glimpse of silvery grey light edging its way around the window. I try to move slightly and cannot, those arms, the arms that held me down and took absolute possession, are still locked against my back. I turn my head to kiss his chest, and that seems to reconnect him back here. I'm about to murmur "Cold" when a hand travels down to the small of my back, making me shiver--it's as though he reads my mind because he gently releases his hold on me and pulls the comforter over us both.

I sleep for hours and hours. At some point I feel Mark gently slide out of bed, I hear phones ringing, I hear his voice behind a closed door. I think about trying to coax myself into consciousness but do not want to leave this place. Just when I'm trying to talk myself into it again, he returns and quietly climbs back into bed next to me, sliding his body behind mine. A hand travels down my arm, down my thigh, and he settles down into what I'm assuming is sleep again.

However, at this point, my body is awake. Very awake. And I turn over to face him. Mark's about to open his mouth to say something but I silence him with a kiss before he can speak. He thinks I am just giving him a good morning kiss and then as I continue, he realizes that I have something else in mind. I don't know that this was even a conscious decision on my part, but I'm not disagreeing with it.

"Oh no, here we go again," he whispers in my ear.

That was pretty much how we spent the remainder of the day. We'd drift off into sleep, one of us would wake up, touch the other, and it would start again. God, this is how sex is supposed to be, I remember thinking at one point. I can't remember doing it more than twice with Ian in one night. I can't remember sex being like this since...

Since James.

I hug Mark tightly and hope he can't feel the tears coming out of my eyes. But I'm not crying for James, I'm crying for me. Or for whoever that Lisa was that I left downstairs last night.

★

I wake up yet again, and this time Mark is propped up in bed, sheet covering him, reading a book.

"You awake for good this time?"

I look up at him and smile.

"Okay. No. We're not starting that again."

I must have looked upset because he put the book down and slid down next to me.

"No, no, that's not it, at all... my god, no. It's just--it's 4:00 p.m. I'm fucking starving, babe. You've got to be hungry, too."

I stop and consider this, and realize that I am famished. I nod.

"Is it really four o'clock?"

He reaches over to the bedside table, grabs a small clock and brings it to my face. Yep. 4:00 p.m.

"4 p.m. as in--Sunday?"

"Yep."

I rest my head against my arm. "Oh, god, I bet the entire world thought we went to Mexico, or something."

Mark laughs. "That was actually what Scott and Jonathan voted."

"Does the *entire band* know about this?" I say, horrified, sitting up.

"No. The entire band knows that we got drunk out of our minds and stayed up all night watching videos. Jake just started to panic around noon when there was no sign of either of us, and I wasn't answering any phones."

I sigh in relief.

"Anyway, no one suspects a thing. I'm not even sure this really happened."

I lean over and kiss him lightly. "Um, I think it did."

"Are we going to talk about this now?"

I shake my head no.

"Good, because right now I have absolutely no words. I'm convinced I fell into some parallel universe."

"That would explain a lot of things," I say, shaking my head, closing my eyes, remembering--a lot of things.

"All right. I'm going to be assertive here," and he slides out of bed, wearing nothing but boxer shorts. He strides over to the closet, takes out a green plaid flannel bathrobe and tosses it on the bed. "Here. You probably want to use the shower in the guest room, it's the yellow room on the right. Chrissie stayed here while they were renovating her condo, and all her girl stuff is still in there."

I nod.

"If you need some clothes, take whatever you like--except my '75 Stones shirt," he says, as an afterthought.

"Damn. I thought this would finally be my chance," I say. He beat me to that shirt by two seconds at a record show, and ever since then, I've tried everything possible to steal it.

"I'm going to hit the shower," Mark says. He looks at me inquisitively, and then walks back over and kisses the top of my head. I'm sitting there with the sheet up to my neck, feeling--well, just weird.

"Are you okay, babe?"

I look up at him and shrug. I notice the change in pronoun, though. Twice. I'm not "kid" any more.

"Do you want to talk about this now? I mean, we can."

I shake myself out of it. "No, no, I'm fine. A shower would be good. Food would be good. I think we both need a little time to--process all of this?"

He kisses me again, nods, and walks towards the bathroom. Jesus god, he looks good.

I wait until the door closed and I hear the water run. I grab the bathrobe, get out of bed, and wrap it around me. It's big and warm and comforting. I pad across the floor, out the door, down the hall, and into the guest room.

I walk into the bathroom and turn on the light. Warm water would be a really good thing right now, I think, turning on the shower. I step underneath the spray and let the hot water try to sort my brain out.

This is a big deal, and we both know it. The trick is going to be figuring out what happens next.

CHAPTER 13: Los Angeles

"Where are we going?" I ask, as the convertible--top up now against the night wind--speeds up some nameless highway.

"My favorite restaurant."

"Do you mind telling me where?" I ask, playfully.

"It's a surprise," he says. "It's not far, I promise." He reaches over and smooths the hair down on the back of my head.

It's all different now. The energy is different, the way we lean towards each other is different. Our bodies have apparently made a decision, even if we haven't quite yet.

Suddenly, the water comes into view, with the sun just starting to drop off the Pacific edge. Ten minutes later, we pull into a dirt parking lot next to what isn't more than a glorified shack.

"It's not fancy," Mark says, "But it's the best sunset view, ever, I swear. It was the most romantic place I could think of."

I am so touched by that statement I am temporarily at a loss for words.

Mark is greeted warmly and by name as we enter the restaurant, which is much larger and more substantial than it appears from the outside. The host says, "Take whatever table you like." There aren't more than half a dozen people in the restaurant, which is definitely not your typical, polished L.A. eatery. It looks like it was built by hand, piece by piece over the years, as the owners had the time and inclination.

"Well?" Mark asks, once we're seated next to the water, as the sun starts to edge everything in pink.

My smile says it all. It's absolutely beautiful.

The waiter strolls over after a few minutes and begins, "I could give you menus but I wouldn't recommend anything on them. Mark, can I just bring out the specials? Some lovely fish tonight."

Mark defers to me, and I nod yes.

"Drinks?"

"Just water, Michel, thanks," Mark answers for me. He's right--there is no way I can even think about alcohol right now.

"It's going to take a while to get the food out here, I'll warn you now," Mark says to me, once Michel had walked away.

"It'll give us time to watch the sunset," I say.

He stares down at his glass and quietly asks, "Can we talk about this now?"

I take a deep breath and nod yes.

Mark begins: "In case it wasn't obvious, last night wasn't an offhand or casual thing. I can't say that this is something I've thought about a lot, but I would be lying if I said I hadn't thought about it more than once over the years."

There is more than a little bit of shock on my part. "Will you be deeply offended if I say I can't say the same thing?"

"I'd be freaked if you said that you could." He pauses. "I hesitate to ask this next question, as normally it would be none of my business, but--what about you and Jake?"

"I've been waiting for this one. No," I say, shaking my head.

"You're not even surprised that I'm asking you this."

"No, because I have recently learned that all of you, apparently, assumed for years that eventually Jake and I would end up together. But--"

"Have you two talked about this?"

"Actually, we have. I think I'm going to have every life-changing discussion this week. On the surface, yeah, sure, we seem like a matched set. But there's no click, Mark, no spark. No fire."

"Wasn't there, once upon a time?" he quietly asks, staring at his ice cubes.

"I don't know how on earth you know about it, but--Mark, we were young, we were drunk, it was a moment. It didn't mean anything."

"It might have, if you guys had been able to keep it going."

"It was lust that night, that's all it was, it would not have lasted." I stop again. "Whoa. I never even said that to myself, until now."

"How will you know if you don't try?"

"Listen: I love Jake, sure. There is great affection and caring, but it is not a love for the ages."

"That's more than a lot of married couples have," he says.

"I know. It's more than I had with Ian, for Christ's sake, but it's not enough. There, I said it. It's not enough for me. I know there is more, I know there can be more. I had it once."

Mark and I have never really talked about James in detail. He knows the basic story, but he wasn't the one I'd sit up crying with--that was Jake. So this is thin ice I'm skating on right now, and my emotions are already fragile and confused enough as it is.

"So how will you know when you find it again?" he asks, still not looking at me.

At that moment, my heart stops. It stops, it does a back flip, turns upside down and inside out, spins around sideways. I try to switch to the eyes that looked at Mark yesterday, throw out everything I have thought or felt or believed, and just feel.

What I feel is a tiny glimmer of something, a small spark, something that could grow if it wasn't neglected.

But it's too soon, and I'm too scared. So I say, "I don't know, Mark. There's no guidebook for this. I'll just know."

At that moment, Michel appears with huge, heaping plates of grilled fish and vegetables and rice and salad, setting them on the table proudly. "Bon appétit," he wishes us both.

We eat quietly, as darkness slowly sets in across the ocean.

Walking back to the car after dinner, arm in arm, Mark asks, "What now?"

"Will you be deeply hurt if I say--I want to go and sleep for three days?" I say.

"No, I'll say that I'm glad you did, because I didn't want to say that and hurt your feelings."

"Then I'm going back to the mansion on the hill. I need to face Jake."

"What are you going to tell him? What are we going to tell anybody?"

"Mark, we're supposed to be grownups. Let's just tell them the truth."

We drive back to Jake's house listening to *Wingless Angels*, this almost gospel reggae album Keith Richards had a hand in (Mark being one of the two dozen people on the planet who own a copy). It's a neutral choice, yet interesting enough that we can just listen without feeling like we have to talk.

As we pull into the driveway, Mark says, "I don't think I'm going in there with you."

I nod. "But you're gonna have to deal with it, Mark."

"I know. I'll see him tomorrow."

I lean over, and he's expecting a kiss on the cheek. But I have something else in mind. I give him a real kiss, it is deep and long and hard and I mean it with every cell in my body.

I break away and look him in the eyes. He nods, and I get out of the car, waving behind me as I do.

Facing the house, I take a deep breath and gather courage. This shouldn't be a big deal, but I know that's stupid. No matter what Jake says he feels or doesn't feel, this has been hanging over our head for years, and for me to walk in there and say, I just spent the night with your best friend--well, let's just say that it's not going to be a small thing.

I straighten my shoulders and open the front door. The house is quiet. I'm not going to try to sneak upstairs or something stupid like that, I'm going to go find him and we're just going to talk about it.

He's lying on the couch in the library, reading a book, or at least pretending to, when I walk in.

"Hi," I say, somewhat weakly.

He drops the open book onto his chest and glares at me. "Hi."

"Is this going to be weird, or what?" I ask.

"It's none of my business," he says, a touch defensively.

I walk over, pick his feet off the couch and drop them on the floor so I can sit down. Collapsing into the depths of the couch, I lean my arm on the back, head on my hand, looking at him. "Let's just say whatever we have to say to each other, even if we end up fighting. Okay? I'd rather fight now than in a year."

"What happened?"

"You can probably guess what happened."

"No, that's not what I mean. I mean, *what happened?* How is it my two best friends in the entire world have had a thing for each other all this time, and I didn't even know it? I don't even really care, I just don't like the sneaking around part of it."

"How, exactly, did we sneak around?"

"You two have been acting like you couldn't give a shit."

"Jake, this was not planned. This was not devious. It just happened."

"Maybe for you it just happened, but nothing 'just happens' to Mark."

"Mark's a lot different than he was years ago."

"Wow, thanks for coming down from Seattle to tell me that!" he says.

I guess we are going to fight.

"I'm not going to apologize for the years with Ian. I'm not going to apologize for trying to be a grown up and have what I thought was a grown up relationship. I'm not going to apologize for being caught up in the real world, trying to manage money and a career and a life, and not being able to be with you guys all the time. I'm not going to berate you for neglecting me, abandoning me by moving down here and going off to be a rock god. Jake! This is what happens to most of the rest of the world!"

"But you're better than that, Lisa. You always were. But James died, and you just--gave up."

With that sentence, the tears finally arrive, hot and sharp. I cry because I know he is right. James died and I just stopped trying. There were some halfhearted attempts, sure, but most of Lisa died when he did.

I shrug his arm off my shoulders and lean back against the couch, looking right at him. "Jake, I don't know what's going to happen with Mark, and neither does he. But we'd like to try to find out."

He looks down, then back up at me, and nods.

"Can you be happy for us?"

"It's not that I'm not happy for you. And grudgingly, I'll be happy for Mark, even if I think he doesn't deserve the most wonderful woman in the world."

"Shut up."

"No, you shut up. He better fucking appreciate what he's got, or he'll have to answer to me."

"Jake, what is it? We talked about this. We both agreed that you and I weren't the great love affair the entire world thought we were."

He pauses and glances sideways, clearly thinking. "I know. And I still agree, more or less..."

"But?"

"But I'm jealous. There, I said it. I'm jealous, even though I believe that you are right, my heart says that you're right. I'm jealous that he has what I don't, I'm jealous that I tried for years to find the right woman and failed miserably, and that motherfucker seemingly just wakes up one day and gets what I've always wanted."

"Me?"

"Not you, but--what you represent I guess? A girl who can be my friend, my partner, my equal..."

"It would help, a lot, if you didn't base your decisions on who you were dating solely on the size of their waist."

"That's not fair," he says.

"Jake, you are dazzled too fast and too easily, and you are too nice."

I crawl over and rest my head on his shoulder, and he slides his arm around me again. We sit that way for a while, quietly, not talking. There isn't much left to say right now, anyway.

After a while, I get up, kiss Jake on the top of his head, and leave the room, heading for bed. I stop in the kitchen to get a glass of water first. Jake must have thought I was already behind closed doors, though, because as I walk up the stairs, I hear Gram Parsons floating out of the library. Gram Parsons plus Jake can only mean, or at least has always meant, only one thing: heartbreak. "A Song For You" is Jake's ultimate lonely hearts song. I've heard him play this song probably a hundred times and it always means the same thing. My heart feels like it's going to rip in two. I stop and think about turning around and walking back in there, but instead, I keep walking upstairs, tears welling up in my eyes as I climb.

★

"YOU DID WHAT??!" Marie says, screeching in my ear the next morning.

"You heard me."

"You slept with MARK? Lisa! That's the GUITAR PLAYER!"

"Bitch, shut the fuck up."

"Okay, take me through this again," she says, and I provide her with an executive summary of the events of my love life over the past few days. When I finish, there is a long silence that I worry is disapproval.

And then: "So was it like incredibly hot sex, or what? Mark is a babe."

I laugh so hard I drop the phone. "It was mind blowing."

"Oooh! I like to hear that. In fact, I do not think I have ever heard you say that."

"Yes, you have."

"Who?" she asks.

"That guy in that big deal, critic's darling band they opened for once."

"Oh! The guy from North Carolina?"

"Yeah. Him. The Keith Richards circa '68 look-a-like. That was probably the best sex I have ever had. Well, until yesterday."

"But Mark?" She's still incredulous.

"Yeah. It was the way I remembered it was supposed to be like."

Another sigh, but it's Marie's big happy ending sigh, the sigh she'd give at the end of movies that she liked.

"Oh, by the way, I'm also probably quitting my job, and leaving Seattle."

"That's the sanest thing you've said in this entire conversation. I don't care if it's New York or L.A. you're moving to, just please tell me you're going to work as a consultant."

"That's exactly what I'm going to do."

"Okay, maybe you haven't totally gone off your rocker."

"Fuck you, again."

"Honey, I'm sorry that I give a shit, okay?"

"So why the hell did you let me stay with Ian all those years?" I say, sharper than I mean to.

Another silence. A big one this time.

"I always told you what I thought," she finally says.

"I know, but you didn't tell me you thought I was wasting my life."

"No, I didn't," she says. "I guess I hoped you would figure that out for yourself eventually."

"Well, eventually is here."

★

Jake is gone by the time I make my way downstairs, showered and dressed, and ready for lunch with Christine. He's left a sheet of paper with his usual, precise directions down to their office. Finally! I get to drive myself somewhere! It's sunny and warm, and a great day to be driving around Los Angeles, windows down, radio blaring. Okay, so KROQ is only a novelty for the first thirty minutes. I'm just not in Seattle, and that's all I care.

I pull up and park behind the bungalow in West Hollywood that's the headquarters for Blue Electric. I walk into the office, and finally, come face to face with Virginia, my nemesis. The battleship of an office manager who never passed my messages on to Jake, or anyone else. I always suspected she had a secret crush on him.

"May I help you?" she asks in clipped tones.

"Hi, you must be Virginia. I'm Lisa Simon, I'm here to meet up with Christine?" I say, extending my hand. She looks at it, and then shakes it carefully once.

"Lisa--yes, I believe Christine is expecting you," she says, as formally as possible.

At that moment Christine appears in her office doorway--I could hear her on the phone the whole time I was trying to be charming to Virginia--headset on, cord trailing behind her. She gestures frantically for me to come in. Virginia glares at me, as I smile at her and walk into Christine's office.

"It'll be just a sec--sit down," she says, pointing at the big leather sectional couch in the corner of the room. "Want something to drink?"

I shake my head no.

"Virginia, can you get Lisa some water, please?" she yells, and then goes back to her call. "Oh, come on, you cannot tell me that some band from Orange County that no one's ever heard of-- Orange Independent, is that what they're called?--can't be bumped from the lineup on Friday for Blue Electric? Ticketing will be via our fan club, limited amount at the door that night, you can handle that, right? Yep, I'll hang on..." She pauses. "You could go across the hall and see if Suzie's in..."

I nod, and get up from the couch. I still don't have my water, and now I actually want it.

I walk back into the outer office, where Virginia is busily staring at a computer screen, pretending she doesn't notice that I'm standing ten feet away from her. I ignore this, and walk to the other side of the office, and push open the door that says FAN CLUB--GO AWAY. Suzie is sitting at a desk surrounded by piles of mail, typing frantically into a computer, a very early Blue Electric bootleg blasting so loudly she didn't hear the door open.

I walk over to the stereo, turn down the volume, and say, loudly, "What is this crap you're listening to??"

Suzie whirls around, alarmed, curly red hair flying, and then her face breaks into this huge grin as she comes tearing around the desk, flinging herself at me in a hug.

"Lisa! "

"How's the queen of the underground?"

"You always called me that!" she says, beaming.

"Well, that is what the song says," I say, smiling back. It's impossible to be in a bad mood around Suzie.

"What are you doing here??"

"I came down for a visit. I've been here about a week. Seattle's kind of gross this time of year."

"Tell me about it! Wow, you never take a vacation, and you're here?" She frowns. "What is up?"

"Nothing, I just wanted to see the guys."

Her eyebrows arch--she's not buying it--and at that moment, Christine walks into the office, beaming. "Okay, Suzie, guess what? Fan club show at the Roxy Friday night."

"Ohhhhh!" she yells, excitedly, still every inch the superfan. "What are we doing about tickets?"

"Email the fan club. The capacity of the Roxy is about 500. I guess three-fourths to locals, the other quarter can go to the rest. We're holding fifty for the door, and another hundred for guest list."

"Lottery?"

"Come up with something creative, but the email has to go out today. Some kind of contest that requires effort."

"Do you want to see the email before it goes out?"

"Nah. You know what you're doing here better than I do."

"I have class at three o'clock, so I need to get to work!" With that, Suzie practically vaults back into her chair and starts busily typing. She stops for a second, and then says: "Oh! Now I understand why you're here, Lisa. This is cool! We will have so much fun!"

"Lunch?" Christine asks.

"Famished."

"Virginia, I'm out. Cell is on. We're gonna get a lot of calls. Any media, please just send them over to the PR firm, okay?"

She nods curtly and continues staring at her computer.

Christine is the only person in the entire Blue Electric organization who actually drives a car from this decade, and we head off onto Sunset in her shiny black BMW. Once again, I have no idea where we are going. We are chattering so much about clothes and shoes and places we need to go shopping--Seattle has no stores that I can ever find anything interesting in--that I don't pay much attention to my surroundings.

Christine turns into a parking lot, a valet takes the car, and we walk into a restaurant that is very upscale, cool and chic, windows and plants and a nice sunny patio out back. We sit down, and order some wine.

"Listen, I don't want to pry," Christine asks. "I didn't ask you lunch to interrogate you, we had this planned anyway."

"I know. But it's okay. Chrissie, we're friends. Just--talk to me. We used to just talk to each other."

The waitress arrives with our glasses of wine, we order salads, and she scurries off.

"Lisa, I have to ask: Have you ever thought about Jake since, well, that night?"

"I still can't believe that you all knew about it. But no. Not seriously, until I started driving down here."

"Before you started driving or after?"

"It wasn't the motivation to come down here, no."

"Damn," she says, sighing. "That was just so romantic and dramatic. I was hoping that you'd decided that you and Jake were meant to be together, and you decided to come down and force the situation." She takes a sip of wine as our salads arrive.

"No, Joey Ramone died, and Ian was a jerk. That's all."

"I knew it was too good to be true. Damn, I just want everyone to be happy. It just made so much sense. Every time Jake would break up with whatever bimbo he was with, and come and sit and wail in my house, I would tell him: call Lisa."

"You've got to be fucking kidding me," I say, fork hovering in midair.

"Not at all. It seemed like the perfect solution. You guys clearly adored each other. He needed a woman who isn't going to take his shit, who isn't going to bolster the wrong parts of his ego, who will kick him in the ass when he needs it. And you needed someone who thought you were great. Seemed like a match made in heaven to me."

"So what would Jake say when you would tell him to call me?"

"He would protest, and say he couldn't, and that you were happy with Ian, and I would tell him that we both knew perfectly well you weren't, and that we needed to get you out before it was too late."

I pause to consider this for a minute.

"So now--Mark?" Christine says, after a few minutes of eating silently.

"I don't know, Chrissie. He's like a totally new person to me."

"He has changed, a lot. Probably the most out of all the guys," she says. "He grew up."

"That surprised me. Just a few hours with him, alone, and it was so obvious, so different."

"Is it one of those things that just happened? I really don't need all the details--it would be like talking about my brother, or something." She shudders slightly.

I laugh. For the first time in this conversation, I laugh.

"Okay. Another glass of wine?"

"Aren't we going shopping?" I ask, anxiously. "I absolutely need some new shoes."

"I'm glad you still have your priorities straight."

★

I'm heading home from an expensive but satisfying bout of shopping, radio blaring, happy as a clam. I switch to what sounds like the classic rock station, and "Wild Horses" by the Stones comes on. At first, it's a welcome visitor, and I'm singing loudly, harmonizing along with Mick.

But then, after a minute or two, the tears are rolling down my face and I have to pull off the road into a gas station. This song hasn't reminded me of James in years, but I'm such a bundle of exposed nerves right now that I guess it shouldn't surprise me that it does. I feel helpless and overwhelmed, like there's a twenty-pound rock lying on the center of my chest.

Impulsively, I take the turnoff to 101, heading towards the ocean. I drive for a while in silence, trying hard not to think. Half an hour later, a left hand turn into a beach parking lot, and I'm here. Zuma Beach, just like the Neil Young album. It's sunny and windy, slightly cool, and the beach is deserted.

I approach within a few feet of the waves, thinking of the line from "Racing In The Street," about the water washing away your sins. I don't think I have any sins to wash away, but I like the symbolism, wonder if it would get rid of old ghosts and maybe cleanse the guilt I have been carrying for all these years over James' death.

More than anything, I have always hated the fact that I could never understand what he did or why, hated the fact that I would never understand. For a long time, I almost thought I was a coward for not ever trying to find the answer. But now I know it's exactly the opposite.

I crouch down at the edge of the waves, where the sand is stained dark and marked by the gentle ebb and flow. Balancing on my toes, water just touching the soles of my sneakers, I let the waves wash over my hands for a few minutes. I take some deep breaths, stand up and stare at the horizon as the afternoon light just begins to fade.

Walking back to the car, I drive back in silence, the rhythm of the waves in my head.

★

Arriving back to the darkened house--I guess they are still busy in the studio--I wander to the kitchen to make a cup of tea, planning to get a book out of the library and go upstairs and read for a while.

While I'm waiting for the water to boil, I hear the front door slam.

"Jake?" I yell. "I'm in the kitchen."

A few seconds later, he comes striding in. "Hey."

"Hey," I answer.

There's an awkward silence hanging like a cloud over our heads.

"Jake, this has got to stop being weird."

"I talked to Mark today," he says, almost offhandedly.

"And?"

He walks around the counter and grabs me in a fierce hug. "It's fine, Lisa, it is. I'm sorry."

"Is it?" I say, muffled into his shoulder.

He breaks the hug, and holds me at arm's length, looks me right in the eyes. "Yes," he says, and then his face erupts in this huge smile.

"What?"

"I'm just fucking with you," he says. "I wanted to get the concerned-Lisa face."

"Asshole!" I smack him in the arm.

"Yeah, I am. But, Lisa, it's all great. Mark's going to be happy, which will be a refreshing change. You're going to be happy, which will also be a relief. And we're going to finish making the best record we have ever made." He stops for a second, and then continues: "And when the record is done, I'm going to go travel around Europe for a few months."

"What?" I am incredulous. Jake is the original comforts-of-home guy.

"Yep." He grins. "I called our travel agent today. I want to see the world for a change, not from inside a tour bus."

"Jake, that is fucking awesome."

"Yeah, and I talked with Mark about how he'd feel if I worked on a solo record."

"And he didn't threaten to slit your throat?"

Jake laughs, hard. "He did say, 'Well, if I'm Keith in this equation, this is the part where I have to threaten your life.' And then he mumbled something in that Keith-imitation voice of his, you know what I mean. It was hysterical. But anyway, I have to do something with all the songs I wrote that we're not using for this record."

"You have more songs than the thirty-six that you guys have already recorded?" I ask with incredulity.

"I've been writing pretty freely, actually. I probably have about fifty that we haven't touched. And a lot of those are Blue Electric songs or they're not, but--yeah."

"Wow."

"Well, it helps that he told me he was thinking about doing one," he grins again. "It just sort of slipped out."

"You guys had a good talk."

"We had a *great* fucking talk. We just sat at this bar not far from the studio and shot the shit for like four hours. We didn't even eat dinner. We just drank beers and talked. It sucks, I can't remember the last time we did that. But, we did tonight."

"Wow." I am astonished.

"Yeah, I think we both thought it was going to end up being shootout at the OK Corral or something, but it turned out to be the best talk we've had in ages."

Now it is my turn to hug him fiercely.

"I think your water has long since boiled," he points out. "What are you doing now?"

"I was going to make some tea, read, go to sleep."

"Or you could come downstairs and I could play you some of these songs, and you could tell me how much they suck."

God. I haven't done that in years. The days of Jake slipping lyrics under the front door in an envelope, or even emailing them to me, seemed so long ago.

"You're on."

We walk out of the kitchen and head for the basement studio.

"Oh, wait," Jake pauses as he's opening the door. "You need to call Mark."

I look at him.

"No, I don't know anything, he just asked me to pass on the message."

"But I want to hear the songs!" I protest.

"Go call him, I'll get everything cued up. I'll wait. I promise."

I nod, head upstairs, pick up the cell phone and dial Mark.

"Well, that was fast," he answers.

"Where are you?"

"Being driven home. I took a cab from the studio to the office, and then called a driver."

"Mark!" I protest.

"No, I'm not that drunk, I'm more giddy than anything. My fucking lead singer and I had a great time tonight," he says, almost crowing.

"So I heard," I say.

"Anyway, I want to take you to dinner tomorrow night."

I don't answer, and he continues:

"Lisa. It's just dinner, babe."

I laugh again, and say, "Sure. I think my dance card is open."

"All right then. Get dressed up. Let's be festive."

"I like the sound of that. See you then."

I hang up, and stand there, bemused. I guess I have to do some heavy thinking between now and then, but--I shrug to myself--not now. Now, I am going to go downstairs and listen to Jake's songs, just like I used to in that basement in the Central District.

The next morning, I manage to get Jake's laptop hooked up in the kitchen, and it was time to get to work. A few hours later, I head down to the band office with a sheaf of documents.

I walk into the office and breeze past Virginia, who acts like she's going to try to say something to stop me. I ignore her, and stride into Christine's office and plop myself down on the sofa. She's on the phone, and I make an asking gesture--should I leave?--but she waves me back down.

"No, I really don't care if the L.A. *Times* covers this show or not. Bob hasn't exactly been a fan of the band, and this is a show for fans." She hangs up.

"I am going to age ten years just dealing with this show," she says in exasperation, standing up. "What's up?"

"I need to fax some paperwork back to Seattle," I say, proffering my folder. "But I need to run a few things by you first."

She sits back down. "Shoot."

"I'm thinking about flying home on Monday."

She nods. "You're not going to drive back?"

"One, I don't think the car will make it home, and then back down here. Two, I'm not driving round-trip alone, and none of you can leave right now. I need to get back quickly so I can pack and get the hell out of Dodge."

"So you're really going to move to Los Angeles," she says in wonderment. "What do you need from me?" That's the manager lady in action.

"Well, I know Jake's offered, but I think given the current situation, it would be better if I don't stay there for an extended period of time. It would be best if I just got my own place, but since I still barely understand this city, I'd like to not jump into things."

She opens up her top desk drawer and throws a set of keys at me. "I had the cleaners open up the spare room today."

"How did you know what I was going to ask?" I say, astonished, catching the keys in midair.

"Lisa. This is me, remember?"

I look at the clock on Christine's desk. "Okay, I need to get these letters faxed."

"You have a hot date tonight, or something?"

"Actually, yes." I grin.

I see her hold herself back from gushing, and the question marks are practically written all over her face, but she stops herself. "Virginia!" she yells. "Let Lisa use the fax machine, that's an order!"

★

Later, as I head back up to Jake's house, I marvel at how everything was working out and falling into place, with very little effort. I decide to take that as a sign that I'm doing the right thing. Now, if I can have some of this universal wisdom to help me decide what I'm going to wear tonight, my life will be complete.

The doorbell rings at 7:30, and I run down the stairs, new shoes in hand. I open it to behold Mark standing there, almost unrecognizable. His hair is slicked back, and he is wearing--"Is that a suit? " I gasp.

"Well, it's a suit jacket," he says, turning around. "I wasn't quite ready to go all the way."

Pinstriped jacket. This great olive green shirt underneath, black vest over it. Black jeans. Black cowboy boots with silver hardware on the tips.

"Actual *shoes*!" I gasp again.

"They're boots, let's not get carried away, they are still rock," he says.

"But they're not sneakers!"

"I hope you're not disappointed," he says. "And, well, let's look at you."

"Wait, let me put the shoes on for the full effect."

Now I turn around slowly for inspection. Low-rise jeans, black sequin tank top that was perfectly form fitting, and the shoes I bought with Christine. They were about as high as I could bear to walk around in.

"Very nice. I approve." His reply is accompanied with that sly grin that got us into so much trouble the other night. I lean over and kiss him gently on the mouth.

"Okay, if we start with that, we're not going anywhere," he says, kissing me back.

"Is this what you meant when you said 'festive'?"

"Well, I guess I was thinking some kind of dress, but you really don't wear dresses, do you?"

"No, I just don't like them. I hate my knees. I'll wear long skirts, but I didn't bring one with."

"Hey, no complaints here. Those jeans look like they were painted on you," he says, looking me up and down slowly. My stomach started doing flip-flops.

"Let me get my jacket and purse, and then I think we need to go," I smile, backing away and heading up the stairs.

★

"Where are we going?" I ask, as Mark expertly backs the Fairlane out of Jake's driveway onto that impossibly windy road.

"Dinner, but a stop first. Something I want you to see."

I look over at him.

"No, you're always going on about how you love surprises-- well, this is a surprise."

But we don't head out onto the freeway. He's cutting through Jake's neighborhood, and then onto one of those huge tree-lined boulevards. A right turn, and we are ascending seriously upwards.

Finally, we reach the top of whatever we were driving up, and then I see a building that looks vaguely familiar. Mark parks the car and gets out, coming around to open the door for me. I climb out and stand next to him, shivering a little. Maybe partly out of some kind of fear or apprehension, but it's breezy up here. He puts his arm around my shoulder, and says, "Do you know where you are?"

"Not really. It looks familiar but I can't quite place it yet."

"Do you want me to tell you?"

"Give me a few more minutes."

"Okay. Let's walk, though," he suggests, so we walk towards a big white building, illuminated with spotlights.

As we approach the building, I can see the reason I think we're up here--there's all of Los Angeles, sprawling underneath us, lit up like a million Christmas lights. I squeal slightly and walk to the wall along the edge.

"This is really gorgeous," I smile at him.

"Have you figured it out?"

I shake my head.

"Griffith Observatory?"

I shake my head again.

"*Rebel Without A Cause?*" he says.

Now I see it. "I can't believe I didn't figure it out sooner. Wow, this is something."

"Yeah. This is one of the coolest things in L.A., as far as I'm concerned," he says, leaning against the wall with me, resting his arms on it.

"So guess what I did today," I ask.

He shakes his head.

"Turned in my resignation at work. And I gave my landlord notice, too. I fly home on Monday to begin packing."

"Wow." He smiled. "You don't waste any time."

"I've wasted enough for an entire lifetime, I think," I say.

"No--don't start that. Present tense only from now on."

I nod in agreement. "Then I turn around and come back down here. I'm going to stay with Chrissie for a while, until I can figure out where I want to live."

"Well, congratulations, Lisa. Good for you."

"Thanks," I smile. "It is an event, isn't it?"

A few more minutes go by, and then Mark turns around, leaning against the concrete, and says, "So, Lisa, what are we doing?"

"What do you mean?"

"I guess I'm putting you on the spot and asking you how you feel. Feel free to tell me to fuck off, however, if it's too soon, or I'm pushing you..."

"About you?" I look at those black eyes, that calm, level gaze that was always quietly full of fire and intensity. My heart stops.

"God. I don't know. Or, I do know, but..."

"But what?"

I turn to lean my back on the wall so I didn't have to look at him. I stare out ahead into the parking lot. "It's all so--new. And sudden. And real. And scary." There. That was honest, at least.

"Scary good, or scary bad?"

"Good. Too good. Amazingly good. I could see this, see us..."

"Is that a yes?"

"Was there a question?" and then I stop. I suddenly have a shock of realization as to where this all might be going. Mark runs his hand through his hair like I have seen him do hundreds of times, that trademark gesture. He takes a deep breath.

"I'm proposing that we try this for real. I am totally serious about going to New York when the record is done, and I would love nothing more than for you to come with me. We'll get a place in the Village. You can show me your city. We can go to shows, you can write, I can play. God! Wouldn't it be great?" The enthusiasm in his voice catches me off guard.

"That was what my life was supposed to be like," I say. "We're back to scary again."

He nods. "It's not like this was anything I planned, either. But--it's what I want. Will you think about it?"

I rest my head on his shoulder and close my eyes. I could see it, I could see us, I could see a life I didn't even know I wanted any more until this moment. The truth is that I just wanted to say yes right then and there, say yes to anything and everything.

I open my eyes and lift my head up. "I just want to make sure that I'm not running away again. I want to be running toward something with both eyes wide open."

He picks up my hand and kissed it. "I understand. It's all right. This was probably a little too much."

"No. Stop apologizing. I think it was perfect." I shiver. It really was cold up here, and I was on the verge of tears, but didn't want him to see that.

Of course, I am lying, I am lying to him and to myself. I know. It was that moment. Just like I knew with Ian that it was over, I already know that Mark is the next chapter. The feeling of knowing is so overwhelming in a way, and so simple and non-dramatic in another. I think it is the quietness with which the realization presents itself that is the most frightening. It's not angels and trumpets and fireworks. It's just that moment in time when the universe gently taps you on the shoulder and says, *here you go.*

As we get into the car, I get a crazy idea. "Mark..." I ask.

"Yeah?" he says, backing the car out of the space, and starting to head back down the hill.

"I know you told me to dress up, and that this was going to be a big fancy dinner, but--"

"But what?" I can hear the disappointment in his voice.

"Well, I've always heard of this place called Oki Dog, it's in all the punk histories of L.A.. And I've always been too, I dunno, afraid of being too much of a tourist to ask someone to take me there. I know it's not quite what you had in mind."

"Oh, god--I thought you were going to tell me that you changed your mind and you wanted to go home! You just want to go to Oki Dog!" He almost giggled. "You are insane."

"Is that okay?"

"Of course it's okay! It's actually a great, crazy idea. I like it. We're a little overdressed, but that won't call any attention to us at Oki Dog."

We drive for a little while, Mark pointing out random landmarks, trying to help me get my bearings.

As we pull into the parking lot at Oki Dog he asks, "You do realize that the original one isn't around anymore, right?"

"I had no idea, no, but I wouldn't know the difference."

"Well, I know how you are for punk rock landmarks. The only thing the new Oki Dogs share is the name."

"And it's not the '80s any more, either," I say, getting out of the car.

"How are you managing in those shoes? I don't think I have ever seen you in heels before," Mark laughs, as I almost fall off the curb.

"You have so."

"When?" he frowns, trying to remember.

"The Grammies."

"Okay, Lisa, I remember absolutely nothing from that evening. It is one big blur."

"You remember Jake slipping ice down Eddie Vedder's back."

"That fucker. Couldn't even wear a tux." He laughs in disbelief. "I do remember that, but barely. I was so zoned out, it did not seem real."

"I also wore high heels to the MTV Awards."

"Another evening I remember nothing of, but this time it was because Jake and I got shitfaced on Jack Daniels in the limo on the way over. We kept toasting each other, and before I knew it, the bottle was empty."

We approach the counter, and he asks, "Do you know what

you want?" he asks.

"I believe the pastrami burrito is the specialty, correct?"

"Shall I order for you?" he asks, bowing elaborately.

"Please."

Gathering the food, we walk over to a table and sit down.

"Oh, my god," I say, looking at the greasy mess in front of me.

"Hey, this is what you wanted," Mark says, taking a sip of soda.

"No, it looks great. I'm sure it's bad for me on every possible level, but--now I can say I've been to Oki Dog."

"We're kind of early. If we were here around 2 a.m., you would notice that most of the customers were in some state of inebriation. That's probably the secret." He pushes his food away too, and stands up. "What do you want to do now? We could go to a bar, or hit the Viper Room or something."

"You know, I don't care. I had my request for the evening fulfilled."

His eyes light up. "I know! Let's go."

We get in the car and head back out. Mark makes some expert turns, crosses some side streets, and then pulls up in front of a record store.

"Record shopping?"

"If we can go to Oki Dog dressed like this, we can go record shopping. Didn't you say you needed a copy of *Alladin Sane*? This is the best used CD store in L.A."

I laugh, and get out of the car. We walk into the bright fluorescence and I'm wishing for sunglasses.

"You should always have them with you, Lisa. You're going to have to learn this lesson if you're going to live here," Mark laughs, pulling his out from his inside jacket pocket.

I go down the racks, idly flipping through sections here and there. Mark, on the other hand, picks up a new disc every few feet.

"I do this every couple of weeks, at least once a month--I want to try to keep up with the competition," he says. He reviews the new releases rack one more time, and decides that he's done. "Are you sure there's nothing that you want?"

"Yeah, the whole store." I pick up one or two new releases I'd been wanting.

We head towards the register. Mark steps up to the counter,

and hands our purchases to the clerk. "Oh, wait. Do you have a copy of *Alladin Sane* in stock?" Mark asks.

"Who?" the clerk says, barely audible.

Mark rolls his eyes. "And you actually work here. David Bowie."

"That section is over there," the clerk says, pointing as unhelpfully as possible.

"Now I remember why I come here--the insults are free. Just ring this up," he says, exasperated. The girl watching the front door glances over, and then does a double take as she clearly recognizes Mark. She's on our side of the counter within a split second.

"I'm sorry, what was it you were you looking for?"

"*Alladin Sane*, David Bowie?"

"I'll be right back," and she zips down the used CD bin.

"Did you want me to wait to ring this up," Mr. Helpful asks, as though it's a dreadful imposition.

"Yes," Mark says.

The other clerk is back within thirty seconds, CD in hand. "Here you are. Sorry about that."

"Thanks, I appreciate it." He hands the CD to Mr. Charm and says, "Okay, now you can ring me up." We complete the transaction, picking the CDs up on the other side of the theft detectors, and walk out the door.

We get in the car, and Mark shuffles through his new purchases. Ripping open the cellophane on one, he asks, "Okay, what are we doing?"

I lean over, slide my hand around the back of his neck, and pull him to me in a sharp, sudden kiss that takes his breath away. He answers with that sly grin that makes my knees week, and starts the car up.

Driving west, we head for Venice, and I feel like I'm on my first date. I'm dizzy, excited, and just plain happy.

CHAPTER 14: Los Angeles

I wake up on Thursday morning, light streaming into the room, and for a split second I don't remember where I am. And then I remember, and then I grin, and then I blush.

I realize that Mark's not next to me. Just when I'm about to get out of bed and go look for him, the bedroom door opens. He's carrying two paper cups of coffee from his espresso joint.

"Well, good morning," he says, grinning.

"Yeah, I feel about the same way," I say, smiling and sitting up. "Is that for me?"

"Yes, it is. Here you go." He sits down on the bed and hands the cup to me. I take a sip.

"Oh, my god, that is the best coffee, ever."

"I don't know that I want to move, just because I am one minute from that coffee place. They'll even deliver for me in extreme circumstances."

"They don't have coffee like this in New York. Well, you can get good, plain coffee just about anywhere, it's just not like this. This is--art." I take another sip.

"Okay, lazy, it's 10:30. I don't want to rush you, but I have to be at the studio at noon, since we are rehearsing all day and into the evening. I have to cart you home still, so you need to get a move on."

"Can I borrow a shirt?" I ask, suddenly glancing on the floor and seeing that flimsy sequined thing lying there.

"Sure, whatever you want, except--"

"I know, I know."

"I'm going downstairs, just come down when you're ready." He leans over and gives me a kiss, and then pulls away. Before he's out of reach, I pull him back and kiss him myself.

"Okay, babe, I am not succumbing to your charms again. Get in the shower," he laughs, sliding out of reach. "There's a robe right there, and I moved all the girlie stuff into my bathroom." He heads for the door, and I wave stupidly as he closes it behind him.

Twenty minutes later, I'm heading downstairs with my shoes in hand, wearing a white button-down shirt, untucked, hair wet and twisted up.

"Ready?"

"Yeah, let's go."

We walk down the stairs and I tiptoe barefoot into the car.

"Are you guys ready for tomorrow night?" I ask as we get on the freeway, heading back to Jake's house.

He snorts. "Barely. It's going to be hell today. We're not even letting Christine come."

"Wow."

"We're gonna have to duke it out. We'll also probably do a really long soundcheck tomorrow. But today is the acid test."

"You know, everyone will be so glad to see you, and no one else knows what the songs are supposed to sound like except you."

"That's just it. We know exactly what the songs are supposed to sound like. And if we play like shit, we will know it, and hate ourselves. Kids are coming from all over the country to watch this show, and for some of them, it may be the only chance they get to see us for a year and a half, or more."

"Your fans are more forgiving then you probably give them credit for," I say.

"They are, and I know that. But I think we owe them the best show we can play. They aren't going to care if the next one is great, they care about if this one is. And I care. I don't care if we fuck up once or twice, I just want to know that we tried as hard as we could." He sighs.

"Mark, it'll be fine."

"It probably will be once we're in front of an audience again. But right now, I know there are at least five songs that are nowhere near ready to play live. And I refuse to get up there and just play all the old stuff that we could sleepwalk through."

With that, we're pulling into Jake's driveway. He stops the car, and I lean over and kiss him briefly, touch his face with the back of my hand.

I head to my room and fall back on the bed. Oh, my god. This guy is something else. This is Mark I'm thinking this about, feeling what I'm feeling. It doesn't seem real.

The next morning, I walk downstairs in search of coffee. Jake and Mark and Scott are already there, way too animated for first thing in the morning, sitting or standing around the kitchen, talking and reading the paper, drinking coffee and eating breakfast. I stroll in, barefoot, hair still wet, and receive applause for my fashion choice: the first Blue Electric shirt. There were maybe thirty of these made. Black with what was bright blue silkscreened print, now faded to almost grey. The front had a photo of the guys standing on the beach down at Alki, the back says "BLUE ELECTRIC: Someday this will be a big deal."

Equally, I applaud Jake, who is wearing a classic issue Ramones shirt.

"Well, the fans have been camped out since last night," Jake says with a grin. "Adam drove by the club on the way to the office."

"I didn't know anyone did that anymore," I say, incredulously.

"Yeah, there was a line since about six last night," Jake says.

"I think we should bring them breakfast," says Mark, with this impish grin.

Everyone stares at him, including me. That sentence should by rights have come out of Jake's mouth.

"What? Wouldn't it be so fucking cool to roll up in the convertible with coffee and doughnuts? They'd fucking freak. I would, if it was my favorite band. C'mon, it's like the Stones announcing the '75 tour. Let's do it!"

So here we are, after a stop for doughnuts and coffee, driving down the Sunset Strip with the top down on the Fairlane (after a brief clash of car egos, Mark's car won over Jake's simply because we could all fit in it). *Sticky Fingers* is blasting out of the stereo and all of us are singing along at the top of our lungs, *yeah-yeah-yeah-WOO*-ing along with Mick. Mark is driving, Jake is riding shotgun, and I am in the middle of the back seat with Jonathan and Scott on either side of me, Jake's video camera at the ready.

We are stopped at a traffic light about a block away from the club. It looks like there are probably about two dozen fans lined up. Mark drives past, slowly, and then does a quick u-turn and pulls up in front of the club, double-parked. Jake hops out first with a box of donuts. I climb out over Jonathan, quickly and ungracefully, because I really want to get the first shots of total incredulity once these kids realize what's going on.

"Hi there! Did you really spend all night out here? What are you waiting for?" Jake says, as bright eyed and bushy tailed as ever. I will never understand how he is such a morning person. "Would you like some breakfast?" he asks, opening the box of doughnuts with a flourish.

The kids in the front of the line have that look on their faces of, "Oh, God, what now," and then a girl at the back of the line jumps up and comes running over. Two seconds later, everyone is on their feet, surrounding Jake. The first girl turns around and looks at the car, and then whirls around again and yells, "OH MY GOD! They are all here!"

Mark and Jonathan and Scott wave, and get out of the car. There is no massive freakout--I think people are in too much shock.

"Coffee, anyone? I bet you guys need it," Mark says as he walks up, holding a stack of cups and the coffee container. I am getting this all on video.

"This is not real. I am dreaming this," says a kid wearing a Rolling Stones shirt.

"Who are you, and where are you from?" I ask from behind the camera.

"I'm Eric, and I'm here from Atlanta, Georgia," he say, taking a cup of coffee from Mark. "What the fuck are you guys doing here?" he asks, incredulously. "And where did you get that shirt!" he exclaims, jaw dropping to the floor. I turn around to model the back for him.

"Original issue," I say, smiling.

"I've never seen one of those! You have to let me take a picture of it," he says, reaching into his backpack to take out a camera.

"We heard there were fans camping all night, and figured you could use some breakfast," says Jake, continuing to hand the box of doughnuts down the line.

These two girls just stare at him, open-mouthed. I move over there. "Hi girls, where are you from, what are your names?"

"I'm Stacey and this is Rachel, we are here from Boston." Rachel starts to cry. Stacey elbows her, clearly annoyed.

"It's okay, Rachel, it's just breakfast. We have other doughnuts if you don't like those." Jake pats her on the head. She looks up in shock and stops crying.

"Come get coffee, everyone, you won't lose your places, I'm just a really bad waiter. That was Jake's specialty, not mine," Mark yells out.

"Oh, fuck you, Genovese," he yells back. "I made pizza! I was not a waiter!"

"No, I was the waiter," Scott says. "If you remember, Grandpa."

"This is really funny," I say, as the fans watch the scene unfold with a mixture of delight and disbelief. "Keep it up."

"Fuck you, Lisa," Jake says, giving the camera the finger.

"Wait, are you Lisa Simon?!" the kid in the Rolling Stones shirt says. "You're the person who named the band! This is too much!"

"That fucking *Rolling Stone* cover story. I'll never live it down," I say, as I drop back to the curb to get some wider shots of the scene.

"You're in the FAQ on the website, Lisa," says Jonathan.

"My mother would be so proud," I say, listening to clicking cameras taking photographs of the back of my t-shirt.

I walk back over to Mark, who is continuing to dispense coffee. "Well, I don't really know when we'll be done with the album," I hear him explaining to two girls who do not look old enough to be here.

"Will you play anything from the first record?" one asks.

"Forget that, will we get to hear new songs tonight?" the other says, sharply.

"That's why we're playing," he says. "We've been playing them for ourselves too long."

"Are you guys playing the Joey Ramone birthday party next month?"

"If they ask us, we will be there in one second flat."

"Is the record really going to be called "What's Next"," asks the other girl.

He stares at her in a brief moment of shock, and then asks, "What's your name?"

"Elizabeth."

"Where are you from, Elizabeth?"

"Nutley, New Jersey."

"Yay, New Jersey!" I reply automatically from behind the camera.

"Well, I'm not going to ask how you heard that, because I know you guys manage to find out just about anything we think, let alone say out loud, but right now it's a joke title more than anything."

"Well, if you keep it, we think you need to do a takeoff on the Who's album cover."

Mark laughs. "That's a great fucking idea. If we do, we will give you a credit, Elizabeth from Nutley, New Jersey."

She drops her coffee, and then starts to apologize, flustered. Mark tries to reassure her. "Don't worry about it! It's okay! Really. We understand. Here, have another cup." As he's handing her the coffee, he looks down at her shirt, which had been hidden by her jacket until that moment, and says, "Lisa, you gotta see this."

I put the camera down and walk around to his vantage point.

"Oh, lord have mercy," I say, smiling.

"Did you know that photograph was taken in Seattle customs?" I hear Mark explain to her, as I move to the back of the line, where Jonathan is engaged in what seems to be a serious conversation with two guys and a girl.

"We don't have any tour plans right now, no," he says.

"I read somewhere that you are going to break up when this album is done," says one of the guys, intently.

"That's just not true. We just don't want to go on another big tour," says Jonathan.

While they're engaged in conversation, the girl takes a doughnut out of the box, and is about to take a bite, when one of the guys shoots her an incredulous look. She looks back at him, and then a look of understanding comes over her face. Taking a bandanna out of her backpack, she carefully wraps the doughnut up and places it gingerly into the front pocket.

"I don't want to see that on eBay, now," Scott says from behind me, clearly having witnessed the entire proceeding.

They think he is serious, and start to protest.

"Eat the doughnut, kids. It's just a doughnut. It won't make it through the night. It'll get crushed, and then you'll be hungry. Better to have the memory of that Blue Electric doughnut than a bunch of squished, sugary crumbs." Scott opens up another box, and offers it to them.

I leave Jonathan and Scott, and move up the line where Mark and Jake are engrossed in a conversation with a tiny girl with long blonde hair. I walk over and assume my journalist role.

"Lisa, this is Alison, she's from Connecticut and is the one with the web site, she had the first web site!" Jake says, introducing her.

"Good for you," I say. She waves at the camera.

"She does it all by herself," Mark says. "I don't know how you do it."

"I have a lot of help," she says. "So many people contribute to it."

"Lisa, have you seen her web site? It's better than the lame one the record company has. I don't know why we bother," Mark says.

I put down the camera. "Hello, I am familiar with the internet. How do you think I know what you play every night?" I grab Mark's wrist to look at his watch. "Okay, guys, we have to wrap this up and get back to the office. If people want autographs or pictures, now is the time."

Someone overhears me, and before I know it, everyone has a camera in hand.

I walk the boys down the line, where they pose with the fans, and I take photographs that I know will be all over the internet in a matter of hours.

Leaving what was left of the doughnuts and coffee with the

line, we head back to the car, waving, and drive to the office. Virginia completely ignores our presence as we walk in.

"Yes, it did happen. No, there was no press call," Christine says into her headset, clearly annoyed, as we troop into her office. "Not everything a band does has to be a media event. I didn't find out until they were already there." She rolls her eyes at us. "Well, tell her she should check our web site in about, oh, fifteen minutes for the full report."

Christine grins and hangs up.

"MTV is pissed they didn't get a press release about this."

Jonathan and Scott high-five each other.

"Okay, gentlemen, I understand we want a rehearsal and a soundcheck," Christine says. "You're going to the studio to rehearse, but will be at the club by two, please?"

"We need to run through the set." Mark says.

"It would help if we had a set," Jake says.

"I thought we were doing all audibles," says Jonathan.

"Dude, I always blank onstage, I suddenly forget our entire catalog. Let's just write down some songs we want to play, it doesn't have to be a formal setlist if you don't want," Jake says in exasperation.

"Guys, you can debate this in the van, get a move on, we'll see you in a few hours, Lisa and I have some work to do." She herds them out of her office and we can still hear them arguing as they walk out the door and down the stairs.

Suzie appears in the office doorway. "Is it true?" she says.

"Is what true?" Christine asks.

"Did the guys bring breakfast to the kids in the line? I have like thirty emails about this, no one thinks it is true. The message board is down from all the traffic, I've got the IT guys at the label working on it."

I hand her the video camera. "Here. See for yourself."

"Can we put this on the web site?" she asks, excitedly, watching through the viewfinder.

"No, just send it to that girl in Connecticut," Christine says. "What do the kids call it? The 'dot org'?"

"This is unbelievable. I'm almost upset you didn't call me, but then I remembered where I work," Suzie said.

Christine looks down at the massive To Do list on her desk. "Suzie, the van will be back here at three to take us to the venue, so everything and everybody has to be ready to leave for the Roxy then."

"I am going to go watch this video and answer email. I cannot believe they did this." Suzie turns to leave, and then stops and asks: "Oh, by the way, whose idea was it? Jake's?"

"No," I say. "Mark's."

She looks at me incredulously.

"Swear to god. I was there."

Shaking her head, she walks out of the room, headed for the fan club office.

"Okay, boss, what do we have to do now?" I ask. I volunteered two days ago to act as Christine's PA, since her usual assistant was on vacation in Maui.

"We need to go over the guest list. I have the fan club list, it's counted and verified. But we have more people who want tickets than we have tickets for on the guest list side of things. Virginia has to call people back and let them know they aren't in." Christine hands me the list, and says, "Okay. Read it to me."

An hour later, Christine has handed off a copy of the list to Virginia. "She likes telling people they aren't on the list. It's weird," she says, coming back in the office.

"Seems consistent to me," I say. "Now what, chief?"

"I don't know. I guess I can tell you what tonight will be like."

I sit down on the couch. "Shoot."

"Insane."

"Somehow, I knew that."

"No, it will really be insane. People will be showing up and demanding to be let in, and I have about ten spaces worth of wiggle room."

"So what do I do?"

"Best judgment. I know you won't be intimidated by flash. If you really don't know what to do, then get me on the walkie-talkie, but I honestly trust your judgment."

"So I can tell Sheryl Crow to fuck off."

"Not in so many words, but yeah, you get the general idea."

"Oh, my god, this could be a total scenario for revenge. 'Blink

182? I don't think so.' Or even better, 'Scott Stapp? Never heard of him.'" I grin evilly.

"If you get us in the papers tomorrow, just make it good is all I ask."

Three o'clock, and we are helping Suzie move boxes of t-shirts into the waiting van. Christine and I climb in, and then Suzie and her two helpers follow. It's a short drive, and we pull in around the back.

"Do you need help, girls?" Christine asks.

"No, we'll be fine," Suzie says, waving her away as she stacked three boxes on top of each other and picked them up like it was nothing.

We walk through a hallway and then emerge into a narrow, dim black space. My eyes adjust to the light and then I realize that this is the club. It's tinier than I anticipated. I walk out into the middle of the floor, and turn around, slowly, taking it all in. The guys are onstage arguing, or having some kind of heated discussion. Mark sees me doing my pirouette and hops off the stage and walks up to me.

"Whoa. So this is the Roxy." I say.

"Yeah? Is that a general 'whoa,' or is there something I'm forgetting?"

"My favorite Springsteen bootleg is from a show he did here in 1978."

"Bruce Springsteen played here?"

"He didn't start out playing Giants Stadium, you know."

"That must have been intense."

"It was an important show for him. Kind of a big deal." I kind of let it all settle, and then ask, "So how's it going?"

"If all of us are still alive tonight, it will be a miracle."

"What's the deal?"

"Oh, no one is happy with how the new songs sound. And since everyone has songs, everyone is pissed, instead of it just being me or Jake who is pissed."

"Well," I say, "At least it's even for a change."

"So what are you on call for tonight?"

"I'm more or less in charge of the guest list, and then I help Suzie with merch, not that she needs anyone's help." I look over at her, supervising her helpers with military precision as they set up the merchandise next to the stage. We both laugh as she hangs up a hand-written sign reading, "ONE SHIRT PER PERSON, I DON'T CARE WHO YOU PROMISED."

Christine walks up to the stage, and gestures at us to come over.

"So, what are we doing? Are you done?"

Jake looks at everyone. "I don't know. Are we done?"

"I don't think six weeks of rehearsal are going to make us any more done than we are now. We are a fucking train wreck," Jonathan says.

"Infinite Trainwreck!" I say.

That breaks some of the tension, and we all laugh.

"You should put that up on the marquee outside," I say.

"That's fucking brilliant," Jake says. "Christine?"

"I'll make it happen." She pauses. "Are we done? What do you want to do about dinner?"

"Can you bring in sushi?" Jake asks, looking for agreement from everyone else. They all nod.

"I'm going to go arrange for food, and go schmooze the staff. Everyone, I'd prefer it if you didn't wander off, but if you do, back here at six." Christine stalks off towards the entrance with authority.

Jake looks at me and says, "What are you doing?"

"I am at Christine's beck and call, so I am here."

"Well, why don't you come upstairs for a while?"

I look around, and realize that I am really not needed at the moment, so I say, "Sure."

We walk to the left of the stage and up a flight of stairs. There are two small dressing rooms, and Jake opens the door to one and we walk inside.

"Any requests?" he says, sitting down with a magic marker and a blank piece of paper.

"No, and I do not even want to see that. If you're working on the setlist, then maybe I should leave."

"Okay, okay," he says, throwing his hands up in the air. He picks up his Gibson Hummingbird acoustic and starts to idly strum, and then abruptly stops and puts the pick down on the table.

I haven't seen his picks in a long time, so I pick it up.

"Those are from last tour," Jake says.

I examine it closer. It says "JMcD" on the front, and the back has a tiny drawing of a pizza slice. I crack up, and pocket it.

"It reminds me of my roots," Jake says. "Keeps me humble." He pauses. "I hate to bring this up tonight, but are you sure you'll be okay flying home on Monday? Being up there all by yourself?"

"I'll have to be. I'm also going to try to talk Marie into coming out for a long weekend."

"When do you think you'll be back?"

"I really hope it doesn't take longer than two weeks." I sigh. "I wish I could wave a magic wand, and be back here instantly with all my stuff."

"Well, you'll be back before you know it." He looks at me, right in the eyes. "And if you somehow manage to lose your mind after you're back there, I will be coming up to kidnap you and bring you back here."

Christine suddenly appears in the doorway, walkie-talkies in hand. "Suddenly there is a whole Japanese delegation from the record company who expects to get into the show tonight. There is no room for even half of them." She hands me a walkie-talkie.

"What are you going to do?"

"Tell the execs here that they can give up their places if it's so important for these folks to get in. They can't call me three hours before showtime and expect twenty-five spaces to magically materialize." She sighs. "Okay, this turns it on--just leave it on. This knob is the volume. You can clip the handset to your shoulder or something and then put the walkie on your belt, that's how I do it."

"Wow, cool," I say, playing with the buttons. "Check, 1,2, check," I say into the handset.

Christine winces. "You won't think it's so cool when I am calling you every five minutes."

"Christine, it's going to be fine," says Jake.

"Yeah, yeah, I know." Her cell phone rings. "Oh, if you can't reach me on the walkie, I will have my phone with me, too."

"Got it."

We hear someone climbing up the stairs, and then Jonathan sticks his head in the doorway. "Dude, can we talk setlist?"

"Yeah, I was just starting it, but Lisa doesn't want to know anything."

"Oooh, a Blue Electric purist! You'll be like those kids on the mailing list who are always freaking when someone doesn't put SPOILER in the subject line."

"I find it curious you know so much about this, Jonathan," Christine says.

"Fine, I lurk. That's all. It's funny sometimes," he says.

"Okay, we will leave you to it," Christine says, and we head down the steps.

"You do know that your phone has been ringing off the hook," I say.

"I do, but I don't care." It rings again, this time with a different ring. She checks the display. "This one, I have to take. It's the president of the label. Can you check on the food status?"

I nod, and toward the office, looking for the woman from earlier. She's talking with Suzie as I come into the show room. I walk over, and extend my hand. "I'm Lisa. I just realized we hadn't been introduced. I'm Christine's assistant for tonight."

"Hi, I'm Heather."

"Heather, did you by any chance have someone you wanted to get into the show tonight?"

Her eyes open wide. "Oh, my god, yes, my brother. He is the biggest fan, but they told us all no guests tonight."

"I don't have the list here, but later, if I don't ask you, remind me, please."

"Thank you so much, Lisa."

"Hey, I'm gonna run you ragged tonight, it's the least I can do."

She smiles wryly, and scurries off again.

Just then, Adam goes walking by, not even recognizing me.

"Adam!" I say.

He stops, and does a double-take. "Oh my god! Lisa!" He

comes over and engulfs me in a bear hug. "The guys said you were here, but I hadn't seen you, and then I saw you standing with the walkie-talkie."

"I'm playing PA tonight."

"Thank god someone is here to help Christine." He stops, and then says, "Wait. Are you the one responsible for the marquee saying INFINITE TRAINWRECK?"

"More or less."

"That is fucking awesome. I took a cab back from my house, and I almost fell out of the car. I just could not believe it."

Just then, Christine comes bounding down the stairs with a clipboard in her hand. "Adam! Thank god."

The walkie-talkie squawks. "Lisa, the food is here," says Heather.

"Can you bring it to the dressing room? Or someone?"

"Roger."

"Here's the guestlist, and here's a laminate," Christine says, handing them both to me. She gives me a hug. "It's going to be really, really great to have you here," she says, relieved.

Her phone starts ringing again.

★

It feels like we're about halfway through the show now, although Jake made some promise earlier in the evening about no curfews. I am at the merch table, covering for Suzie, who has gone into the crowd for a song or two. The table is amply manned by the two fan club members that Suzie entrusted, not that there's any business now; everyone here is watching the damn show, and all that's left to buy are some posters from the last tour.

"Is there a balcony tonight?" Jake asks, with a trace of British accent.

This line makes me stand at attention, because I know exactly which Stones bootleg Jake is quoting, and I also have a good idea as to what is most likely coming next.

"I'll be right back," I say to the girls. "Tell Suzie to call me on the walkie-talkie if she needs me."

I am heading into the crowd just as Mark leans back, drops his left hand from the fretboard, and as the right hand falls down to the strings, I lose it slightly. I lose it because I know who he's imitating: Keith Richards during the intro to "Honky Tonk Women," which is precisely what the band begin playing.

Jake snarls the opening lyrics in his most perfect Jagger imitation, and the audience goes nuts, singing the chorus so loudly they are outsinging Jake. He looks pleased, and holds the microphone out into the crowd to let them continue.

I move further into the crowd. It's unfair, almost; while it's not that tightly packed or rough, I am using the presence of the walkie-talkie to get people to move out of my way. I feel horribly devious, but I also do not care. I cannot remember the last time I watched Blue Electric in a club, in the middle of a crowd, out of the sightlines of any of the guys. I am anonymous, just another fan in the crowd. It is the most delicious feeling. I'm bouncing up and down, and singing along at the top of my lungs, just like everybody else. I could not be having any more fun right now than if the Rolling Stones themselves were on that stage.

Blue Electric are enjoying themselves so much that they are literally falling on the floor and laughing. Mark walks backwards and almost falls into the drum riser, which cracks up Jonathan so much he stops playing for a split second. Scott is shaking his head with that "Oh, my god, what are these idiots up to now," expression on his face. Jake is breaking into his painfully bad imitation of the Mick Jagger strut, but then falls over laughing himself. He never could get that down with a straight face.

I overhear a conversation behind me:

"I can't believe we're seeing this!" a girl says to her friend.

"I know! A Rolling Stones cover! We are so lucky!"

They squeal a little bit, and hug each other. It almost makes me a little misty. I could be them. I have been them. I have felt that. I have said that.

"I love your shirt!" says the other one, tapping me on the shoulder. I smile and nod in acknowledgement. She is wearing a shirt from the first time they went to New York, the blue shirts I helped design that just said "blue electric" in typewriter font across the front. "I like yours too!" I say. She grins proudly from ear to ear.

"Okay, this is an old one, and yes this is one of ours for a change. I wrote it a long time ago, back when I didn't ever think that anyone would ever really come see us... it's about our hometown, Seattle..." There's a huge shout in response. "Yeah, we know you traveled, we know there are people here from New York, and Georgia, and Chicago..." More cheers. "And we love you for coming to see us. We don't think we deserve it, but we thank you kindly."

A glance at Mark, his arm goes overhead into pre-windmill position, and I think it at the same moment as the kid next to me gasps, "Antique Mirror!"

That song. One of the first real Blue Electric songs Jake ever wrote, when he was depressed and dejected and trying to get drunk on whatever money he had left, sitting at the bar at the OK Hotel. The OK, lost to us in the earthquake earlier this year. But I remember it, I remember the bar, I remember seeing the guys play there, at first at the miniscule stage in the front, and then later, on the only slightly bigger stage in the back room. And now they are here at the Roxy, and all these people are here to see them, freaking out, jumping up and down and singing along to every word. I have seen them play this song so many times, in so many places, in front of so many different audiences. And each and every time, I love it.

Second chorus, and the audience starts to jump up and down, and Jake sees them and starts pogoing with them, which starts *everyone* pogoing--including me. I stick the walkie-talkie in my back pocket and start singing along, louder and louder and louder, losing myself in the crowd. I think: how fucking great, how much fun. This is part of who I am, this is the world to which I have always somehow belonged. I would not want to be any other place in the world right now, I would not want my life to be any different than it is right now.

I stop jumping, and realize what thought just flashed through my head.

I look at Mark, playing guitar like he was born with it. And Jake. And Jonathan. And Scott. Christine is sidestage, behind the monitor board, laughing as hard as I am right now. Adam is somewhere behind the amps. Part of me wants to go join them, be where I can laugh with everyone onstage, but the other part of me is so fucking happy to be lost in the crowd like this, drowning in the music and the energy and the lights and the happiness. Just like I did when I saw the Who for the first time. Blue electric. They chose their name well.

Jake steps up to the mic: "I know you are all cool enough to know who Joey Ramone is, I mean, was--"

"Gabba gabba hey!" Scott yells into his microphone.

The crowd cheers in acknowledgement, and a group of kids down front, all wearing homemade Ramones shirts, starts a "Hey, ho, let's go!" chant.

(I spotted them waiting in the drop line earlier, and promptly gave the last five places on the guest list to them.)

Jonathan picks up the beat on the bass drum, and Jake turns his mic out to face the audience, while Mark walks along the edge of the stage, encouraging the cheer.

"This is for Joey, and for you, and for friends, and for us--take it, Dee Dee!"

"1-2-3-4!" yells Scott.

They crash into "Blitzkrieg Bop," Jake holding the microphone just like Joey would (he was even a little taller than Joey was), and the audience goes absolutely insane. The crowd starts pogoing, and throwing caution to the wind, I decide to join them again. It isn't a mosh pit, people are laughing and singing along and my sadness at not being in New York to do anything in tribute to Joey vanishes.

The Ramones were a fucking great band: their razor sharp timing between chorus and verse, Joey's impeccable phrasing, Johnny's waves and waves of power chords, Dee Dee's bass lines somehow both fluid and solid at the same time. I stand there for a moment, flooded with memories. And then the song finishes, but then Jonathan hits a drumbeat and all four of them start chanting: "Lobotomy! Lobotomy!" It's "Teenage Lobotomy" next, and I realize this is going to be a freaking Ramones medley, and is likely one of the reasons I was banned from rehearsals. Fuckers.

"Sheena Is A Punk Rocker" follows, and I don't know whether Jake encouraged it, if it was spontaneous, or a little of both, but all of a sudden one kid is dancing onstage, just to the right of Scott, and then a girl with pink hair is up on the drum riser, doing the Frug, and in what seems like a flash the stage is filled with dancing, pogoing, ecstatic fans. No one is diving off the stage or bothering the band or hurting the equipment--although I can see Adam in attack position just to the right of Mark's amps--they are just dancing like crazy. It is anarchic and joyful and spontaneous and crazy, and one of the most beautiful sights in rock and roll I have ever witnessed. It's the best possible tribute to Joey and the spirit of the Ramones. I sing along, just like I did when I was 14 years old, and feel happy and free.

The song finishes, and although it wasn't planned that way, the show has clearly ended, because nothing else could possibly follow that moment. The kids carefully climb back into the audience, shaking hands or high-fiving the guys as they do, some posing for the occasional picture and others getting an autograph quickly scrawled onto a t-shirt. Mark and Scott and Jake are handing out guitar picks to everyone they can reach, and Jonathan walks to the front of the stage to hand out drumsticks to the entire Ramones-shirt contingent.

Once the stage has cleared off, the guys walk front and center, put their arms around each other, and bow. They separate and continue waving at the crowd, shaking hands, crouching down to accept gifts or talk to fans. In the midst of it all, I glance over, and see Mark looking right at me, his expression both bemused and pleased. I wave, blow him a kiss, and then start walking towards backstage.

I'm home.

ABOUT THE AUTHOR

Caryn Rose is a Brooklyn-based writer and photographer who documents rock-and-roll, baseball and urban life. She covers the ups and downs of the New York Mets at metsgrrl.com, reports on Bruce Springsteen for Backstreets Magazine and brucespringsteen.net, and ruminates about music at jukeboxgraduate.com. She lives in Greenpoint with her boyfriend and her cat, Jackie Wilson. *B-Sides And Broken Hearts* is her first novel.

Made in the USA
Lexington, KY
23 March 2012